City of Flami

and King of the Fleshless Legion

THE TWO CLASSIC ADVENTURES OF

by Norvell W. Page
writing as Grant Stockbridge

plus a new historical essay
by Will Murray

SANCTUM BOOKS

This Sanctum Books edition is an unabridged republication of the text and illustrations of two stories from *The Spider* magazine, as originally published by Popular Publications, Inc., N.Y.: *City of Flaming Shadows* from the January 1934 issue, and *King of the Fleshless Legion* from the May 1939 issue. These stories are works of their time. Consequently, the text is reprinted intact in its original historical form, including occasional out-of-date ethnic and cultural stereotyping. Typographical errors have been tacitly corrected in this edition.

International Standard Book Number: 978-1-60877-173-8

First printing: June 2015

Series editor/publisher: Anthony Tollin
anthonytollin@shadowsanctum.com

Consulting editor: Will Murray

Copy editor: Joseph Wrzos

Proofreader: Carl Gafford

OCR text reconstruction: Rich Harvey

Cover restoration: Michael Piper

The editors gratefully acknowledge the contributions of
Chris Kalb (www.spiderreturns.com) and Rebecca Searson.

Published by Sanctum Books
P.O. Box 761474, San Antonio, TX 78245-1474

Volume 6

Thrilling Tales and Features

Cover art by John Newton Howitt

Back cover art by Raphael de Soto
and John Newton Howitt

Interior illustrations by J. T. Fleming-Gould

ABOVE THE LAW ... SWORN ENEMY OF THE UNDERWORLD ... HATED BY BOTH ...

City of Flaming Shadows

Feature Length Spider Novel

By

Grant Stockbridge

Like the blighting shadows of descending doom, the "darkness" fell upon the city, shrouding section after section in a flame-shot gloom—wherein walked screaming death and swift, unmerciful destruction . . . . Go with the SPIDER as he battles, single-handed, the Flaming Shadows—to save a populace which nightly prays for his destruction!

CHAPTER ONE
"Talk or Die!"

THE road ahead was black. Trees crowded close, reached down leafless, skeleton arms. The low-hanging clouds of the night seemed to squat on their tops.

Richard Wentworth sent the rented Ford roadster bumping up a rutted hill, leaned forward and switched off engine and lights. The car, in total darkness now, sped on with its momentum, topped the rise and scooted creaking down the steep grade beyond. Wentworth watched the parting of treetops overhead that marked the direction of the road, a lighter gray streak amid the darkness.

Without warning, he wrenched the wheel violently to the right. The car's tires whined and popped on the gravel, struck a ditch violently and the Ford jounced with a rattle and crash into the woods. It battered through the underbrush, found almost miraculously a break in the thick trees and jerked to a halt.

Wentworth sat motionless, listening. That swerve from the road had not been blind. A break in the treetops had revealed the small opening into which he had wedged the Ford. Above him a cold wind rattled leafless branches. Shrubbery creaked, springing back into place behind the Ford, concealing it from the road. Distantly a dog howled. That was all.

No sound of that car which, hanging persistently at his heels for ten miles, had finally sent him crashing into hiding.

No sound? That was the answer for which Wentworth had hoped. He was pursued. Detecting that trailing car, he had spurted on past his goal, doubled back. But the car had persisted, and there was work to do. He had no more time for dodging through country roads. If they found him now, they would find the *Spider*.

And crooks who overtook the *Spider* often lived—briefly—to regret it!

Wentworth's lips were smiling thinly as he slipped from the car, a hand brushing the twin guns that nestled in the pockets of his black leather jacket. The shadows reached out and absorbed him.

A half mile away a cottage gleamed white in a small clearing. A single yellow light peeped through the denuded shrubbery that clattered hard switches against its side.

The gleam of the house was not paint. Once it had been bravely white. Now it was lopsided and loose shingles slapped in the wind. Its sides were polished by wind and rain.

A shadow detached itself from the encircling woods, drifted to a shrub where the darkness was thickest. The man's hands went to his face, and a black silk mask slipped into place.

The *Spider* crept toward the lonely cottage.

Months had passed since last he had donned that mask to battle with the Black Death, months in which it had seemed to him and to Nita van Sloan that at last their dreams were to be realized: that the *Spider*'s single-handed battle against crime had wiped out the masterminds of the underworld, had left only petty criminals with whom the police could cope. It had seemed that at long last he and Nita could consummate the love that had been forced to wait upon Wentworth's crusades of justice.

Now, once more, the tocsin had sounded.

Not in New York itself, but in Hamlettown, far upstate. Wentworth had read in the newspapers of the crime there and his face had grown grim. For in those few lines of type describing the looting of a small—but very rich bank—Wentworth had seen a menace that threatened to strip the nation of its wealth, to impoverish millions and send the nation plunging back into the depths of Depression from which it had just begun to climb!

The robber gang had a system that even the *Spider* would be at a loss to combat. Working with uncanny knowledge and precision, the criminals had isolated all Hamlettown, had severed all connection with the world. Telephones had been useless, alarm systems disconnected and, adding to the mad confusion, even the lights had been dimmed throughout the city.

The looting of the bank itself had been simple. The guard had been murdered, as had two police, who finally stumbled on the crime, and Joseph Ringer, the president of the bank. Working with a flaming electrical torch of incredible heat, which apparently had been hooked into the city's electrical system by a powerful transformer, the gang then had burned through steel doors and vaults as if they were so much butter.

The treasury of the United States itself could not resist such an attack!

No wonder the *Spider*, stern defender of humanity and nemesis of the underworld, had dropped everything to race to Hamlettown and take up the trail, a trail that led him now to this lone cottage.

WENTWORTH made a slow, careful circuit of the house, but found no lurking guard. Touching his guns, he stole forward. In his body was no crouching stealth, no furtiveness; directly he moved, with swift strides, yet without a sound.

At the lighted window he paused an instant, listening, heard a man's slow, heavy feet pacing, pacing. Then he crossed to the door, and his hand slid to a compact kit of chrome steel tools beneath his arm. From it he drew a lock pick, a slender long flat rod with a hooked end. A moment he manipulated it in the keyhole; there was a soft rasp and the door yielded beneath his hand.

He closed it softly behind him and located the slow, heavy footsteps. At the end of a short hall a narrow line of light slitted beneath a door.

Wentworth glided to it, peered through the keyhole. On a table an unshaded lamp flickered. Back and forth before it moved the slow shadow of the pacing man, a heavy, hunch-shouldered figure. As Wentworth watched, the man checked suddenly, ground out a curse and pounded to the right out of sight. He was gone a moment, then his body blotted out the lamp again.

He was crouched forward now, with bent head and elbows close to his sides. Slowly he moved aside, dropped into a chair. He stared at the table—and Wentworth stared, too, his lips twisted in a mirthless smile.

On the table was something that glittered warmly in the lamp light. On the table, mingled with sheafs of banknotes, were heaps of gold coins!

The *Spider* straightened and flung open the door. The man cried out, whirled, a crouching menace, eyes glaring in a weather-reddened face. He stepped quickly in front of the table so his body hid the money. Wentworth shut the door slowly. He stood with hands empty of weapons, without movement and without a word, watching the man through the slits of his black mask.

The man's arms were half raised for attack, his

big fingers opening and closing slowly, his breath pumping the chest that showed hairy and thick in the opening of his shirt. A small tin stove glowed red to his left. There was a cot in a corner, the chair and the table. That was all.

"Who—who are you?" the man asked uncertainly. "What do you want?" His voice was a growl.

Wentworth did not answer, but faced him with utter calm. He was taller than the man, his body tapering athletically from broad, fluid shoulders that seemed slight beside the bulk and crude strength of the man he confronted.

The man became disconcerted by the silent regard of those slitted eyes, the blank expressionless mask. He took a half step forward, fists clenching.

"Speak up, damn you!" he roared. "What do you want?"

"Less noise," said Wentworth gently.

"What!" It was a shout.

"Less noise," Wentworth repeated, "and sit down. You're going to give me some information."

In the other's eyes, he read mounting desperation and fear. Suddenly the fellow hunched his shoulders and without warning lunged forward.

Wentworth's right hand moved like a flash. A pistol crashed. The flame of the lamp jumped smokily. The man reeled backward, clapping a hand to his head. Uncertainly he took it away and stared at his palm. It showed no blood. He blinked at the masked, erect figure by the door, a gun held carelessly now in its right hand.

"Just by way of warning," Wentworth said casually. "I clipped a lock of your hair. The next bullet might be an inch lower."

FEAR made the man's face work. Creases showed white against the leathery red of his skin. His eyes flitted about as if seeking escape.

"In God's name," he gasped hoarsely, "who are you?"

Wentworth stared at him fixedly and did not speak.

The man's fear grew frenzied.

"You're not—not from them. I know it. Who — please—"

"My time grows short," Wentworth said curtly. "And there is certain information you must give me."

The man's head shook slowly from side to side. "I don't know nothing," he said. "I don't know nothing."

"You know plenty, Reardon," said Wentworth. "I'll tell you what you know. You are a linesman of the electric company. You know where the main feed wires of the town are, the telephone and burglar alarm cables."

"No!" cried the man. "No!"

Wentworth's voice went on coldly. "A while ago a man came to you and offered to pay you for that information. Last night they used it—and men died."

"I didn't know why they wanted it," the man cried. "I didn't know."

He was kneading his strong hands before him.

"You are the one who is responsible," said Wentworth.

The man took an uncertain step forward. There was no menace in it. There was only pleading in his half-outstretched hands.

"You're not a crook," he said. "You don't talk like a crook. You talk—you talk more like a cop. But you've got that damned mask on. Who are you? Who are you?" he cried.

The gun in Wentworth's hand advanced two inches. "Take a step backward," he ordered.

The man's hands locked together so the muscles quivered in his hairy forearms.

"Who are you?" he pleaded.

Wentworth's lips behind the black mask twisted into a thin smile. "Over by the fireplace," he ordered.

A light footfall sounded in the hall, and Wentworth's eyes glinted. So the occupant of the pursuing car had come at last! But the *Spider* was ready. He had been alert for that sound, but he gave no sign of having heard.

Slowly, pressed back by a superior strength, Reardon retreated. Wentworth's left hand slid into his vest pocket, extracted a cigarette lighter, and his thumb pried off the base. Masking the entire lighter in his hand, he pressed it on the stack of money on the table, stepped back.

The man's eyes fixed on the money. On the top bill a spot glowed like a drop of blood, a tiny red seal—the Seal of the *Spider*!

THE man's breath came hoarsely through his open mouth. "Good God!" he gasped. Suddenly he was on his knees. "In God's name, *Spider*," he said, "don't kill me. I didn't know. I *didn't know*!"

Wentworth's eyes glinted. This was splendid hearing for whomever lurked in the hall. Ears tautly attuned, he listened for the first sound of attack. He had moved out of range of a pistol shot through the door. Well, on with the play. He eyed Reardon.

"Yet," said Wentworth softly, "you helped to rob a bank and four men were murdered."

"Listen," pleaded the man. "Listen to me. I know I did wrong, but listen. A year ago my wife was ill. I went to the bank for money. They wouldn't give it to me, and my wife died because of that. The only reason I kept on living after that was because of my boy, and he's sick now. I tell you that old man Ringer who was killed was responsible for my wife's death. You're supposed to be just, *Spider*. Tell me, didn't Ringer deserve to die?"

Wentworth's tones were cold. "There is something in what you say. Perhaps I won't kill you."

"Oh thank you, thank you," the man babbled.

"But there is a condition," the *Spider* rasped. "Tell me the man who paid you for the knowledge of where the wires were."

The man's hand crept slowly to his throat. His head began to sway from side to side.

"No, not that," he said. "Not that! They'll kill me!"

Wentworth's words leaped at the man. "Then die now!" His gun jutted forward.

There came a slight rasp of the doorknob. Wentworth was ready. He whirled as the door fanned open and squeezed the trigger. Then, even as he fired, he jerked up his hand so that the shot blazed harmlessly into the ceiling. For dashing through the doorway, hurling straight at him was no armed enemy. It was a girl!

Her blue eyes were desperate. Blonde, long hair streamed backward as she sprang, snatching for the gun. Wentworth whirled aside, dodging. The girl plunged on past him, caught herself and spun to face him again. Her breasts panted beneath the mackinaw coat that covered a cheap gingham dress. Her eyes were narrowed in anger. Her mouth was never meant to be as thin and bitter as now.

"You leave him alone," she gulped out. "Leave him alone now."

Wentworth's eyes gleamed with admiration.

"Why didn't you tell me, Reardon," he said softly, "that you had so lovely a defender? We might have had her in to plead for you."

The girl's face was white, except for the spots on her cheeks where the wind had kissed them. She was erect, with a proudly carried head. She began to walk slowly toward Wentworth. He thrust forward the gun.

"Get back," he snapped.

The girl looked straight into his eyes behind the mask.

"You wouldn't shoot me," she said slowly. The cords in her throat were tight. "You wouldn't shoot a woman. The *Spider* doesn't."

SHE continued to advance. Wentworth laughed softly and turned his gun toward Reardon who still, in a seeming daze, crouched on the floor.

"But I kill criminals," Wentworth said softly, "and this man has helped murder four others."

The girl checked, her hand going slowly to her throat. She swallowed with difficulty. "Oh, you couldn't! You couldn't!" she cried.

Wentworth did not answer her. He watched her intently and spoke to Reardon.

"Who is this?" he demanded.

"It's—it's my son's friend," he said. "Elsie—Elsie Thompson."

"I see," Wentworth said softly. "Now, Elsie, suppose you get over by the stove and keep warm until I finish my little talk with Reardon."

The girl shook her head dumbly.

"Quickly," Wentworth ordered. He turned the gun toward Reardon, and the girl moved backward in a panic.

"Now," said Wentworth, "talk, Reardon."

The man closed his eyes. "I'll talk," he said.

The strength seemed to go out of him. He sat upon his heels, his shoulders slumped, his head hanging. His words came almost inaudibly.

"The man who gave me the money said his name was Wiggard. I never saw him before he came up to my house one night and offered me money. He was the only man of the gang I ever saw."

"What did he look like?"

"Short, wide shoulders, bushy black hair—and he had long fingers. If I ever talked about him, he said—" Reardon's hand went to his throat once more—"he'd strangle the life out of me."

"Have you seen him since?"

The man shook his head. "No. The money came by mail. I was supposed to leave the country right away. But my boy—Jack—is sick."

Wentworth acted quickly then. He strode to the table, scooped money and gold into his pocket. The girl cried out softly, but Reardon did not protest.

Wentworth drew his wallet and from it fingered five hundred dollar bills and laid them on the table.

"That will get you away," he said. "Don't worry about your son. Tell me where he is and I'll see that he's taken care of."

THE man gazed up at Wentworth with baffled eyes.

"Don't tell him!" exclaimed the girl.

"I'm returning this money to the bank," Wentworth said quickly. "Where is your son?"

Reardon spoke dully.

"He's at the hospital of St. Vincent de Paul in New York."

"Right," said Wentworth. He backed across the room. "Stay here," he warned, "or the bogeyman might get you!"

He laughed shortly and strode out into the dark hallway, closing the door behind him. Two strides took him to the front door. Another and he was off the porch. But he moved alertly. He had not forgotten the auto that had trailed him. He crouched beside the bole of a huge oak tree that leaned above the house, searching. Then, from behind, fingers plucked suddenly at his throat!

Before they could clamp shut, Wentworth had

seized the wrists and jerked sharply forward. A short curse, and a man hurtled over Wentworth's head and landed heavily on the ground. He was up in an instant, and Wentworth made out his vague figure. A short man with abnormally wide shoulders; his hat had been knocked off, and bushy hair made his head enormous. Wiggard! The man with the strangling fingers!

These things Wentworth grasped in a flash as the man charged. Grim laughter poured from the *Spider*'s lips. He had scarcely counted on such luck as this. This was a man higher up in the chain by which the gang communicated with its underlings. He would capture this one—

He ducked aside from the swift bull-like rush of Wiggard; lashed out with his fist and caught the man on the chin. Wiggard shook his head, retreated a half pace. There was a gleam of metal. The *Spider* sprang forward, seized the man's right wrist and twisted. A sharp pain shot through his hand. A knife had sliced it. Straining arms locked. Their breaths came hoarsely. They fought in the darkness for possession of the weapon.

The man's strength was enormous, but slowly Wentworth forced his knife arm down and up again behind his back. Forced it up until breath panted in hoarse pain from his opponent's lips, upward until the man screamed and the weapon dropped from his fingers.

Wiggard panted out a single hoarse curse and, flailing around with his left fist, caught the *Spider* a violent blow on the throat. Wentworth reeled back, but the man, one arm disabled, did not press his attack. He raced off.

Wentworth braced against a tree, dragged out his gun. The man had disappeared into the blackness. The *Spider* ran after him. A motor roared out into the night, gears clashed, but no lights showed. Wentworth crouched and fired twice at the sound. The motor raced off, dwindled.

Wentworth whirled and raced toward where his own car was parked, a half mile away. He crashed through snagging underbrush, battled through trees that whipped knifelike switches across his face. Panting, he reached the Ford, flung into the seat and fought the cold motor to life. He jerked it raging into the road, then cut it, listening for that fleeing auto.

The wind moaned through the bare tree limbs, rattling them like dry bones; mournfully the dog still howled. All else was silence.

CHAPTER TWO
A Man Is Hanged

THE room was in darkness except for a low-swung light that funneled white glare down upon a mahogany table. That lamp revealed two human beings, one with hands resting on the table, fingers pyramided calmly, the other a man being hanged.

Behind those pyramided hands gleamed the formal white of a dress shirt. But that was all that was visible. The sharp edge of the light's white shaft cut across just below the shoulders. The face was in black shadow. A low, musical voice hummed softly, the fingers tapped soundlessly together.

They were sensuous, long fingers and their tips bent backward slightly, tapering from thick bases to slender points. They were corpse white, and the hands from which they stemmed were covered with thick black hair that curled and seemed to crawl as if every individual hair were endowed with separate life.

The man who was being hanged was perhaps ten feet from the foot of the table, at the opposite end from those hairy hands. His arms were bound behind him, and his whole body seemed stretched. His neck was abnormally long, strained by the noose that dragged upward from behind. And the man was not dead.

The rope about his neck, swinging from the ceiling, was just long enough to allow him to touch the tips of his shoes to the floor, and frantically the man was balancing himself on his toes. He wavered, fell off balance, and the rope yanked tight about his throat. His neck corded with pain; his weathered face turned dark red with congested blood; his eyes bulged.

Desperately the man's shoes pecked at the floor. Finally he got his toes on the proper spot and strained upward, relieving the drag on his neck. It was not enough entirely to loosen the noose, just enough to allow frantic breath to whistle hoarsely through his restricted windpipe.

The humming stopped.

"Bravo!" cried the man softly and the corpse-white palms beat together softly in applause. "Bravo, Reardon! Never have I seen a man last so long!"

Reardon—for it was the linesman Wentworth had forced to talk—fixed glazing eyes on the speaker's hairy hands. Murderous hate was in his stare, but he was helpless. He fought to keep his balance on straining legs, breath rasping.

"You are stubborn, Reardon," the soft voice went on, "but not quite stubborn enough to resist talking to the *Spider*." A chuckle of gentle mirth interrupted the words. "But stubborn or not, in the end you will die, too, Reardon. They all do."

For a few moments the hands pyramided again, and the tableau continued in silence—silence save for the creak of the rope and Reardon's hoarse breath. Then one of the hands moved slowly and touched a button, returned to its former position, fingertips against those of the other hand.

Light showed in a narrow streak on the far side of the room. It widened, a door opened, and three men walked across the deep-piled carpet to the table and sat down silently beside it. They too placed their hands upon its top, but unlike the one of the hairy hands they were entirely visible in the glare of the light, visible except for their faces, which were covered by black masks.

The masked faces stared intently into the darkness above those hands, then swung to regard the man who slowly strangled, swinging in the noose of torture. No one spoke. They waited.

A husky chuckle rippled out, and the white- shirt bosom behind those hairy hands leaned forward slightly. The hands pressed their tips upon the table. The chuckle turned into a low voice that intoned:

"Dearly beloved, we are gathered in this place—" laughter bubbled through the words, "to separate a man from his soul. Perhaps it would be more accurate to say, two men from two souls."

The voice was mild. "This fool who is dying betrayed us to the man who calls himself the *Spider*. After he investigated our little play in Hamlettown, he traced Reardon—and Reardon talked. He won't again."

As if that had been a signal the three men turned their masked faces toward the man strangling. His eyes were closing painfully; the dark red of his face was turning slowly blue, and the tip of his tongue was thrust out between his teeth that were clamped upon it. His struggle for balance was weakening, but stubbornly he fought on.

"I shall not attempt," the one with the hairy hands went on, "to bring the *Spider* here for punishment. It will be enough that he dies. But die he must, if we are to reap the harvest that awaits us. The police are as nothing; Commissioner Kirkpatrick is smart, but he is not smart enough to catch us. Only one man is—and he already is on our trail—the *Spider*. Tonight, the *Spider* must die."

THE white hands slowly clasped. "There are millions in this—millions," said the voice behind them. "Perpetual wealth for all of us. Not one man nor one thousand men can stand in our way."

One of the masked men spoke up for the first time. His voice was deep.

"A thousand murders? Yes, that I agree to. But the *Spider*—he is a dangerous man. More plots of genuine genius have fallen through on that man's account than for any other reason. If we could get by without antagonizing him—"

One of the hairy hands waved in a small gesture, cut off the man's words.

"Without antagonizing him! My dear fellow, let's be sensible. The man already is on our trail. There is no choice but to kill him, before he kills us. I personally have no desire to be put on a morgue slab with that villainous little red Spider of his printed on my forehead!"

One hairy hand balled into a fist and slammed down on the table top.

"Even the *Spider* shall not foil us. There's not a bank in the city that can withstand us—not even the treasury of the United States itself!"

The one who had first spoken among the masked men stirred uneasily.

"It's true our first venture came off all right," he said. "But there we had a linesman to point out which telephone and burglar alarm cables to cut, and the wire for our torch. But here in the city no one person could possibly know all the wires that run beneath it."

One of the hairy hands disappeared beneath the table, and in the silence that followed Reardon's rasping breath grew loud.

The masked man stirred and turned to glower at Reardon.

"I wish he'd die and quit that confounded noise," he grunted impatiently.

His eyes swung back to the table. The hairy hands held now a scroll of oiled paper, which they slowly unrolled, revealing a map of Manhattan Island, crisscrossed with red, blue, black and green traceries.

"No one person knows," said the man at the head of the table softly, "but someone has taken very good pains to record where these things are. This map shows in detail every main wire in the city and where every connection is made. It shows every burglar alarm, every telephone connection, every main feed wire. It shows tunnels through which these go beneath the streets.

"I have enlargements covering all of this and showing in even more minute detail every inch of the tunnels and wires beneath the city.

"Do you see now why the *Spider* must die?"

There was a trembling in the voice of the masked man. He cried, "The *Spider*? My God, I'd wipe out the whole police force single-handed for that map, and what it means!"

Once more the bubbling chuckle issued from the darkness behind the light.

"Splendid! But fortunately that will not be necessary. Only the *Spider* must die—and the Tarantula will gobble up the *Spider*."

He chuckled again as though he had made some great joke.

"Ah yes, the Tarantula." The shirt front leaned forward again, and one hand ticked off fingers on the other as he spoke.

"First, we know certain things about the *Spider*. We know he is a man of wealth and refinement, a member of society. He has appeared often in the underworld in evening dress, in expensive clothes. There can be no doubt that these are facts.

"Secondly, we know that when he fought Wiggard, Wiggard slashed his left hand with a knife. Also, we succeeded in convincing Elsie Thompson, the fiancée of Reardon's son, that the *Spider* had done away with Reardon. She is working for us, and she is certain she will recognize his voice when she hears it.

"Now then. Earl Carroll's 'Vanities' are opening tonight. Every member of fashionable society will be there. The *Spider* will be there. Do you think it likely that in that assembly there will be two men who have a knife gash on their left hands and who talk like the *Spider*?"

THE speaker paused and the heavy, tense breathing of the three masked men became audible. Behind them Reardon struggled weakly in the noose, but his breath could not be heard. He wasn't breathing.

"This, then, is the plan," the low, smooth voice went on. "When the girl has spotted the *Spider*, she will signal and all the lights of Broadway will be turned off. While three men take care of the *Spider*, our boys will take jewels from the women in the lobbies, get the money from the box office; it will help finance us in our further ventures. And"—the Tarantula's voice sank a full note—"if any of our men sees that he had been identified, or if he even suspects anyone has seen his face, kill the witness!"

A murmur from one of the masked men. The Tarantula's fist slapped down upon the table.

"Kill the witness!" he snapped out. "There can be no hesitancy about this. We are modern pirates. The ancient pirates survived because there were no witnesses. They killed every victim. It is the only safe way. There is too much at stake in this to haggle over a few lives.

"Are the instructions understood?"

One asked slowly, "Can we trust the girl?"

A hairy hand waved. "She merely has to identify the man. After that, she does not concern us. Wiggard has a fancy for her—"

"Knives for the *Spider*?" asked another.

"Knives," the Tarantula rolled the word on his tongue. "Usually I prefer them. They are silent and you know where they're going in the dark. But for the *Spider*—machine guns!"

And once more the Tarantula queried softly, "Are the instructions understood?"

Slowly, one at a time, the three nodded, and the Tarantula leaned forward so that a black mask loomed behind the brilliant light, so that the hands with their hairs that seemed to crawl and be alive upon their backs were pressed flat upon the surface of the table.

"Understand this. When the *Spider* is spotted, the three chosen to kill him follow—and the *Spider* dies. There must be no botching of it. Wait until the *Spider* is in a place where our killers can make sure he is dead.

"If our killers fail, no matter for what reason, if they fail to kill the *Spider*—"

One of the hairy hands raised slowly, and a long finger pointed toward Reardon, hanging dead in his noose. "If they fail, they shall die like that—the penalty for all who fail the Tarantula!"

The black-masked head loomed behind the light, turned slowly from one to another of the three masked men about the table, and each in turn nodded.

"Tonight," repeated the Tarantula softly, "tonight, we kill the *Spider!*"

CHAPTER THREE
"For the Spider—!"

THE Broadway that soon was to go black at the bidding of the Tarantula, that soon was to hear men scream, and screaming die, because they had seen too much—Broadway blazed with light. The Great White Way danced with blue, green, red, and dazzling yellow signs. The front of a motion picture house was a solid mass of bulbs spelling "Berkeley Square." Another blazoned "Dinner at 8." And the figure "8" glowed and died, leaped and glowed and died again.

Streams of taxis and limousines flowed with the green lights, panted impatiently when they turned red, and another lane of traffic equally heavy and dense streamed across. Two police at each of the four corners of each crossing; sidewalks thronged with crowds; five minutes to walk a block. Barkers shouting the movies: "Plenty of room. Feature just starting."

Queues at the ticket office, waiting, another double line thronging the lobby, waiting. A burlesque house flaunting coy nudes. "Hold Your Horses," ballyhooing Joe Cook in a thousand lights. Bing Crosby's voice crooning from a loudspeaker in front of "Too Much Harmony." Gobbling voices, raucous horns. And over all, the dancing, flickering, pulsating lights. Bright as day—brighter.

Down the river of light to Forty-Second Street, where a string of words in lights went sliding endlessly along the news bulletin board about the Times Building.

> THE BODY OF A MAN MURDERED BY HANGING WAS FOUND TONIGHT IN AN EAST SIDE STREET. THE POLICE FEAR THAT THIS INAUGURATES ANOTHER GANG WAR.

If the crowds could have known what Reardon's death heralded! A gang war? Wholesale murder

and looting! And somewhere, the Tarantula was waiting to strike, biding his time until the *Spider* was in his trap—patient fingers folded, horrid corpse-like white hands with hair that seemed to crawl.

Around the corner from Broadway and that warning news sign into Forty-Second Street, the New Amsterdam theatre was a living mass of light. Earl Carroll's "Vanities," opening tonight. Curious throngs watching the fashionable first nighters. Full length posters in the lobby of girls coquettishly exposing seven-eighths of their bodies; a sort of glorified burlesque.

At the curb, a constant procession of expensive motors, pausing a moment to discharge men in high silk hats and women in furs and jewels; a glimpse of dazzling white shoulders; cars drawing away to make room for others; Packard, Rolls Royce, Minerva, Lincoln, a Duesenberg, a long-nosed Lancia....

The Lancia purred to the curb; a dark-faced Hindu sprang from the seat beside the liveried chauffeur, flung wide the door, his face impassive, but his eyes glittering beneath his dark turban. This was how Ram Singh liked his master to live: amid the luxury that was native to Richard Wentworth; elaborate ostentation; glittering wealth on every side. It pleased Ram Singh's Oriental soul.

Richard Wentworth alighted, silk-hatted, an Inverness cape showing its white satin lining, white gloves in his hand; a tall, distinguished man, notable even among that rich assembly; an alert man with an intensely vital, alive face. He handed out Nita van Sloan, Nita of the clustering lustrous hair, Nita of the blue eyes of mystery.

Her hand on his arm, she smiled up into his face, red lips apart. Only one thing marred the perfection of the couple, as they strolled in through the elaborate, pestered lobby. On Wentworth's left hand, along the joint between the thumb and forefinger, was a conspicuous strip of court plaster, covering the wound that Wiggard's knife had inflicted.

Presently the curtain rose and eventually, after the swift passing of many entertaining minutes, it fell again. Everywhere a spontaneous applause burst from the wealthy bon vivant audience. The intermission was on, the intermission when the Tarantula would strike.

Wentworth and Nita rose and made their way to the lobby, joining a slow line of dozens of others such as they. Unobtrusively, a girl with piled blonde hair, garbed in a clinging black dress, filed out also with a bushy-headed man.

If Wentworth saw them, he seemed to pay no heed. He and Nita nodded to many acquaintances. Stanley Kirkpatrick, Commissioner of Police, smiled behind the suave points of his mustache. Big Tim Lally, a stout and polished politician, waved a negligent hand and introduced the woman beside him, a woman with hair that flamed like fire above the pure, gleaming white of her dress, Tamara Lamaris.

A thin, bespectacled man with a gray, narrow face stood with him and nodded also; Professor Johnson Hague, an electrical engineer; a blond,

"You are the *Spider*!" she screamed. "You killed—"

excessively muscled young man who had lost a thumb from his left hand, Russell Daliot, swimming instructor at an athletic club.

All these and many more Wentworth saluted as he stood chatting with Nita. He drew a platinum cigarette case and proffered it to Nita, flicked flame to her cigarette and his with his light. And across the lobby the girl with massed blonde hair, the girl in the clinging black, gripped the arm of the man with her and stared at the court plaster on the hand that held the lighter. The two drifted closer to Wentworth, passing just behind him and listened as Wentworth bent close above Nita, murmuring in her ear.

"*M'amie*," he whispered, "in just about two minutes, all hell is going to pop loose! Get to Ram Singh, go to my apartment. I'll join you there later."

He turned slowly toward the blonde girl. She pulled her hand out of her bag and pointed a revolver at Wentworth's breast. Her eyes were wild, her face distorted with rage.

"You are the *Spider!*" she screamed. "You killed—"

Wentworth sprang in, seized her hand and forced it straight up. The bullet spattered tile work in the ceiling.

"The *Spider*! The *Spider*!" men cried.

Screams tore out. The bushy headed man who had been with the girl raced for the door, ploughing through chatting people, bowling over a woman.

The girl clung to the gun, striking at Wentworth with her free hand. Over her head, Wentworth saw Kirkpatrick struggling toward him through the crowd. He twisted the revolver, still in a vertical position so that no one would be wounded, jerked it free and tossed it to Nita.

"Keep the girl here," he cried.

He raced headlong toward the door after the man who had fled. The theatre lobby was in wild disorder. The murmur of shouts swelled to a screaming hysteria. Wentworth tangled with three men and two women bolting for the door, saw Kirkpatrick reach the girl and Nita.

Then the lights went out.

It was as if a great black hand had suddenly throttled that entire throng. The dark smote silence over the theatre for an instant. Then a woman screamed. A man shouted, "Thief!"

Bedlam rioted through the house. Ushers flashed on hand torches, and their minute spots of light flickered weirdly over the audience.

Wentworth fought frantically to get through the tangle. He was certain the man who had fled was Wiggard. He must capture him! About Wentworth, men shouted angrily, and suddenly another woman screamed, and another.

"My jewels!" one screeched.

A sharp cry tore from Nita. Wentworth whirled toward her, arms thrown out protectingly. His charge knocked down a man. He raced on, saw the gleam of a raised knife. Wentworth lashed out savagely. His fist crunched upon flesh and bone and a body struck the floor.

"Nita!" cried Wentworth. "Nita!"

The gleam of an usher's light spotted her. Her dress had been stripped almost from her body. Her gleaming topaz necklace was gone. Wentworth jerked off his coat and threw it about her, stooped over the unconscious man on the floor. The necklace was in his grasp. He seized the man, hauled him to his feet.

"Where's the girl?" he asked Nita swiftly.

"With Kirkpatrick," she gasped, "outside."

"Follow me," Wentworth shouted.

With Nita behind him, he once more battled the surging, screaming mass of humanity to the street. Not a light on it except the crazy beams of auto lamps. Forty-Second Street was dark. Broadway was dark.

All the flickering dance of lights was stilled. Darkness lay thick as soot upon the entire district. But it had not silenced the voices of the multitude. From theatres and shops people poured. A mob charged from a subway entrance. Trains were stalled, and darkness below the earth meant terror. Women fell in the panic and were trampled. Their screams added to the bedlam.

Wentworth shielded Nita with his body, fought off surging masses of people and inched gradually to the curb, still dragging his unconscious captive. A man screamed in mortal agony. A woman ran by, her clothes hanging in rags.

The headlights of autos gashed bizarrely through the gloom, showing the masses of panic-stricken people, dashing wildly one way, turning and rushing back; revealed Kirkpatrick upon the curb, alone except for one traffic officer.

"Every phone and burglar alarm in the district is dead," he shouted, as Wentworth finally reached his side. "I've sent a man for help."

"The girl," cried Wentworth, "where is the girl?"

Kirkpatrick stared at him blankly, then jerked a hand impatiently.

"I couldn't fool with her in this panic," he shouted back above the chaos.

Wentworth cursed, then shrugged. One more possible clue wasted. He dumped his captive at Kirkpatrick's feet.

"Here's one of the gang," he shouted.

The sharp clap of a pistol bit through the confusion of sound and the man on the pavement jerked convulsively, threw out a hand and rolled over on his back. A bullet had ploughed between his eyes. The gang had removed a witness!

Wentworth whirled, angry eyes searching the mob-choked darkened street, but found no trace of the gunman. His eyes held an ugly light. His last possible clue had been wiped out.

Out of the tangled mass of traffic, Wentworth's Lancia nosed its way to the curb. Wentworth thrust Nita into it.

"Ram Singh," he snapped in Hindustani, "guard the *Missie Sahib* with your life! Home, fast!"

The Hindu's eyes glittered. *"Han, Sahib!"* he said, and sprang to the seat. The car spurted away.

In the distance police sirens were at last wailing. Wentworth shoved off into the crowd, his white vest and shirt-front gleaming.

"Wait!" cried Kirkpatrick, "Wait, help me here! You're the only cool head about."

Wentworth grinned crookedly at him, the glimmer of auto headlights showing his lean face.

"Sorry, Kirk," he said, "I have business out there." He darted off into the darkness, Kirkpatrick's shout ringing after him.

He found a taxi, ordered out a frightened, pinch-faced man.

"No, no!" the man cried, "I got this first!"

Wentworth caught him by the coat, jerked him out.

"Police business," Wentworth snapped, whirled to the driver.

"Somewhere in this district," he told him, "there's an emergency service truck of the electric company. Find it!" He thrust a twenty dollar bill into the man's hand.

WENTWORTH'S mind was racing. He recognized the technique of this wholesale robbery and knew that his fears had been realized. The gang that had staged the Hamlettown bank holdup had struck New York.

Yet this had been an excessively elaborate setup for the small loot they could have hoped to obtain. There had been some other motive, Wentworth was sure. And the attempt of the blonde girl—Elsie Thompson it had been—to kill him? What did that signify? He was certain Wiggard had been with her. A smack against the back window of the cab and a tinkling of glass punctuated his thoughts.

Wentworth crouched, peered back. A bullethole was in the glass. But behind them was a tangle of cars; there was no way of telling from which it had come.

The taxi driver looked back with a frightened face. He jammed on the gas, and the car leaped ahead. Wentworth was unarmed. He rarely carried a gun when in evening dress and had not tonight. Nothing to do but run for it.

The taxi slewed around a corner, jammed on brakes, and the driver turned a white face.

"You got to get out, mister," he chattered.

Wentworth snaked his cigarette lighter from his pocket, leveled it at the man.

"Get going," he ordered. "Fifty dollars if you do as I tell you. If you don't—" he thrust the lighter forward like a gun.

The man's mouth sagged. He gasped a curse, sent the taxi hurtling forward. He was just in time. Around the corner behind lunged a heavy sedan. Tires squealing, it slammed against the curb and spurted after them.

A gun hammered behind. Lead plunked into the back of the cab as it did a two-wheel skid into Fifth Avenue. Traffic was jammed ahead from curb to curb. No passage there, and the death car behind!

The driver flung a glance over his shoulder, jerked on the emergency brake, and in the same movement threw himself out and behind another car. Wentworth spotted the murder car sweeping into the Avenue. He leaped to the runningboard, into the driver's seat, and jammed on the gas.

A solid rank of cars blocked his way. He twisted the wheel, headed for the sidewalk. People scattered before him. The taxi hurtled the curb, did acrobatics turning on the walk. Fifty feet, and it shot off into 39th Street. Cut gas! Jam brakes! Wrench the wheel and give her the gas again! The cab, shivering and rocking, pounded westward.

He hurtled south on Sixth, roared downtown for several blocks, got back to Fifth and headed north.

He had left the area of darkness now. Street lights blazed. People, huddled in overcoats, stared curiously at the coatless man with his gleaming formal shirt and vest driving a taxi. The bitter wind knifed him. Traffic was congested as in the rush hour, but Wentworth expertly wove through it. He turned east when he reached the block on which his apartment house stood and braked up to its back entrance. He stepped from the cab, started across the sidewalk. Then he shot a swift look behind him and bolted for the door at a dead run. But before reaching it, he checked abruptly and dived to the pavement.

The staccato laughter of a machine gun filled the street... machine guns for the *Spider!*

CHAPTER FOUR
The Tarantula Strikes

MACHINE gun bullets blasted chips from the wall of the apartment house before which, a moment before, Wentworth had stood. They turned the door into a sieve. Wentworth, flat on the pavement, rolled frantically back toward the taxi.

Flakes of cement flew past his head. The stream of lead raced toward him, followed with a vicious splatting on the walk as he flung himself beneath the taxi. Bullets ploughed up the asphalt, beat a drum roll on the cab, but Wentworth, huddled far forward where the thick iron of the engine shielded him, was safe for the moment.

For the moment, yes, but there was nothing to keep that death car from stopping, nothing to keep the killers from thrusting the muzzle of their fast-speaking gun beneath the cab and sending a dozen slugs to tear the life out of him.

Wentworth, face on the cold pavement, peered out cautiously. The death car had halted a hundred feet behind, snubbed to a stop to allow the gunner better aim. But now it lurched forward again, gears screaming with speed.

Wentworth threw a desperate glance about. The men in the car didn't know he was unarmed, but they would suspect it, if he did not soon return their fire. Then he would be doomed. The car's headlights glinted on something in the gutter, a broken milk bottle. Wentworth seized it with an exclamation. A pitifully weak weapon against a machine gun? Yet the *Spider* smiled.

The flying wheels of the death car raced closer. Once more bullets tore into the cab, probing for their prey beneath it. Wentworth calculated carefully, swung his arm horizontally and sent the bottle slithering across the pavement. His aim was true. It struck point first against a tire. The jagged points bit through the soft rubber.

A hiss of air! A wild swerve! At fifty miles an hour, the death auto careened across the street, the driver fighting a crazy steering wheel. The car hurdled the curb. With a rending crash, it rammed a steel lamppost. The post slammed down. The car's rear slithered about and smashed broadside against the stone wall of a building.

Instantly, Wentworth was out from beneath the taxi, sprinting toward the wreck. The engine was killed. A headlight sent its beam straight upward. Over the steering wheel a man lay like a discarded rag. Wentworth ignored him. He jerked open the battered rear door, scooped up the machine gun, looked swiftly for the second man.

A face stared at him through the opposite window. Wentworth jerked up the muzzle, then with a grim smile lowered it. It was the face of a corpse!

The gunner had tried to leap out and been pinned between a two-ton car and the wall. He was held upright like that.

Wentworth spun to the other man limp across the steering wheel, caught his hair and hauled back his head. The steering post had speared into his chest. As Wentworth grimly implanted the *Spider*'s seal upon the man's brow, the eyes fluttered open a moment, blood dribbled, then poured from the mouth and the man doubled forward, dying.

Wentworth leaned through the car and imprinted the seal on the face of the corpse that stared at him unblinkingly through the window. Queer that police had not come yet, he thought. But probably the force was stripped down to throw as many as possible into the Broadway area.

Wentworth climbed out, then whirled, dodging as he turned. A knife flashed over his shoulder, grated against the side of the car. A brutal face was within inches of his own.

GRINNING, the *Spider* dropped the machine gun and struck out savagely. His fist smacked the face, sent the man reeling. Only a knife? Here was an easy capture, a witness against this murderous gang. Wentworth's glance shot beyond him. A small car was parked behind the taxi. It was empty.

The man recovered, threw up his knife hand and flung the blade, a fleeting gleam of light, straight at Wentworth. The *Spider* twisted his body aside and laughed aloud.

"Now," he taunted the man, "you haven't even a knife. Want to surrender?"

The man's answer was a headlong charge, and Wentworth waited his attack with lips thin and eyes alight with the joy of battle. As the man rushed in, he stepped close and slammed two blows against his body.

His assailant made no effort to ward them, but locked his arms about Wentworth's body, pinioning him. The arms were like steel. The man rammed his head under Wentworth's chin, thrust upward savagely. Wentworth was bent irresistibly backward. Pain shot through his spine.

And now, finally, the cold winter air rang with the whine of police sirens, a whistle screamed and a half block away a policeman pounded toward them at a dead run. No help for the *Spider* there. That seal on the dead men's foreheads would doom him as surely as this man's arms would snap his spine unless he broke the hold.

Wentworth's arms were pinned helpless at his sides, but were free below the elbow. He gouged his thumbs into the man's sides, groping for the nerve center that would paralyze him, a jiu- jitsu trick. But the man's muscles were hard and tense with the fury of his struggle. He writhed in pain but held on, tightened his arms until Wentworth's breath gasped hoarsely, until his spine seemed about to snap.

Without warning then, the *Spider* allowed himself to go lax, let all his weight sag upon the man's arms. His assailant was thrown off balance. The two men lurched to the street together.

The policeman was close now, but the man made no effort to escape. He seemed intent only upon killing Wentworth. His hold had been weakened. He released it, flung himself upon the *Spider* and seized his throat. Wentworth doubled up his knees, struck savagely with them. The man pitched backward with a scream of agony, and Wentworth reeled to his feet.

The policeman was fifty feet away. He threw up his gun.

"Halt!" he shouted.

Wentworth dodged like a jackrabbit and sprang to the taxi. The officer could easily take his assailant captive now, and that would serve Wentworth equally as well as holding the man himself. And the *Spider* must vanish. Those seals on the brows of two dead men spelled doom if he were caught.

Behind him the cop's gun roared. The windshield cracked, as the cab behind surged forward. Again the gun boomed. Lead whined by.

Wentworth twisted his head, stared back and saw the man who had attacked him rise up in back of the policeman—saw a knife slash down. The killer snatched the policeman's gun, leaped into his own machine that had been parked behind the taxi. The chase was on again.

POLICE cars skidded into the streets behind. Wentworth, low over the wheel of the taxi, sped north again, twisting and turning. Knife-like wind stabbed him with cold, but he did not feel it. His blood raced with excitement. The man behind him made no effort to escape from the police who were hard upon his heels, seemed intent only upon one thing—the death of the *Spider*.

The *Spider* smiled grimly. If he could lead this man away from the police for a few moments, he still might capture a witness against the gang.

Wentworth jerked around a corner on two wheels, squeezed between two trucks and spun north, took another corner, cut through an alley and turned west. He flung a half-second glance back over his shoulder and, smiling, found the killer's roadster still burning along in his wake.

South again, ploughing through the heavy trucking of First Avenue. Slamming brakes, crashing fenders through holes a motorcycle would have feared to try, Wentworth drove as only a fearless man who knows he is master of his car would dare. And always behind him, he drew the roadster, never quite within striking distance, yet never lost.

Without warning a tower of steam geysered from the radiator of the taxi, gushing hot water over the windshield. Wentworth's lips tightened. Bullets had drilled the radiator. A few blocks now and the cab would stall. He had to act at once. He must overcome this man despite gun and knife, take him prisoner and escape from the police. Their cars were everywhere now. On all sides sirens wailed.

But police must not take the *Spider*. The taxi marked him as the fugitive from the spot where the *Spider* had twice killed. Wentworth knew he would be blamed also for the stabbing of the policeman. And the *Spider* must be entirely unhampered, if he were to save the city from this murderous gang—if he were to avert the peril that only he could see towering over the very nation itself.

Wentworth flung another glance backward. The killer's car was only a half block behind now, and gaining. A tight smile lifted Wentworth's mouth. He let the man creep even nearer, then slammed around a corner into a deserted street, locked brakes and leaped from the taxi. He landed in a foot-slapping run, seized a lamppost and pivoted behind it.

Tires squealed as the killer spun his car into the street. Too late he saw the taxi. His brakes shrieked, the back end of the car swayed wildly and the roadster slammed into the cab. The rear of the cab crumpled. The roadster reared like a horse, its front wheels climbing the taxi.

The killer dived head first into the windshield. The shatterproof glass sagged, radiated cracks, but did not break and the man bounced back into the seat like an explosion-tossed sack of meal.

Wentworth darted to the car, hauled him out. Working swiftly, he stripped off the man's coat, dragged him to the lamppost and rapidly bound him to it with the man's own belt. Then he laid just beyond reach of the police gun and the knife.

Wentworth bent then and on the unconscious man's forehead printed the small red seal of the *Spider*.

If the police would only believe, here was evidence to clear the *Spider*. Here was the killer and the weapons with which he had slain the policeman. And he had put into their hands, where he also could question him, a member of the robber band.

WENTWORTH jammed arms into the coat he had taken from his victim and raced off into the shadows. The sirens were at hand now and a police car skidded, swaying into the street, dodged the two crashed cars by a hair's breadth and slid to a frantic halt.

But Wentworth was already a block away, not running with pounding feet, but slipping from shadow to shadow, weaving back toward First Avenue. The dress shirt and white vest were hidden now by his victim's coat. And as he glided along, he tore off the formal winged collar and tie, thrust them into his pockets. He dug his patent leather shoes into gutter slime, splashed mud over his trousers, slouched his shoulders.

Wentworth was gone. The *Spider* was gone. A bum shuffled out among the stacked crates of produce that lined the sidewalks of the First Avenue market district.

A half empty truck jammed to a halt to avoid a racing police car. Wentworth shuffled out and swung up on the tailgate, sat jolting laxly with the rumble of the truck as it roared into motion again, watched other police cars zip futilely by, followed by the muttered imprecations of the truck driver.

Wentworth swayed patiently. Now that he was quiet, he felt the still cold of early morning. His breath made white funnels of fog from his nostrils. He shrugged his shoulders higher about his ears, content. In good time he would get in touch with Kirkpatrick. Together they would worm out this killer's secrets.

Then, abruptly, Wentworth straightened, his eyes narrowed. If these criminals could trail his taxi, why could they not also have trailed the Lancia in which he had sent Nita van Sloan to his home? Why could they not have struck at her to make doubly sure of his elimination from the chase?

His lips grim, Wentworth slid from the truck and ducked into the warmth of a subway, hurried to a telephone booth. He dropped a coin in the slot and zipped the dial. His head was steady, but in his eyes there was dread.

The clickings of the phone mechanism buzzed in his ear. Then the intermittent, fixed ringing the bell began. Began, and went on and on. Half dazedly he counted the rings, *five—six—seven—eight!* Good Lord, why didn't Jenkyns answer? Even if

Nita herself were not there, the faithful old butler never would leave without Wentworth's express permission—*eleven—twelve—thirteen!* Wentworth slammed up the receiver as a train hammered into the station. He darted across and squeezed through closing doors, stood tensely on the rear platform watching gleaming steel rails race backward into blackness.

His eyes did not see the tracks. His eyes were pinpoints of rage. Freely he risked his own life in the service of humanity in the foiling of the underworld. But when the slimy hand of crookdom reached for Nita... !

THE night train crawled, clacking over switches, rumbling to slow halts at stations. Wentworth's fists clenched in impatience. He beat one with slow tension against the side of the door. Finally the train jolted into Twenty-Third Street.

Wentworth streaked across the platform, up steps three at a time, swung into a taxi, flinging a Fifth Avenue address at the man. The fellow stared at him, snarled: "Get out of there, you bum!"

Wentworth thrust a bill at the man.

"Get moving!" he snapped.

The driver hesitated. The man looked like a bum, but that voice crackled with command, and the bill in his hand—he looked down at it—was twenty dollars! The driver kicked his motor into life, sent the taxi leaping forward like a race horse when the barrier is sprung. Wentworth sat tightly forward on the edge of his seat, hands white-clenched fists on his knees. Wind whistled past.

"Faster!" he shouted. "Faster, and you get another twenty!"

The cab roared down a side street, as the lights switched red ahead. The driver clapped his hand on the horn button, held it there and ripped through the already moving traffic. Shouts rang after him. A police whistle burbled. The cab darted on, got a break on the next light, just changing, and stormed

Wentworth dragged him to the lamp-post, rapidly bound him to it.

down Sixth Avenue among the elevated pillars. One more frantic two-wheel turn, another that tore the tires and they skated with locked brakes to a halt. The address Wentworth had given was two doors from his apartment. He flung the second twenty at the man, but for all the fear that tore his breast, for all his impatience, he got out slowly, slouched past his own doorway and to the back entrance.

For five minutes, while the watchman stood chewing a toothpick, Wentworth was forced to wait. Twice he started to identify himself and thrust past. There could be some excuse.... but caution forbade—

caution and the certainty of Kirkpatrick's keenly suspicious inquiries when he learned the *Spider* had killed at Wentworth's very back door. The wrecked car still lay across the street, Wentworth saw.

Finally, the watchman vanished into the building and Wentworth slid in, raced upstairs. Panting, he reached his floor. He sprang with a rush for the knob, then jerked himself to a halt, chest against the door. Suppose all this was a trap, suppose Nita van Sloan was a prisoner within, held pending his return, bait for a trap?

Wentworth crouched to one side of the door, unlocked it and thrust strongly. There was an explosion like dynamite. Hot air blasted past within inches of his face, protected behind the wall. A great slab of plaster cracked and tumbled from the doorway and Wentworth dived inside the room, rolled and came up ready to attack.

No one in sight, but on a table directly across from the door rested a sawed off double-barreled shotgun, braced against the wall. A heavy bookend had jerked a wire fastened to the triggers when the door's opening had yanked a string, pulling the bookend off the table. A simple, but effective, death trap.

Wentworth took that in in a flash, raced through the apartment.

"Nita!" he called. "Nita!"

Silence answered him, broken only by the rapid slap of his own hurrying feet. He ran on, searching one after another of the fifteen rooms. Finally, by the kitchen door, he found a trace of the men who had come and gone, found Jenkyns, his old white head torn by a bloody wound, crumpled on the floor.

Wentworth went down on his knees instantly. Life still fluttered in a feeble pulse. Fury distorted Wentworth's face.

Jenkyns slugged, perhaps fatally wounded—and Nita van Sloan vanished!

CHAPTER FIVE
Orders From the Tarantula

WENTWORTH sprang up from beside the injured butler, raced to the phone in the hall. This was once the *Spider* could legitimately call on the police for help, once when the wide-flung police organization could work better than the *Spider* alone.

He snatched up the phone, dialed the police swiftly.

"This is Richard Wentworth," he told the man who answered, and he gave his Fifth Avenue address. "I want—"

Then his eyes spotted a crude drawing that hung on the wall, and his voice choked. His hand tightened about the phone until it ached with strain, and rage burned over him in a white-hot tide. He swallowed hard, stilled his racing pulses.

"I want," he continued, voice cold and utterly without expression, "an ambulance from the hospital of St. Vincent de Paul rushed at once to my apartment. There's a man here injured seriously, a blow on the head. That's all, thank you."

And he hung up without asking that police throw out their wide-flung dragnet for Nita van Sloan, hung up the phone and stared with bitter eyes at the drawing on the wall.

It was hasty work, but done by a fiendishly clever hand. It depicted Nita van Sloan being hanged!

There was a rope about her soft throat, and her toes barely touched the floor, so that she was strangling slowly, dying as had died the man who first had given information to the *Spider*.

The drawing showed Nita's face distorted, eyes bulging, skin darkening with congested blood. It sent chill fingers of fear probing through Wentworth's veins. Nita—his Nita—

He tore his eyes from the fearful fascination of that drawing, saw then a folded paper attached to its lower edge. He tore it loose, read with eyes of dread:

> Dear *Spider*,
>
> When a man strangles slowly, it is unbelievable torture. But you probably know that already, don't you, *Spider*? I have tried to show you with my humble art how your charming lady will strangle. You will notice that her tongue is between her lips, and that she has bitten completely through her tongue. This is not unusual in cases of slow strangulation. I would not advise, dear *Spider*, that you call the police. Better wait until we phone you.
>
> THE TARANTULA

Wentworth reached out a slow hand to that horrible drawing, placed it, carefully folded, in his pocket. He snatched up dressing gown then, to hide his telltale clothing from police, kicked off muddy shoes and toed into house slippers, hurried to Jenkyns' side. He placed a pillow beneath the bleeding head, got water and bathed the wound.

Soft footfalls jerked him about. Ram Singh, eyes narrow beneath his dark turban, stared down at Jenkyns. His figure stiffened.

"*Wah!* Ram Singh is a bungler, a fool!" he berated himself. "I go search for you and this happen!"

"You left the *Missie Sahib!*" Wentworth's voice was accusing.

Ram Singh touched his forehead. "*Han, Sahib!* She send me for you."

No help here—and no blame. That was like Nita. Wentworth turned back to Jenkyns. He was still working over him when the heavy thump of feet in the hallway heralded police. A surgeon rapidly completed the first aid Wentworth had begun, ordered Jenkyns carried to the ambulance.

Wentworth touched the surgeon's arm.

"A private room, doctor, and spare no expense to pull him through."

The doctor nodded, eyes curious behind thick glasses, and strode out. But two policemen remained on guard at the door, and when the elevator returned, Stanley Kirkpatrick stepped from it.

Wentworth spoke to Ram Singh without moving his lips.

"Not a word," he said. "Understand?"

Ram Singh said nothing, but seemed to recede into the shadows, motionless as a statue.

KIRKPATRICK was immaculate as always, a gardenia gracing the lapel of his elegant evening dress, Chesterfield coat over an arm. He glanced down at his clothing apologetically.

"This is not really a formal call, Dick," he said. "It's just that I've not had time to change yet. It's been rather a busy evening."

His keen glance strayed about the hall, spotted the shotgun trap. He turned and surveyed the shot-peppered wall of the hall.

"You, too, seem to have had a busy evening. Damnable of them to slug old Jenkyns." His voice was careless, too careless. "Any idea who did it?"

"Not the slightest."

Kirkpatrick touched his pointed mustache with a thumbnail, crossed to the gun and fingered its mechanism. Wentworth watched him narrowly. He knew the commissioner, knew that when he was most casual, he was most keenly alert.

"Any luck in that chase of yours?" Kirkpatrick asked over his shoulder.

Wentworth shook his head slowly. "No." His crisp hair was disordered and his fists were thrust savagely down into the pockets of his black silk robe. There was a slight smile on his face, but there was tension in his breast. It was an effort to keep himself in hand. Within him was only the thought that Nita—his Nita of the blue eyes of mystery and the red, red lips—was in the clutches of that ruthless gang, of a band of wanton murderers. Nita in peril, and he was forced to remain inactive, unable to ask help of this man who could assist so mightily—able to do nothing but seek to get rid of Kirkpatrick so that the *Spider* might search.

And Kirkpatrick was questioning him in his cannily indirect way. That girl's cry in the lobby of the theater: "You're the *Spider*," which apparently had signaled the robbers' attack, two killings by the *Spider* in a single night, had renewed Kirkpatrick's always active suspicions, Wentworth knew. He smiled casually, took out his platinum cigarette case and offered it.

"You're hinting at something, Kirk," he said lightly, "out with it."

The police commissioner allowed him to light both cigarettes before he spoke again.

"Just curious about that chase of yours, Dick. Tell me about it."

Wentworth compelled patience in himself, kept his voice calm.

"I saw a suspicious looking car," he said. "I trailed it for a long while, but apparently I was wrong in my hunch. I came home, rang the bell. When Jenkyns didn't answer, I became suspicious and in that way avoided this gun trap. I found Jenkyns unconscious and phoned at once. I didn't ask for you because I thought you'd be busy."

"Nonsense, Dick," Kirkpatrick, waving his cigarette so that the blue thread of smoke spiraled. "Never too busy for you. In fact, I was going to look you up, anyway. You must let me reimburse you for that long taxi drive on police business."

Wentworth veiled his eyes. He must put his mind more directly on Kirkpatrick. Worried about Nita, he had been paying only half attention to the Police Commissioner and this was getting serious. So they had traced the taxi!

"That would be difficult," he laughed, "I changed taxis four times and I've forgotten the amounts."

Kirkpatrick dragged on the cigarette. His eyes glinted. "So you changed four times?" he asked softly. "Curious. That taxi in which you first rode tonight was mixed up in a shooting affray at the back door of your apartment. Machine guns apparently.

"Then a car was wrecked, two men killed in it, and the seal of the *Spider* put on their foreheads. A policeman came up and was stabbed to death. In other words, the *Spider* is running wild again."

He looked directly into Wentworth's level gaze.

"Was I mistaken tonight, or didn't the girl who pointed that gun at you in the theatre say, 'You're the *Spider*'?"

WENTWORTH smiled slowly. "She did." He vouchsafed nothing further.

Kirkpatrick continued to stare at him. "Hmmm," he said, "I thought so." He crossed to the table and ground out his cigarette on an ivory ashtray.

Wentworth's pulses throbbed hard and slowly. He knew that thin old scar upon his right temple was glowing red. His heart cried out against the delay. Nita! Nita was in peril. He looked down at his own cigarette, his lips twitching mockingly.

"Do you want to examine my cigarette lighter again, Stanley?"

Kirkpatrick shook his head. "I've done that at least three times. Do you care to hear the further adventures of your taxicab?"

"You mean the taxi that I first rode in tonight, I take it?" Wentworth said precisely.

"Yes," said Kirkpatrick, his mouth grim. "The *Spider* escaped in that same taxi and later it was in a smashup down on the Lower East Side. Another man was injured and tied to a post, and the seal of the *Spider* was found on his forehead, too."

Abruptly all Wentworth's attention riveted on Kirkpatrick. Here was hope, here was a trail that might lead to Nita. He had feared the man was dead.

"You said 'injured,' I think, Stanley?" he asked, restraining his anxiety.

"Yes, he's in Bellevue," said the police commissioner. "This time it served the *Spider*'s purpose to let the man live. Beside him he planted the weapon with which the *Spider* had killed the policeman, trying to pin his crime on the man. The man—he's a lad named Corey—recovered consciousness in the hospital. Said he turned the corner, saw a taxi ahead and tried to stop. That's all he remembers."

"Perhaps," ventured Wentworth, "perhaps this time the *Spider* was not guilty. It looks as though he had turned the murderer of the policeman over to you."

Kirkpatrick watched him narrowly. "It's more likely," he said slowly, "that the *Spider* wanted us to think he had done that."

Wentworth shrugged. His voice was light. "Perhaps you're right. But you know, I'd like to question that man Corey. It's just possible he might be tied up in some way with those crooks who robbed the people in the theatre tonight."

Kirkpatrick's face grew grave.

"Robbery," he said, "is the least of the crimes committed tonight. Eight persons were murdered. Apparently they got in the way, or saw the robbers' faces."

Wentworth's gravity matched his own. This was part of the horror he had foreseen in that robbery upstate. "Do you realize the potentialities of this business of turning off lights, telephones and alarm systems?" he asked slowly. "Do you realize what that means in looting banks? Unless we find some way to foil that gang they'll strip the city. Man, the very financial structure of the nation is in danger!"

"You're telling me!" said Kirkpatrick, but his voice was deadly serious.

Wentworth pressed a heavy palm to his forehead. It was close to four in the morning. He was weary, his mind besieged with worry. "Something must be done at once," he said. "I think possibly the first thing to do is question Corey. If you'll give me a few moments' time, I'll change and be with you."

He had started for an inner room, when the telephone's ring stopped him. Its low metallic buzz was like the whirring of a rattlesnake. Wentworth's thoughts flashed to that warning from the Tarantula. But his hand, picking up the phone, was steady, his voice expressionless.

"Richard Wentworth speaking."

The answer was a low, mocking laugh. "The Tarantula speaking! We have your Nita here!"

Nita! Nita! Wentworth's heart cried. He heard Kirkpatrick's light tread, and his mouth corners tightened. He was watched on every side, by the police, by the underworld—

"May I speak to her, please," he said to the Tarantula in a conventionally polite tone.

Again came low laughter. "Why not?"

ABRUPTLY Nita's voice was vibrant in his ear: "Don't let them coerce you, Dick, I don't matter—"

Confusion over the wire. No chance to say a word. Kirkpatrick listening. When the phone transmitted a voice again, it was the Tarantula's hatefully dulcet tones.

"A brave woman, and a clever man! Allow me to congratulate you. I did not think you would fall into the crude traps my rather less intelligent workers set for you. But there was no harm in trying. It is imperative that you cease to interfere with our plans. There is too much at stake, too big a fortune for myself.

"This is what you must do, *Spider*, and Nita van Sloan is our hostage to force you to obey to the letter. You will book passage on the *Europa*, sailing Thursday, day after tomorrow. I will tell you later what I wish you to do in Europe, and there will be someone on hand on the boat to see that you do your part. Nita will talk with you every day, to assure you that we are fulfilling our side of the bargain.

"But at the first disobedience on your part, the first day the man we send to watch fails to report to us, on that day *Nita van Sloan dies!"*

It was fortunate Wentworth's face was turned toward the wall. It was distorted with anger too strong for even his masterly control to hide, anger the more furious because it was impotent. He thought frantically. There was no way out.

"Well?" came the Tarantula's voice, sharper, more commanding. "What do you say?"

And Wentworth, teeth locked, jaw muscles ridged, forced himself to speak casually. Kirkpatrick must not suspect.

"I agree," he said slowly, forced a laugh, and added, "let me compliment you on your art. Your technique is irreproachable, but I cannot say that I like your choice of subject matter. If what you painted should ever come to be a reality"—his voice rasped suddenly—"I do not think that even you would find the Earth a very pleasant place to live."

The mocking laughter of the Tarantula answered him.

"Very clever, *Spider*. If I had not known how clever you could be, I should not have phoned you while the commissioner of police was at your elbow!"

A *click* of disconnection and the line went dead. Wentworth stared at the mouthpiece.

"Yes," he said, "I should be glad to see more of your work. That's a date, then."

He hung up and turned slowly to Kirkpatrick, his face calm again despite the mad whirl of his thoughts.

"I think I shall have to reconsider, Kirkpatrick, that little trip I was to make with you. An artist friend has just invited me to go abroad and view an exhibit in Paris. We shall be sailing almost at once, and I have quite a number of things to wind up before I leave."

Kirkpatrick's smile faded slowly. His searching eyes inspected Wentworth. "It is absolutely necessary for you to go at this time?"

Wentworth nodded. "It is absolutely necessary."

"It seems a little strange," said Kirkpatrick, "that you should change your plans so suddenly. A little strange."

The eyes of the two men fixed unwaveringly on one another. Kirkpatrick raised a freshly lighted cigarette to his mouth, funneled smoke from his nostrils. A thin blue veil drifted between them.

Wentworth nodded affably. "I'll admit it must seem strange. However, as I said, it is necessary."

"I see," said Kirkpatrick. He bowed slowly. "If you'll excuse me, Mr. Wentworth," he said, "I'll be going."

Wentworth half raised a hand. "Don't be like that, Stanley."

Kirkpatrick raised a quizzical eyebrow, turned on his heel and strode away, calling his men behind him.

Wentworth started after him, stopped, shook his head. He couldn't blame Kirkpatrick. He turned slowly to his dressing room, then shook off his lethargy and swiftly donned dark tweeds and a soft shirt. Yes, what he had done had been necessary. The Tarantula had known Kirkpatrick was in the house. Wentworth could not afford to leave with him, lest the Tarantula exact payment for that violation of his agreement—payment that would mean suffering for Nita.

Wentworth's face was bitterly lined. As always, the *Spider* must play a lone hand.

"Stay here," he ordered Ram Singh. He caught down a dark soft felt from a shelf and pulled its brim down over his eyes. Automatics slid into twin holsters beneath his arms. A loose topcoat that would not hamper his movements, and the *Spider* stalked from the apartment.

Out through the service entrance, down four flights of stairs before he signaled an elevator—in case the Tarantula watched. He left the building by the trade entrance, strolled with slow, casual steps along the avenue until he was out of sight of the apartment building, then he sprang to a cab.

"Bellevue Hospital," he snapped.

THERE was no need to go by the desk. He knew where the prison ward was. He strode swiftly into the gray stone pile, entered the elevator and on the third floor paced rapidly, with the oddly muffled sound that hospital floors give out, to the prison ward. Against the door a policeman was seated in a tilted back chair, a gun upon his knees.

Wentworth strode swiftly to him, taking out his wallet. He held out the wallet with his police card showing. "I'm Richard Wentworth," he said, "I want to see Corey."

No answer from the man. No indication that he saw Wentworth at all. What the devil? Was the man asleep at his post? Wentworth caught him by the shoulder, shook him violently. The gun clattered to the floor. The policeman's body lurched sideways, the chair tilted with it, and both plunged to the floor. Then Wentworth saw the reason. A knife had been driven through the man's neck into his brain!

Wentworth seized the door and thrust it inward. His groping hand found the light switch, clicked it and a thin smiled twisted his lips. The Tarantula took no chances of his gangsters' confessing. Corey was dead—hanged—with a rope about his throat drawn up over a closet door!

Wentworth moved swiftly down the hall, took the stairs to a side entrance. No need for Kirkpatrick to know he had come. He caught another taxi several blocks from the hospital, sped back to his apartment. Nita was safe, for the present, he reassured himself; safe as long as Wentworth left the city and remained inactive; safe until the Tarantula had looted the nation and no longer needed a hostage from the *Spider*.

Then, Wentworth knew, Nita and himself would both die.

Alighting from the taxi a few blocks from his apartment, Wentworth re-entered the same way he had left. He strode swiftly to his music room, caught up his violin with eager hands, tucked it beneath his chin. Strident, angry music whipped from it as he shot his bow across the strings. Music was his one consolation in time of trouble.

The whir of the telephone interrupted him. Wentworth did not wait for Ram Singh to answer. Violin beneath his arm, he crossed to the phone in two strides.

"Wentworth speaking."

"The Tarantula speaking," words snarled at him. "You agreed not to enter this case, to keep hands off. You broke that agreement!"

The voice stopped, but another sound reached Wentworth's ears. He heard Nita cry out, heard her cry out again, in pain. She was struggling for breath; a sob caught in her throat; the breathing ceased!

"In God's name, Tarantula," Wentworth pleaded, "stop! I'll drop the case, I'll—"

A sob of pain, a gasped breath from Nita, quickly hushed as though she were ashamed of that cry, and over the wire came the Tarantula's voice again.

"That is a little warning of what will happen to your Nita if you repeat tonight's attempt. One more such errand and the strangling will continue until Nita's little white teeth bite through her tongue!"

CHAPTER SIX
The Altar of Duty

WENTWORTH'S face was haggard. During those few moments in which Nita had suffered, years had written their agony across his face. He spoke slowly, his voice calm as death, his eyes like glacial ice.

"You harm her, Tarantula," he said distinctly, "and all hell will not be able to hide you from my vengeance."

The transmitter rasped with his vehemence. For a full minute then, the only sound over the wire was the faint buzzing of the current. Wentworth's face was rigid, his nostrils dilated and rimmed with white. He waited. Finally other sound filtered through the phone. Laughter. The Tarantula was laughing!

"You have a nice knack of expression, *Spider*," the voice mocked. "I find it a little startling. Your warning is accepted at face value. However, in the meantime—" and the voice turned brittle with command—"you will obey!"

Wentworth controlled himself rigorously. "I have agreed to that, but I would like to make you another proposition."

"And that is?"

Wentworth drew a deep breath. "Let me ransom Miss van Sloan."

"Of course," the Tarantula answered. "That was my intention...."

"How much?" Wentworth snapped out.

"Ah, but you grow impatient," there was a tantalizing slowness in the Tarantula's drawled words, something feline, womanish, in the way he dragged out the torture. "The payment I demand is not in money, but in service."

"I am rich."

A bubbling chuckle cut off his words. "Rich? Of course you are, *Spider*—but not rich enough! Not all your millions could comprise one-tenth the money I shall take. One-tenth? Not one- twentieth! For when New York is stripped, there is London, and Paris, and..." the laughter burst through again. "But you get my point, I fancy, *Spider*?"

Wentworth cursed, a single tearing oath. Despite all his efforts at control, fury poked hot irons into his brain; fury at his own helplessness; fury at the enormity of the crimes proposed, crimes that the *Spider* would be helpless to prevent.

"Yes, *Spider*, it is unpleasant," the Tarantula drawled again, "but you will obey. Ah, yes, I think you will obey, for any deviation from strict neutrality will mean—"

"It is unnecessary to repeat that," Wentworth snapped.

"Ah, you do not like to hear what will happen to—Nita?"

"Miss van Sloan, *vermin!*"

"Vermin, yourself!" mocked the Tarantula

Wentworth held himself rigidly in check. This would not do. He was allowing the Tarantula to goad him, and that was a disadvantage. There was high good humor and self-satisfaction in the Tarantula's voice when he spoke again.

"The conversation is pleasant, Wentworth, but time grows short." The tone became crisp. "Here are your final instructions. When you reach London, you will immediately determine the best way to obtain maps of its wiring systems. Your brain is too valuable to keep merely idle. I have decided to let you assist me. If you don't—"

WEARILY, Wentworth hung up and stared into the blank wall ahead of him, seeing in imagination again that dread sketch of Nita, hanging. His face was set in a grim mask. It was obvious that every time he left the house, a henchman of the Tarantula trailed him. At the *Spider*'s first counterattack, Nita would suffer.

Wentworth walked slowly to the music room, picked up his violin again. But his music was uncertain. Wentworth's mind was torn between duty and his love. On one side he placed the nation's bankruptcy, which undoubtedly was threatened through the lootings of the Tarantula. He placed there, too, the scores of murders those lootings would mean, the misery of an impoverished populace.

A few more robberies, and long lines of depositors would form at the doors of the banks. Runs would destroy more than the robbers stripped, and penury would spread throughout the land. The Tarantula was endangering the recovery of the entire nation, finally beginning to fight its way up out of the depths of Depression!

That was the weight he must place on one side of the balance, and on the other—good God!—the life of one woman! Wentworth's music grew wild, half mad in its throbbing. What did it matter if one life was that of the woman who above all others meant everything to him? What did it matter if her death would tear his heart in two? It was one life against scores, one life against the life of a nation.

Wentworth's music faltered and died. He stood with the violin hanging at his side, his shoulders bowed. Between his love for Nita and his service to the nation, there could be no choice. Nita must be sacrificed on the high altar of duty, must die that the nation might live!

Wentworth's hands became huge knots at his sides. There was a dry cracking, and the neck of the violin snapped in his hand. He looked down at it slowly, touched the jagged ends with a finger and woodenly placed the broken instrument in its case. He turned and strode from the room, draped a hat down over his brows, almost subconsciously caught up his sword cane, and paced to the door. Silently as a shadow, Ram Singh strode after him.

"No, Ram Singh," Wentworth said dully.

Ram Singh bowed submissively, touching cupped hands to his brow, but Wentworth saw determination in his face. He started to insist, then lifted wide shoulders in a half shrug. What difference did it make? He moved blindly to the elevator and out of the apartment house, walking with weighted feet, his head bowed.

Cold wind moaned between the buildings. It made street lights sway and circle. The air was sharp with frost. Wentworth, without his overcoat, did not notice. He strode on, scarcely realizing where his feet led. He stumbled once and peered about curiously with vacant eyes. Abruptly, then, his head snapped up and his gaze sharpened.

All about him, street lights were dim! They had not gone out, but seemed drained of all current, showed only as faint yellow blobs choked by darkness. Alertly, Wentworth peered about. He was at the corner of Eighteenth Street and Fifth Avenue. Neighboring apartment houses and shops displayed only dying lights. Wentworth knew what that portended. The Tarantula had struck again!

A SWIFTLY moving figure across the avenue caught his eye. A policeman pounded up to an alarm box, clanged open the door and grasped the lever. The metallic rattle of it reached Wentworth. The policeman cursed, slammed the box shut, plunged up the dark, deserted street with slapping feet.

Wentworth watched him go, turned back to survey the street. A man slipped from nearby shadows and stalked toward him, his shoulders furtive. Wentworth faced him, his hands hanging ready at his sides, the sword cane with its tip forward. The call to action stirred his blood.

The man came on unhurriedly. The shadow of a pulled down hat hid his face. Three feet away he stopped.

"Go back to your apartment," he ordered.

"And just why?" A curious lightness crept into Wentworth's voice.

"You know why," the man said. "These are orders."

Wentworth spoke with mocking humility. "I hear and obey." He bowed, sweeping his left palm to his forehead. There was no anger in him. He had found the way out. For the present he would obey. But afterward—

He turned and strode back the way he had come. Distantly in the north now he heard the growling moan of police sirens. From the west came a sound that made Wentworth's heart contract, the staccato death laughter of machine guns!

An armored motorcycle with blue-clad police crouched low behind the shield, shot past and skittered into a cross street. Wentworth, a small smile unwavering on his lips, strode steadily northward. This was the kind of thing police could do. The *Spider*'s battle would come later.

Ahead, a police squad car halted at Twenty-Sixth Street. Men spilled from it. Behind, bedlam broke loose. The pop and chatter of guns was continuous. There were screams and shootings. Wentworth pushed steadily on, walked deliberately up to the police who had thrown a cordon across the avenue at Twenty-Sixth.

"Halt!" a stocky cop challenged.

"Righto," said Wentworth lightly, "but I can't give the countersign."

"What are you doing in there?"

"Just taking a morning stroll," Wentworth explained.

"Yeah," growled the officer, "well, you just stroll along over here until the sergeant comes back." He was an alert youngster, getting a huge kick out of his job.

Wentworth nodded affably and went with the cop, watched as other men of the squad commandeered autos from a nearby parking lot and placed them in a barricade across Fifth Avenue, headlights streaming full strength into the darkened area.

"Commissioner Kirkpatrick has ideas, I see," Wentworth commented.

The policeman peered at him suspiciously. He held his gun ready. Presently the sergeant strode across, glared at Wentworth beneath truculent eyebrows.

"What the hell are you doing here?" he demanded.

Wentworth slid a card from his vest pocket and presented it between two fingers. The sergeant grunted at it, read by flashlight and looked sharply back at Wentworth.

"I'm sorry, sir," he said, "but you'll have to wait. Commissioner's orders. No one to leave the area until he's looked them over."

Wentworth bowed silently, and the stocky young policeman marched him to a small, picket-fenced yard, standing guard with a tensely held gun. Wentworth peered down the avenue now brilliantly illuminated by the headlights. Where was Ram Singh, he wondered. A thin smile twisted his mouth. No need to worry. If Ram Singh wished to,

he could penetrate a cordon held by the entire police force of New York.

Shots continued to echo from the distance, then a tearing explosion ripped out. A momentary lull in the firing, and a heavy car skidded out of Twenty-Fourth Street into Fifth. Two others squealed behind it, and the three raced toward the barricade.

POLICE opened a spattering fire. The cars charged on unwaveringly. An arm thrust out a car window and a small black object arched ahead through the headlight glare.

Wentworth shouted a warning, threw himself to the ground. His guard dived, too. White flame blossomed among the parked cars. There was a terrific detonation. Two autos heaved up like flung toys, black against the white and red burst of fire. Wentworth reared up, snaking guns from beneath his arms.

Men, torn by steel and blast, screamed in the street. A body lay in a bloody puddle on the walk. There was a gap in the barricade. The cordon was broken.

There was a terrific detonation; two autos heaved up like flung toys.

With scarcely slackened speed, the escaping gang cars skirted the pit the grenade had torn in the pavement and roared on up the avenue. Wentworth, crouching, banged at the tires of the foremost car.

The stocky police guard cursed beside him, hurdled the fence and ran, firing, toward the autos. A machine gun spat from the second car. The cop stopped, took two quick steps backward, hands gripping his stomach. He folded over slowly. His face skidded on the pavement.

The first car in the line yawed wildly as Wentworth continued his careful fire. It wobbled around a corner, the other two closing up behind it. Wentworth hurdled the fence, gun ready. An armored motorcycle burst past, took the corner with its side car in the air. Its machine gun stuttered into action.

Wentworth went slowly back to the policeman, turned him over and stared down into his youthful face. No chance for life there. A dozen slugs had torn through belly and chest.

Holstering his guns, he paced to the yard and picked up his sword cane. He went back beside the body. His face was austere, lined. Wholesale murder—and his hands were tied! The twist of his lips showed his teeth in a smile that was half snarl. But not for long, not for long!

Wentworth looked up sharply as a big Cadillac snubbed its nose to the curbing. Commissioner Kirkpatrick's dark, striding figure, thick in a black camelhair coat, pounded up the street, and presently returned more heavily to where Wentworth stood beside the body. Kirkpatrick peered up from under his derby.

"Lord, Dick!" he exclaimed. "What are you doing here?"

"Just out for an early morning stroll," Wentworth said casually. "Got stopped by your cordon on my way home."

"Stroll, oh, at six A.M.?" Kirkpatrick was distraught, his words seemed preoccupied. "You picked an unfortunate locality. I'll have to ask you to return to headquarters with me."

Wentworth raised a shoulder in a slight shrug. "Whatever you say, Stanley, but can't we get this over with here? I very foolishly came without my coat—and it's chilly."

The wind moaned as if to confirm him. Kirkpatrick's coattails flapped against his legs. He eyed Wentworth steadily a moment, began talking monotonously.

"One of my men punctured a tire of the lead gang car. They abandoned it around the corner and got away in the other two. They left two of my motorcycle men there dead. That makes eighteen tonight. Eighteen of my men and twelve others. They looted a bank on Fourteenth Street, burned through doors and vault like so much butter. God knows how many millions were stolen."

His words had come out slowly, like the report of an automaton. Now he spoke with a forceful directness that told he had made a decision.

"It is queer, Dick," he said, "that you always manage to be on hand when this gang gets busy."

Wentworth's alert eyes took in the police commissioner's forward thrust shoulders, his suspicious glance.

"Yes, it is queer," Wentworth said. "Scarcely seems it could be coincidence, does it?"

"That was what I was thinking." Kirkpatrick's voice was soft. "There is another thing that I should like to have explained. The watchman at the bank was stabbed in the back, and in the wound I found this."

He held out his hand and across it lay a thin blade of steel, perhaps twelve inches long, jagged at the end.

"This is obviously," said Kirkpatrick, "the end of a sword, broken off in the wound. It is a queer weapon for a criminal."

The commissioner took a step nearer.

"Dick," he said, "you are one of the few men I know who carries a sword cane. That is it in your hand now, isn't it? Let me see it."

And he reached out his hand for the cane that Wentworth carried.

CHAPTER SEVEN
Reardon's Son

WENTWORTH looked down at his stick as if he were seeing it for the first time. It was of simple dark wood with a slender amber handle that fitted as neatly as a foil's hilt across the palm. Where the amber ended, a jerk would separate hilt from scabbard and a thin blade of fine steel would be instantly ready for offense or protection.

As Kirkpatrick had said, a strange weapon, but one that Wentworth, skilled in fencing, had found tremendously effective. Yet Wentworth, so familiar with its excellence, stared at it strangely. He felt as if he had grasped a venomous snake in the dark. Until now he scarcely had been conscious he carried the stick, had picked it up as a matter of habit when he left the house. But now he knew suddenly that this well-loved weapon had become a thing of peril.

He knew, just as surely as if he held that blade bared in his hands, that its tip was broken off and that the jagged steel would match this murderous fragment that Kirkpatrick held in one hand while the other reached out for the cane.

Wentworth remembered with a sense of shock the shadow who had ordered him back to the apartment. Of course, the Tarantula could not have known he would carry the cane, would want him at home to receive Kirkpatrick when the police commissioner came. He knew—even as he smiled suavely and told Kirkpatrick, "Of course,"—that the Tarantula had planted this trap for the *Spider*, was seeking to involve him in his own crimes and tighten his stranglehold.

"Of course," Wentworth said again to Kirkpatrick. "My stick."

He lifted it from the ground, but in the act of surrendering it, hesitated, looking at the commissioner sorrowfully. "Why do you distrust me so, Kirkpatrick? Do you think I am the sort to stab an innocent man in the back?" There was bitterness in Wentworth's voice.

He was stalling for time, thinking furiously to find some way out. Short of running away, a thing that would condemn him more surely than the broken point of his sword, how could he escape this trap of the Tarantula?

Kirkpatrick's eyes did not falter; his hand outstretched for the cane was no less demanding.

"Eighteen police were killed tonight and twelve bystanders," he said heavily. "That's thirty lives, thirty wiped out by this gang of criminals. I cannot do less than investigate every possible clue. Even if it pointed to myself, I would feel compelled to demand that my men investigate it."

Wentworth laughed aloud, and again there was a bitter note in his voice. But his eyes were sparkling. He had glimpsed the shadow of a man beside the adjoining building. "Friendship," he said, "the golden love. There is a proverb about that." His words were harsh, unnaturally loud as he quoted in

Hindustani. He finished the phrase and said, "Since you demand it, here's my cane, Kirkpatrick," and once more he lifted the stick.

There was a sharp, muffled sound of a blow and, without warning, Wentworth pitched forward on his face, the cane beneath his body. Kirkpatrick cursed once, staring down in bewilderment. On the ground beside his fallen friend a knife gleamed. In the darkness at the corner, a shadowed form showed an instant, then fled. Police guns banged. Kirkpatrick pounded after that fleeting shadow. Wentworth's eyes opened carefully. From beneath his body he whisked the sword cane, sent it slithering along the gutter into a sewer opening.

He pulled his hand back beneath him and lay as before.

PRESENTLY feet pounded back beside him and Kirkpatrick dropped his prostrate friend over into his arms. His breath was short.

"Dick!" he called urgently. "Dick!"

Wentworth flickered his eyelids, opened them slowly. He muttered, rolled his head.

"What—what happened?" he asked weakly.

"Someone threw a knife," Kirkpatrick said. "Luckily it turned. The hilt knocked you out."

Wentworth sat up heavily and squeezed his temples between his palms, propped elbows on his knees. His voice was muffled.

"Now, in the name of Heaven," he mumbled, "why do you suppose anyone did that?"

"I'm trying to figure that myself," said Kirkpatrick, his voice sharpened. "Where is your sword cane?"

"Sword cane?" said Wentworth slowly. He took one hand from his head and groped about on the ground, turned heavily and looked on the pavement. "Got a light?" he mumbled. A detective splashed the beam of a hand torch.

Wentworth scrambled to his feet, stared around.

"The damned thing's gone," he exclaimed. "Now I see why that knife was thrown!"

He whirled toward Kirkpatrick.

"Don't you see?" he demanded. "Someone is trying to throw suspicion on me. A sword is broken off in a man's back. When I'm about to clear myself by giving you my sword, unbroken, they knock me unconscious and steal the sword cane so that I can't prove my innocence."

Kirkpatrick stared directly into Wentworth's eyes.

"A very clever trick," he said.

"You're dealing with a very clever criminal," Wentworth told him.

Kirkpatrick nodded slowly, his gaze still on Wentworth's.

"A very clever criminal," he agreed. "That should make you the more anxious, Dick, to help me capture him."

Wentworth rubbed the back of his head gingerly. His voice was regretful.

"Yes, it should," he said, "but unfortunately I've promised my artist friend to sail Thursday." He sighed. "It's too bad. This case does seem quite interesting."

Kirkpatrick's voice was harsh. "I never thought," he said bitterly, "I'd live to see the day Richard Wentworth would run from danger."

Wentworth allowed his hand to fall to his side. "Neither did I," he said quietly. "Do you want me any longer? As I pointed out before, it's chilly."

Kirkpatrick's gray-blue eyes were scornful.

"No," he said shortly. "I want you no longer."

Wentworth nodded, picked up his hat from the pavement and walked slowly up the avenue to his apartment house. He strode in jubilantly. Ram Singh bowed impassively, eyes glittering beneath the spotless white of his house turban.

Wentworth grinned boyishly. "The next time I tell you to throw a knife at me, Ram Singh," he said, "don't throw it so confounded hard!"

THERE was very little sleep for Wentworth that night. He and Ram Singh packed. They threw together two compact theatrical makeup kits, then flung themselves down for a nap. At ten o'clock, Wentworth roused, found Ram Singh had prepared a simple breakfast. He ate hurriedly.

"You have on two suits of clothing, Ram Singh?" he asked.

"Han, Sahib!" the Hindu bowed.

Wentworth nodded. "Good. Now have the florist make up some flowers, order a big basket of fruit and have Jackson bring the Lancia around at once."

"Han, Sahib!" Ram Singh was gone. Ten minutes later, Wentworth descended and entered the Lancia.

"The hospital of St. Vincent de Paul," he told the chauffeur and Jackson, tanned, square-cut face smiling, saluted and sped the Lancia on its way.

A bespectacled, stout nurse directed him to Jenkyns' room and he went directly there with Ram Singh carrying the baskets of fruit and flowers. Jenkyns was conscious, but white and weak. His head was swathed in bandages. He told Wentworth in whispers that he had not seen the assailants who had knocked at the door and struck him down when he answered.

Wentworth glanced over Jenkyns' chart with a practiced eye.

"You'll be up and about soon," he assured him.

Behind Wentworth, Ram Singh was rapidly unpacking the basket of fruit. He deposited half on Jenkyns' dresser, then together Wentworth and Ram Singh left the room, signaled a nurse.

"Jenkyns has asked me," Wentworth told her,

"to give part of his fruit to the son of an old friend who, he says, is in the hospital. Jack Reardon is the name. Will you find out where he is, please? I want to deliver it personally."

The nurse hurried off, came back in a few moments and led them to another wing of the hospital, to a public solarium where a gaunt young man sat in a wheelchair. Ram Singh deposited the fruit on a table beside him, and the nurse left.

Young Reardon stared curiously at the two. His identity was apparent in the modeling of face and head, but his forehead was more intelligent than his father's.

Wentworth looked him over slowly, nodded in approval. He pulled up a chair.

"I'm Richard Wentworrth," he said. "I promised your father I'd look you up to see if I could help—"

Reardon continued to study him, hostility creeping into his gaze.

"My father wrote me about someone who had promised help, but didn't identify him. Elsie—that's my fiancée—doesn't..."

Wentworth nodded. "She doesn't believe my intentions are good, eh? I gathered as much when she tried to shoot me last night."

Reardon frowned, eyes wide.

"Elsie tried—Oh, I don't believe that!"

Wentworth smiled quietly. "Can you stand?" he asked.

Reardon's surprise was still large upon his face.

"Elsie wouldn't do a thing like that," he said stubbornly.

Wentworth waved a hand.

"Let's not quarrel over it," he urged. "I haven't filed any charges against her and won't. But she is in danger from another source, the people who have deceived her about me. Right now, I want to do something for you. Can you stand?"

Reardon stared fixedly at Wentworth. The *Spider*'s keen, vital countenance was the sort to inspire confidence. After a few moments of study, Reardon nodded slowly.

"Yes," he said. "I'm leaving the hospital tomorrow."

Wentworth looked him over slowly. Despite his recent illness and the poorly-fitting hospital pajamas, it was apparent that Reardon was well-built. He and Wentworth were of about the same size.

Wentworth nodded. "I think a sea trip would do you a world of good," he said. "You're sailing tomorrow."

THE youth stared at him, his eyes, as gray as Wentworth's, going wide. "Gee, that's swell of you, Mr. Wentworth!" he said. "But I got to get to work and send Dad some money. He ain't making much these days, and—"

Wentworth measured the boy with his eyes again, took in the firm line of the jaw.

"Your father doesn't need your help," he said slowly.

The boy's chin got stubborn. "It's kind of you, of course, but I can take care of him. I don't want him to have to depend on charity."

Wentworth shook his head slowly, his eyes kind.

"He's not on charity," he said. "But he doesn't need your help."

Wentworth's sympathetic tone penetrated the boy's consciousness. He stared into the older man's face and his eyes got wider. He put a hand on the chair arm to steady himself.

"You mean something," he got out with difficulty. "You mean something you're not saying."

Wentworth nodded slowly. "Your father is dead," he said gently.

The words did not seem to register with young Reardon. He shook his head, pressed his right palm to his forehead, looked up quickly at Wentworth as if he suspected some joke, realized then what had been said and slumped back into the chair.

"Dead," he said. "Dad's dead. But how? What?"

Wentworth's face went grim. "How much guts have you got?" he demanded.

Reardon's questioning eyes narrowed slowly. His jaw clenched.

"I'm no kid," he said quietly. "I can take it."

Wentworth inspected him closely. "I think you can," he said. "You'll have to. Your father was murdered by a gang of criminals."

The boy's posture did not change. But the pallor of his face deepened and an ugly light glinted in his eyes.

"You know who did it?" the words rasped.

Wentworth shook his head slowly. "I know the gang that did it, but I don't know its identity, its whereabouts, or its leaders. I need your help to find out."

Reardon said slowly, "Will you tell me about it?"

And Wentworth did, sparing the youth nothing.

"You can help me catch those criminals if you will," he said. "But it will require courage and fortitude."

The boy struck a clenched fist upon his knee.

"Try me," he demanded.

Wentworth had been studying the youth throughout their conversation, and he was satisfied. He nodded.

"You will take a sea trip, disguised as myself. This will permit me to work against the gang unhampered by shadowers."

"But—" Reardon began.

"Yes, I know," said Wentworth, "You want to come to grips with the gang yourself. I said this would require fortitude."

"It seems more like running away," the boy said, and the stubbornness of his jaw became more emphatic.

Wentworth locked gaze with him. Reardon was no youth to be browbeaten, but Wentworth willed to dominate—and the *Spider* was Master of Men! Reardon's eyes dropped.

"You're right, sir, of course," he said. "It is foolish of me to attempt to butt into a thing like this. I'll—I'll do as you say."

"Fine!" said Wentworth. "Let's go to your room."

REARDON got up and moved steadily to a nearby door.

Wentworth gestured to Ram Singh. The Hindu entered, began to unwind his sash. He seated the boy on a chair, took a makeup kit from the fruit basket and rapidly tinted Reardon's face the same hue as his own. He reshaped the nose with wax, built the cheekbones higher, gave Reardon one of the two suits he wore, took shoes also from the basket. In ten minutes there were two Ram Singhs. Wentworth looked Reardon over carefully.

"Fold your arms," he instructed. Reardon did so. "Now bow slowly and say *Han, Sahib!*"

Reardon did as bidden, and Ram Singh's white teeth showed in the flash of a smile. Wentworth spoke rapidly to the true Ram Singh in Hindustani, then he and the false Ram Singh went down the stairs, out past an unsuspicious nurse. In the Lancia they sped to Wentworth's apartment. Much later, the true Ram Singh returned.

"You were not seen?" Wentworth asked.

Ram Singh's smile was proud. "I was not seen, *sahib.*"

"Good," Wentworth nodded. Immediately he set about instructing Reardon in posing as Wentworth, imitating his voice, gestures and posture. The makeup would do the rest. There was a day and a half in which to prepare him.

He had a struggle with Reardon over the impossibility of notifying Elsie, but finally prevailed. "I promise to restore Elsie to you unharmed," Wentworth pledged. "And what I promise, I fulfill."

He had Ram Singh keep watch for her at the hospital, to follow her and perhaps obtain a clue to the Tarantula's whereabouts. But Reardon's disappearance from the hospital had been in the papers and apparently she had taken alarm. She did not show up.

Finally, an hour before sailing time, on the second day, Wentworth made up Reardon as himself. Then, giving final instructions to Ram Singh, which he made the Hindu repeat after him, he watched as the two of them left the building and entered the taxi that would take them to the *Europa.*

Each day he had been allowed to talk for a few moments with Nita. She was unharmed and fairly comfortable except for her close confinement, but over her head always hung the threat of death. Once she had tried to beg Wentworth not to go, to sacrifice her and fight the criminals, and the connection had been broken abruptly. Later the Tarantula had telephoned a warning.

Using the marvelous dictaphone that Professor Brownlee had invented for him, Wentworth had made records of his love making, of his violin, enough to last a full month of daily conversations with Nita. These Reardon had taken with him. Wentworth knew he could count on Nita's ready wit to fill in any gaps.

Late that night the *Spider*, in slouch hat and worn clothes, left his apartment building by the tradesmen's entrance. He took a cab, left it at midtown and took another. Left the second cab at Ninety-Sixth Street and took a downtown Seventh Avenue local to Brooklyn. There he hired a Ford at a self-drive station and headed, along night- darkened roads, toward his Long Island estate, secure in the knowledge that the Tarantula thought him miles at sea on the *Europa* bound for England.

A MAN darted from the shadowed porch as Wentworth brought the hired car to a stop in his own driveway and stepped out.

"Put the car up, Jackson, and have my large cruiser ready in twenty minutes."

The man's tanned, square-cut face was smiling. He had firm lips, trustworthy eyes. "Yes, sir," he said. "In ten minutes, Mr. Richard."

But Wentworth was already a dozen feet away, racing toward the porch steps. He kept his servants to a minimum; the fewer there were, the fewer could discover his secret enterprises. And of them all, only Ram Singh and Jenkyns knew that Wentworth was the *Spider*.

But Jackson was trustworthy. He would give service without question, doing whatever Wentworth commanded. Jackson had been in the Army with him, a first sergeant in his company originally, a sergeant major when Wentworth had become colonel, and he had followed Wentworth back to civilian life. All the tortures of the Inquisition could not drag from him one syllable of Wentworth's secrets.

So Wentworth had not hesitated to enlist Jackson's help in his scheme to trick the Tarantula. He raced into the house, seized a phone, and put through an emergency call to Kirkpatrick. In less than five minutes the commissioner's precise accents vibrated over the wire.

"This is Commissioner Kirkpatrick."

RICHARD WENTWORTH

Wentworth's lips twisted in a slight smile. Stanley was in for a surprise.

"Richard Wentworth speaking."

He heard Kirkpatrick's breath catch, rushed on without giving him an opportunity to speak. "I'm at my Long Island estate," he said. "Tell you later how I contrived it. This is the important thing now. The gang that have been terrorizing the city kidnapped Nita the night of the theatre holdup. They are holding her hostage and forced me to leave town and to keep hands off their depredations.

"That was why I told you I was leaving town."

Kirkpatrick broke through the torrent of words. There was a buoyancy in his voice apparent even through his sharp, clipped speech.

"Bully for you, Dick. I should have known you wouldn't desert."

Wentworth's voice was grave. "You don't know how near I was to deserting you, Stanley, with Nita in danger."

"Couldn't blame you," Kirkpatrick snapped.

"But I need your help, now, Stanley. I can't return to town as Wentworth. This is my plan. The *Britannic* docks late this afternoon. I'm taking my fast cruiser, and I'll board her somewhere around Montauk. I'll be in disguise and under the name of Rupert Barton, from Scotland Yard. I'm supposed to have been called in by you for consultation. Will you radio the captain for me and meet me at Quarantine?"

Kirkpatrick's tones were lively with hope.

"I will. And what we won't do to this gang, won't be worth doing."

There was no gaiety in Wentworth's tone. The battle plan was laid, the rival forces were poised on the verge of conflict, but even before the fight started the Tarantula held the strategic points—Nita was in his power.

"Don't underestimate the Tarantula," Wentworth said heavily. "He is a shrewd conspirator, and very powerful. Till tonight, Stan."

"Till tonight."

CHAPTER EIGHT
"I Know the Spider"

WENTWORTH hung up and in the same movement whirled and darted from the house again. There was no time to be lost if he were to reach Montauk and board the *Britannic* while it was still dark, before even the sunrise passengers were aboard to detect his subterfuge.

Pounding out onto the dock, he heard the low-throated mutter of the cruiser's powerful engine, but the cautious Jackson had not turned on the boat's lights. Wentworth sprang into the cockpit.

"Montauk, Jackson," he called, "and two hours to make it in."

Jackson's firm-lipped face was ruddy in the hooded light from the binnacle. Wentworth's feet had hardly touched the deck when, with a deepening hum, the cruiser sheered off from the dock. Spinning the wheel with a practised hand, Jackson turned to smile at Wentworth.

"I'll have you there with a half hour to spare, sir," he promised.

His hand went to the throttle. Deeper roared the motor. The prow of the cruiser lifted, a white crested wave curled back from the cut-water.

Wentworth walked slowly forward, glimpsed dark sea water sliding past. Going down into the cabin, he called back, "Wake me when we reach the light," then flung himself down on a locker and was almost instantly asleep. When Jackson aroused him an hour and a half later, they were rounding Montauk and dead ahead on the southern horizon the yellow lights of a liner gleamed. Wentworth studied her carefully through night glasses, picked out the familiar silhouette with its two squat funnels, a black stripe near their tops. It was the *Britannic*.

"Lay me alongside that liner, Jackson," he said, "then get back to the estate and forget this little excursion."

Half an hour later, clad in brown English tweeds, his hair bleached yellow, his features altered with a makeup kit, he hailed and boarded the *Britannic* and found the way paved for him by Kirkpatrick. He remained out of sight through the day in the captain's cabin, resting and planning.

At Quarantine, Kirkpatrick boarded the liner from a swift police launch and greeted Wentworth formally as Inspector Rupert Barton of Scotland Yard. Chatting carelessly, Wentworth in the clipped English drawl that he knew so well, they descended to the launch, and not until they were in Kirkpatrick's private office, did either man betray Wentworth's true identity. Then their palms met in a solid grip of friendship.

"I want you to forgive me, Dick, for—"

"Nonsense," interrupted Wentworth. "You were fully justified. Now let's get busy." There was a grimness about his face that not even the pleasure at being back on the scene, able to battle again, could lighten. His eyes gleamed like dull gray steel.

KIRKPATRICK, eyeing him keenly, nodded. "You won't mind if I have Joe Roberts in on this, will you? You know, the president of the Board of Aldermen."

Wentworth shook his head. "He's honest and keen. Let's have him in by all means."

Kirkpatrick touched a buzzer and Roberts was ushered in, a bluff, heavily built man with a strong face. After brief introductions, Wentworth dropped into a seat by Kirkpatrick's desk and put a palm flat on its top.

"First of all, I have no clues to the Tarantula. I have only a plan. Since this gang worked first of all by cutting wires, it must have an intimate knowledge, or among its members must be someone who has an intimate knowledge, of the city's wire system.

"Such a person must be connected with either the telephone or electric company. And that person must be of sufficient influence and importance to have access to those maps freely and without question. That gives us something to work on.

"Now as to foiling the gang of the Tarantula, let's get a master map of the city's wiring system, and see what we can do toward guarding those wires."

Kirkpatrick's gravity matched Wentworth's own. "I think you've got something," he said slowly. He picked up his phone, got in touch with the two companies and requested that they send over maps and the heads of their mapping departments at once.

"If you need any added authority, gentlemen, I'll get it for you," Roberts put in. "Meantime, if you'll excuse me, the Board is meeting."

Wentworth and Kirkpatrick nodded farewell. "Don't forget to call on me if you need me," Roberts said as he went out.

His help was not needed, however, in obtaining the maps. The Tarantula had the city by the throat, and officials were frightened.

Within half an hour, the phone company's representative arrived. His name was Peter MacPherson, a short, beetle-browed Scotsman, who came with a long roll of oiled paper beneath his arm.

"This is damn foolishness," he snapped without waiting for Kirkpatrick to speak. "Carting maps like this through the streets. Man, these things have got valuable information in them!"

Kirkpatrick ignored the outburst. He arose, and Wentworth did also. "Mr. MacPherson," said Kirkpatrick, "this is Inspector Barton of Scotland Yard. He's cooperating with us in stopping these burglaries."

"And about time you did something about it, too," said MacPherson testily.

Kirkpatrick's eyes glinted, but once more he overlooked the man's attitude. His desk was clear. He indicated it with a wave of his hand. "Spread the map here," he ordered.

Glumly, his beetling brows working, MacPherson unrolled the map, placing weights to hold it down. Wentworth watched him curiously. The man's hands accorded ill with his person. Instead of being square and gnarled, they were beautifully kept, with tapering fingers. But their backs were incongruously covered with wiry hair, sandy like his head.

Wentworth and Kirkpatrick bent over the chart. "Would it be possible," Wentworth asked, "to guard central points of your telephone cables so we could prevent their being cut?"

"Certainly," MacPherson grunted, "if you had fifty thousand men."

Wentworth raised his brows. "Fancy, fifty thousand men! It seems to me, Mr.—ah—MacPherson, that you order things very poorly here in America. Now in Lond'n—"

MacPherson sniffed. "London be damned. This is New York—"

"Precisely the point I was making," said Wentworth and turned again to the map.

MacPherson turned, muttered under his breath, and Wentworth, for all his appearance of scrutinizing the map, studied him carefully. The man had a thin, cruel mouth with pursing lips from which a score of lines radiated. The eyes were deep-set and sharp behind thick glasses; but it was the hands that chiefly drew Wentworth's attention, the tapering, delicate, incongruous hands with their strangely hairy backs.

A KNOCK on the door, and a policeman walked in with a fatuous grin on his face. "From the electric company," he said.

Wentworth looked at him quickly, glanced beyond. The other official was a woman, a singularly charming woman, her cheeks flushed with cold. He saw a smiling mouth and a small but intelligent face nestling in the turned up collar of her mink coat. Hair like flame peeped out beneath a small close toque of brown. Her green eyes met Kirkpatrick's directly.

"I came as soon as I could," she said, her voice low, full of soft throat tones.

"Miss Lamaris," cried Kirkpatrick, "this is a surprise. I didn't know that your duties included the mapping."

The woman laughed. "Oh, I do a little of everything." She turned to Wentworth, and Kirkpatrick hastily introduced her.

"Inspector Barton of Scotland Yard."

Wentworth bowed. "Charmed, I'm sure."

She held out a straightforward hand. "The name is Lamaris—Tamara Lamaris. Commissioners are so careless about those things."

Wentworth took her hand, bent low over it.

"One often hears of the charming women of America. One meets one such as you so rarely."

Tamara Lamaris pressed her left palm to her heart, closed her eyes and sighed ostentatiously. "Positively you make me blush," she said.

She turned toward the door. "But you wanted to see my maps, I believe." The policeman was still standing there, gazing at her. "Oh, there you are," she smiled at him. "Would you mind telling Charles—he's the man in uniform outside—to bring my maps in? That's a dear."

She unfastened her coat and Wentworth expertly relieved her of it. Her dress was woolen, of dark blue. Modishly snug, it subtly emphasized the rounded maturity of her figure. She walked toward the desk, smoothing her hips, and Wentworth thrust forward a chair, conscious of Kirkpatrick's quizzical glance.

MacPherson broke in dryly. "When you've quite finished being gallant in the Lond'n manner, Mr. Inspector Barton," he said, "would you mind telling me whether you're through with my maps so that I can be getting back to my work."

"I think," said Kirkpatrick, "that we can let you go now, Mr. MacPherson. I believe Miss Lamaris has all the necessary information, and"—his voice rasped—"I believe she's more inclined to cooperate. Let me tell you, Mr. MacPherson, that it is men such as yourself who make it increasingly difficult to keep down crime in this country. You want crime suppressed, but you are willing to do nothing to put it down."

MacPherson frowned his beetling brows at Kirkpatrick. His sharp eyes behind the thick lenses were angry. "Listen, Mr. Commissioner," he began.

"That will be all," Kirkpatrick snapped. "You may go. We have work to do."

Still glowering, MacPherson rolled up his map and strode to the door.

"You may call it work," he grumbled back, turning. "But it's just plain gallivanting."

He slammed the door on Tamara Lamaris' laughter.

FOR an hour then when the policeman had brought in the maps, Wentworth, Kirkpatrick and the woman pored over the charts. But it was even as MacPherson had said, unlimited men would be required to guard the wires. Wentworth straightened slowly.

"That makes it rather difficult," he said. "We'll have to work another way. May we have, Miss Lamaris, a list of all persons who have access to these maps? And by the way, Miss Lamaris, there is a request I'd like to make. Couldn't you give a reception of some sort and invite major officials of the company? I'd like to look them over, without their being aware of the scrutiny."

The woman turned wide green eyes on Wentworth. "Why, Inspector, surely you don't suspect—"

Wentworth smiled dryly. "I'll suspect even my friend, Commissioner Kirkpatrick here, until I have eliminated him."

Tamara Lamaris looked into his face quite seriously, her folded hands resting upon the maps, smooth soft hands with delicately tinted nails. "Then you suspect me, too, Inspector?"

Wentworth nodded gravely. "Of course." And then he smiled. "In fact I think I had better keep you under close personal surveillance from now on."

Her green eyes smiled at him.

She rose, and Wentworth helped her into her coat, murmured something about dinner that evening. But she laughed and shook her head. "Positively," she said, "not a single time until the reception, which will be on Wednesday. That's four days from now."

Wentworth sighed. "I don't see how I can stand it," he said. "But I'll try to bear up."

"Stout fellah!" she said and clapped him on the shoulder. She shook hands with Kirkpatrick and left with a smile.

Kirkpatrick's gaze was curious. He touched his mustache points and sat down, surveying the maps that Tamara Lamaris had left. "I must say," he laughed, "that for a man on such a serious case—"

"Don't be a fool, Stanley," Wentworth growled, "the woman may be useful. Now we have free access to the maps at any time—the more detailed maps, I mean, and this reception will give us an excellent chance to look over the suspects. And by the way—" he leaned forward and tapped the desk with a forefinger, "—in a day or so, will you ask her to invite also Tim Lally and Johnson Hague. I've seen both with her and either might have obtained the information about the maps without her having any idea she was being pumped."

Kirkpatrick looked at Wentworth intently. "You suspect those two, then?"

"I suspect everybody," drawled Wentworth, "just as I told this woman."

The buzz of the phone at Kirkpatrick's elbow interrupted them, and the commissioner picked up the receiver impatiently.

"Yes," he said, then all his impatience vanished into concentrated attention, as he caught the phone excitedly with both hands. "Yes," he said again, "but can't you tell me more than that. I—"

He hung up quickly, rapidly signaled the operator. "Have that call traced immediately," he snapped, "and shoot men out on it. A woman was calling. I want her taken into custody and brought here." He replaced the receiver on the hook, raised his eyes slowly to Wentworth's questioning gaze.

"That was a woman," he said, "who gave the name of Elsie Thompson. She said," he hesitated—"she said she was the woman who pointed a pistol at you in the lobby of the theatre the other night. She says you are the *Spider*, and that she has evidence that you killed two men, Jack Reardon and his son. Then she said that Wentworth, the *Spider*, apparently had sailed for Europe, but actually was back in town now!"

Wentworth was holding a cigarette in his left hand, his lighter in his right. The cigarette crumbled.

"Careless of me," he muttered, dropped it into a wastebasket and drew on another, lighting it with steady hands.

"That means," he said slowly, "that the Tarantula knows I'm back in town." His voice suddenly went hoarse, broke despite his effort at control. "God knows what it means to Nita!"

Kirkpatrick snapped to his feet. "I'm not forgetting that *Spider* charge," he said, "but that must wait. First, we must save Nita."

The phone buzzed again, and he caught it up in a clenched fist. "Yes," and he listened. "Very well," and he hung up with a heavy hand.

"The phone company reported that call came from a pay station, Fifty-Sixth Street. My men got there—too late. Elsie Thompson was gone."

CHAPTER NINE
Kirkpatrick Misses a Date

WENTWORTH regarded the end of his cigarette, casually streamed smoke from his nose. But a rap on the door spun him with a tenseness that betrayed his anxiety. A man in uniform stood there, nearly filling the entrance with his broad shoulders. Their width made him seem even less than his five feet six.

"Yes, Penrose?" asked Kirkpatrick.

The man's eyes were small and glittering in a face that was heavy without fatness. His bristling hair was almost white, not gray with age, but blond. He stared fixedly at Wentworth.

"Oh," said Kirkpatrick, "you have not met Inspector Barton. Inspector, my deputy, Shane Penrose." Their nods were equally curt. Penrose turned back to Kirkpatrick.

"I tuned in on that telephone conversation of yours as per your orders," he said. "Why in the hell don't you arrest that guy, Wentworth? You've had proof forty times over that he's the *Spider*."

Kirkpatrick waved a weary hand. "I know how you feel about that," he said. "But this is scarcely the time to fight that battle again, with these crooks looting and killing right and left. Besides, regardless of how many suspicious circumstances there are, you know there has been no actual proof that Wentworth is the *Spider*. Anonymous calls can't convict a man."

Penrose strode forward. He was ponderous, but his movements were quick. He slapped a palm on the desk. "Kirkpatrick," he said, "I'm telling you the *Spider* is behind all this new crime in the city. He's the guy we've got to catch if we're going to stop this looting business."

Wentworth turned to a chair and lolled in it, crossing his knees. "You seem frightfully positive, Mr. Penrose. Any reasons for it?"

Penrose's turn was like a boxer's. He shot out a fist with a pointed index finger. Kirkpatrick's cool voice drawled between them before he could answer.

"Penrose has a sort of private feud with the *Spider*. Every time he and I think we've just about got a criminal, and he slips out of our hands, the *Spider* catches him and all we have for our pains is a corpse with the red seal of the *Spider* on his forehead. It's handy, but naturally," he laughed, "this upsets Mr. Penrose."

Penrose whirled back to Kirkpatrick, flung his hand in a violent gesture, a square hand with knotty fingers. "Laugh at it if you like, and just as long as you do, the *Spider* is going to make us the laughing stock of the city!" Red-faced and angry, he stalked from the office.

Wentworth got slowly to his feet. Facing Kirkpatrick, he spoke of that subject which was for the moment uppermost in the minds of each.

"I have received no new threat," he said, "against Nita's life. Somehow I do not believe the Tarantula would strike against her without seizing the opportunity to mock at and torture me. He would love the chance to gloat."

Kirkpatrick regarded him steadily. "I hope you're right," he said solemnly.

Circles were smudged beneath Kirkpatrick's eyes. There were lines about his mouth that even the militant points of his mustache could not disguise. He reached into the top drawer of his desk and tossed out a sheaf of papers. "Here are the lists from the telephone and electric companies of all employees who have access to the maps."

Wentworth picked them up slowly, his eyes still fixed on his friend's face. "I appreciate your confidence," he said, "more than I can tell you, Stanley." With a small gesture of his hand he seemed to dismiss the idea. He caught up a chair, pulled it forward and sat down across the desk from Kirkpatrick. As he skimmed through the pages, his voice became brisk.

"There are several hundred names here," he said. "If you agree, Stanley, I think we should have your men check over the entire list for possible suspects, get history, financial standing, personal data on all of them."

Kirkpatrick nodded.

"And another thing," said Wentworth, "I suggest that the wires are being cut by men who operate in a truck disguised as a repair wagon of one of these companies. Let's put a tail on every one of those wagons and give orders to patrolmen that every wagon not being followed by your men shall be seized."

Kirkpatrick agreed and threw his entire force into the search. But days dragged by without any new attack by the Tarantula. Kirkpatrick's appearance of strain increased. Thin lines of apprehension etched themselves into Wentworth's face, showing even through the disguise.

THE night of the reception at the home of Tamara Lamaris found him grim and burning- eyed. Ram Singh and Reardon had arrived in London and, since he had not heard from them, Wentworth knew the daily calls from Nita were continuing. He feared to communicate again with Ram Singh lest he betray a connection between the false Wentworth and the real.

Swiftly he dressed in dinner clothes, made a precise adjustment of his tie, descended to the lobby and left for the Park Avenue home of Tamara Lamaris.

Every effort to check the Tarantula so far had proved futile. Tonight he and Kirkpatrick must discover some lead or... But there must be no "or." They *must!*

Resolutely he thrust all thought of failure from his mind, masked his worries behind a smiling face. It was a debonair suave man-of-the-world without a care except the pleasant destruction of hours that bowed above the lovely white hand of Tamara Lamaris.

"I'm afraid I'm a little late," he said. "Is the commissioner here before me?"

Tamara reproved him with a glance, a toss of her flame red head. "Is that a proper greeting?" she demanded.

Wentworth laughed. "Forgive me this once, won't you... Tamara?"

He stepped back a pace and surveyed her, resplendent in a close gown of green sequins and she waved a fan of green plumes before her face, dropped her eyes in mock coquetry.

"Oh, Inspector," she said, and sighed, "you Englishmen—"

They laughed together, Wentworth offered his arm, and they strolled across the already well filled room, the center of curious gazes. "But seriously... Tamara, much as I hate to intrude business upon so pleasant an occasion, Kirkpatrick's presence is important."

"Important?" She turned frank green eyes to his. "I'm sorry," she said, "or I would not have joked about it. Commissioner Kirkpatrick phoned a short while ago and said it would be impossible for him to come this evening. He asked for you, said you had left your hotel. I offered to have you call, but he said it would be impossible to wait."

Wentworth stared at her blankly, swiftly hid his surprise beneath a shrug. "Doubtless something unexpected turned up." His eyes grew bantering. "The life of a policeman always interferes with his"—a bow—"greatest pleasure. That is the case now. I'm afraid I'm going to have to ask you to excuse me."

The woman turned squarely to face him. "But this is impossible," she said. "These people are here expressly to meet you."

But Wentworth already was on the way to the door. "I'll see you later," he called back. "If I may use your phone—"

He did not wait for a response, but went to the instrument in the hall. He called Kirkpatrick's home, but drew a blank there. At the office he succeeded only in getting Penrose.

"Yeah, I know about it," Penrose growled, "he left word to tell you that dame Elsie Thompson had phoned again and offered him evidence. He said he was sure she was mixed up with the Tarantula, but she insisted he come alone to some dump or other to get the evidence. He wouldn't tell me where he was going. I put a tail on him and Kirkpatrick discovered the man and sent him back. That's all I know."

"It's plenty," rasped Wentworth. "As sure as you're living, Kirkpatrick's work has been bothering the Tarantula and he's going to remove him. In God's name, throw every man you've got on the job of tracing Kirkpatrick!"

Penrose's voice rasped into the receiver. "Listen, John Bull," he said, "get this in your bean. I'm running this police department while Kirkpatrick's not here. You're not. When I need your help I'll ask for it."

Wentworth's eyes glinted, but his voice was calm. "For heaven's sake, man," he urged, "forget the personal element in this. Kirkpatrick's life is at stake, I tell you. Take any action you like, but do something right away."

Penrose was stubborn. "I'm running the police department," he reiterated, "and—"

"Yes, you're running the police department," Wentworth broke in, "and you're responsible. But I'm warning you, if anything happens to Kirkpatrick as a result of your pigheadedness, you'll answer to me for it—personally!"

He hung up on Penrose's shouting anger, strode swiftly to the street. He signaled a taxi, then abruptly whirled and stared down the thronged, two-lane avenue. Was it his imagination, or were the lights dimmer?

As he watched with narrowed eyes, the lights flickered and paled until they were only small yellow gleams in the blackness of the night. There was a moment of utter silence, broken only by the swish of passing cars. Then, from the house behind him, from passing couples on the pavement, came a rising murmur of startled excitement. The taxi driver Wentworth had hailed cursed fearfully. He knew, they all knew, what those dimming lights meant. The Tarantula had struck again!

CHAPTER TEN
Flaming Loot

THE Tarantula had struck again! Fifteen minutes before Wentworth saw the lights dim, a red electric company truck, loaded with repair equipment and bearing the regular insignia of the company, had rolled slowly down Madison Avenue. Upon it two men lounged carelessly, the driver and a helper. It turned into a side street, halted, and the men got down with the slow, time- killing motion of men who are working on somebody else's time. They took down a red stand made of pipes, set it about a manhole, and removed the lid.

On the corner was a bank, a branch of a powerful and wealthy institution. On its side was a large red box surmounted by a bell, labeled "Burglar Alarm." Stout iron bars covered its window; the doors were massive, steel with an embossed bronze covering. And within, lights burned, and two watchmen made regular rounds.

In the street outside the two electrical workers descended into the manhole. Down Madison Avenue a heavy sedan rolled, shades low. From the opposite direction came a light roadster, its top down, a man in a sporty gray fedora at the wheel with a second, equally sporting young man at his side. On the crosstown street on which the electric truck was parked, another curtained sedan rolled slowly.

Moving with the precision of barrage fire, the three converged on the bank together.

Meanwhile, on Madison, a policeman alighted from a small roadster, turned to his companion. "You keep an eye out, I'm going to see what these linesmen are doing now. It's too near the bank to suit me."

"Boloney!" said his companion. "Every time that truck has stopped today, you've had to go up and peep over their shoulders."

"Yeah, well, that's our job," the first cop growled back.

He slid his hands into his coat pockets. There was a slit in the right-hand one, and through that his fingers touched the butt of his gun. His walk was casual, yet there was an alertness about him that betrayed his excitement to the gray-hatted men in the sport roadster, which turned into the street just then. The policeman reached the stand about the manhole, peered down into the lighted pit.

"Aren't you boys working pretty late?" he asked.

One of the workmen below grinned up at him. "There ain't no end to this job," he said.

A pistol spat from the night. The patrolman straightened, a cry gasping in his throat, a startled expression on his face. His hand went to the small of his back, his head flung backward and he collapsed in a huddle on the pavement.

The second policeman in the car started at the sound of the shot, jerked his gun from its holster. A footstep rasped beside him and he whirled, revolver leaping up. That was his last movement. A pistol exploded two inches from his head. The slug slammed him to the seat. He did not stir.

The two gray-hatted men who had fired, killing the two policemen, darted back to the roadster. They flung open the rumble seat and a mounted machine gun rose behind a shield of steel.

The two sedans braked to a halt before the bank at the same instant. A dozen men sprang from them. Instantly, the sedans raced away. The linesmen climbed from the manhole, unreeling wire toward the door of the bank at a fast run.

From the electric truck four men seized and lifted a heavy piece of machinery. They staggered with it to the door of the bank. All was in readiness there. Working swiftly, electricians attached wires to the machinery; another man slipped on a headgear like a medieval helmet, colored glass for eyeholes. He thrust forward a tube, and a blue-hot flame bit into that massive door of steel and bronze.

In the same instant, all lights of the area went dim. That powerful torch was draining the main feed wire of the district. And a mile away on Park Avenue, Wentworth, hailing a taxi, stiffened to attention, watching the lights fade, and knew the Tarantula was busy.

THE bank's doors withstood only a few seconds of that intolerably hot flame. The lock, carved completely out, clanked to the floor, and four crouching men poured gunfire through the opening.

From within other guns blazed. The two watchmen were returning their fire. The metal doors swung outward. Still the alarm at the side of the bank did not sound, nor was there any indication of police interference. The Tarantula's men had done their work well. The alarms were useless, their wires cut.

The street was in pandemonium; people fled shouting or raced in silent fear through darkened streets. The machine gun mounted on the back of the roadster coughed and chattered, and frantic cars detoured. In all that darkened area people fled, panic-stricken, seeking the light.

At the door of the bank, no more bullets came from within. The two guards were stretched dead upon the floor, their bodies struck a dozen times by the raiders' bullets. The Tarantula's men thrust in, lugging their machinery, reached the door of the vault, and once more the hooded man knelt before it like some gargoyle figure out of a demon-ridden past. From the tool in his hands once more that sharp tongue of fire licked out, and before its kiss the steel melted away.

The vault was of tempered steel, built to withstand ordinary torches, but never before had the genius of the underworld contrived a portable transformer which could produce so hot a flame. The safe resisted scarcely longer than had the massive doors of the bank.

The instant they swung open, the torchman and four others seized the transformer and darted to the street. A convoy of armed men surrounded them. They reached the door. From the walk opposite a lone policeman's gun spoke. The muzzle of the roadster's machine gun swept around; it chattered and cackled with a fiendish glee.

The police gun did not speak again. The transformer was loaded into the electric truck and it rolled away.

The two sedans already had disappeared. Those who had carried the transformer ducked into the manhole where the electricians had worked, and scarcely had they disappeared when others from the bank rushed out carrying bags of gold and money from the vault. One by one they popped into the manhole, and the last men dragged down the cover into place behind them.

Of all that crew of robbers, only that single car remained visible, an innocent-seeming auto with two neatly dressed men, without weapons now except for that masked and secret tool of death folded into the rumble seat.

Dim in the distance, the first police sirens growled into life. From the fringes of the darkened district alarms had sped. But they could not designate the exact spot where the Tarantula had struck. As police cars filtered into the area, they would pick up clues from the fleeing people, news of the chattering guns, of the death cries of men. And finally they would find the bank, empty except for the dead.

The driver of the machine gun roadster pulled down the brim of his light gray fedora. He smiled evilly and drove leisurely away, minutes ahead of those frantic, questing police.

"The Tarantula sure knows his stuff," he chuckled to his companion.

CHAPTER ELEVEN
Empty, Save For the Dead

BEFORE the home of Tamara Lamaris, Wentworth darted through the panic of the pedestrians, sprang for the taxi he had signaled. The driver ground into gear, lunged away before Wentworth could grab a hold, fleeing in fear with the rest from the scene of the Tarantula crime.

Wentworth plunged to the middle of the street. A private car swerved past him, darted on with a deep roaring motor. Savagely, Wentworth grabbed out a gun, stood squarely in the path of a taxi. The car raced straight for him, blinding headlights glaring. Wentworth swayed aside just in time. Every driver on the avenue seemed suddenly to have gone mad. They were mad, Wentworth thought bitterly, mad with fear!

Desperately he ran down the street, seeking a car. He saw a man run from a building to an auto at the curb. Before he could start, Wentworth was on the runningboard, gun leveled.

"Outside," he ordered.

The man stared, mouth gaping, words stuttering from his lips.

"Get out, damn you!" Wentworth ordered.

The man spilled out, stumbled and fell to his knees. Before he was up, Wentworth had prodded the stubbornly cold motor to life, whirled around the corner toward Madison. He did not know what loot the Tarantula sought, but he conjectured a bank. And there were a number of them on Madison.

He spun into Madison, skating half across its width on shrieking tires, righted the swaying car with a wrench, and roared down the street.

A constant stream of cars poured at top speed in the opposite direction. A taxi took a corner on two wheels, rammed another head-on with fearful concussion. Two other autos locked wheels. Their drivers wrenched frantically, trying to get free. Behind them horns grated and squealed. A trumpet horn sounded endlessly its polite *ta-te-ta-ta*. These things Wentworth saw with a half glance as, low over the wheel, he jockeyed the coupé at top speed down Madison.

Far ahead now he could hear the rattle and cough of a machine gun, hear pistols blasting. But suddenly, as he raced on, the sounds of battle ceased. All was silent except for the bellow of his own racing motor. The street now was clear of cars.

A man lying dead on the walk, his white face catching a gleam from the headlights, was Wentworth's first warning that he neared the scene of the Tarantula's attack. Bullet-shattered windows glinted silver on the sidewalk, then the gaping doors of the bank sprang into view. Wentworth slapped on brakes with such force that the car did a half turn and skated to a halt, almost nose on to the curbing.

Wentworth plunged out with drawn gun, peering, listening. Here was not even the clatter of fleeing cars; here was only silence, and death.

WENTWORTH raced to the corner, peered around it. Here, too, was death. A policeman slain in his auto, another crumpled in the middle of the street. Wentworth heard distantly now the wail of police sirens and went heavily back to the car. Nothing to be gained by racing madly through the traffic-cluttered streets. The police could do that better than he.

Nothing could be gained either by dashing into that bank with its blank, gaping doors like the mouth of a hideously surprised man. He would only lay himself open to the bullets of police, racing up in wild excitement too late to do anything but blunder—and bury the dead.

He went back and climbed into the coupé, sat there and waited until the sirens' wail became a scream; until foot-pounding cops dashed up to him and thrust guns in his face; until the wide-shouldered Penrose stuck his heavy face in, recognized "Inspector Barton" with a grunt, and called off the police.

"Where's Kirkpatrick?" Wentworth snapped at him.

Penrose had lost some of his stubbornness, but none of his pigheaded belligerency. "How the hell do I know?" he growled back and whirled to direct the hurried search of his men.

Wentworth climbed from the car and strode over after him. "I'll show you the way they went," he said.

Penrose whirled toward him. "I'll bet you will," he spat out. "I want to know how the hell you got here ahead of us. I believe you're mixed up with that gang."

"Your acumen does you credit," said Wentworth, smiling. "I'd been wondering how long it would take you to find out that I was the Tarantula."

Penrose snarled and pounded off, moving his heavy, broad body with the singular alertness that characterized all his actions.

"If you're afraid to go yourself," Wentworth called after him, "you might at least give me a few men to follow up the gang."

That brought Penrose stamping back, fists clenched at his sides. "One more crack like that," he said, "and you're going to land in jail."

"I scarcely think so," Wentworth told him. "There's the little matter of diplomatic courtesy with Scotland Yard. Now listen, Penrose, I'm aware that you dislike me, that you feel slighted because I was called into conference by Kirkpatrick instead of yourself. But if you've got one grain of sense left in that blockhead of yours, you'll realize that I'm at least trying to do the same thing you are: catch the Tarantula."

Penrose sputtered, actually too angry to get out words, but Wentworth cut even that short. "Your men found no autos escaping, did they?"

Penrose growled a negative.

"And they won't," Wentworth said. "Their autos were gone before you got the alarm. I am convinced the Tarantula's men escaped this time through the tunnels beneath the street. They know the wiring systems of the city. Those wires go through tunnels. The chances are they know those tunnels, too. If you don't want to investigate that possibility yourself, give me a couple of men and I will."

Glittering small eyes glared into Wentworth's. There was fury and hate there, but also there was an uncertainty. "I'll settle with you later," he snarled.

"That's fine," said Wentworth. "I've got a little account to settle with you anyway over failing to protect Kirkpatrick. But later. Now, give me men."

Penrose turned his back on Wentworth. "Donahue!" he howled. "Schwartz! O'Flaherty!" Three men came pounding toward him. "This is Inspector Barton of Scotland Yard," there was a sneer in his words. "He thinks he knows how the gangsters got away. Go with him." He stalked off.

Wentworth looked at the three men individually, his face determined and set, showing in the reflected glare of many headlights. His clipped voice was sharp, commanding, and, as always when Wentworth used those tones, he got obedience. There was a compelling power about the man, a vital force that men of action recognized. Here was a leader. When he chose to lead, others followed readily. Now he sized up the three before him, had each identify himself in turn.

"All right," he said briefly. "Listen, Donohue, Schwartz, O'Flaherty! I have reason to believe these crooks escaped through the tunnels beneath the city. I do not know these tunnels. There are wires on every side. If you touch the wrong one, you die. Beneath the streets we may meet gunmen who have killed a half dozen men tonight. They'll be working in territory they know. We won't. I want instant, and immediate obedience. Those are my reasons for it. Understand?"

He looked at each man individually and each nodded as he met his eyes. "Follow me," said Wentworth.

He turned and strode to the spot where the policeman lay dead in the middle of the street beside the manhole.

"Take that cover off," he ordered.

CHAPTER TWELVE
Beneath City Streets

THE policeman who had identified himself as Donohue bent swiftly over, dug his fingers into the lock holes of the cover and strained upward. His back arched. His neck corded. The cover stirred slightly, but did not lift.

"Schwartz," barked Wentworth, "fire axe from the bank."

The cop darted away, panted back with the axe. With its hooked point they lifted the cover until they could get their fingers under its edge and heave it to one side. The three straightened then and faced Wentworth.

"The fact that this cover was unlocked proves we are right," Wentworth told them. "The gangsters undoubtedly went this way. O'Flaherty, let me have your light." He held out his hand and received the long-barreled powerful hand torch that was police equipment. He smiled briefly into the faces of the three men, and once more said, "Follow me."

He sat on the edge of the hole, his legs dangling inside and threw the beam downward. He thrust the light inside his coat, caught the edge with his hands, hung and dropped. He held the light so the three policemen could follow, flashed it upon the batteries of wires on all sides. Certain ones of them had been cut.

"Further proof," said Wentworth.

They were in a room about six feet by seven, hollowed out beneath the street. At its end a pipe perhaps three feet high opened a round black mouth. On this Wentworth focused the light. He went toward it swiftly, dropped to all fours and crawled, the men trailing behind him. Fifteen feet of this, and the pipe became larger so it was possible to move at a crouch. The pipe sloped sharply downward. Wentworth halted.

"Go carefully," he called back, his voice booming in the tunnel, "but do not hold to any of the wires. Some are charged. Anyone might kill you."

Slowly then he moved downward. His light, probing ahead, found the end of the tube, revealed a larger cavern below. He reached the end, flashed his light. There was a damp, fetid smell. Water glinted below. They were looking down into one of the main sewers of the city. There were narrow walks on either side of the sluggish stream. Slime dripped from the walls, and moving twin points of light that were rat's eyes gave back the glitter of his hand torch.

The nearest walk was four feet to one side of the pipe in which they crouched, the conduit through which the wires ran opening in the middle of the arched roof. Wentworth sat down, feet dangling. Donohue thrust up behind him.

"Focus your light," Wentworth said. "I'm going to try to swing and throw myself so I land on that ledge. If I slip, I'm going to get rather unpleasantly wet." He laughed lightly and Donohue echoed it. It reverberated hollowly down the length of the sewer and abruptly Donohue stopped. "Jeez," he said, "I don't like the sound of that."

Wentworth turned about then, placing his hands on the bottom of the pipe and slowly lowered himself until he hung at arms' length. The end of the pipe was slimy, and his fingers slipped on the wet surface. Clinging with all his strength, he began to swing slowly from side to side.

With each movement his hold on the edge of the pipe became more difficult to maintain. With a final effort he launched himself through the air, his feet struck the walkway and he teetered precariously, swinging his arms in wild circles. His back arched. He leaned out over the scummy stream. Finally he recovered his balance and stood panting on the narrow walk. He focused his light.

"All right, Donohue," he called calmly.

Without hesitation, the patrolman did as Wentworth had, and when he flung himself through the air, Wentworth seized his hands and pulled him to safety. O'Flaherty slipped waist deep into the sewage, but Schwartz managed the maneuver with only a wet foot. Then with O'Flaherty squashing along in the rear, cursing under his breath, the four pushed on, Wentworth, as always, in the lead.

SMALLER sewers opened at frequent intervals, pouring filth sluggishly from pipes, and once, at the junction of another main sewer, they were forced to pause until Wentworth's questing light picked out a damp footstep that pointed them the way. On and on for what seemed hours they threaded the tunnels beneath the city, twice pushing into pipes that ended in apertures too small for human exit and being forced to retrace their steps.

At long last they found an iron ladderway that led upward into an open tunnel where they could walk nearly erect. Through it echoed a distant rumble and roar that Wentworth instantly identified as a subway train. The tube led them, after two wide turns, to the tracks.

Along the rails, they made their way, squeezing aside as a local pounded by, to a station platform where waiting throngs eyed their disheveled and slimy clothing with curious eyes.

This then was the end of the trail. They had come from Madison Avenue near Thirty-Fourth Street to the Twenty-Third Street station of the East Side subway. Wearily Wentworth led the men to the street above, and a reluctant cab driver carried them to headquarters and Penrose.

Wentworth took the three before the deputy

commissioner and made a concise report of what they had found. "There isn't much doubt," he concluded, "that this is the way they escaped."

"What do you want me to do about it?" Penrose growled. "Post cops in the sewers to watch for them?"

Wentworth smiled grimly, turned his back and faced the three men, thanked each of them by name. "I'll pay the cleaning bills," he said with a quick smile, and the men grinned back at him. "Dismissed," he clipped out and faced Penrose again.

"I want to compliment you on the morale of the department," he said, "but I doubt you have anything to do with it."

But Penrose, apparently, would not be angry. His heavy face creased into a satisfied smile. "While you were chasing rats in the sewers," he said, "I've been doing good work." He reached into his drawer and laid on the desk a silver-mounted and pearl-handled revolver. "We found that in the bank," he said. "Can you guess who it belongs to?"

"Is it Professor Johnson Hague or Big Tim Lally?" Wentworth asked casually.

Penrose started to his feet, his mouth sagging. For moments his mouth opened and closed like a goldfish tipping air on the surface of a bowl. When he finally got out sound it was a roar. "By God, you must be a member of the gang! How did you know that?"

Wentworth waved a hand. "The processes of deduction, my dear Penrose, might be a trifle difficult for you to follow. I prefer to remain mysterious. But you haven't told me to which of the two gentlemen in question the gun belonged."

Penrose still glared, but he was too surprised to continue his tirade. "Lally," he got out.

"Then take my advice," said Wentworth, "and follow Professor Hague."

Penrose sat down slowly, his heavy face working. It finally twisted into the semblance of a smile. "Here's another little item of information, Mr. Inspector from Scotland Yard. I learned that Lally was at the same party you were going to tonight, and he left just about ten minutes before you did. Got a phone call, he said. Now isn't that funny as hell?"

WENTWORTH flipped open his platinum cigarette case and extracted a cigarette, tapped it against his thumbnail.

"And what does Lally's departure in answer to a phone call signify?" He flicked flame to his lighter, puffed at the cigarette.

Penrose's broad face was frowning. "You know as well as I do," he growled. "It means he ain't got no alibi. He can't prove he wasn't at the scene and dropped this here revolver."

"Neither could I prove an alibi," Wentworth pointed out.

Penrose leaned across the desk. "I know that," he said softly. "But you have got an alibi for the second holdup tonight."

"The second holdup!"

Wentworth held the cigarette rigidly. Its thin thread of smoke made an unwavering column.

"Yes," Penrose admitted grudgingly, as if that was something he hadn't intended to reveal. "The Tarantula knocked over another bank a little while after the first and in another part of town. Both had a load of dough, too. This damned Tarantula seems to know just where to hit."

"Two banks robbed," muttered Wentworth, "the same night that Kirkpatrick goes to a mysterious engagement and fails to return. Have you started a search for him?"

"Yes," Penrose was sullen.

"When?"

"What the hell difference does it make?"

Wentworth's smile was acid. "I thought so. You didn't do a damned thing until the second holdup frightened you, isn't that it?"

"That's my business," Penrose snapped.

Wentworth walked up to the desk and tapped it with a rigid forefinger. "And mine also," he said sternly. "Kirkpatrick is my friend. I warned you I'd hold you accountable, and I will."

Penrose slammed belligerently to his feet. His chair caromed against the wall and smashed to the floor. A policeman thrust in a startled face.

"Get out!" Penrose roared at him. The door clapped shut. He circled his desk on his wary boxer's feet, great shoulders rolling. Small eyes glittering in his flat, wide face, he glowed up at Wentworth and, despite his lesser height, seemed the more powerful man.

"Any time you say, Mister Inspector," he snarled. "Any time. Until then, stay out of my office, see? And stay out of headquarters. There's a leak here somewhere and I think you're it!"

There was an ugly light deep in Wentworth's eyes. He had patience for all human faults except inefficiency in high places.

"There's something rotten here," he admitted, then wrinkled his nose. "I think you're it!"

"Damn you!" Penrose roared out. "Damn you, I'll smash your face for that!" But his clenched fist did not strike again. The light in Wentworth's gray eyes was like the glint of a sword point.

"This is not the time for it, Penrose," said Wentworth softly. "When the time is ripe, I'll be glad to oblige you. And—" his voice rasped suddenly—"if Kirkpatrick hasn't been found by then, come prepared to kill me. That's the only way you'll survive that meeting."

Penrose's pig eyes got wide. "That... that's a threat!" he stammered out.

Wentworth bowed stiffly. "Quite right," he said, and strode from the office.

CHAPTER THIRTEEN
Hairy Hands

Outside, Wentworth glanced at the white gold dial of his watch, saw that the hands stood at three minutes to twelve. It was late, but not too late to return to the reception of Tamara Lamaris. Ten minutes to change at the Waldorf, ten more for a taxi.

At precisely twelve-seventeen, Wentworth—his bleached hair glinting blandly in subdued lights, his made-up face seeming even more sallow in artificial illumination—was bending again over the hand of Tamara Lamaris. She placed her other hand in his also.

"It was really nice of you to remember your promise after all that has happened," she smiled.

Wentworth looked at her slowly, from head of flame, over the shimmering green of her dress that seemed part of her, an actual soft iridescent skin like a gorgeous snake—but Tamara's flesh would be warm!—down to the shapely small ankles, the high-arched feet in slippers of dull red.

"Nice?" he repeated softly. "Nice to myself!"

She laughed in her low throaty laughter that would have seemed almost masculine in its depth, if a man could utter such seductive, soft sounds.

"It is a pity such men as you must die," she told him, "and all policemen die someday, don't they?"

Wentworth frowned. "You have to mention death," he complained, "and remind me of duty." He sighed. "Well, you'll suffer for it. I must straightway turn to business. Is Lally here?"

She nodded slowly, eyes intent. "Is your business with him?"

Wentworth shook his head. "Come along and find out." He offered her his arm.

They passed through crowded rooms. A grave-faced youth sat cross-legged in a chair, thumbing a guitar with a muscular hand, and sang bawdily to its uncertain accompaniment. Five women stood about him with intertwined arms and giggled.

Tamara's green eyes flashed at the man. Wentworth looked, too. The youth was familiar. He noticed then that he'd lost a thumb off his left hand and memory flooded back. This was Russell Daliot, one of those who had met with Tamara in the theatre the night of the Tarantula's first raid. Wentworth turned veiled, curious eyes on Tamara. What was the connection between these two, he wondered.

They moved on.

Wentworth, leading his partner deftly, brought up presently before the skillfully tailored paunch of Big Tim Lally. His whole person was polished, from the nascent baldness of his red, sloping forehead, to the tips of his patent leather shoes. His voice was polished, too—with oil.

"Inspector Barton," Lally bowed with extreme unction, his murmuring tones like a moist-palmed caress.

Wentworth surveyed him through expressionless eyes.

"You'd better surrender to Deputy Commissioner Penrose right away," Wentworth told him in conversational tones. "He found your gun in a bank the Tarantula robbed tonight."

Lally jerked erect, his mouth gaping, his vague

eyes popping with surprise.

"My... gun?"

Wentworth heard Tamara exclaim, too, but did not turn. He nodded. "Yes, a pretty, rather useless thing, all plate and mother of pearl. And Penrose told me you didn't have an alibi."

"But... but..." Lally mopped his reddened forehead with an ample silk handkerchief held in a fat-padded, heavy hand.

Wentworth offered his arm to Tamara. "Now," he said calmly, "let's go have a little chat with Professor Hague."

The green eyes that regarded him were slightly puzzled. She glanced toward the beet-countenanced Lally. "I think the Inspector gave you straight dope," she said, then took Wentworth's arm and walked off with him. "Now what could you possibly accomplish by scaring that man to death?" she asked slowly.

WENTWORTH grinned, but did not answer. He had satisfied himself that Lally lacked the mentality to direct the Tarantula's gang. He might be a tool connected with it, but Wentworth doubted even that. Penrose's clue was obviously a plant to turn suspicion from someone. And Professor Hague.... Wentworth had learned that the gray-faced scientist was making a study of electrical systems. That would undoubtedly include the mapping of New York's underground conduits!

Skillfully he led Tamara back through her guests. Professor Hague came into view. Scarcely taller than Tamara's five feet five, he held an amber drink.

He lifted it, and the color made his gray face doubly pale, deadened his mouse-colored hair. Everything about the man was neutral toned—except his eyes. They were black, and behind thick glasses, rarely blinked. They did not blink as they met Wentworth's keen gray gaze. He set down the amber glass and shook hands as Tamara murmured, "Inspector Rupert Barton of Scotland Yard."

Wentworth had difficulty concealing disgust at touch of that hand. It was cold and his fingers, gripping it, were conscious of wiry hair. The backs were alive with it, black and thick, so virile it seemed to crawl.

He plunged into conversation. "Professor, you are studying the wiring system of the city, I believe."

Hague nodded, his oddly staring black eyes unwavering

"Have you any theories as to how these robberies might be prevented?"

Hague raised one shoulder in a slight shrug. "The wires are poorly organized," he said, speaking in a voice that, while masculine enough, had a slightly womanish quality. Wentworth, listening to it acutely, did not like it. "I've been toying with an idea," Hague went on, twirling the amber-filled glass between tapered fingers, "an idea of rigging the wires so that the touch of a wire cutter—without proper preparation—would cause a short circuit blast. But I've discarded it. Obviously the Tarantula and his men know the system thoroughly, they could make those 'proper preparations.' The only suggestion I have—" his chuckle, low, throaty, and again startlingly feminine in its overtones—"is to catch the Tarantula!"

Wentworth nodded. "I'm going to."

Hague's black eyes regarded him fixedly. "I wish you luck," he said without warmth.

WENTWORTH bowed and walked on with Tamara, frowning. Her exquisite hand was light on his arm. Her long green eyes sought his.

"And now," she said, "which other suspect do you want to talk with?"

Wentworth smiled absently, his eyes preoccupied. "Our friend, Peter MacPherson, must be about."

This time it was she who guided him through the growing congestion in the rooms, till they finally located the sour-faced Scot. He drew down his beetling brows as they stopped before him.

"It's all evening I've been waiting to see you," MacPherson's burr was thick. "If Scotland Yarrrd pays you a salary, and if our city has to foot the bill for you to come herrre, I'm going to write a letter aboot it to the *Times*."

Wentworth eyed the man keenly. Was he drunk, or acting cleverly? It seemed impossible that a man of his important position could behave as foolishly as had MacPherson, first in Kirkpatrick's office and now, downing Tamara's excellent amber drinks.

"Yes, Mr. MacPherson," Wentworth said slowly, "both items of your arraignment are true, but even if I seem to be gadding about, actually I am on the trail of the Tarantula."

MacPherson sputtered. "Tarantula! Tarrrantula! Another damned *Spider*! This town is overrun with the vermin. If I were police commissioner, I'd exterm–extermi–I'd kill every damned one of them!"

His eyes were owlish. His incongruous hand with its sandy-haired back was wrapped completely around a glass.

"Yes, sir, I would!" He nodded his head.

Wentworth shook his head slowly. If the man was acting, he was quite clever enough to be the Tarantula several times over. He strolled away with Tamara, MacPherson's drink-thickened burr buzzing after them.

Wentworth spent the better part of that night roving Tamara's luxurious apartment, apparently getting thoroughly drunk, but actually watching closely every person in the house. Hague and a girl, all amber like the drinks; Tamara of the green eyes and hair of flame; that splendid young animal of a man

Daliot, who played the guitar with a thumbless hand. But he learned nothing more than his first casual survey had shown. Lally had got hold of his lawyer and gone down to headquarters. Hague stayed on and continued to drink until the girl in amber began to weaken at the pace he set. Then he smiled at her thinly and took her home. MacPherson had passed out, apparently.

CHAPTER FOURTEEN
Panic!

THE next morning at nine, Wentworth presented himself at the offices of the electric company with a note he had got from Tamara, permitting him to inspect detailed wire maps. From these, he picked out a dozen spots that seemed to him to control lights, alarms and phones in vital sectors, spots where controlling wires converged at one point so all could be cut at one time.

He rented a car and set out to patrol these dozen points, ranging from Broadway and Maiden Lane, near the lower tip of Manhattan Island, to St. Nicholas and 110th Street, halfway up its length. North of that, Wentworth doubted there was anything rich enough to lure the Tarantula.

He sent the rented Ford roadster in a swift sweep up the express highway that strode on stilts along the west side, up curving Riverside Drive, cut across 110th. He passed a bank. Before it there stretched a long double line of people, shoulders hunched against the cold.

A dumpy woman waved a bankbook in the air, exclaiming to a white-haired man who stood stolidly with shoulders drooping. Her words seemed to become visible in puffs of white frost-vapor from her mouth. A fellow with a black, stringy beard mounted a soap box and harangued about "the bosses" until a blue-coated cop sauntered up with a lifted, pugnacious chin and growled, "Move on." Wentworth stewed to the curbing by the cop, flashed his credentials.

"What's the trouble?" he demanded.

"The Tarantula," the cop said laconically. "His last two robberies broke an insurance company. Can't say as I blame the depositors much." He rubbed a speculative hand along a blue-shaven jaw. "Phoned my wife to get ours out as soon as I heard the news."

Wentworth nodded somberly, eyeing the line. The cop had "phoned his wife." So had many other men apparently. Every moment the line lengthened. Gesticulating women and excited men grabbed and quarreled over places. As he watched, a bank guard in a gray uniform barred the passage of more into the building, shouldered shut the doors. A black-lettered sign was hung on the glass.

"Closed—This bank is in the hands of the state examiners, called in by the Board of Directors to conserve assets."

Wentworth started the car with a lurch as the crowd began to howl at the closed doors.

Someone threw a stone, and a window smashed. A woman, gashed by a fragment, screamed. The policeman charged into the crowd, reached over the heads of two men and cracked a third with his stick. Another cop dashed to an alarm box, jerked it open. The reserves would make a siren-heralded dash.

Wentworth sped on. Nothing he could do here. Three blocks away was another bank, a branch of the one the Tarantula had robbed the night before. Before it excited depositors clustered also. An armored truck drew up and men stood with leveled revolvers while others lugged boxes of money across the walk. Wentworth shook his head. That would be in vain, too.

A boy screamed an extra and Wentworth signaled him.

TARANTULA'S RAIDS SHUT BANKS

Wentworth skimmed through headlines. Both banks the Tarantula had struck the night before had been insured with one company against robbery. The company had made good the losses then suspended further payments. Runs were on at nearly every bank in town. Bankers issued reassuring statements, saying there was ample cash on hand, that the insurance company was sound and merely wished a chance to straighten its accounts. Front page editorials urged the depositors to have faith, demanded the police instantly capture the Tarantula.

Wentworth read on:

BANKS WATCHED BY ROOSEVELT
President Keeps Touch With New York
Crisis by Telephone

WENTWORTH'S face was grim, the line of his jaw lean. For he knew that the crisis would soon become chaos, despite Roosevelt and the police and the remaining statements of the bankers. The Tarantula had the city by the throat. The millions he had taken had made a painful dent in the bank's reserves, and now that the insurance companies were failing, there was nothing to guarantee the people's money. Banks collapsing here would shake others throughout the country. This was the nation's financial capital. If it fell, the nation fell with it. Well might President Roosevelt "keep an eye" on the bank crisis here.

With coldly shining eyes, Wentworth resumed his patrol, going from danger point to danger point on his mental map of the wiring. All day long he watched depositors rioting about closing banks, watched police, more than half in sympathy with the people, forced to charge in with flying clubs to turn aside raids. And no clue developed. He found no gleam of hope in all his long patrol. No gleam of hope until late in the afternoon, driving down Sixth Avenue, beneath the slam-banging elevated.

Wentworth's left hand tightened on the steering wheel. His right dropped down and slapped the gear shift into neutral, fingered it back into low gear as he idled up to a red light at Ninth Street. Just ahead where Eighth Street right-angled into Sixth and slanted off on the other side as Greenwich Avenue, an electric company truck was parked directly beside one of the manholes which opened on a danger point. The light turned green and Wentworth coasted on past the truck, turned into a parking yard just below Eighth and walked slowly back to a luncheonette on the corner where Greenwich forked off.

He slid into a booth beside a window, ordered a steak sandwich and coffee. It was drawing close to the evening rush hour. In twenty minutes, subways and thrashing elevated would be jammed. He frowned and watched the men on the electric truck. They moved leisurely, stopping to light cigarettes before they unlocked and lifted the manhole cover. Only one climbed slowly down the red ladder they thrust into the tunnel below, a youngish, wiry chap with a greasy cap dragged over his right eye, a heavy leather jacket about his ears.

Wentworth told himself it was all foolish. They would not be attempting an attack on a bank in the rush hour. It would be suicide. They couldn't kill off the whole street full of witnesses. Yet this was one of the danger points.

Peering about, he located the police car that was trailing the truck, parked some little distance down the street.

The waitress slammed down the plate before him, slopped coffee into his saucer and gave him a gold-toothed grin. She raised a hand coquettishly to lifeless, hennaed hair. "Anything else, sir?"

Wentworth shook his head and turned back to the truck. The heavy smell of hot grease rose from the steak sandwich. He glanced at it, picked up half and munched, watching the linesmen. Only one went beneath the street. The other stayed by the truck, a nonchalantly held red flag signaling the open manhole.

FINALLY the workman crawled up the ladder and the two reloaded their apparatus. Wentworth left half the steak and all the coffee, paid his check and hurried to his car. He still told himself it was foolish, a ridiculous supposition that these linesmen had done anything to wires beneath the street. Still, timing devices were easily possible. A wire, for instance, might be attached to the street light cable. That wire, half an hour later, might set off a bomb; it might be attached to a filament that would melt cables in two when current sizzled through it.

Wentworth followed the police car that followed the truck. It worked a leisurely way through thickening traffic, bluffed through tight jams in the way truck drivers have. Finally it turned into the electric company garage. There Wentworth parked and waited, eyeing each man who left the shop.

He was waiting for the man who had gone down into the manhole. Many men came out, walking heavily with heads bowed into the cold wind. When the man he sought came out, jumped into a rattletrap Chevrolet and gassed it around a corner on two wheels, Wentworth trailed.

The swift Winter dusk was falling. A biting wind pushed Wentworth's Ford on the nose, slid around the windshield and gnawed at his face. A few bewildered snowflakes blundered into the funnel of the headlights.

No lolling back in the seat to follow this man. He was making time, slamming the Chevrolet along like a ten-ton truck, crashing through traffic on sheer nerve. Wentworth, sitting tensely behind his wheel, writhing through behind him, began to smile thinly. The trail looked better. This man had idled back to the garage. Now that he was away from there, he was racing. His eyes were grim. If Kirkpatrick and Nita were to live, he must find a trail quickly.

Into Eleventh Avenue the chase led, rattling along beside a crawling freight train, cutting short across its nose and nicking into Forty-First, slanting west. That meant the elevated highway, southward. Wentworth was forced to shoot on to Forty-Second to get around the locomotive. He took the highway a good two blocks behind, jouncing over the hillocked cobbles at the entrance to the upward ramp, holding himself to the seat by main strength.

The Ford scooted up the ramp. Through the scattering white flakes, Wentworth spotted his man by his swift, reckless cutting in and out through traffic, toed the accelerator to the floor and let the Ford roar down the center of the three-laned road. A police whistle got excited behind him. A glance in the rear-vision mirror showed a belted, putteed cop running to his parked motorcycle. A signboard flashed by. Speed limit, thirty five miles. Wentworth's cold-stiffened lips twisted again. The speedometer read seventy.

THE Chevrolet ahead slithered around a sharp turn, rear swinging wild. Wentworth circled a droning Packard to his left, wrenched to dodge a slow-moving Buick and slammed into the curve with the speedometer still at seventy. Jammed brakes, shrieking tires. Another wrench and the Ford, swaying madly, took the gas and jackrabbited ahead. The Chevrolet ducked into a ramp, slanting to West Street at Nineteenth. Wentworth swooped behind him, the siren of the motorcycle dinning in his ears. His credentials would calm the policeman, but it would lose him his quarry. He couldn't wait.

He heard the Chevrolet's brakes take hold with a squeal, saw it U-whirl back toward Twenty-Third. He stood on the brake pedal, shot east across Nineteenth. The siren's whine was muffled, then lost entirely as Wentworth swung north, took the next corner west again and, cutting his mad speed, loafed at twenty back into West Street and picked up the Chevrolet's taillight sliding onto the Hoboken ferry. A whistle blew then and Wentworth kicked the accelerator again, palmed the horn and held it squawking as he made a dash for it.

The chains were clanking as they lifted the draw. Wentworth slid by a wildly waving guard, bumped over six inches of black water and slowed to a halt with his fenders rubbing the Chevie's. The linesman was crawling slowly out, grinning beneath his cocky, greasy cap.

"What's your hurry?" he asked.

Wentworth grinned back. "Jeez," he said, "I just got a hankering to let the old boat out—*you* know how it is, and then that cop got on my tail." He shrugged, his grin widened and he peered back through the thickening snow to see the motorcycle cop jerk to a halt as the ferry cleared the slip. A ferry man pounded up to Wentworth.

"What the hell—" he roared.

The linesman sidled away. Wentworth turned to meet the man, argued with him till the Chevie's driver had disappeared, then took the man by the arm and led him toward the cabin. He showed his police credentials. The man's bluster evaporated.

"I'm going off the boat on foot," Wentworth told him. "I want you to drive that car of mine off and take care of the police when that motorcycle cop gets on the phone."

The man backed off. "Ixnay," he said, "I ain't wanting to get mixed up in this business."

Wentworth caught his hand and crisp paper crackled between their palms. Wentworth grinned at him.

"I could get hard about it, but maybe—"

"Okay, okay," the boat man sliced the air with the edge of his hand. "That makes it different."

Wentworth was the first person off the boat. He walked swiftly ahead, got a cab and took up the chase when the linesman drove off. The man had calmed down now. Apparently Wentworth's close shave had had a sobering effect, or the need of haste was gone.

He drove without loss of time, however, straight out Jersey's express highway that stretched ninety miles to Camden, but turned off at the Newark airport, an acres-huge plot of ground full of lights blinking red and green around the close spiraling of wind-blown snow. Wentworth had his taxi close up. The Chevrolet parked, its driver got out with a grip, ran toward a plane in the line, its motor idling. Wentworth leaped out and sprinted after him, coat-tails flapping against his calves.

As he raced, he dug under his arm and snaked out his gun. When the man stopped to buckle into a parachute harness, Wentworth would get his chance. He was a hundred and fifty yards away. The man twisted, glimpsed Wentworth. He sprang to the wing, legged into the forward seat. A gun glinted in his hand.

Instantly the motor of the plane revved up. The snow blew toward its nose. Already it was pointed into the wind, ready for the takeoff. It began to trundle forward, the propeller clawing the cold air for momentum!

CHAPTER FIFTEEN
The Spider Spins

WENTWORTH was less than fifty yards now from the slowly moving plane. Head flung back, legs thrusting like pistons, he sprinted like the champion he was. Wentworth could shade ten seconds for a hundred yards. But with an overcoat flopping about him, and the knifing wind in his face—

Orange flame lanced from the forward cockpit of the plane. Wentworth's own gun was ready, but he did not fire. He wanted that man alive. Again the gun ahead blazed and lead plucked at his coat. The plane was picking up speed. Wentworth swerved in his stride, dived headforemost and landed on its tail. An instant later, it would have lifted, and seconds later the ship would skim free of earth. Wentworth's calculated leap jammed the controls.

In imminent danger of a crackup, the pilot cut the throttle, fought his wobbling plane. The linesman reared up in front of him, thrust the gun against his head, yelling. The flier threw a gesticulating hand backward. In that instant the plane tilted dangerously. Wentworth threw himself clear. The ship dug a wing into the earth, did a cartwheeling ground loop.

Wentworth plunged forward even as the motor choked its bellow. The plane flopped over on its back. The pilot hung in his straps, but the linesman tumbled out. Struggling to get to his feet, he flung out the gun, thrusting it almost point-blank toward Wentworth. He was not quick enough. Wentworth lashed out with his own pistol, caught the man's wrist. The gun thumped to the frozen ground.

Across the field sirens moaned. The crash wagon, with blinking red eyes, banged toward them. One-eyed motorcycles spurted past it. Wentworth caught the man by the collar and, yanking him to his feet, jabbed a gun into the small of his back. A swift but thorough frisking found no more weapons. Grimly then, Wentworth awaited the field officials.

His credentials satisfied the police. A check put a grin back on the face of the pilot, and Wentworth herded his prisoner toward the administration building. He turned him over to a cop there, but kept his own gun leveled while he put through a hurried call for Penrose. There was no doubt in Wentworth's mind now that the linesman was a henchman of the Tarantula, a man whose capture might mean much. But even more important at that moment was the necessity of warning Penrose of impending trouble in the neighborhood where this man had worked. In view of the man's attempted flight, there could be no doubting the accuracy of his own wild guess—a time mechanism attached to electric cables beneath the street!

Wentworth had trouble getting Penrose, but finally the deputy commissioner's voice rasped over the wire.

"This is Barton," Wentworth said swiftly. "There's going to be another Tarantula robbery somewhere about Eighth Street and Sixth Avenue. You can—"

"So there's going to be, eh?" Penrose snarled into the midst of the words. "Are you trying to pull a crude joke, Barton, or are you trying to alibi yourself? That robbery was pulled off an hour ago, and at least forty people got bumped off!"

"Forty, Good God!" For an instant the news stunned Wentworth. "I called as soon as I could," he said slowly. "I was trailing—"

"Oh, sure," Penrose broke in again. "Don't let a little thing like forty lives interfere with an important thing like trailing. Listen, Barton, I'll be damned if I don't believe you're in cahoots with that gang. You knew too damned much about how they worked that last raid, and now you phone too late. Are you trying to make me think you're okay, by calling too late?"

PENROSE was fairly howling with anger. Wentworth opened his mouth twice to interrupt, but finally hung up. No use telling the deputy that he had at last succeeded in capturing a member of the Tarantula's gang!

He slammed out of the booth, his mouth twisted in a savage grin. He seized the manacled hands of his prisoner, nodded to the cop and roughed the linesman out of the building into a waiting taxi.

"My bag!" cried the linesman. The cop tossed it in.

"Head for New York," Wentworth ordered. "Holland Tunnel."

He booted the linesman into the cab, sat on a kick seat facing him with a leveled gun in his hand... and said nothing. There was a ruthless ferocity on his face. Lights along the express highway threw crooked shadows across it. His eyes gleamed. Forty dead!

He leaned forward and deliberately crashed his left fist into the prisoner's face.

The man moaned, whimpered. "Jeez! Why'd you do that? You ruined my nose... Jeez!"

Wentworth raised his fist again. The linesman winced.

"Cripes, don't do that!"

He took another glancing blow on the cheek, beat his manacled hands upon his knees. He slumped down further in the corner, eyes rolling up. The cab slid to a halt.

"Lookit here," the driver protested, "you can't do that in my cab, cop or no cop."

Wentworth's gun persuaded him. The cab rolled on, the driver keeping his eyes steadily on the snow-barred road, fearful even to stare into the mirror that reflected that gloomy back seat. The prisoner sat up feebly.

"You ain't no cop!" he quavered. "You come from *them!*"

A chuckle bubbled from Wentworth's lips. The cab slanted down off the highway, hacked through thick traffic, ducked into the crashing fury of the Holland traffic tube beneath the Hudson. The roar of the ventilators, the drumming of auto exhausts, drowned all other sound. Wentworth raised the gun and pointed it directly at the man's stomach. The fellow doubled over as if shot, lifted a bloody, pleading face. They darted out of the tube into snow-sprinkled darkness again.

"North," Wentworth ordered. "Take the express highway."

"Jeez," half sobbed the manacled man. "That ain't the way to police headquarters."

Then for the first time Wentworth spoke to him. He said, "You're telling me!" and his grin was mocking.

"But I never failed them," the man babbled. "I did just what they said and when my job was done I cut and run like hell."

Wentworth leaned forward. "Who do you mean by *they*?"

His prisoner cowered back on his seat. "Oh, Lord, I done it now. I done it now!"

"You have," Wentworth said grimly. "You've admitted you're a member of the Tarantula's gang, and that means death. I shouldn't be surprised if the police killed you without ever letting you go to trial. They wouldn't need to tell anybody they'd taken a prisoner."

THE man whimpered and rocked slowly backward and forward. A driblet of blood trickled from his smashed nose. "Oh, Lord, I done it now," he moaned again.

Abruptly he stopped his rocking. "Where's my bag?" he demanded.

Wentworth jerked his head sideways, indicating the floor.

"I'll give you all of it to let me go free," the man whispered with sudden intensity. "There's fifteen grand in that bag."

"You'll give it to me!" jeered Wentworth. "Man, I got it!"

"You can't take it!" It was a cry, but there was no belief in it. Wentworth only laughed.

"Listen," the man leaned forward again, lifted his manacled hands. "I'll get you fifteen grand more if you'll let me go. I can get it." Words spilled out. "They owe it to me. They were sending it to me when I got away. They'll let me have it. Honest, I'm not fooling—"

Wentworth looked at him fixedly. "Fifteen more would be thirty thousand," he muttered.

The prisoner's voice took on life. "Thirty thousand is a lot of dough," he said eagerly. "Cripes, what I could do with thirty thousand!"

"And all I got to do is turn you loose, huh?"

"Yeah, that's all." Hope breathed in the man's tones. His eyes were bright.

Revulsion was strong in Wentworth's breast. This man had assisted in the murder of forty human beings for the sake of money. Thirty thousand dollars. That meant—a grim twist of his mouth made his prisoner shrink back in his seat with a little moan—that meant $800 a head. The Tarantula paid well for murder.

Wentworth said slowly, "That's a deal. How do we get the other fifteen grand?"

"Take me somewhere and let me phone," the man's words poured out in a stumbling stream. "They'll bring it to me when I tell them how I need it."

"Yeah, and rub me out when they get there!"

"Then I won't tell them why I need it. I'll just tell them to bring it, and—"

"Okay, okay," growled Wentworth, "we'll see how it works." He barked over his shoulder at the taxi driver. "Hit west on Forty-second. Find a phone booth."

While the cab's tires purred on the temporary steel ramp that slanted to the street at 38th Street, Wentworth opened the bag and in the uncertain light counted the money. "Fifteen grand is right," he grunted.

The cab jounced over rough cobbles and headed west, braked to a quick stop beside a small drugstore. Wentworth paid him off. "And keep your mug shut, see?" he told the driver, flashing a badge.

The chauffeur grinned crookedly. "I been driving for ten years, Mac. I want to keep on." He shot the cab away.

WENTWORTH, carrying the bag of money tucked greedily under his arm, stopped in the shadows and unlocked one handcuff, let the prisoner thrust the other hand and manacle into his pocket. He gave him a handkerchief to daub at his face and walked with him into the store.

They wedged together into a phone booth and Wentworth listened. His prisoner called the Doctor's Exchange and asked where he could locate Dr. Fauquier. He called the number they gave him and was told the doctor had just left. "Try Fenwick 3-9748." And then finally the call went through. The prisoner asked again for Dr. Fauquier, then talked excitedly.

"Listen, Hague," he spilled out, "I got to have that other fifteen grand. Yeah, I know it ain't due—"

Hague! Wentworth's eyes were pinpoints as he eased out of the booth and stood waiting until the man, mopping his gashed forehead gingerly, came out and looked up sourly at his captor.

"What's Hague look like?" Wentworth demanded.

The man took his hand away from his forehead. "Listen," he rasped, "you're getting your dough, and that's all. I ain't squealing."

Wentworth glowered at him in his best police manner, but finally shrugged. "Okay," he said. "Now listen, I'm sliding out of here, but I'm going to be watching you. When you get that dough, you walk up the street,

NITA VAN SLOAN

any sort of way. If any of that gang follows you, I'm going to put a bullet in you, see? I ain't walking onto no spot for thirty grand, nor three hundred."

Fright shadows returned to the man's eyes. "Jeez," he said, "I ain't the boss of the gang. If they want to put a tail on me—"

Wentworth grinned crookedly. "It's okay by me," he said softly. "I'd rather put a bullet in you anyhow. You might open that trap of yours—"

"I'll keep 'em away!" the man promised frantically. "I'll keep 'em away."

"You better!" Wentworth backed away from him and slipped out a side door. He found a red-and-black cab and gave the driver five dollars. "Park across from that drugstore, with your flag down," he said. "Pretty soon a car's going to come along, and some men will go into that drugstore and come out with another man. Follow them. I'll be following you in another cab."

The driver leered. "For five bucks? Not me, mister. That sounds like gang stuff to me."

Wentworth looked at him steadily. "I was going to say if they got rough to drop it. If you want to stick with it, regardless, I'll give you fifty."

"Yeah?" the driver was unshaven, his eyes suspicious beneath a broken-rimmed cap.

"Yes," said Wentworth. He drew out the fifty dollar bill and held it in the light. The driver licked his lips nervously. "Okay," he said and grabbed for the money.

"Not so fast," said Wentworth softly. He held the money where the driver could see it, but not reach it. "Just remember I'm on your tail and—" he touched his side overcoat pocket— "don't try to skip out on me." He handed over the bill.

The driver touched his cap. "Okay, Lieutenant."

WENTWORTH drifted backward into shadows. The snow had stopped now. The pavement was wet with it, reflecting lights in long shimmering lines. The air grew colder. Wentworth found an orange taxi—the first had been red-and-black—and parked it two blocks away, around a corner.

Watching, he shivered in the shadow of a doorway. Within five minutes, a powerful gray sedan drew up before the drugstore and two men, one wearing a white felt hat, went in. In a minute they were out with a third man, walking stiffly between them. They got in the sedan, pulled away. The red-and-black taxi jerked into motion.

Wentworth climbed into the orange cab and ordered, "Follow the red-and-black."

They got going. The sedan did tricks. It rolled along slowly, spun a corner with its motor roaring into sudden speed. Wentworth sent his own cab to the right a block behind, and they caught the sedan flashing into a skidding left turn and trailed casually along. The red-and-black held to the trail, passed Wentworth's orange at forty-five.

They kept that up for thirty city blocks, the gray sedan doubling and turning, crashing red lights, turning about in thick cross-street traffic, trying to jam the red-and-black to the curb and gun out the driver. But that unshaven, city-wise cabbie was too wary. Finally, the gray sedan raced uptown to the ramp where Fourth Avenue becomes Park, headed for the viaduct for vehicles which weaves through the Grand Central Station building itself and lets cars out into Park Avenue proper.

Wentworth's driver got stopped by the last light before the viaduct. The sedan and the red-and-black cab swung into the right-angled drive through the station building. And a moment later, the sedan came scampering back through the downtown passage alone, having somehow dodged the red-and-black in making a complete circuit of the station building.

The sedan cut to its right into a one-way street, and Wentworth sent his driver after it.

A red-and-black had been trailing. Now an orange followed, leisurely. The men in the sedan ahead were evidently satisfied they had lost their shadow. They turned at normal speed down Fifth Avenue, crossed town in the thirties, wove up Eleventh Avenue to Seventy-Second and coasted into Riverside Drive, turned up a side street in the Nineties and parked.

Wentworth's cab muttered past. He saw three men with another in their midst enter an apartment building.

"Turn the corner and park," he ordered.

CHAPTER SIXTEEN
Spider Bait

FROM the compact kit beneath his arm the *Spider* took a few simple makeup articles, a black pencil, powder to gray his hair. Five minutes later he got out, paid the driver, then took a $500 bill from his pocket and tore it in two, while the driver watched with staring eyes. Wentworth gave half the $500 bill to the driver with some detailed instructions, put the other half of the bill in an envelope, pocketed it, and walked away.

As he walked, the youth went out of his shoulders and out of his step, and an old man slow-footed down the hill toward the apartment where the men had disappeared. An expensive felt hat had been left behind in the taxi, and on his grayed locks reposed a battered hat from his pocket. His topcoat was reversible. It had been gray herringbone, now it was black and a distortion of one shoulder made it a sad misfit.

There was no resemblance between the belligerent cop who had seized a man at Newark airport and this shambling, but dignified-seeming old man.

He entered the apartment house where the Tarantula's men had gone, his heart thumping in slow, long pulses in his temples. It was not that he was going into battle against long odds. The *Spider* was used to such battles for high stakes. It was the thought that, possibly somewhere in this building, Kirkpatrick, or—or Nita might be held prisoner. Lord, how long it had been since last her blue eyes had smiled into his! How long—

Wentworth choked, shook his shoulders. He must not allow himself to think of that. Emotion slowed the brain, cut down the split-second reactions and coordination upon which the *Spider* so often was forced to depend on for life and victory over the underworld. One precaution he took: after surveying the name cards and selecting one, after entering the elevator and telling the operator "three," he took his hat and held it in both hands before him. And into a strap in its high crown, he slid a revolver.

He got off at the third floor, walked along the hall until the elevator had gone down, then concealed himself in a dark corner and waited, watching the indicator above the door which showed the location of the elevator. Five minutes later, Wentworth saw the elevator rise to the seventh floor. When it came down, he spotted three men in the cage, and one wore a white hat. The linesman was not with them.

As soon as the car was out of sight, Wentworth went swiftly upstairs to the seventh floor. There were four apartment doors and he rang each bell in turn mumbling a name when a woman came to the door of the first, being scooted by a maid in a second, and failing to get any answer at the third. He slid his hand again to the toolkit beneath his arm and extracted a lockpick, took out also a black mask that hid his entire face, the mask of the *Spider*.

The door did not resist a minute. Wentworth entered slowly, gun in hand. The stab of a small pencil flashlight revealed a room furnished in installment-store style. The air was close and hot with steam radiators. There was a faint smell of paint. Wentworth went swiftly through a living room, dining room, a kitchen—where he halted suddenly, muscles tensing.

He stood motionless, listening. The sound came from the bathroom, a hoarse, rasping breathing. It shut off suddenly, and there came a tapping, frantic and panicky. Then again the panting respirations. Wentworth kicked the door open, pocketed his gun and sprang into the room.

From the shower curtain rod a man was being hanged, a man with a battered nose, the linesman he had captured at the airport!

WENTWORTH lifted him, loosened the rope, let the man sag to the floor. He had fainted. A splash of water remedied that. The man's eyes blinked open, words creaked painfully from his throat.

"Who... are... you?"

Wentworth regarded him unwaveringly. He was bitterly disappointed. He had hoped to find here Nita, or at least Kirkpatrick, and some clue to the identity of the Tarantula or his whereabouts. Instead there was only this small-time crook he might have questioned before.

Again the man gasped, "Who are you?"

"What do you care?" Wentworth asked. "I saved your life. Now I want payment." His voice was mocking, brittle.

"Jeez!" the man gulped painfully, rolling his head, got out more words. "I ain't got no money. I–I—"

Wentworth crouched beside him, the noose in his hands. "I don't want money," he said softly. "I want information."

As often before, his blank, masked face, the slitted hard eyes, struck terror to the criminal heart.

"But who—who—"

Wentworth rose swiftly from beside the man, crossed to the door and slid the cigarette lighter from his pocket. Its base touched the door for an instant and when it had been removed, a vermilion spot glowed there like a drop of blood, a vermilion spot that had hairy, venomous legs—the Seal of the *Spider*!

The man on the floor struggled to a sitting position, stared at the spot. He swallowed loudly.

"The *Spider*!" It was a cry.

Wentworth went back to him slowly, the noose in his hands. He tossed the rope about the man's throat, tightened it a little.

"You killed forty people tonight," said the *Spider* softly. "You should die—"

"But you took me down," the man protested hoarsely.

"I want information," Wentworth pulled on the rope with his fingers, and the man leaned forward frantically, easing the strain. "Talk, and you live. Refuse, and—" again he tugged at the rope.

"I'll talk, I'll talk!" the man gasped. "What do you want—"

Wentworth stiffened abruptly. He had felt a slight motion in the close, unventilated air of the apartment. Someone had entered, someone of the Tarantula's men. Wentworth did not move from his crouch beside the man on the floor. Instead he placed both hands where they could be seen from the door behind him, placed his gun at a distance on the tile floor, and waited.

Forty lives had been sacrificed this night while he trailed this man, and at the end had been only an empty apartment. He knew this man before him had little information. He was one of the lesser workers of the gang. Those who came now might be higher up in the chain. He did not think they would kill the *Spider*. They would save him for the Tarantula.

So Wentworth waited, gun at a distance from his hand, risked a shot in the back, and spoke softly to the man in the noose.

"Quickly," he said, "I have little time. The name of the man who first approached you!"

"Wiggard," gasped his prisoner.

"Know where to find him?"

The man shook his head silently. "Always called Doctor's Exchange, asked for Dr. Fauquier, got a number to call, talked to a guy named Hague—"

"Ever see him?"

The head shook slowly in the noose. Then the eyes bulged, staring in fright over Wentworth's shoulder.

"Oh, God—" he moaned.

"Just hold that," a voice behind Wentworth was sharp. "Raise your hands. That's it. Now turn around, and turn slow."

WENTWORTH did as he was ordered, faced about, eyes expressionless behind the slits of his mask. Three men were in the doorway. The one in front held a leveled gun. He wore a pinch-waisted blue coat. Gray spats graced his shoes, a white felt drooped a jaunty brim over the right eye. His face was thin, skin taut across the cheek bones, and the eyes were the flat, fishy eyes of a man who kills, coldly and without feeling.

"Well, well," he said slowly. "Now what have we here in the pretty little mask?"

Behind Wentworth the man he had saved from hanging gasped out words. "It's the *Spider*," he got out. "The *Spider*! I knew you was coming back, and I was holding him till you got here. Honest to God! You tell the Tarantula that, and he'll turn me loose. Honest, I—"

"Shut up," said the cold-eyed man in the white hat. He said it without emphasis, but the pleading voice choked off instantly. "The *Spider*, eh? With that kid's mask on? Nuts."

"Look on the door," said one of the men behind. He had a fat voice, and his face was rosy and padded. He wheezed out the words.

Cold Eyes said, "Okay, pull your rod." And when two more guns were covering the *Spider*, he took a swift glance at the door, glimpsed that venomous red seal. Nervousness crept into the motions of his hands then. They shook slightly. A nerve twitched in his upper lip on the left side. It twitched and was still, twitched again.

Wentworth said nothing at all. He stood with elevated hands, staring fixedly through the slits. Cold Eyes licked his upper lip.

"One of you scout through the apartment," he said hoarsely, cleared his throat. When he spoke again, there was a higher pitch to his voice. "It ain't like this guy to walk into a trap without a back door out."

Fat Boy walked away, his footsteps heavy on bare floors. The feet moved slowly, a little reluctantly. Cold Eyes stooped and, left-handed, snaked the gun up from the floor.

"Come out of that," he ordered Wentworth. And as the *Spider* moved calmly forward, he backed away, keeping always six feet or more between them, the gun ready. "Hang Sethol up again," he grated to the man who remained in the hall with leveled pistol. "And hang him high this time."

There was a choked cry from the bathroom. Wentworth walked slowly after Cold Eyes, ugly light deep in his eyes. The hanging of Sethol was just enough. But when police found that hanged man and the seal of the *Spider* on the door— The frightened protests of Sethol were cut off suddenly, and the third man came back into the room, his lips lifting evilly from wolf teeth. It was meant for a smile.

"He's hanging high," he said dryly.

Fat Boy's heavy feet came back. "There ain't nobody in here," he said. "I looked the whole damned place over."

Cold Eyes was still nervous. "I don't like it anyway," he said. "Lucky I got suspicious of this old boy the elevator operator was telling us about." He stared at the mask, licked his lip again. "Take off that mask," he ordered.

Wentworth lowered his hands slowly. The gun was in his hat if he wanted it. He could pretend he had knocked his hat off accidentally, grab it and the gun, be out of this fix in a moment.

Instead he unfastened the mask and took it off. His face was the face of an old man, creased about the mouth, lined about the eyes.

"Cripes, he's old!" said Cold Eyes. "Okay, now let's get out of here. Listen, *Spider*, one of us is going to be on each side of you and one behind, and all of us will have our guns ready. Don't try no funny business, *Spider*. We want to take you alive to the Tarantula, but"—the fishy eyes got more shallow, the nerve twitched in his upper lip— "it ain't necessary to take you—alive."

Wentworth still answered nothing.

"Jeez," Fat Boy wheezed. "Why don't he talk?"

"Maybe he ain't got nothing to say," Cold Eyes jeered. He prodded the gun barrel into Wentworth's belly, but scarcely dented the muscle. "Cripes, he's hard for an old one." He patted expertly over the *Spider* for weapons, but missed that gun in his hat, and he missed that compact tool kit beneath his arm. The coat was built so that they'd always miss that, unless they stripped him. It was padded so that the kit seemed part of his hard-muscled body.

The search over, Fat Boy took Wentworth by one arm, Wolf Teeth by the other, and Cold Eyes walked behind with a ready gun.

"I think," he said, "the Tarantula will be tickled to death to see you." His laughter rasped. "Tickled to death!"

CHAPTER SEVENTEEN
Face to Face

WITH three guns pointed at him and two men gripping his arms, Wentworth strolled casually to the gray sedan. He was thrust into the front seat beside Fat Boy, who did the driving. The other two sat behind with drawn guns.

They went silently along for a few blocks, then Cold Eyes stepped into a drugstore for five minutes.

"The Tarantula says he'll be delighted to welcome you to his humble quarters," he told Wentworth on his return. He drew from his pocket a pair of "snatch" glasses, spectacles with smoked lenses through which it was impossible to see, with side strips that fitted snugly against the face. He leaned forward and adjusted these on Wentworth.

A simple matter for the *Spider* to seize those wrists, yank the man toward him as a shield, and grab that gun in his hat. But he submitted calmly to the glasses. It would do no good to strike now, to take command of these three hirelings. He must first let them guide him to the Tarantula's lair. Once there, he would take his chances as they came. One thing he knew: this time he must not fail!

So Wentworth submitted. Half an hour later, after many turning and twistings, which Wentworth knew were intended to confuse him, the gray sedan halted and he was led with guns ever prodding his ribs through a court that echoed; upstairs and through a door that creaked into a musty hall; then up more creaking stairs, through a door into a room.

As they entered, one of his guards snatched off Wentworth's hat. "Jeez!" Fat Boy breathed. "This guy had a gun in his hat all the time. Guess he just didn't get a chance to use it." He laughed wheezingly. "Guess we was too smart for him, huh?"

Wentworth's mouth twitched wryly.

"What's that?" a sharp voice demanded ahead of him.

Fat Boy drew a stuttering breath. "I just found a gun in this guy's hat," he said.

Wentworth lifted his mouth corners in a conventional smile and bowed formally from the waist.

"Haven't we met before, Tarantula?"

A chuckle answered him. "Take the glasses off," said the voice that Wentworth had heard many times over the phone. A hand that shook slightly removed the spectacles.

For an instant, light dazzled Wentworth's eyes; then he made out before him a long heavy table over which a low shaded lamp funneled white glare. Behind that lamp he saw the white bosom of a formal shirt, the satin gleam of lapels... and the hands of the Tarantula. They were folded calmly beneath the lamp, tapered, sensuous fingers resting tip against tip, corpse-white, with black hair on their backs that seemed to crawl with individual life.

Wentworth saw the shirt bosom lean forward. "I didn't know this was to be a formal occasion," he said mockingly. "You'll have to pardon my clothing."

The Tarantula's voice was sharp.

"This is not the *Spider*," his voice clipped out. "What is this?"

The man called Cold Eyes spoke up from just behind Wentworth. "We were executing Sethol the way you told us. When we go away this guy slips in and cuts him down. He was pumping Sethol about you when we walked in on him. Sethol said this guy's the *Spider* and his seal was on the door, a little red seal like a spider."

There was silence in the room for two full minutes, silence that was thick and perilous. Then one of those hairy hands turned the light so its glare struck directly into Wentworth's face.

"Five feet eleven," said the Tarantula softly. "Weight 175 or 80. Carriage might very well be erect. Eyes, gray. Lips firm and straight. Ears long and close to the head, tops on a level with the eyes.

"Strange as it may seem, the description I have just given is that of Richard Wentworth and it fits precisely. However, I have a way to know definitely whether you are Wentworth or some impostor seeking to muscle in on our enterprise." The Tarantula's voice crackled in sudden command. "Tie his hands behind him."

WENTWORTH had just time to swell his wrists against the bands when his arms were wrenched back and ropes bit into them.

"Fine," said the Tarantula softly. One of the hairy hands held a gun now. "Now, Mr. *Spider*, or whatever your name is, you will kindly go where I indicate."

The Tarantula rose, and walked slowly toward Wentworth, who saw now that a black hood hid the Tarantula's head as well as his face. Shadows hid even the color of the eyes. The figure was smallish, not above five feet five. Over formal evening dress the Tarantula wore a robe like a judge—or an executioner—draping from shoulders to floor. Not much chance to locate an identifying feature except for those corpse-like hands with their crawling black hair.

If that hair were sandy-colored instead of black, those hands and figure might be MacPherson's. Put an amber colored drink in one of those hands and the Tarantula might be Professor Hague. Both had the necessary knowledge; both had the requisite intelligence.

Wentworth, arms bound, walked stolidly ahead of the Tarantula through a door that revealed a dimly lighted room. Hands seized Wentworth's shoulders, forced him backward into a chair. Ropes bound his ankles, looped about his already pinioned arms, and secured them to the chair back.

"You may go," the Tarantula said softly, and the door clicked shut. The two were left alone in the dimly lighted room.

It was a queer room. Its walls, without openings, were hung in gray velvet. It was empty of all furnishings save the chair upon which Wentworth sat and, in the far corner, an iron beam that ran up the wall and out upon the ceiling—an iron beam fitted with pulleys and a rope with a noose dangling from the end.

"Do you recognize my little gibbet, Spider?" the Tarantula asked softly. "You know its usage, don't you?" Chuckling laughter bubbled out. "My drawing showed you that, eh, Spider?"

That drawing, the one that had sent cold fear through Wentworth's veins, a drawing of Nita, hanging!

"Your drawing meant something else to me," the Spider said softly. Behind him he strained at his ropes. Swelling his wrist had saved a fraction of an inch. Not much, but with effort and time—

"Yes?" queried the Tarantula. "That drawing is a foretaste of your own doom!"

The Tarantula laughed at that, too, but Wentworth had not spoken in threatening tones. His voice had been calm as if he stated only facts. The laughter was not convincing. The Tarantula seemed to realize, and grew vicious.

"I had planned to substitute yourself on that gibbet in actuality," the words spat out so vehemently the black mask quivered. "I know all your plans. I knew when you returned and your disguise. At any time I could have killed you, but—"

"So you tapped the police phones, did you, Tarantula?" Wentworth cut in. "I wondered if you'd think of that."

The vehement voice of the Tarantula broke with anger, grew high. "Think of it! Why you—" Abruptly the voice checked, and for moments there was silence. Then the Tarantula laughed!

"Very clever, O *Spider*, but you shall not goad me into forgetting my purpose. You shall live, Spider, until my biggest raid. Then I shall shoot you with a police gun and leave you to take the blame for the Tarantula's crimes.

"Our mutual friend, Penrose, is very anxious to accuse you, *Spider*, and I—I am not anxious to have both the honor and the money. I will take the money."

The taunting voice ceased and for a full moment there was silence in the room. Wentworth stopped working at his ropes for a moment, lest their creaking become audible. His lips were mocking.

"I appreciate the—honor you bestow, vermin," he said lightly. "I would appreciate it more if it did not confuse your identity with mine."

"Doubtless," murmured the Tarantula, "but we must get about proving your identity. I no longer need Nita since she has lured you into my trap. So—"

WENTWORTH felt throbbing rage, felt the thin white scar on his right temple grow red and angry. He had been fighting to spare Nita, fighting for time to work on the ropes.

"Just what is it that you want, Tarantula?" he demanded, forcing his voice to calmness.

The Tarantula had reached the gray curtains. Wentworth's words brought the masked face about. "Ah, you admit your identity!"

Wentworth's face was rigid. "I haven't denied it."

The Tarantula turned to him. "That is true. I was the one to deny it." Patent leather shoes gleamed beneath the long black robe as the Tarantula paced toward Wentworth. "You are a man of discernment, my dear *Spider*. You see that I want something."

Wentworth's eyes glittered coldly. He said nothing.

"What I want is this: there are three men whose intelligence thwarts me. There was Kirkpatrick, whom I have. Another, yourself. As you see, I have you. And the third—the third is Roberts, president of the Board of Aldermen. A very shrewd and honest man, who in addition to an armed guard, a steel vest and an armored car, seems to have a charmed life. I am afraid Roberts will have Penrose removed and substitute an intelligent man in his place.

"Now this is the plan, *Spider*. Promise me to kill Roberts and to leave the country permanently and I will restore Nita to you."

Pain stabbed Wentworth. But his cold eyes never wavered from the Tarantula's. "You know that is impossible," he said quietly.

The Tarantula shrugged, shoulders lifting the black robe. "I'm afraid I can't see why. You have killed many men. What does one more matter?"

Wentworth's lips clipped off words like sword blades. "I kill only vermin such as yourself."

The Tarantula laughed. "Stout fellah! But I think that after you have seen my little demonstration you will change your attitude."

Wentworth's jaw was clenched until the muscles bulged. "There are some things, Tarantula," he said, "that nothing on Earth could force me to do. One of those things is to kill an innocent man. Another is to do anything that might assist your plans!

"I want you to know that if I had not been able to fight you better by appearing to sail from this country, neither your threats, nor the actual death of Nita van Sloan, could have forced me to go."

THE Tarantula continued to regard him through the slits of his mask. "We'll see." The robed figure moved across the room again, ducked under the gray drapes. Wentworth yanked at his bonds. They did not yield. The curtains were thrust aside again, and Nita van Sloan stood there—and behind her was the leering black mask of the Tarantula.

Nita's eyes leaped to Wentworth, but she gave no indication that she recognized him. She did not know the *Spider*'s plans, nor did she know whether or not he had identified himself. And though she knew those gray eyes that met hers so lovingly, though she would have known them anywhere, she gave Wentworth only a casual glance and turned back to the Tarantula.

Laughter bubbled from behind the mask. "Very clever, my dear. Very clever indeed. You don't know whether Wentworth wants you to recognize him, so you don't."

Wentworth's jaw was still tightly clamped. His face was pale. Torture for Nita was ahead. Torture he would be forced to witness. Duty and love, and love must die!

"Nita, darling," he said, "I have admitted my identity."

The girl jerked her head about and smiled bravely. Her face was pale from long confinement. Dark circles beneath her eyes made them more vivid. She held herself proudly, though her arms were bound behind her. "It's good to see you again, Dick," she said.

"What's this animal up to now?" Nita's voice was scorn itself.

The Tarantula's laughter bubbled over again. "Just this, my dear: your Dick is proving a bit stubborn. I want him to do a very simple thing for me—remove a troublesome man. He refuses, so—"

"So you're going to torture me to force Dick to act," Nita broke in. There was courage in her voice. "I tell you in advance," she said. "It won't do any good." Her head rose proudly. "I wouldn't have it otherwise."

The Tarantula looked from one to the other. "You may be right, but I always find it wise in such matters to experiment. He knows you are no longer useful to me. He knows you must die. Death of a loved one a man can face. But sometimes his resolution weakens before the actuality of—torture."

The Tarantula reached up and caught the noose that dangled from the gibbet, seized Nita by the shoulder and dropped the rope about her neck. Wentworth strained at his bonds, but they had been well tied. They would not give. The noose drew tight about Nita's soft white throat!

CHAPTER EIGHTEEN
The Pit of Bayonets

THE Tarantula swiftly tightened the noose about Nita's throat, but left her room to breathe. Standing behind her with the rope cleverly rigged so that little effort was required to lift considerable weight, he peered past Nita's head with its clustering brown wealth of curls into Wentworth's eyes.

"Shall I pull the rope, *Spider*, or will you kill Roberts for me?"

Wentworth's teeth were ground together. His shoulders swelled. His hands fought frantically against the ropes. Time he must have. Time—

His eyes were riveted on Nita's face. Her blue eyes met his with an effort at calmness, but Wentworth could see the haunting fear that forced itself into them.

"Make up your mind," the Tarantula urged, voice sharpening. "Time grows short."

Tentatively he tugged at the rope. The noose wrinkled the white flesh of Nita's throat. Wentworth saw her try to swallow and fail, saw her mouth open for breath. Then Nita did a courageous thing. She lifted her feet from the floor, throwing her entire weight upon the rope, seeking immediate death to prevent torture—to save Wentworth from a decision that, either way, would torture him all his days.

The Tarantula cursed, paid out rope and allowed Nita to crumple to the floor. It was not part of his plan to let her die easily. Her death, he knew, would remove his last hold upon the *Spider*.

Wentworth bit back words that raged on his lips. His struggling hands had gained a fraction of an inch leeway from the bonds! If he could only stall off the Tarantula's torture a few moments more—

The Tarantula's chuckling laughter was the only sound in the room. "Very good, Nita. But the rope works just as well when you are lying on the floor," and slowly once more he pulled it tight, not heavily, not savagely, but with a feline cruelty that tightened the noose just enough to half strangle Nita. It pulled her pretty head up from the floor, bit into her flesh.

Resolutely Nita made no effort to ease the strain, let her full weight sag against the rope.

"Wait!" gasped out Wentworth, fighting for time. "Wait!"

"Yes?" The hand did not ease the tension on the noose as the Tarantula turned toward him, slitted eyes glinting.

"Give me time," cried Wentworth, "time to think!"

His eyes were riveted on Nita's face. It was growing dark with congested blood. Her eyes were closed, her mouth open, and he could hear no sound of breathing. The Tarantula did not relax the rope. The robed body leaned back against Nita's weight.

"Sorry," came the casual voice from behind the mask, "I can't give you any time." The voice crackled. "Decide now!"

Wentworth was fighting two battles; one against the bonds—which in time he would win; one in his heart—Nita against his promise to kill. One innocent life against another—and Nita, Nita was dying!

THE noose did not loosen. The Tarantula's body still leaned against its pull. That loved face was bluish now with suffocation. Her tongue forced itself out between clenched teeth.

Wentworth tossed his body in the chair, thrust out elbows as if already the ropes were free. The Tarantula uttered a startled exclamation, released the ropes and sprang toward Wentworth, a gun flashing out from beneath the black robe. In his heart the *Spider* cried, "Thank God!"

Nita sagged to the floor as the noose fell limp. Breath hissed from the girl's suffocating lungs. She stirred feebly.

"Shall I pull the rope, *Spider*, or will you carry out my orders?"

Wentworth flung himself forward on his feet, lifting the chair from the floor. He whirled so the legs struck out savagely at the Tarantula. The robed figure dodged aside, the gun glinted, the edged voice barked out, "Get back, Wentworth, or I'll shoot."

"Shoot and be damned to you!" cried Wentworth.

"I'll shoot... Nita," the Tarantula cried.

Without warning a buzzer rasped in the room. The Tarantula whirled toward the gray curtains, and in that instant Wentworth threw all his strength upon one straining wrist. Slowly at first, then with a tearing of flesh, his hand pulled free from the ropes. He sprang toward the Tarantula, though still crouched awkwardly in his ropes against the chair.

The Tarantula whirled. Wentworth's fist struck over the heart. The Tarantula reeled back, flung up the gun, and—the lights went out.

Wentworth dropped to the floor, and an orange lance of flame stabbed the spot where he had stood. Distantly now came shouts and cries of fright. Gruff men's voices rang out, a riot gun blasted, and the stuttering savage voice of a machine gun burst out. Once more the Tarantula's gun spoke, and then again, pointed straight at the floor where Wentworth lay. An axe crashed against the door of the room itself. The gun fell silent.

Again and again the axe smashed, biting into metal and wood. Men's feet stumbled into the room. The velvet curtain ripped, and a hand torch flung its broad ray of light into the darkness. Wentworth thrust himself up with his one free hand, struggled to get on his feet, looking like some awkward turtle with his heavy chair.

"What the hell," he heard a man's voice, and blinking into the glare of the light he saw it glint upon brass buttons.

"I'm Inspector Barton," Wentworth said. "Get me out of this quick. One of you get to Miss van Sloan over there and resuscitate her. She's been strangled."

The light left him and swept the room, found the iron gibbet with its dangling noose. The noose was empty. The room was empty, except for Wentworth and the policeman with the light. The Tarantula and Nita were gone!

"THERE ain't nobody in here," the cop said.

"Behind the curtains, doors!" Wentworth snapped out.

The cop bounded across the room. Gray velvet rippled. Nothing there. Around the whole room, the policeman went, tearing down the drapes. Except for the door through which he had hacked a way, there was no opening in the walls.

"There's a door there," Wentworth declared grimly "The Tarantula went out it, and Miss van Sloan is with him. Here, cut me loose!"

The cop crossed to his side, used the axe to saw through the ropes. As he worked he laughed grimly. "There's two bullet holes in the bottom of this chair," he said. "Looks like somebody tried to burn the seat of your pants."

Wentworth's voice was grim. "The Tarantula shot at me three times. I dropped under the first one, then rolled over so the chair shielded me."

The ropes fell away and he tossed the chair aside, sprang up, grabbed the axe. He was across the room in a bound, hacking savagely at the walls. A panel of wood split beneath his assault, revealed plaster. He attacked the second panel and that, too, showed no opening. A third blow bounced back with a ring of steel. The edge of the axe was chipped.

Wentworth pried at the wood with the blade, stripped it away and revealed a door like a safety deposit vault. He tossed the axe to the floor. It was useless now. His hand slid beneath his arm to the tool kit that still nestled there. Swiftly he extracted two small vials and—finding the slit along the top of the door—he poured part of their contents into it, dribbled some of it down across the face of the barrier.

"Stand clear," he sang out, "there's going to be an explosion."

The cop darted through the door he had hacked open, leaving the room in blackness. Wentworth touched a match to the wet place across the door, leaped after the policeman. He caught the edge of the door and swung through just as a terrific detonation ripped out behind him. A blast of air like the discharge of a cannon cycloned past. Within the room of the gibbet there was a heavy thud. Wentworth snatched the policeman's light, darted back.

The secret door lay twisted and torn on the floor. Wentworth leaped over it, sprang into the dark space beyond. His light revealed a room. This had been Nita's prison. On the far side a panel of wood swung open, disclosing a passageway. He raced to it, plunged into narrow stairs. Down and down the steps spiraled. Wentworth took them three at a time, one hand pressing lightly against the wall for balance.

The air became dank and stale. A wet chill bit through his clothing. Still the stairs led downward. Then Wentworth checked in mid-leap, stopping himself with that hand pressed against the wall, flung frantically backward so that he sprawled on the dank stairs. A pit yawned at his feet, a pit of bayonets fixed with their points up! Another step and he would have flung himself to instant death upon those hungry needle blades!

WENTWORTH crouched and flung the beam of light ahead. For twenty feet the pit extended and there seemed no way over it. He flashed his light upward. There hung the flooring that had covered the pit. It was suspended on ropes, and these ran over pulleys that operated it from the opposite end. There was no ledge on either side, apparently the ropes had been the floor's sole support.

He swept the strip of boards with his light. Along each side there was a narrow space, less than an inch wide, between the wood and the wall.

Wentworth thrust the light into his coat so that its beam slanted obliquely the length of the passageway. He sprang up and caught the end of the flooring, worked to one side and wriggled his fingers into the narrow crack between it and the wall. He could not force his hand through far enough to get a full hold, only the ends of his fingers gripped the flooring. Below, the bayonets thrust up their thirsty points. Twenty feet! It looked like twenty miles. Wentworth's jaw locked grimly. This was the only way. He swung out over the pit.

Each hand must be worked into that narrow crack each time he slid it along a few inches. He advanced his right hand six inches while he clung with the aching fingers of his left. He wriggled the right hand as far into the crack as possible, pulled the left up against it, then repeated.

Slow work, slow tendon-tearing, strength-sapping work. Wentworth's breath gasped through locked teeth. Feeling fled from his fingers, left them numb and aching. Still he fought on over the yawning pit of bayonets. Right hand six inches, strain and tug, left hand up beside it, right—left—right—left. Then, at long last, fingers seeming torn from his hands, a weak swing, a fumbling leap. His feet struck the far edge of the pit, slipped. He arched backwards, over the bayonets!

Wentworth swung his arms wildly. One hand brushed the wall, reeled, pitched forward on his face. For seconds he lay there panting, then scrambled up and raced on.

The pit of bayonets was past, but valuable time had been lost.

He ran with heaving chest. Another fifty feet, and the light stabbing ahead of him struck a closed door. He flung his weight against it, bounced back, reeling. The door did not even shiver. Once more with fingers that were like sticks, Wentworth brought out his two small vials. He allowed a little of the liquids to pour into the crack above the door. It was a desperate chance. The explosive was terrifically powerful, and in this narrow passage he had no way of dodging the blast.

He laid a long trail as a fuse down the entire length of the door, struck a match to it and sprinted back to the pit, dropped over its edge and hung by his tortured hands. Scarcely had he taken his position when the explosion came.

Fan of hot rushing air! Concussion like a blow on the head! Deafening sound! Wentworth was half stunned as the blast swept through the tunnel. One hand tore loose from its grip on the edge, and he hung perilously over the bed of bayonet points. There was a creak overhead, another. Wentworth's light was gone, but he knew what those sounds meant. The ropes that alone supported the flooring over his head had been torn loose by the explosion!

DESPERATELY, Wentworth seized the damp slippery flooring, muscled himself upward until he got his elbows over the top. Another creek of the heavy flooring above his head! With a frantic heave, Wentworth dragged his body clear of the opening and rolled. Air gushed past him, a slamming crash! The flooring had fallen, missing Wentworth by inches.

He thrust to his feet, bolted for the door that he had blasted. Dim light from beyond showed it sagging on one hinge. Wentworth, with a single wrench, pulled it loose and ducked through. He was in the cluttered cellar of a building.

Ladderlike stairs climbed the far wall. Wentworth plunged toward them, swarmed up and found himself in a vacant house. He pounded forward, out into the street.

At the corner was a swirling crowd, all peering curiously the other way. Nearby was an orange cab, but the street was empty of other cars. Wentworth raced toward the cab. No one was in it. He ran on to the crowd.

"Did you see anybody come out of that house down there?" he demanded, catching a man by the shoulder.

The man looked blankly into his eyes. "What house?"

Swiftly Wentworth asked a dozen more in the crowd and finally found a woman who had seen six people leave in a gray sedan—ten minutes before.

Wentworth raced back to the house where the tunnel ended, slammed through the door and bumped chest to chest into the bulky-shouldered Penrose. The deputy commissioner's hand shot out, seized Wentworth's shoulder.

"Thought you'd get away, eh?"

"I'm Inspector Barton," Wentworth said hurriedly. He poured out words. "Six people got away in a gray sedan. Let's broadcast right away. It's ten minutes since they left, but we may pick them up. The Tarantula and Nita van Sloan in the car. Kirkpatrick may be, too."

Penrose's glittering small eyes stared hostilely from his broad face. He made no move to do as Wentworth demanded, nor did the grip of his fingers weaken.

"So you're Barton, are you? Got your credentials?"

Wentworth bit out a single bitter curse. He stooped, turned up his trouser leg, revealed there the badge of Scotland Yard.

Penrose grunted in obvious disappointment. “All right,” he said, “we’ll get out that broadcast. But I want to see you at headquarters.” He turned to a cop at his side. “Cohen, stay with this man and see that he comes to headquarters.”

The cop saluted. Wentworth stared into Penrose’s face. “What’s up?” he asked quietly. Penrose grinned, but made no direct reply.

“I’ll be seeing you,” he said, and stumped out of the building.

CHAPTER NINETEEN
Jail for the Spider

WENTWORTH watched him go with narrowed eyes. He glanced at the officer assigned to watch him, then he, too, left the building and walked slowly up to the orange taxi at the corner. The driver grinned at him.

“Did I do O.K.?” he asked. “You said wait an hour and call police, or follow you if you came out with some other guys and send the cops wherever they took you.”

“You did just right.” Wentworth nodded. “But if you’d followed that gray sedan from here instead of coming to the door and looking for your five hundred, I’d have given you ten thousand.”

The driver’s face went blank. He jerked a glance up the street. “Jeez,” he said. “I never figgered they’d get through the police.”

Wentworth smiled wearily. He took an envelope from his pocket, borrowed a pencil, and scrawled words in Hindustani across its cover.

“What’s that?” demanded officer Cohen suspiciously.

Wentworth grinned at him. “That’s a report to Scotland Yard,” he said.

Cohen’s thin face was dubious. “I don’t know as I ought to let you send that,” he said.

“Listen,” Wentworth snapped, “your orders are to see that I get back to headquarters. As long as I get to headquarters, you’ve got nothing to do with my movements, and you’ll keep that long nose out of my business, see?”

“Oh, is that so?”

Wentworth looked the policeman in the eye. “It is.”

The policeman tried to stare him down but failed, shuffled feet and looked away. He said nothing more and Wentworth gave the envelope with its scrawled words, English transliteration of Hindustani characters, to the driver, gave him the other half of the five hundred dollar bill he had promised and added another hundred dollars. “Get that to a cable office right away.”

The driver grinned at him, looked at the cop with contemptuous eyes, and shot the cab away.

For two hours then, Wentworth, in another cab, cruised about the city seeking some trace of the Tarantula and Nita—and allowing ample time for his cable message to be sent without interference from Penrose.

Newspaper boys were screaming the police raid on the Tarantula’s headquarters, the facts of the escape. Soldiers with bayonetted guns were on guard at every bank they passed, and Wentworth, buying a paper, found that Governor Lehman of New York was prepared to put the city under martial law at the first evidence of a new attack by the Tarantula.

President Roosevelt had closed every bank in the city to prevent their being bankrupted by the panicky runs which had filled the streets with frightened depositors. As a precaution against the Tarantula, the money was being transported by armed convoys surrounded by an entire troop of cavalry to some secret central depository in the city.

At several points, companies of militia were stationed with armored trucks which would rush to any threatened area at the first news of a raid by the Tarantula.

Wentworth, reading the details of the city’s preparation to battle the Tarantula and his gang, was not reassured. There were loopholes in the preparations.

FINALLY Wentworth ordered his cab to police headquarters and confronted Penrose. “If you’ll call off your watchdog long enough,” he said, “I want to get rid of this makeup. It’s not especially pleasant.”

Penrose nodded affably, and directed Wentworth to a small private lavatory which adjoined his office. Wentworth secured the door, speedily creamed off the makeup of the old man which he had assumed to pursue the Tarantula, and with a few deft touches restored that of Inspector Barton. He still wore the small rubber discs that plumped his cheeks, the wax that distorted his nostrils. These were part of the Barton makeup. It was necessary to wash his hair to remove the traces of the powder he had combed into his locks. But it was swiftly done, and within ten minutes Wentworth emerged in his former character of Inspector Barton of Scotland Yard.

He dropped into a chair and surveyed Penrose with veiled eyes. “I gathered,” he said, “that you wished to see me about something or other.”

Penrose, seated behind his desk, knotty fingers upon its top, glowered at Wentworth. He began to speak with careful slowness that indicated he had planned in detail what he was to say.

“I have just about decided,” he said, “that the *Spider* and the Tarantula are the same person. Their names are alike and we know from what this Elsie

Thompson phoned Kirkpatrick that the *Spider* is back in town."

Wentworth drew a cigarette from his platinum case and lighted it. "You seem to forget," he pointed out, "that it was Elsie Thompson who helped put Kirkpatrick in the Tarantula's power. If the Tarantula were the *Spider*, it scarcely seems that anyone connected with him would have tipped you off."

Penrose seemed to hear this joyfully. There was an exuberance about his small, pursed mouth. "It's my theory," he said, "that this Elsie Thompson started to do the *Spider* in and is helping him only when she is forced to. Another thing which points to the *Spider* is the fact that we found a linesman who turned off the lights for that last raid, a fellow named Sethol, hanged in an apartment house up near Riverside Drive with the seal of the *Spider* on the door. If that doesn't prove the *Spider* guilty, I don't know what does!"

Wentworth leaned forward, gesturing with his cigarette. "That's absolutely ridiculous," he said, "to me that indicates very clearly that the *Spider* is fighting the Tarantula."

"Oh, it does, does it?" Penrose growled. But instead of rancor there was an increased exuberance that marked his small glittering eyes and heavy stolid face. "That's what I'd expect you to say." He touched a button on his desk, and a policeman opened the door.

"Bring me a basin of water, soap, a wash rag and a towel," said Penrose.

Wentworth frowned at him. "What is this, a minstrel show?" he asked.

Penrose chuckled. "Well, it's something like a show, at any rate," he said with satisfaction.

The policeman brought in the basin of water and set it on the desk. "Now call a couple more men in here," Penrose ordered, and when they had arrived he leaned across the desk with a complacent smile on his face.

"I've had a tip," he said, "that you're Wentworth in disguise—that is, the *Spider*. Every word you say confirms this, and when I saw how completely you assumed the makeup of an old man to hunt, as you said, the Tarantula, I began to think perhaps it was true. I phoned Scotland Yard a little while ago, but they could give out no information, even to us, about any Inspector Barton, and that sounds damned funny. If you are Barton," Penrose grinned, "I can't do anything to you. Diplomatic courtesy, as you pointed out. But even if you are Barton, you can't object to washing your face."

WENTWORTH rose slowly. "This is the most ridiculous thing I've ever heard," he said. He was thinking swiftly. If his disguise were penetrated, his identity as Wentworth revealed, nothing on Earth could save him. It was fortunate that Scotland Yard had so valued his services in the past that they had given him the fictitious title of Inspector Barton and promised not to give out any information about him to anyone at all, including the police of the world.

It had saved him before. Now it had balked Penrose in that one particular. But if his makeup were removed—

Wentworth stalled. "This is absolutely silly," he said. "You know that I just removed the makeup of that old man a few minutes ago. How could I put on another one?"

"I'm sorry, Inspector, if this inconveniences you," said Penrose firmly. "But I insist that you wash your face and clear up some little uncertainty that has arisen in my mind."

"This is outrageous," Wentworth declared. "I will not tolerate such an imposition, such a reflection upon my integrity. Scotland Yard shall hear about this, and so shall Kirkpatrick."

"If Kirkpatrick ever comes back," said Penrose softly. "Will you wash your face, or shall I have it washed for you?"

Wentworth looked about him at the three police. Apparently they had been told in advance what was intended, and there was no amusement in their faces. Their grim eyes were fixed upon Wentworth, and their guns were conspicuous in their holsters.

"Very well," said Wentworth. "I'll do this, but I'm warning you that you'll live to regret it, Penrose."

"Sure," Penrose agreed, "sure. Now wash your face."

Wentworth walked slowly forward to the desk, dipped the washrag into the water. "Now then, watch closely," he said.

He scrubbed his face with the lathered washrag. He did a thorough job of it, rinsed his face in the basin, mopped it dry with the towel. Penrose was leaning forward excitedly above the desk, staring. Wentworth lowered the towel, and the unchanged, indignant face of Inspector Barton stared hostilely into Penrose's gaze.

Penrose's mouth gaped open. "Lord!" he said, "it didn't come off."

"I hope you're satisfied now," said Wentworth severely. "I'll see that you hear about this from Washington."

Inwardly, Wentworth was congratulating himself upon having recently substituted waterproof makeup in all his kits. More than once he had been forced to plunge into water in various adventures of his, and he had taken that precaution against the betrayal of his identity. It had served him well. He caught up his hat and stalked toward the door.

"Now perhaps," he said, "you will turn your attention to catching the real Tarantula." He opened the door.

"Wait!" snapped Penrose.

Wentworth turned.

"It just occurred to me," said Penrose, "speaking of shows, that actors and actresses use cold cream to remove makeup—"

"Dashed if I'll submit to another such indignity!" Wentworth exclaimed, and started from the room.

"Seize him!" Penrose barked.

THE three policemen sprang upon Wentworth, wrenched him about and thrust him back into the office. Wentworth railed in his traditionally English manner, but without effect. A large jar of cold cream was brought in and one of the policemen crudely but effectively massaged his face.

With the cream came off also the surface makeup, all the sallow paint that Wentworth had applied to his face, but certain other articles of makeup remained. There were tiny disks of rubber in his cheeks, there were bits of wax in his nostrils which dilated them—and he had reshaped his eyebrows to remove the quizzical points that were typical of Wentworth.

Certainly he was no longer Inspector Barton, except for the bright blond hair. But certainly also he was not Wentworth.

Penrose glowered at him. "That takes care of you," he said, "Mr. *Spider*."

Wentworth smiled calmly at him. "You have removed Inspector Barton," he said. "I had found it necessary to assume that because of certain criminals in your country whom I did not wish to identify me. I am actually from Scotland Yard. My name is Richards. You can confirm that by phoning the Yard, and letting me speak with them."

Penrose shook his head obstinately. "You're Wentworth. There's something about you that ain't quite like him, but you're the man, all right. I can't prove it, yet. I ain't got nothing to prove you're the Tarantula. But I'm going to hold you in jail, together with a couple of other birds, and see if the Tarantula doesn't stop working while you're there."

"This is ridiculous, Penrose," Wentworth snapped. "Just phone the Yard and they'll tell you who I am."

Wentworth had a shrewd plan in mind; his friend, Inspector Ferguson, had a keen mind. If Wentworth asked him over the phone to identify him as Richards, the Inspector would do it. But Penrose waved aside his protests.

Wentworth leaned forward, pounded a fist into his palm. "Who," he demanded, "found the Tarantula's hideout the only time it was found? I did. I had that taxicab driver trail me and phone you to come. That is the only time you have come near catching the Tarantula. If you lock me up, Miss van Sloan will die, Kirkpatrick will be killed, and not all the precautions that the soldiers and you together can take will prevent the Tarantula from looting the city of its wealth."

Penrose sneered. "Hate yourself, don't you?"

Wentworth straightened. "I'm telling you facts. Do you want to take upon yourself the responsibility for these lives and that money?"

Penrose straightened, too, his short heavy body tense. "Sure I'll take it," he said. "And I'll take it a lot more gladly with you in jail, along with a couple of other birds I know."

Wentworth shook his head, his face contemptuous. He had a very definite clue now to the Tarantula. But he would have to work on it himself. Penrose would only bungle and allow the gang to escape.

"Who are these other two birds as you call them?" he asked.

A self-satisfied grin spread over Penrose's face. "They'll be here any minute now," he said. A buzzer sounded. "Ah, here they are now. Come in!" he bellowed.

The door opened and police thrust into the office the corpulent, polished Big Tim Lally and Professor Hague of the gray face and the tapering, hairy hands.

"What is the meaning of this?" blustered Lally.

"It means," said Penrose, blustering back, "that you three are suspected of being the Tarantula. You will be held secretly, without being allowed to communicate with anyone, until I can make sure which of you it is."

CHAPTER TWENTY
The Hanging of Nita

NITA VAN SLOAN had kept her gaze on Wentworth's face as the rope bit into her throat, and his suffering eyes had been the last thing she saw as darkness closed upon her. Then the rope relaxed, and she had struggled back to consciousness.

She heard noise and confusion as from a great distance, heard shots, shouts. Then blackness settled over the room. She felt herself lifted as if with great difficulty and half dragged across the floor. Draperies brushed her face, a door swung heavily shut.

"Here," she heard the Tarantula's panting voice. "Take this girl and carry her to the car. I don't know whether I killed the *Spider* or not. I shot him three times. If he's still alive, the girl will prove useful."

Nita pulled herself back to consciousness. Dick shot! She started to struggle vigorously, screamed. Close walls clapped the sound back at her, smothered it. A man growled harshly. "Do that again and I'll slug you!"

She was tossed to his shoulder, and a long

descent down many stairs began. She screamed again, "Downstairs, Dick!"

A violent blow caught her on the head, sent dazzling lights, then darkness swooping upon her brain.

When consciousness returned to her a second time, she was being jolted on the floor of a car. It seemed to continue for hours, then she was hustled, only half aware of her surroundings into an unlighted house, dumped upon a hard cot.

Dimly, she heard the voice she recognized as the Tarantula's swearing, "Your friend, the *Spider,* chased us out of comfortable quarters," it said harshly. "You'll have to suffer the consequences along with the rest of us. I'm afraid this room won't be up to your tastes in luxuries."

Long days dragged past, days in which, though she did not know it, Wentworth was helpless in a police cell. The Tarantula was waiting. On the rare occasions when the hooded, robed figure thrust into Nita's room, worry was in the voice that issued from behind the mask.

"Your friend the *Spider* has disappeared," the voice that tried hard to gloat stated. "Either I shot him to death, in which case I have nothing to worry about, or he has run away from the Tarantula."

Nita's haggard blue eyes were scornful. "Run away from you!" She threw back her lovely head and laughed. "I think both your theories are wrong. He has found he can work better if he works secretly. That is why you can't find him. Is that why you are afraid to loot any more banks?"

The hooded, robed figure was like an executioner's. The slitted eyes gleamed. They were shadowed so it was impossible to tell their color. "No, darling," said the Tarantula softly, "I'm just waiting until the government very kindly has assisted me by moving all the money in the city into one bank. They think they can guard it better that way. Guard it!" The hooded head was thrown back in genuine laughter.

"Not all the armies and navies of the world could prevent me from taking the money. And as for the *Spider*—" the voice grew firm—"he is either dead or in hiding. At least the police will cooperate with him no longer. I had them informed that Inspector Barton was really the *Spider*."

Nita's arms were still held by handcuffs behind her, but the wristlets were padded to prevent them from galling. She got up and paced back and forth across the narrow, windowless room. She had been given an ill-fitting cheap little wash dress, but her proud carriage made even its gaudy colors seem glamorous.

"Worried, dear?" asked the Tarantula. "Well, you have reason to be. The moment I am convinced the *Spider* is dead, it will be necessary for me to remove you, too."

The girl's shoulders lifted in a listless shrug. "If Dick is dead, I do not care to live anyway," she said levelly.

A DISTANT buzzer sounded, and the Tarantula let out an exclamation. He ducked from the room, pulling at the door. Nita ran on soundless feet after the robed figure, thrust her foot into the opening of the slamming door. It was heavy and inflicted a painful blow. Nita bit her lips to choke back a cry of pain—but the door with its spring lock did not close. Nita stole out.

She was in a dark hallway. No one was in sight. Nita drifted soundlessly to her right, saw a wall panel open a crack. A secret escape passage! She slipped into it, kicking the panel shut behind her. A light clicked on over her head, apparently operated by the closing door, and she found herself in a small, luxuriously furnished room. It had no other exit than the one by which she had entered. Nita whirled back toward the door, heard footsteps. She was trapped!

Her eyes swept swiftly over the room, and she let out a little gasp of hope. By a chaise lounge on the far side of the room was a French phone. Nita raced to it, turned her back and lifted the phone off its cradle with her manacled hands, then she lay down on the chaise, pressed her ear to the earpiece and could talk into the transmitter.

Seconds of clicking silence passed. Nita's breath quickened, her eyes fixed on the door. If only the Tarantula would stay out of the room for a few moments. Finally the operator answered, and Nita hurriedly gave the police number, saying, "Emergency," to speed the call through.

In seconds a gruff voice answered.

"This is Nita van Sloan," she said swiftly, "I am a prisoner in the Tarantula's headquarters. The phone number here is Chelsea 7-0965. Tell Inspector Barton or the commissioner right away, I—" And suddenly the door swung open and the Tarantula's eyes glared at her from the slits of the hood. Nita poured out words in a frenzy of haste. "Can't you get hold of Mr. Wentworth? No, no, I don't know where to reach him, I—"

The Tarantula wrenched the phone from her with such force that it was ripped from its wires, slapped her heavily in the face.

"You little tramp!" the voice came out muffled from behind the mask.

Nita dropped her head as if in despair, one cheek reddening from the blow. "Oh, you're right, you're right," she moaned. "Dick has disappeared. I tried to get him through his apartment, but they didn't know—"

"You're lying," there was a small break in the Tarantula's voice.

"No, no, it's true. Dick has run away. Oh, how could he do such a thing! How could he—"

"Shut up," said the Tarantula. "You're not fooling me." The Tarantula dashed across the room, flung open the door. "The police are coming. We'll have to clear out of here, too, at once! This little tart phoned them. You know what to do."

The robed figure whirled at the door, strode back to Nita, stood glaring down at her an instant. "For this," the Tarantula said, "you die, even if I lose your valued services in trapping the *Spider*. Kirkpatrick will have to take his place and die in my big raid to take the blame for the crimes. It's not as good. My build-up has been for the *Spider*. But it will have to serve. The public is ready to believe anything about a man in a high office."

A noose appeared from under the Tarantula's robe, snaked over Nita's head before she could move to prevent it. The Tarantula ran across the room, dragged the rope over a closet and door and threw full weight upon it. Nita, strangling, her hands helpless behind her, ran toward the door. She did not want to die now that police were on their way. The Tarantula hauled in the rope too swiftly for her rush to save her. Nita felt herself lifted, strangling.

She fought for breath, kicked out frantically. The Tarantula eased the rope until her toes just touched the floor, until by desperate effort, Nita could ease the strain of the noose about her throat. The rope was fastened that way.

The Tarantula stood before her, gloating as Nita fought to save herself.

"You want to live now, eh, my dear?" the voice chuckled. "Well, it will do you no good. Even if the police come here, they won't be able to find you in this secret room. And there is planted beneath this building a powerful bomb which will go off precisely five minutes after the lights go out."

As the Tarantula spoke, the lights went out. Nita, through the drumming blood in her ears, heard swift feet cross the floor, heard the door close. She fought the noose. Five minutes. If she could keep from strangling that long, there would be the bomb. Dear God, if Dick only knew.

CHAPTER TWENTY-ONE
Spider to the Rescue

FACED with Lally and Hague, in Penrose's office, Wentworth made no further protest against the deputy commissioner's intention of imprisoning him. Lally blustered on and Professor Hague added his dignified complaint. But the three of them were locked in isolated cells and a guard took up his slow, vigilant patrol before them. Regularly once each day, Penrose came to inform them gloatingly that since their imprisonment the crimes of the Tarantula had ceased.

"One of you is guilty," he said finally on the fifth day. "The fact that the raids have stopped proves it."

"Or else," said Wentworth dryly, "it proves the Tarantula is waiting until all the money is put together in one place before he strikes."

Penrose glared at him. "That's what the President and the bankers are afraid of, according to the newspapers. Is that what you instructed your men to do, Mr. Tarantula?"

"If I may permit myself some peculiarly apt American slang," said Wentworth, "nuts to you."

Penrose snorted and left. The guard resumed his slow pacing.

Hague called to Wentworth. "How long do you suppose this fool is going to keep us here? I haven't even been able to get a lawyer."

"I'm leaving today," Wentworth replied.

The guard spun toward him. He was tall and gangling. A bleak nose crowded watery blue eyes that seemed to protrude as he stared at Wentworth. "The hell you say!" he growled.

Wentworth smiled at him. "Yes. The real Wentworth is coming in on the *Bremen* today. He knows I am imprisoned, and he is a fair man. He would not let another be locked up in his place."

"Baloney," said the guard. "You're Wentworth; you're the *Spider*!"

Wentworth's smile was confident. "As I told your estimable chief, I am Richards of Scotland Yard."

The guard walked argumentatively toward the cell. "Now listen," he began.

"You know," Wentworth interrupted, "I like that American phrase."

"What d'yuh mean?" demanded the guard.

"Nuts to you," said Wentworth, and strolled to a seat on his hard cot.

Two hours later, Penrose came excitedly down the long corridor, followed by the calm-faced Ram Singh and Reardon in disguise as Wentworth. Penrose fairly puffed up to Wentworth's cell. "I'm sorry as the devil about this, Richards," he said. "I hope you'll understand that I've been only trying to do my duty as I saw it."

"The trouble with you," said Wentworth calmly, watching Penrose, important in brass-buttoned blue, unlock the cell, "—the trouble is that you see only what you want to see, Penrose, and what you want to see is dashed stupid."

The door clanged open, and Wentworth strode out.

"Dashed white of you, Wentworth," he said grasping Reardon's hand. "I was telling this bully guard here you'd do precisely this as soon as you landed. If Kirkpatrick had been here this never would have happened."

"I came as soon as I got your cable," Reardon turned and strolled off, arm linked with the real Wentworth, while Penrose tagged remorsefully along at their heels.

They climbed the stairs to the main hall of Police Headquarters. Without warning, a policeman flung open a door. "Commissioner!" he yelled. "A dame on the phone says she's Nita van Sloan, and—"

Wentworth spun through the door ahead of Penrose, snatched up the receiver, heard Nita cry out: "The phone number here is Chelsea 7-0965. Tell Inspector Barton or the commissioner right away. I—" Her voice broke suddenly, became desperate. "Can't you get hold of Mr. Wentworth? No, no, I don't know where to reach him. I—"

Crashing noise came over the wire, then silence, Wentworth flashed up and down on the receiver hook. "Have that call traced at once," he snapped.

He whirled toward Penrose, his voice crackling. "That was Nita van Sloan. She's bound to have been calling from the hideout of the Tarantula. I've ordered the call traced. As soon as you find out where it is, rush men there."

Penrose was too startled, too recently humiliated, to bristle his usual protest against orders. He nodded, and Wentworth dashed to the door, Ram Singh and Reardon behind him. At the curb, Wentworth signaled a cab, spun toward Ram Singh, spitting out Hindustani words. Ram Singh's eyes glittered. His hands slid beneath his coat and drew out a small kit—a duplicate of the one police had seized from Wentworth—and handed it over. He gave Wentworth a gun and a wallet of money also.

"You stay here," Wentworth snapped at Reardon, "you and Ram Singh. I know the district from which that call came. I think I can get there ahead of the police. You stay here and find out definitely where the house is. I'll get to the neighborhood, phone you—"

"I got you!" said Reardon.

Wentworth leaped to the cab. "Get going, north! Wide open," he shouted and flashed a badge from his kit. The taxi jerked into startled speed.

Wentworth, sitting tensely forward on the seat, peered ahead through the darkening streets and watched traffic lights. Rapidly he strapped the kit beneath his arm, checked it over, drew out a cigarette lighter with his *Spider* seal in its base, tested the gun. He thrust a mask into his topcoat pocket. He was going into action, and tonight he would go as the *Spider.*

He knew the Tarantula feared no one in the world as he did the *Spider*, and he was fighting against desperate odds. The second's advantage he might gain by frightening his enemy, reappearing as the *Spider* after a long absence, might mean the difference between life and death for Nita and himself, the difference between salvation of the city and its utter ruin.

THE light turned red as they reached an eastbound street. "Crash that light," Wentworth ordered. "Turn west." They raced across town, shot over Broadway, raced on across Sixth and Seventh Avenues. Wentworth was in a fever of anxiety.

"North again," he ordered as the cab struck Hudson, then: "that corner drugstore."

He slammed into it, grabbed the phone and called headquarters, got Reardon.

"West Twenty-First," said Reardon, and he barked out a number.

The phone went dead in Wentworth's hands. In the same instant lights flickered out in the store. The druggist shouted in alarm. A woman screamed. "The Tarantula!"

Wentworth darted the length of the store, crashed out the door. Traffic lights were out now, all lights were out. The mad panic the Tarantula's raids always brought reigned everywhere.

The taxi driver turned a startled face as Wentworth leaped into the cab. "Listen," he said, "the Tarantula is getting busy again. They'll shoot everything in sight!"

"Not this time," Wentworth said grimly. "They're on the run. Get me to Twenty-First Street in nothing flat."

"Cripes, boss, I—"

Wentworth jabbed a gun against the driver's neck. "Get north, damn you, or I'll blow the head off your shoulders!"

The taxi reached Twenty-First Street in a little over nothing flat, whirled west at Wentworth's command, skidded to a halt before the address Reardon had given. Wentworth leaped out while the car still moved and instantly the driver shot it forward again. Wentworth cursed, but let him go.

Slipping on his mask, he bounded across the pavement. Two more leaps, and he was up the steps. His shoulder struck the door. It splintered, crashed inward, red flame lanced from the dark hall. Wentworth's gun answered. A coughing scream tore out. A body fell.

Wentworth's eyes were gimlets behind the slits of his mask. He pounded in, his pencil light stabbing a thin ray through the hall. No one in sight, no one but the body of the man who had tried to stop him. Wentworth raced like a whirlwind through the first floor, found a phone. But it had not been wrenched from its wires, and Wentworth knew from the sound of the one Nita had talked over that it had been torn loose.

Down on his knees he went, followed the wires of the phone; they pierced the floor. Downstairs he raced, took up the wires again. They slanted across the basement, through an outer wall. There was a small window giving onto the back yard. Wentworth squirmed through. Wires ran up the side of the house. Wentworth went up them hand over hand, crawled through a window that he smashed with his elbow. The wires crossed a room, went through the baseboard. Wentworth slammed to the hall, into the next room. The wires did not exit there.

Wentworth did not hesitate an instant. That meant a secret room such as in that other hideout of the Tarantula. He whirled out into the hall again. His light found a fire axe in a glass case against the wall. He smashed the glass, whirled the axe above his head and struck it into the wall. Plaster rained to the floor. Again he struck. Wood splintered.

HE was slashing like a demon now. The axe was one continual whirl of glinting light, reflected from the flashlight he had dropped to the floor. A narrow segment of wood crashed through. Wentworth snatched up the light, shot its beam through the hole, and saw Nita, Nita hanging with a rope biting into the tender white of her throat!

"Courage, Nita!" shouted Wentworth. He saw that she was struggling on tip-toes to loosen the noose. "One minute now."

The axe whirled again. If it had been fast before, it was a blur of light now. The hole he had hacked widened with dragging slowness. Plaster and wood gripped the axe, impeded its withdrawal. Desperately Wentworth hacked on. His breath was panting, his hands numb with the furious jarring of the axe.

The street was filled now with shrieking sirens, the shouts of police. Heavy feet pounded below. Wentworth slammed the axe again and again into the wall, wrenched it free a final time and wedged himself into the narrow hole he had made.

Jagged splinters held him back. Wentworth seized the wall with his hands, forced himself through, felt clothing and flesh tear. He pitched forward into the room. He sprang up, jumped to Nita's side and lifted her free of that hideous noose. She could not stand, and he laid her on the floor, knelt over her, pillowing her curl-clustered head on his lap. The pencil light in the hall still threw in dim illumination, made grotesque shadows.

"Nita, darling," cried Wentworth, "Nita, Nita!"

The girl was breathing heavily, air rasping in her throat. She fought to speak.

"Not now," said Wentworth, "Wait."

Nita shook her head. "Bomb!" she flashed out finally. "Bomb under building, five minutes after lights out."

A bomb under the building! Set to explode five minutes after the lights went out! Wentworth had raced blocks since then, traced down a wire, hacked his way through a wall. No more than seconds could remain.

"Oh, Dick," gasped Nita. "Hurry, hurry!"

A flashlight bathed them in white glare, a flashlight like a baleful eye glaring through the hole that Wentworth had hacked.

"Dick and Nita," jeered a voice. "Dick Wentworth in person. The *Spider*!"

It was Penrose's voice, gloating. Wentworth picked up Nita, whirled toward the opening.

"That was a neat trick of yours," Penrose went on, "having somebody disguised like Wentworth come and get you out of jail, Mr. Barton—Richards—Wentworth—*Spider*."

"One side, Penrose," Wentworth bit out. "There's a bomb under this building. It's due to explode any second."

Penrose laughed, blocking that only exit with gun and light. "That trick won't work, Mr. *Spider*, you just wait there until a man that can get through this hole comes and takes you prisoner."

"But the bomb!" Wentworth cried. "Bomb?" said Penrose, grinning. "Baloney!"

CHAPTER TWENTY-TWO
Nita's Sacrifice

WENTWORTH let Nita's feet touch the floor. His hand, behind her, caught out his gun. It was his one chance. Penrose was holding the flashlight level, its three-battery base directly behind the lens. A straight shot would smash the light, but would not wound Penrose. A desperate chance, but the only way his and their lives could be saved.

Wentworth snapped up the gun and fired in the same motion. The light smashed out. Penrose's cry was half a scream, but he didn't sound hurt. Wentworth plunged to the opening. He thrust his left arm through, seized Penrose's tunic and jerked him forward. His right fist caught the deputy commissioner's chin, and the man's weight sagged. Wentworth squirmed out the opening.

"Nita," he called, "can you—"

"I'm here," she gasped by his side, and with Wentworth's help she, too, wriggled out. Wentworth caught up Penrose's bulky body, heaved it across his shoulder, caught Nita up in his other arm and, reeling beneath their double weight, raced down the stairs. His feet beat heavy time on the treads. Their sound was to him like the racing seconds of time, any one of which might explode a bomb beneath the house, blow them all to extinction.

"Clear the house!" he shouted as he ran. "Bomb! Clear the house! Bomb! Clear the house!"

Below him he heard startled shouts, then slapping feet as men raced from the building. Wentworth stumbled, reeled and almost fell. He jabbed Penrose against a wall, caught his balance, pounded on through the darkness. He was down one flight now, panting along the hall. With this heavyweight his best pace was a shuffling trot. He whirled another corner, down again. His breath rasped.

The spattered lights of auto lamps showed through the broken front door. Toward it he shuffled, gasping, cleared the final steps and reeled out into the open. He staggered, but lurched heavily forward toward the scant protection offered by a parked auto.

The sky seemed to collapse about his ears. A rush of air hurled him flat with Nita and Penrose. Then an earshattering explosion struck over them. Dazzling white and red filled the world. First a thunderous clap, then a rumbling beat, then a vast unbroken silence.

It lasted for seconds. The spattering rain of debris broke it. Fragments beat upon houses, street and cars. Men shouted, and the sound was muted by deafened eardrums.

Wentworth ripped off his mask, staggered to his feet. He left Penrose lying, caught up Nita. Staggering, stumbling like a drunken man, he weaved an uncertain way along the street. His feet seemed weighted. Not a man was in sight. The wrecks of two automobiles were tumbled on their sides. Behind them, the house of the Tarantula had disappeared. A jagged hole gaped where it had stood.

On Wentworth fought his way, muttering broken words in Nita's ear. He turned a corner. The street was thick with police cars, parked almost fender to fender. Wentworth made his way to the nearest one, placed Nita in the seat. With fumbling hands, he started the motor. He jerked the car backward, swung it in a skidding whirl and shot off into the black night.

BEHIND him now came shouts and the frantic bleating of police whistles. Cold air knifed through past temples, clearing his head, bracing him like strong liquor. Beside him on the seat Nita stirred, sat erect and looked about her. She tried to speak. But wind snatched the words from her mouth; the roar of the motor drowned them out.

Wentworth, low over the wheel, sent the car skidding and sliding around the corners, finally lost the disorganized and halfhearted pursuit that had started. He cut then the frantic speed, but still hurled swiftly through darkened streets. Finally he turned and parked in a dark alley.

Wentworth turned to Nita then, dug implements from the kit beneath his arm and went to work on the handcuffs. The padding that the Tarantula had placed there made it a simple job. He ripped that out, thrust a slender piece of steel into the opening where the ratchet was, lifting the catch that held it in place. Then he would squeeze the cuff shut another notch, hold the steel in place, and remove the manacles from Nita's wrists.

Desperately Wentworth longed to take Nita in his arms to console her for the pain and privation she had been forced to undergo. Desperately Nita longed for that consolation. But both knew there was stern danger and peril ahead. Swift work must be done if they were to snare the Tarantula and avert the fearful threat to the city and nation. As always, their personal desires and feelings must wait upon the *Spider*'s ruthless crusades.

Nita's words were not thanks to Dick, not happiness at their being together again, but rapid information. "The Tarantula," she said, "is only waiting for all the money to be centralized before he strikes again and for the last time. He says he has ways of beating even the guards of soldiers."

"I guessed that," said Wentworth, words crackling as he worked on the handcuffs. "The money must be moved now. If I were he I would strike tonight while Penrose is absorbed in chasing me. I think, Nita, the Tarantula will not be less keen than myself. So far he has proved smarter.

"This is what we must do. We will steal a plane, steal because Penrose will put a guard upon all the airports. You must cruise over the city. Do not watch where the lights go out, but when they grow dim as if the current was being drained off, fire a signal rocket toward the part of town where that is happening. That will be where the Tarantula is striking.

"The government has kept secret the exact place where the money is being accumulated. They have guards about three such places. One is in Harlem, one on the top floors of the Empire State Building, one at the lower end of the Island, the Federal Reserve Bank.

"I do not doubt that the Tarantula knows the exact spot where the money is being accumulated. With his marvelous facilities for tapping wires, there is little doubt he would learn the truth. There," he finished, removing the cuffs. "I'm going to see if there isn't a coat in this car for you."

His own topcoat had been left behind, discarded as he hacked at the wall. He clambered out, jerked open the back of the car. There were two raincoats there, and one of these with his suit coat he gave to Nita, while he donned the other raincoat. The wind was bitter cold. Crystalline snow was filtering down as they swung out of the alley, headed for a ferry and a New Jersey airport.

"Do you know who the Tarantula is or what he looks like?" Wentworth asked as they rolled on the ferry.

Nita thought a while in silence. "I only know," she said, "those hairy hands and his immense strength. He lifted me once with one arm as if I were a child." She frowned. "And yet I have an impression that when we were together in that other hideout and he carried me off that I was dragged, not carried. But I was only half conscious then, and—"

"Thanks," said Wentworth softly, "you've helped a lot."

WENTWORTH sped off the ferry, but did not go to one of the large air fields. Instead, he selected a small one farther inland, where it proved a simple matter to steal up and overcome the lone guard. That done, he located signal flares and warm clothing, buckled Nita into a parachute harness, and watched her take off into the face of the wind-driven snow.

Then he turned back to the hangar and placed money, much more than enough to pay for the plane, beside the bound caretaker. He left the police car there and took the man's own machine back to New York. He raced, bundled in a coat with high-turned collar that concealed his face, to a Ninth Avenue elevated station at Houston Street. He must get in touch with Penrose, yet he must talk over a phone from which he could watch the sky for Nita's signal. Up the stairs to the elevated station he hastened, paid his fare, and on the southbound platform found a telephone booth from which he could see a large portion of the sky over New York City.

He called police headquarters, got Penrose's snarling voice in a few seconds. Wentworth's lips lifted in a mocking grin.

"This is Richards, Penrose. I am sure the Tarantula will strike tonight."

"Will strike?" shouted Penrose's voice. "He already has struck. Every policeman in town and all the reserves of soldiers have been rushed to Harlem. The lights are out up there; the phones are dead; gunmen are shooting from windows and autos!"

"Did you say the lights were out?" Wentworth asked swiftly.

"Yes, out."

"Not just turning yellow, but actually out?" Wentworth insisted.

"Yes, damn it, out!" roared Penrose. "And you're just pulling your old trick of calling too late to do any good, to build up an alibi for yourself."

Wentworth ignored that. "For God's sake, man, call in all your forces! Have them ready to rush to another part of town at an instant's notice. That Harlem business is just a trick of the Tarantula to pull your forces away from the real object of his attack. When the Tarantula actually strikes, the lights don't go out, they only turn dim. I have a plane over the town right now which will signal when the lights go dim and where the Tarantula really strikes."

Penrose's voice was heavy with suspicion. "Do you think I'm as dumb as that?" he demanded. "Think I'd call in all my policemen at your say-so and give the Tarantula a chance to loot the city without a single cop to prevent him? You must think I'm getting crazy."

Wentworth snapped at him, "You are crazy. For God's sake, man, can't I pound any sense into your head? I tell you this is all a trick. The Tarantula has created this disturbance in Harlem, started a riot, just to pull your men away from the real object of his attack. I wouldn't call you if I could fight the whole Tarantula gang single-handed, but I can't. You must listen, and—"

Heavy feet pounding across the platform cut his words short. He slammed up the receiver. Now he knew the purpose of Penrose's slow, argumentative words. He had held him until men could trace the phone call and send the radio patrol to capture him.

Wentworth darted from the booth. Four policemen were within a few feet of him, guns leveled. But Wentworth could still escape. He could leap behind the telephone booth, over the railing, slide down a steel pillar. On the verge of leaping, his eyes caught a red flare in the skies, saw a signal rocket spurt toward the southern tip of the island.

Nita's signal! The Federal Reserve Bank was there! The Tarantula had struck!

Wentworth jabbed his hand upward, pointing at the signal. Police closed in, ignoring that. "Watch him, men! He's tricky," growled the leader.

Even then, Wentworth might have escaped. The men were too close to him, walking too closely together. A leap at the leader, a quick thrust, and they would all tangle in a heap on the floor, leaving a way to escape down the elevated pillars still open.

But as he was in the act of leaping, new light from the sky caught his eye and struck him motionless, his face distorted with horror. The light was the lurid, angry blaze of a plane in flames!

It was plunging swiftly down, whirling, long red tongues of fire licking back behind it, a flaming comet diving out of control toward the Earth. And Wentworth, hands clenched at his sides, staring up into the heavens, stood rigidly, while the police clamped hands upon his shoulders; stood without protest while they searched him roughly and took his gun—clamped handcuffs upon his wrists.

Nita, brave darling Nita, had plunged to her death in a flame-wrapped plane!

CHAPTER TWENTY-THREE

Spider vs. Tarantula

WENTWORTH was insensible to the hostile hands that roughed him down the elevated stairs. He moved mechanically, without feeling. His heart was a vast, dull ache. In his brain was a thought that he refused to visualize. Nita dead! Nita killed in a fury of flames, shot down probably by the ripping, tearing slugs of machine guns.

Slowly a white rage replaced that numbness in his breast. A cold tide of anger flooded over him. In his brain was only one cry, that if Nita had died, she should not have died in vain. The Tarantula and all his murderous crew should die also—or the *Spider* himself would perish.

As his anger mounted, Wentworth took himself in rigid control. He continued to move like an automaton, feet shambling, shoulders slouched, chin upon his breast. He was thrust into a two-seater radio patrol car, one man beside him, another hanging on the runningboard with a leveled gun. Wentworth went docilely enough, but his mind was working now.

When he had unlocked Nita's handcuffs he had dropped into his trouser pocket the slim piece of steel with which he had worked. Police, taking his gun, had missed that, and Wentworth moved his manacled hands until he felt it through the cloth of his trousers. Its corners were sharp. Wentworth pressed the cloth against one until the point came through the pocket and cloth of his trousers—and he had in his hand the key to the handcuffs.

His shoulders slumped forward to conceal what he was doing, as he slid the tiny piece of steel into the opening where the adjustable ratchet held the cuffs together. Manipulating it as he had when he freed Nita, he worked the cuff off one wrist. He did not wait to release his other hand, but clenched the bracelet in his free fist. With one movement he smashed the cuff against the jaw of the patrolman to his left, and with the other hand seized the gun that was leveled at him by the man on the runningboard.

The car ran wild. Wentworth kicked the gear shift into neutral and its speed dwindled. He thrust the man on the runningboard, striking again with the cuff and the cop sprawled to the street, shouting.

The auto was barely crawling now. Wentworth tumbled the unconscious driver to the street, then flung behind the wheel, jerked the car into gear, and stamped the accelerator to the floor.

The machine lunged forward like a wild thing, took a corner on two squealing tires and Wentworth was away, racing south like a madman.

He did not bother to shake off the police who, in a second car, whined a siren at his heels. He only jerked the throttle wider, depended on his superior mastery of the car, his greater courage, to escape. And, slowly at first, then more rapidly, he drew away from the pursuing car. Slamming through half-deserted streets, he raced to fight the Tarantula.

Long before he reached the battle scene, the heavy coughing of machine guns dominated even the roar of his motor. He cut across town, skidded swaying into Broadway and raced south again. The Federal Reserve Bank, focal point of the Tarantula's attack, was not more than a half mile away.

All about him was darkness except at a point far ahead, where three sets of headlights sent their blinding glare up Broadway. The headlights did not advance and, racing nearer, Wentworth made out above them the pale flickering tongues of flame that marked the muzzles of death-spitting machine guns.

BULLETS began to plunk into his car, to smash holes in the windshield. Wentworth pivoted left into the shelter of buildings. The bodies of soldiers littered Broadway, headlights streaming fantastic shadows about their death-distorted forms. Here and there lay a stiff, blue-coated policeman. Wentworth slammed on brakes, climbed out and from the shadows a half dozen men came slowly forward, the remnants of those who had guarded the wealth of the city.

Wentworth circled his car, jerked open the back, and fished out a half dozen hand grenades, standard equipment for all radio cars since the Tarantula had come to harry New York. He dropped two into his pockets, held one and gave two to the nearest soldier.

He glanced over the men. They were stalwart, but lacked leadership. A leader had come now.

"No use trying to go through the streets," Wentworth said. "Those are heavy machine guns from the sound of them. Even armored cars wouldn't be proof against them. The city's entire reserve force is in Harlem. It will take them twenty minutes at top speed to get here, even after they learn that attack uptown is a sham."

One of the policemen stepped forward and saluted. "Where to, sir?" he asked.

Wentworth's grim eyes swung to the man. "Donohue?" he exclaimed. "Good lad. O'Flaherty's here, and Schwartz?"

O'Flaherty's long-nosed face showed behind Donohue. "Schwartz is dead," he said quietly.

"It's through the sewers again," Wentworth told them.

Donohue shook his head. "We remember what you did, sir, and have already tried to open a manhole. We couldn't get it open."

"No?" Wentworth grinned. "Show me the manhole."

They pointed.

"Stand clear," Wentworth ordered. He jerked the pin from a grenade, tossed it with a practiced overhead swing. There was a tearing concussion, and where the manhole had been was a gaping hole.

Wentworth looked at the man. "This probably means death," he said. "But at least we'll get a few of them." He stooped and picked up a pistol and ammunition from a fallen policeman, straightened with the gun in his hand.

"Follow me," he rasped, and raced to the manhole.

WITH a borrowed flashlight he led the way south through wirelined tunnels, crawling, crouching, wriggling on his belly, walking half erect again. A gun blazed ahead in the black darkness, and behind Wentworth a man gasped, "God!"

Wentworth's pistol roared, deafening in the narrow tunnel. The gun ahead did not fire again. Wentworth pounded on in a crouch. He halted sharply, gun flying up again. He checked it, went forward with a grim face. Two men lay prone on the floor. One was dead. The other had wide shoulders, an intelligent head which Wentworth thought he recognized. He turned the man over.

"Kirkpatrick!" he gasped. "In God's name, man!" He dropped beside him, tore loose a gag and ripped off the ropes that bound him.

"Thank the Lord you've come," Kirkpatrick said hoarsely. He reeled to his feet, massaging rope-chafed wrists. "I've been wondering when you'd manage to rescue me."

"Rescue!" Wentworth's voice was a sharp bark of laughter. "It's a massacre. Every cop and soldier on guard at the Federal Reserve have been killed except these six—five now. That one shot killed a man."

"Not killed, sir," came Donohue's sharp voice. "Just caught me in the shoulder."

"Good," said Wentworth. He turned back to Kirkpatrick and explained the Tarantula's feint in Harlem. "That dumb deputy of yours, Penrose, has sent every man in the city up there after I warned him it was all a trick."

"Then it's we eight," said Kirkpatrick slowly, "against the entire Tarantula gang?"

"Yes," said Wentworth.

Kirkpatrick stooped and caught up the gun of the man Wentworth had killed. "Lead on, Dick," he said. "They planted me here during the raid. I was supposed to be taken to the bank and killed there, to take the rap for all these robberies."

Wentworth nodded. "The Tarantula picked me first for that honor. You're the substitute." He pushed on, and the seven trailed, walking almost erect now in a larger tunnel.

The sound of firing became louder, and presently fresh air fanned into the dark tunnel through which they walked. Wentworth led the way more slowly, spotted an open manhole overhead—a round gray spot amid blackness. He crept up an iron ladder.

"Let me go first, sir," pleaded Donohue's low voice. "I'm wounded anyway. If they get me, it won't matter so much."

Wentworth laughed shortly. "If they get me, it doesn't matter at all!"

He peered out of the hole. No guards about. Only the backs of three trucks that carried heavy shields of armor. Two had machine guns that blasted up Broadway. They had penetrated the Tarantula's lines!

"Stay here," Wentworth ordered. He crawled out, gun in one hand, bomb in the other, moved on his belly to the curb and snaked on.

Wentworth's eyes were fixed on the nearest trucks. Heavy firing came from beyond them now. Apparently the troops had been recalled from their mad dash to Harlem. But Wentworth doubted if they would avail against those heavy, chattering guns.

A man on one of the trucks turned, saw Wentworth's creeping figure throw up a gun. Wentworth's pistol spat, and the man plunged headlong to the street.

But the alarm had been given. Others whirled now. Wentworth raised one arm. His other hand flew back and a grenade arched through the air. The men shouted and ran, leaping from the trucks. Too late! The grenade let go with a tearing blast, hurling bodies in a bloody welter to the street, wrecking one gun truck, jamming the other.

From beyond the trucks came a cheer, a shrill whistle.

Wentworth sprang up and raced back to the manhole. Kirkpatrick already was climbing out, the others behind.

"The troops are here," Wentworth reported. "Let's get on with our work."

AROUND the corner at a dead run he led his small band. But the streets were deserted before them. Not a man of all the Tarantula's crew showed a head. They found a police motorcycle, its two occupants dead. Wentworth pulled the bodies out, forked the saddle. Kirkpatrick piled into the sidecar.

"Get to cover," Wentworth ordered to the men. "Soldiers and police will be here in a moment. They might shoot you by mistake."

He kicked the engine to life, roared full speed down Broadway.

At the side street where the Federal Reserve Bank stood, Wentworth paused a moment, turned the spotlight. The doors of the bank gaped, its steps studded with dead. A yawning pit marked where a bomb had been thrown. Near at hand, a dozen of the Tarantula's gang sprawled dead about a manhole as if they had been slain racing toward its safety. No use going down that street. The Tarantula had looted and fled. Fled? Yes, but where?

On down Broadway Wentworth raced the motorcycle. Kirkpatrick shouted above the stutter of the motor. "I've got this machine gun working."

Wentworth nodded, sped on.

Ahead he saw dim figures on the sea wall at Battery Park, which covered the southernmost tip of Manhattan. As he watched, they clambered over the edge, out of sight.

Wentworth bounded the motorcycle over the curbing, raced along the walkways of the Park, slammed up to the stringpiece along the sea wall.

Out there in the darkness, a seaplane's motor roared into life. Kirkpatrick opened fire with the machine gun. Wentworth leaped clear and snatched out one of the two grenades that remained, balanced it on his palm and let go. The seaplane vanished in a burst of red and white fire.

Wentworth whirled back to the motorcycle. Kirkpatrick was slumped over the machine gun. As Wentworth turned, he raised his hand weakly. "I'll be okay," he said. "Get the Tarantula. Couldn't all—get away—in planes."

"Right," jerked out Wentworth. He whirled and sprinted along the Battery wall, rounded the circular building which housed the aquarium. Help would come soon for Kirkpatrick, and seconds were precious if he were to catch the Tarantula and recover the city's stolen wealth.

No question now of saving Nita. She was dead. But the Tarantula had got away with all the city's gold and cash. The news of that loss would rock the nation, increase the rioting that already threatened revolution. And only the *Spider*, working alone, could prevent final, grim calamity. He alone had any grasp of the situation; he alone knew the Tarantula. He threw back his head and sprinted on.

The city's prize fire boat, the John Purroy Mitchel, should be docked just beyond the aquarium. It was fast, and steam was always up. He whirled around the building to the city dock. The fire boat was gone!

Wentworth stood motionless on the wharf, looking out over black waters. Somewhere out there the Tarantula must have fled, in the city's most powerful fire boat—leaving scores of dead and taking with him a fifth of the nation's wealth. And Wentworth had no better than a rowboat for pursuit!

CHAPTER TWENTY-FOUR
The Tarantula's Yacht

WENTWORTH'S eyes scanned the dark river. He was desperate. Somehow, single-handed, he must find and catch the Tarantula.

If the Tarantula got away with the gold, revolution would raise its bloody venomous head on the morrow. The nation would rock on its foundations.

Once more, Wentworth's keen eyes swept the river. No sign of any fast boat, no sign of another plane. Yet those machine gunners he had killed on the trucks must have had some method for escape, some such swift craft as that seaplane which he and Kirkpatrick had blown to pieces. Naturally it would be further north than the Battery, more convenient for their escape.

Wentworth ran northward along the docks, peering into the dark strips of water visible now and then between the high warehouses that covered almost the entire waterfront. He was using a steady, jogging run that carried him swiftly, but which he could keep up for miles.

Where Liberty Street ran down to the water, he found what he sought behind a broken fence heading a slimed moored seaplane. Wentworth clambered through the break in the fence. A gun spat from the plane. The bullet plumped into wood beside his head, and Wentworth's gun snaked out and spat. A dark figure reared from the cockpit of the plane, plunged into the black water.

Wentworth climbed swiftly around the edges of the pier, hauled in the plane by the rope which secured it. He clambered to a wing, untied the rope and let it fall into the water, swarmed over that into the cockpit, touched the familiar levers and jabbed the compression starter.

A whistling whine, a jerking start of the propeller, and the motor roared. Seconds later, Wentworth was streaking down the slip. He burst out onto the bosom of the river and jerked the ship free of the water, circled in a slow climb. The seaplane sped him back over Manhattan Island. His teeth were chattering with cold, his body trembling, but he was scarcely conscious of it. He peered downward, scanning the gleaming waters that girded Manhattan. Down the East River a speedboat raced. Behind it he made out the rippling white wake.

The boat had swung off from the shoreline of Manhattan, two others behind it, and was steering a course for the open sea. He spotted the fire boat also, drifting aimlessly, apparently loosed only to prevent pursuit. In those three motorboats would be the raiders who had left first. The planes were for the last guard, those left behind to delay the troops and make sure the Tarantula and his gang escaped.

Wentworth swung the plane and trailed. The boats were making forty knots or better. They rounded Governor's Island and, with Wentworth swinging in wide circles as he watched, they spurted up to a rakish yacht, long and black on the water, that was steaming slowly through the channel. One by one the boats ran alongside. Men scrambled up the sides of the yacht. A derrick boom swung over the side, hauled up many heavy bags in a net.

Wentworth nosed down as the yacht picked up speed, leaving the fast motorboats adrift. He knew he would have no trouble in landing beside the boat and getting aboard. They would take him for a gangster. But what could he, single-handed, do against the Tarantula's many?

Abruptly he made up his mind, slanted the plane in a long smooth dive for Governor's Island, took the water and taxied to the ferry slip. He pulled out his gun and fired three shots into the air. Soldiers came running.

Wentworth megaphoned his hands. "A yacht!" he shouted. "Steaming out into the channel now. Tarantula and all gang aboard."

The soldiers shouted back. "We'll blow her out of the water."

"No!" Wentworth shouted back. "All the gold is aboard. All the money in the city. Phone Mitchell Field and the Coast Guard."

He whirled the plane, sent it skittering out over the water and up again in lone pursuit of the yacht.

THE cold was bitter now. It numbed Wentworth's face and hands. He pushed on. The yacht was making amazing time, cutting the water at better than thirty knots, black smoke pouring from her rakish stack.

Help was on the way, but Wentworth knew the yacht would be too fast for Coast Guard boats. Only planes could overtake her, and planes would hesitate to use bombs, lest they destroy the wealth which somehow must be recovered. Paper money could be reprinted, but the gold would be scattered throughout the harbor. No replacing that—and most of the city's wealth had been transferred into gold by the government to restore the confidence of the people and avert the vast catastrophe that threatened. No it was still up to the *Spider*, single-handed.

Impossible? Wentworth did not know or care. Nita must be avenged, the gold recovered. If the *Spider* died in doing that, it did not matter. Lips smiling grimly, Wentworth reloaded his pistol, put his plane again into a long dive and took the water ahead of the yacht. While it sped toward him he taxied swiftly to keep pace, veering closer and closer. The yacht checked speed; the water that curled from its prow made a smaller wave; and finally Wentworth, clambering down from the cockpit, grasped a rope and was hauled aboard.

He caught the railing, sprang aboard and snatched out the one remaining hand grenade, brandishing the pistol in his free hand.

"I am the *Spider*!" he shouted. "I have pulled the pin from this hand grenade. If you shoot me, it means death for us all."

White-faced men retreated before him.

"Not too far," said Wentworth. "Stay there. Now, where is the Tarantula?"

A soft voice chuckled into the silence that fell then upon the yacht. "Welcome aboard, *Spider*. Now the family party is complete. Nita is here, too."

Nita here, too! The words half stunned Wentworth, for he had seen Nita plunge to her death in the flaming plane. True, she had had a parachute.

"No, she is not dead," the Tarantula spoke again. "It is true we shot down her plane, but you thoughtfully had prepared her with a parachute. She fell so near the yacht it seemed a shame to let her drown when I could dispose of her so much more pleasantly. You've interrupted that as usual. Also Nita once more gives me an ace in the hole, a check on you. And our friends the Coast Guard and the Aviation Corps will be too gallant to bomb into oblivion a yacht that carries Nita van Sloan... not to mention a good portion of the nation's gold.

"The army base has already radioed us to surrender under pain of turning loose the big guns of Governor's Island. I told them of the gold—and your Nita. I also told them there was enough explosive aboard to scatter the ship—and the gold—over the whole harbor. That is why the guns have not spoken. That is why your little hand grenade caused more alarm than it should have among my stalwart men."

Wentworth's gun spoke sharply and a man who had crept too near died. His eyes probed the darkness about him, searched the cabins that lined the deck.

"COME, *Spider*," the Tarantula said, "Toss your bomb overboard. It's true I cannot shoot you lest you blow us up with you. But you can't remain forever alert, and the moment you relax for an instant we'll get you."

Wentworth threw back his head and laughed.

"Fine words, Tarantula, but I do not think you, or any of these gentlemen, care to die as you would if I let this grenade go." He laughed again, and the sound was not pleasant.

"I'll trouble you, Tarantula, to turn the yacht back to Governor's Island and surrender. Otherwise—" and he walked slowly forward, the circle of men widening before him. He stepped inside the cabin, and the Tarantula, black robed and hooded as always stood before him in the white circle of an overhead light. "Otherwise," Wentworth repeated, "I'll be forced to lift my fingers from this little lever on the bomb." And he held the grenade up before him, held it between the thumb and fingers of his left hand—released his fingers the fraction of an inch so that the lever rose with them.

"Ah, but then," the Tarantula gestured with a hairy hand, and Wentworth saw that it lacked a thumb, "—then you would die, too. And I do not think you want to die, now."

A sharp order, and Nita was thrust into the room. "I do not think that you want Nita to die—that way."

Wentworth's eyes glittered. He was watching the Tarantula closely, and that masked gaze was fixed above the *Spider*'s shoulder on a spot high up on the wall.

"Nita," said Wentworth softly, "come here, dear."

Nita crossed to him swiftly, and Wentworth's voice dropped to a whisper that only she could hear. "What is the Tarantula looking at over my shoulder?"

Nita looked at the hooded face, looked at the wall.

"A clock," she said quietly.

The Tarantula caught the significance of the whispers and Nita's movements, turned eyes away. "I'll give you until I count ten to surrender," the mocking voice said.

"*One...*" The Tarantula began. Wentworth said grimly, "And what are you going to do when you have counted ten?"

"*Two...*" The Tarantula's eyes strayed again to the clock.

Wentworth was thinking furiously. Some trickery was underway here. The *Spider*'s mind flashed back to the scene of the yacht from the air. There had been no boats anywhere near. He thought backfurther.

"*Three...*"

The dead littering the street, the dozen men of the Tarantula sprawled about a closed manhole. He shook his head sharply. No, the answer was not on shore, but here.

"*Four...*"

Wentworth's eyes were sharp on the robed figure before him. Tension was apparent in the body, and there was a shrill strain in the voice. The counting was more rapid.

"*Five...*"

The Tarantula was getting ready to spring! Wentworth saw it in the slight crouching of the legs, in the stooping shoulders. But somehow, there was no threat of attack in the eyes behind that hood. They were fixed on the clock.

"*Six!*"

The Tarantula sprang, but not toward Wentworth. The robed figure went through the door like a flash, poised an instant on the rail, the robe fluttering in the biting night wind.

Wentworth's pistol swung upward, spat flame. But even as it discharged, the Tarantula had disappeared, arching out in a perfect dive toward the icy waters!

CHAPTER TWENTY-FIVE
Pandemonium!

FOR an instant, Wentworth stood transfixed, staring. Then the blood drained from his face. He caught Nita about the waist and, dropping his gun, plunged toward the door.

"Abandon ship!" he shouted. "She's doomed!"

He swung Nita to the rail. "Dive!" he told her. "Dive deep, and swim fast!"

Nita cleaved the air in a swift, straight dive, and Wentworth plunged behind her, still clinging to the grenade. The frigid water cut like razors of ice, sent instantaneous stabs of pain through Wentworth's body. He checked his dive, spurted to the surface. He thrust high from the water, keen eyes searching for the Tarantula.

He caught sight of a white froth of water ahead, a head and shoulders ripping the sea in a powerful crawl. Wentworth thrust the grenade into his trouser pocket where the tight cloth held the lever down, skinned out of his coat and shoes.

Nita's head broke through the water a short distance away.

"All right?" Wentworth called.

"Y-y-yes," chattered Nita.

"Then dive again, and swim on." Wentworth was free of clinging garments now. He flung himself forward in a crawl as strong and swift as that of the Tarantula's. Swinging his head about to catch breath, he glimpsed the ship. Men were running about like lunatics, trying to lower boats.

Wentworth sprinted on. The furious action chased some of the numbness from his limbs. He tossed up his head, searched for the Tarantula. Then he spotted something he had not detected before, a small, low boat in which a single man stood erect. Wentworth made out his bulk against the brightening sky—the bushy head and wide, heavy shoulders of Wiggard!

As Wentworth stared, still swimming on, he saw Wiggard stoop and haul the Tarantula from the water. The Tarantula spun about, a gun glinting. Fire spat from it, and lead gouged the water beside Wentworth. The *Spider* dived and swam frantically forward. He heard the beating vibration of the motor nearing, turned sharply upward.

As he rose, he dug into his trouser pocket, fished out the grenade. It was watertight, made to withstand long soaking in the rain. He burst the surface, spotted the boat not thirty feet away, wrenched back his arm and heaved. He dived again instantly.

The concussion of the blast shook him even below the surface. Then, like an echo of the first explosion, an overwhelming convulsion shuddered through the water. Wentworth felt that two huge hammers had struck simultaneously on each side of his head. Feebly he fought his way to the surface of the freezing water, stared about. The launch had disappeared, and with it had died the Tarantula and Wiggard.

Wreckage rained upon the water. The surface churned and swirled about him. He peered back. The yacht also had vanished, blown to bits by the huge mine the Tarantula had planted in her.

"Nita!" Wentworth shouted. "Nita!"

If there had been gold aboard, it was scattered over the entire harbor. But where was Nita?

A weak hail answered him from his left. Throwing himself forward, Wentworth swam frantically toward the sound, found Nita clinging, almost exhausted, to a heavy spar. Her teeth chattered, and she was half-dazed from the concussion of the explosion aboard the yacht.

WENTWORTH looked about. From all directions, red and green lights showed boats racing head-on for the scene of the wreck. In fifteen minutes Wentworth and Nita had been fished out by a Coast Guard patrol boat.

Nita was rushed into the cabin, fed hot liquor and wrapped in warm blankets. Wentworth, shaking with cold, his lips and hands blue, resisted efforts to doctor him.

"Where's the skipper?" he demanded.

"You'll die of pneumonia," a sailor urged. "Get inside, I'll call him."

Wentworth shook his head stubbornly, insisted. The sailor shrugged, escorted him to the bridge. The *Spider*'s teeth were chattering so that he could not speak intelligibly; with an effort, he checked the trembling.

"It's imperative we get back to land at once," he said.

"I'm searching for survivors," the skipper told him, his weathered face frowning.

"There are other boats," Wentworth insisted. "I must get to shore at once." He fixed the officer's dark eyes unwaveringly. "I am Richard Wentworth," he said. "I have police powers. I know they aren't in force here. But I assure you it is absolutely necessary to get ashore."

The skipper eyed him, started to shake his head. Wentworth's eyes flamed, but he spoke quietly. "It's not often I say or do a thing like this," he said. "But I'm telling you that if you don't get back to shore and get there as fast as this boat can move, you're through with the service."

Anger flared in the man's face. "I'll see you in hell!"

"Or yourself," Wentworth flashed. He snatched the pistol from the man's belt. "Order this boat to shore, or—"

The captain's face was twisted with anger, his eyes as cold and furious as Wentworth's. But he bowed before the muzzle of death. He changed the course to shore.

"The instant we land," he said, "I'll see to it that you're put in irons, and—"

"To do that," said Wentworth, "you'll have to communicate with superiors and that's what I want. When you get them, tell them to send the arresting squad to the corner of Broadway and Pine Street. And tell them to send an entire company of men to do it."

Still trembling with cold, pain stabbing his muscles and chest, Wentworth stayed beside the skipper, held a gun on him until the boat docked at the Battery. There he exacted a reluctant promise that the captain would have a company of soldiers rushed to Broadway and Pine, but meantime would not interfere. Then Wentworth sprang ashore, ran up the seawall.

The motorcycle he had used before was still there, but Kirkpatrick was gone. Wentworth leaped into the machine, sent it sputtering up Broadway to the corner he had designated. He slowed it to a halt. The dead of the Tarantula's gang still lay sprawled about the manhole. Wentworth sat upon the cover until soldiers came. The Coast Guard officer was with them.

"Now what the hell is this all about?" he demanded.

Wentworth got up slowly. "Open this manhole," he said, "and I'll show you."

The skipper stared at him, then with a grim smile ordered the cover removed. "I'm curious enough to go through with this thing, just to please you," he said.

WENTWORTH smiled despite the chattering cold. He watched while the manhole cover was lifted, borrowed a hand torch then and focused its beam downward. The Coast Guard officer peered down, too.

The tunnel beneath was filed with canvas bags, heaped and sprawled one upon another. One had torn open, and from its ripped side spilled gold coins. The officer stared wide-eyed into Wentworth's smiling face.

"It's gold!" he stammered.

Wentworth nodded. "This is the gold—all of it—that the Tarantula stole from the Federal Reserve Bank tonight," he said.

IT was two days later that Wentworth and Nita, leaving the hospital where Kirkpatrick was recuperating from a chest wound, rode uptown in the Lancia with Jackson at the wheel and Ram Singh, his dark face inscrutable as always, beside him.

"But where are we going?" Nita demanded.

"First we are going to call on the widow Penrose," said Wentworth. "I want to do something for her. In the end her husband died a hero in the battle downtown, trying to wipe out his mistakes. I want to set at rest the rumors that he was the Tarantula."

"Penrose the Tarantula!" Nita gasped.

"Just a rumor," Wentworth smiled. "The Tarantula who died on the yacht—only a part-time Tarantula, it's true—was one Russell Daliot, a thumbless lad with a predilection for a guitar and foolish songs. You remember we met him at the theatre the night of the first raid. He was the Tarantula who lifted you so easily, as you told me. He had very muscular arms."

He dived head-first into the icy waters.

Nita's blue eyes were cold. "He got what he deserved. But, Dick, you've been putting off telling me how you guessed where the gold was. I thought it had been blown up, thought your grenade had jarred the explosives aboard the ship or something."

Wentworth smiled, patted her hand, raised it to his lips. "It was really simple enough, Nita. Daliot kept looking at the clock. There were no boats near. I had seen that from the plane. Yet he expected something. When he jumped overboard, I knew what it was. The explosives he had mentioned were a bomb to blow up the yacht!

"Now I knew the Tarantula wasn't going to blow up all that gold after working so hard to get it, and I had been suspicious of this escape in a yacht all along. A yacht is a slow thing at best, and easily overtaken. Why, then, would the Tarantula, surely a super-intelligent crook, choose that way to escape?

"The answer was that the Tarantula hadn't. When I knew that, I knew the gold was still ashore, hidden somewhere, and the first thing that I thought of was the tunnels the Tarantula knew so well. It would be a simple matter to cache the gold there, and remove it through the tunnels without ever having to show himself on the surface."

Nita was still frowning. "But I don't see how you found the exact spot so easily."

Wentworth took out cigarettes, lit one for Nita and himself. His eyebrows were quizzical. "The Tarantula did that for me," he explained. "Apparently the gold was loaded into a coal truck the police found later for transportation to the dock. When it was all loaded, the Tarantula simply machine gunned all the men who had helped him, then slid the gold down a coal slide into the manhole.

"It was easy enough for him to get away with that. You know that each crew of the Tarantula's men had a specific job. When they finished that, they left for the yacht. The gold carriers were the last to leave, except for the rear guard of machine gunners, and they were too far away to see what was happening.

"The Tarantula then took a boat, already loaded with fake gold in bags, I imagine, and raced that to the yacht. He loaded the fake gold aboard, planning to slip overboard to the boat Wiggard had waiting, and to blow up the yacht and every last member of his gang. He wouldn't have to split the gold then, and there would be no one left to accuse him."

The Lancia swung out of the line of traffic, drew up in front of an apartment house. "Here's where you get out, Nita," Wentworth said. "I want you to see Mrs. Penrose and tell her of the trust fund I'm setting up for her."

"But you?"

"I'll see you later. Jenkyns is fixing us one of those inimitable midnight lunches, and meantime—" he grinned but there was little humor in his eyes—"meantime I'm going to call on the real brains of the gang—the other Tarantula!"

WENTWORTH tipped his hat, reentered the Lancia and left Nita staring after him. He ordered Jackson to take him to a Park Avenue address, where he alighted and, smiling at Ram Singh, said, "I'll leave the door unlocked."

Then he went alone into the luxurious building.

When the elevator had left him, Wentworth did not ring a bell. He took out a lock pick and unfastened a door, slipped inside. He removed coat and hat, and his hair was blond. Two touches for cheek plumpers, wax to his nostrils, and he was Inspector Barton.

He strolled casually down a hall.

"What are you doing here?" a voice demanded, a woman's voice.

Wentworth turned slowly, raised his eyebrows. A blonde young woman stood there with a leveled gun.

"Sorry," said Wentworth, "I don't believe I know you."

But he did know her. It was the girl he had burst in on when he was first bearding Reardon, the girl who had pointed a gun at him in the theatre, who had led Kirkpatrick into a trap.

"What are you doing here?" the girl demanded again.

"I just dropped in to see an old friend of mine," said Wentworth slowly. Then the drapes behind the girl parted and another woman strolled in, a woman in shimmering green with bare, splendid arms, with hair of flame, with long green eyes that saluted his—Tamara Lamaris.

"Ah, Inspector Barton," she said.

Wentworth bowed. "Ah, Madame Tarantula."

The green eyes widened, then narrowed, glinting. "The Tarantula died on the yacht."

Wentworth nodded. "One Tarantula died on the yacht. The one with no thumb on one hand, the one who lifted Nita easily with one arm—Russell Daliot, in fact—but not the Tarantula who tried to hang Nita while I was bound to a chair."

Tamara stared at him fixedly. "I see. It was your punch, your punch that struck me in the chest, that betrayed me."

"Perfect, Tamara," Wentworth murmured, bowing, "that punch in the... er... ah, chest revealed you as a woman. There could be no woman except yourself with the brain and knowledge to do the job. Then, too, the Tarantula's occasional lack of strength—and your mapwork. They talked, too."

"I see," said Tamara. Her voice was the calm, chuckling voice of the Tarantula. "And my hands?"

"A simple trick," said Wentworth, "though

rarely used. The skin from a corpse's hands, tanned like glove leather. The hair could be either natural or fastened on. After one glance, I knew that skin was not natural. It had the peculiar whiteness that only tanned human skin acquires. So, my dear, I looked for someone who did not have hairy hands. And I could only think of yours. They are beautiful."

Tamara Lamaris for once did not acknowledge a compliment. She was pale, but composed. "Elsie," she said. "This man is the *Spider*, the man who killed your lover. You have been longing to shoot him—"

ELSIE THOMPSON'S blue eyes became like twin flames. Her lovely mouth thinned. She pointed the gun.

"Reardon is not dead," said Wentworth quietly. "I will give him to you presently, but first we must settle with this woman. She hanged Jack's father. She is a murderess a hundred times over. She tortured the woman I love. She sent to their death on a mined yacht the men who had worked to give her millions. And Elsie, you have a score to settle. You nearly lured Kirkpatrick to his death. You assisted, by removing him from the head of the police, in the murder of men.

"I think, Elsie, that you could wipe out most of that score, by—"

Elsie stood with the gun wavering from Wentworth to her.

"But how," she gasped, "how can I know that you tell the truth? One of you is lying."

"He lies!" said Tamara, stabbing one of her white hands at Wentworth. The girl still stared at her. "Many funny things have happened," she said, "lots of things I haven't been able to understand. I didn't know that this was a trap for Kirkpatrick. I really wanted to tell him about the *Spider*... but Kirkpatrick never came—

"Yes!" Elsie pointed at Wentworth. "He must be telling the truth!"

Tamara's voice was soft. "My dear," she said, "you are distraught and nervous. You are grieved by the death of Jack, your sweetheart." As she spoke, she moved slowly toward the girl. There was a vast calm in her voice. Her green eyes were deep and sympathetic. Elsie seemed lulled.

Then Tamara moved sharply. She seized Elsie's gun wrist. There was a moment of tense struggle, as feminine bodies strained in distorted postures, a head of flame against a head of gold. For a moment only it continued. Then Elsie broke free. She was a farm-reared girl, and strong. She leaped clear, thrust out the gun—and fired!

Tamara took a small step backward. She looked down at her figure, gorgeous in the shimmering green she had worn so long ago. There was a spot of blood upon its breast, blood that spread as she looked, her flame head bowed. She smiled.

"It... is... just," she said, and wilted to the floor. "*Spider...*" Her green eyes turned up, seemed not to see Wentworth and the girl. Her voice rose suddenly to a shriek. *"Spider, you win!"*

Wentworth looked down at her, and in his eyes there was no pity.

"Jack," he called, "you may come out now. Your gun won't be needed."

And Jack Reardon came out from behind a curtain back of Wentworth, a gun in his hand.

"But Elsie, Elsie killed her!" he cried.

The girl sobbed, her head on Reardon's chest. Wentworth took her gun, wiped it clean of fingerprints, and placed it beside Tamara. He put his hand to his vest pocket, took from it a cigarette lighter and, walking across, stopped over the body of resplendent Tamara Lamaris. When he straightened, the vermilion seal of the *Spider* glowed on her pale, white forehead, dimming even the glory of her head of flame.

"The *Spider* killed her," he said softly. His mouth twisted into a wry smile. "Your crimes are expatiated. Go and sin no more."

THE END

THE WEB by Will Murray

Supervillains are the theme of this suspenseful *Spider* volume.

Pulp mystery men such as the *Spider* were without question the forerunners of the comic book superheroes now dominating the global popular culture. The themes and tropes are virtually identical: heroic, self-sacrificing protagonist who fights for the greater good and not because he is paid to do so, versus arch-criminal who operates on a level of ferocious evil of such magnitude that ordinary law enforcement professionals are baffled and helpless.

Sometimes, the hero is sanctioned by officialdom. In *Batman*, for example, the Dark Knight works in close cooperation with Police Commissioner James Gordon. In the *Spider* series, hero Richard Wentworth is close friends with New York's police commissioner by day. Stanley Kirkpatrick is a bitter enemy to the *Spider*, beliving him to be a murdering outlaw, but also recognizes that the Master of Men preys on criminals that the police are often unable to defeat. The tension of their association hinges on the bitter conflict between Kirkpatrick's sworn duty to uphold the law against Wentworth's personal pledge to champion a higher calling.

In comic books, which tell briefer and simpler stories, Gordon's alliance with Batman works perfectly, despite the undeniable fact that the premise is preposterous on the face of it. For a novel—even if it is pulp fiction—the more realistic Grant Stockbridge approach is mandatory. Even in The Shadow series, Commissioner Weston and The Shadow are often at odds, although Weston is on social terms with The Shadow's daylight identities, Lamont Cranston and Kent Allard.

City of Flaming Shadows was the fourth *Spider* novel, and only the second penned by Norvell W. Page, who in 1933 was still holding down his day job as a newspaperman at the New York *Herald-Tribune*, while pounding out pulp fiction for Popular Publications. Page had been associated with *The Spider* since the first issue, having had a short story in the back of that inaugural issue. Very soon after he began writing as "Grant Stockbridge," Page abandoned his newspaper career to write the *Spider* full time. He never went back to journalism.

After a stunning debut with *Wings of the Black Death*, Page hit another home run with *City of Flaming Shadows*, which Page submitted under the working title of "Flaming Loot," and which ran in the January 1934 issue of *The Spider* magazine.

Here, Richard Wentworth takes on the threat of an evil arachnid, the Tarantula, as Norvell Page revisits his grand theme of threatening the entire metropolis of Manhattan with an existential menace. His great writing strength—blistering white-heat drama—is present from the exciting first chapter to the memorable dying line uttered by the defeated Tarantula.

Here, also, Wentworth first dons the guise of an alternate identity as Inspector Rupert Barton of Scotland Yard. This persona will crop up again in the next *Spider* tale, *Empire of Doom*, but afterword vanishes forever into the limbo of secret identities that have outlived their usefulness. Page is quickly leaving behind the old 1920s-style thriller novel tone established by R.T.M. Scott.

Spider sales must have skyrocketed, for all through 1934, Norvell Page received regular raises. Starting at $500 per manuscript, he jumped to $550, then $600, closing out the year at $625 a novel. That was a lot of quick raises for the Great Depression.

In the following years, the *Spider* went on to tackle recurring foes like the Fly, the Living Pharaoh, the Faceless One and other colorful

Norvell W. Page

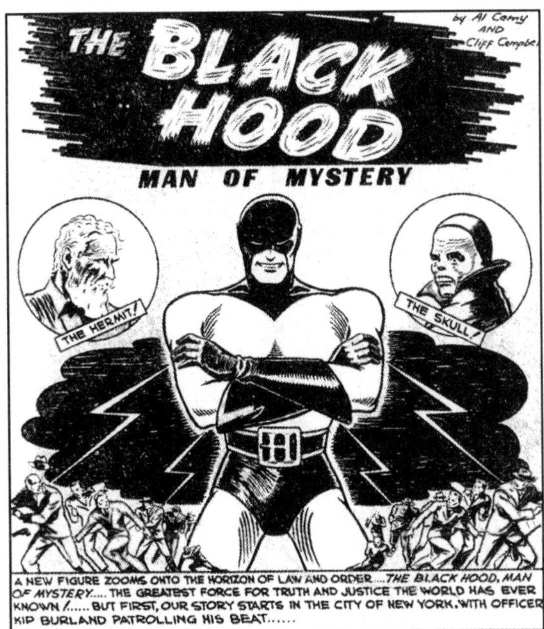

opponents who resembled comic book villains yet to be created. Some, like the Butcher and Judge Torture, were too strong for comic books since they were inspired by the Weird Menace magazines Popular Publications also published back then.

Our second *Spider* selection revisits the theme of Manhattan being terrorized by a merciless master villain. *King of the Fleshless Legion* originally appeared in the May, 1939 issue of *The Spider*, about a year after Superman's debut in *Action Comics* #1 and the same month that Batman debuted in *Detective Comics* #27.

In the early years of the comic book superheroes, that four-color cohort fought an array of grisly bad guys. Going back to the days of Dime Novels—if not before—skull-faced or skeletal villains were a popular staple. It was a natural disguise, for the hollow-eyed death's head of the Grim Reaper symbolized death and piracy in equal measure.

In *King of the Fleshless Legion*, the *Spider* battles the nefarious Skull and his bony minions, all of whom glow as green as radium. Only a year later in 1940, in MLJ's *Top-Notch Comics*, patrolman Kip Burland is framed by a green-faced supercriminal called the Skull, forcing him to become that masked mystery man, the Black Hood. They have a series of recurring and ongoing battles until, in 1941, the Skull is captured and executed in the electric chair in the story titled "The Skull Walks the Last Mile." Mysteriously, he later returns without explanation.

One of the most visible Golden Age superheroes, the Black Hood had his own radio program and a short-lived pulp magazine where he again battled the Skull in his 1941 pulp origin story, *Death's Five Faces*. The character was created by former pulp writer Harry Shorten and artist Al Camy, although the pulp novels were credited to G.T. Fleming-Roberts.

Also in 1941, Captain America fought the Nazi supermenace known as the Red Skull, and that seemingly endless feud continues well into the 21st century. There were numerous other skull-visaged villains who followed, ranging from the Smiling Skull to Batman's the Outsider.

Nita van Sloan's cousin, Melissa Moulin of New Orleans, is introduced in *King of the Fleshless Legion*, but does not continue as a series regular—despite all indications that she will be a recurring heroine. This was just another of Norvell Page's false starts. In the rush to meet the monthly *Spider* magazine deadline, threads were woven and cast aside like a manic spider weaving a disorganized web. Such was the nature of pulp writing at times. The rush to bang out this month's story while thinking ahead to next's month's plot seldom

allowed the luxury of reflection on last month's manuscript.

The creators of the Golden Age of Comics were often pulp readers. Many plundered back issues of *The Spider*, *The Shadow* and other heroic titles for plot and character inspiration. Early four-color features such as "Alias the Spider" and "The Web" were imitations of the *Spider*, although modified to avoid infringing on Popular's trademark.

"Alias the Spider" was not very arachnid-like. He wore an athletic outfit and fought crime with a longbow and trick arrows as Green Arrow later did. Why he called himself "Alias the Spider" remains a mystery, but he employed a special arrow called the *Spider*'s seal to disarm gunmen and drove a car

he called the Black Widow in apparent emulation of the Green Hornet's Black Beauty. The Paul Gustavson strip ran in Quality Comics' *Crack Comics* from its first 1940 issue into 1943, the same year *The Spider* pulp folded.

"The Web" ran in MLJ's *Zip Comics* for about a year in 1942-43. Artist John Cassone launched the short-lived feature about college professor and criminologist John Raymond, who dons a piebald green and yellow costume with a webbed cape and snares criminals in his metaphorical "web." The Web was revived in the 1960s and continues to appear sporadically, at one point being scripted by Superman's Jerry Siegel.

The Tarantula was DC Comics' entry into the

brief Spider-sweepstakes. Concocted by editor Mort Weisinger and artist Harold Sharp, this character was really mystery author John Law, who becomes a masked mystery man in order to write a book about the subject. Unlike the other characters, the

Carol Forman as the Spider Lady in the 1948 *Superman* serial

Tarantula took his namesake seriously, using suction cups like The Shadow's to climb buildings and packing a web-shooting pistol to snare his opponents. He ran in *Star-Spangled Comics* from 1941 to 1943—a bad year for superheroes.

Then there were the distaff versions, the Spider Woman, the Spider Queen and the Spider Widow—the last of whom dressed like a Halloween crone, in much the same way Wentworth donned the fright wig and hunched back that became the *Spider*'s public persona, and who telepathically controlled black widow spiders. Few *Spider* clones survived World War 2.

Were *all* these characters knockoffs of the *Spider*? Probably not. For in the frantic rush to cash in on the demand for superhero strips during the early 1940s, writers and artists were bound to turn to the arachnid theme, making spider-inspired heroes all but inevitable, without or without the example of the *Spider* before them. But the webby cape of the Web sure looks like someone took inspiration from the two *Spider* movie serials Columbia released in 1938 and 1941.

Popular Publications never entered the comic book field. They considered doing so circa 1942, but publisher Harry Steeger decided against it. One of their planned projects was a version of the *Spider* set in the future, in which a descendant of Dick Wentworth, called Rick Worth, fought crime as a 22nd century incarnation of the Master of Men. Norvell Page penned a short story featuring this unrealized character in the back of the June 1942 issue, "Blood Bond."

In 1941, after comic book superheroes like Superman and Batman began stealing away some of *The Spider*'s loyal readers, the magazine published the following letter:

> Dear Mr. Stockbridge:
>
> It seems to me that you go to great lengths to devise logical ways in which the *Spider* can extricate himself from the various and dangerous difficulties in which you place him. Why not let him be more of the miraculous, or super-man type?
>
> I would like to have Dick Wentworth so strong he could heave automobiles around, break gun barrels and tear down buildings!
>
> Yours for a Super-*Spider*!
>
> (Signed) Ben Rayburn

Rayburn had to wait twenty years for his Super-*Spider*. About a year after Norvell Page's death in 1961, dedicated *Spider* magazine reader Stan Lee and artist Steve Ditko presented him to the world. As Spider-Man.

In that light, we cannot assert with confidence that the originators of the Skull, or the Red Skull, skimmed *King of the Fleshless Legion* for villainous inspiration. But as you read through this exciting story, see if you don't feel the tingle of diabolical familiarity race through your *Spider*-stimulated nerves... •

KING OF THE FLESHLESS LEGIONS

Poisoned medicine had flooded New York — and overnight all hospitals had been turned into a hell of helpless human sufferers! For a strange and incredible horror had gripped the metropolis. Men gazed, terrified, upon a greenish Skull glowing evilly in the darkness, then died! And no physician nor science could save them from unbelievable agony and death! Where once happy, healthy citizens had dwelt, was now a city of *defleshed* corpses. No help could come from the baffled police; and mercy in Manhattan was a forgotten word. Yet one man did not fear to challenge the Terror. Richard Wentworth, as the *Spider*, set out to find the way to battle the Skull—and save an entire city from an Epidemic of Poison!

King of the Fleshless Legion

A Feature-Length *Spider* Novel

By Grant Stockbridge

The Spider faces a grim mass murderer who holds sway over Manhattan—when poisoned drugs paralyze the medical profession and turn New York's hospitals into a hell of betrayed human sufferers!

CHAPTER ONE

Death at Midnight

THE angry roar of the mob was ominous in the softness of the Spring night. Its first sullen rumble changed as it swept closer to high-tossing waves of furious sound. Hurrying rapidly along Sutton Place, Richard Wentworth checked to peer narrowly through the midnight dark toward Second Avenue where the violence seemed to center.

"Hurry on, Nita," he urged the woman who clung to his arm. "Get to the drugstore phone. Tell the police to make all possible speed. It's serious."

Nita van Sloan hesitated at Wentworth's side, her white hand sensing the tautening of the lithe muscles of his arm while her eyes took in the increasing gravity of his hawkish profile. She shivered a little at the bestial quality of the mob howl.

"Dick, promise you won't do anything foolish. Remember, you're unarmed."

"Yes, yes—hurry, dear." Wentworth waved her on without turning his eyes from the corner where he thought the mob would show first.

In heaven's name, what could send men marching so fiercely through the soft night of Spring? He must find their object, turn them aside until the police came or someone might be hurt. It was typical of the man, that echo of his thoughts. *Someone might be hurt.* He did not think of danger to himself, only of the possible service he might render.

Nita was running now, her sables flung wide, her silver gown caught high about her silken knees. The gem-glittering heels of her slippers clicked out sharp explosions of sound against the pavement. There was need to hurry: a long crosstown block away, the mob was turning the corner toward where Wentworth stood!

Wentworth swore softly as he watched the thick-pressed ranks of the men swell like a monstrous black serpent around the distant corner. Even from this distance, he could feel the impact of their single-minded hatred. It was like a tangible thing. It beat in upon him with the fresher, wilder surge of their voices. Then a single, thinner sound cut across it... a woman's scream. *Nita's scream!*

Wentworth's head whipped about and he saw Nita, poised in rigid fright before the pharmacy. Her white arms were twisted defensively before her face as if she would thrust her backward-arching body away from some horror behind the doors. The neon sign smeared bloody light across the swirling silver of her dress.

An instant, Wentworth hesitated, then glass crashed from the pharmacy entrance, one door swung outward a little way, flung back. With a suppressed shout, Wentworth hurled himself into a sprint.

"Coming, Nita," he shouted.

As if she gained courage from his voice, Nita took a slow step toward the door. She had time for no more before Wentworth reached her and peered in through the shattered glass.

Just inside, a man crouched in a tortured posture of agonized pain. His hat lay on the floor, and there was blood upon his scalp where his head had smashed against the glass. Slowly, as Wentworth stared, the man's head twisted upward. His face was hideously distorted. His eyes puckered and his lips shrank back from his teeth. Even as Wentworth sprang forward, the man slipped to the floor. His limbs writhed in slow contortions and a tearing groan squeezed out between his locked teeth.

"Quickly," Wentworth shouted at the druggist. "A hypodermic needle. Strychnine. Hurry, man. He's dying!"

The druggist was leaning across the counter, both hands planted there, his whole body shaking. His thin, pale face was sagging in astonishment. Nita sprang toward him, repeating Wentworth's order, and the man staggered away from the counter, began to fumble in drawers. Nita snatched the things from under his awkward hands.

"What's the matter?" the druggist was panting. "Oh, what's the matter? He just asked for a drink and no—"

Nita had the hypodermic filled and she ran back to Wentworth's side. The man's face was mottled, purplish with congested blood. Wentworth ripped open his vest and shirt, plunged the needle home with deft hands. For an instant, the man's eyes flared wide. He stared up into Wentworth's kindly, intent face.

"Poison!" the man gasped. "I've been—" He shuddered and a terrific convulsion made his body writhe.

Nita's hand gripped Wentworth's shoulder achingly. "Oh," she whispered. "Oh, he's... dying."

Wentworth shook his head and pushed heavily to his feet. "He's dead," he said, and his head lifted sharply. The mob-howl—Lord, it was just outside! Men's feet were tramping heavily and he could make out individual sharp shouts.

"Lynch him!" a hoarse voice bellowed. *"Lynch the poisoner!"*

The druggist had come stumblingly forward and stood wringing small, ineffective hands. "Oh, what's the matter?" he whispered. "I haven't done anything. I haven't, so help me God. The man just came in and asked for something for a headache. I gave him one of those fizz drinks, and... he was just a customer... I—"

Wentworth's keen eyes probed the pharmacist's weak face. "Know this man?" he demanded.

The druggist backed away, flapping his hands. "I never saw him before. He just came in and asked for a drink, and—"

"Hide," Wentworth ordered sharply. "Nita, phone the police. Try to find a back way out of this place. I'll hold off this mob. It looks very much as if someone else had been poisoned by drugs from this place today." Nita was already hurrying toward the phone booth. "Don't let him get away," Wentworth ordered grimly. "He'll have some questions to answer. If you can reach the house—"

A side window crashed and a half-brick bounded across the store, smashed heavily through a showcase. The druggist squealed and ran. Wentworth reached the door in two long strides and stepped outside to face the mob as it trooped toward him. His hands were empty; he was unarmed. He lifted both arms there, a tall, commanding figure with an intense, intelligent face. He was in evening dress and when he lifted his arms the light topcoat he wore swung open.

"Just a moment, men," he said quietly. "What's the matter here?"

HIS calm eyes swept over the mob. There were fully a score of men with clubs in their hands; their faces were ugly with rage. He tried to pick out their leader and his gaze centered on a broad-shouldered workingman in the front ranks.

"You tell me," Wentworth ordered. "What's the matter? Don't you realize you're apt to get in trouble like this?"

"Trouble?" The man's voice was heavy and thick. "Trouble? What the hell do I care? That man... that man in there—"

He shook his great, empty fists. "He kill my two babies! He kill my wife!" He surged forward and behind him the mob moved with the singleness of a great, many-legged beast. Wentworth went to meet the man, smiling, arms hanging idly at his sides.

"Wait a minute," he urged. "Tell me about it. How did this happen?"

He was playing desperately for time. If he could get this man to expend his rage in words; there was horror here. This was more than a deadly mistake on the pharmacist's part in making up a prescription. There was this other man, dead on the floor, to testify to that! In God's name, what was happening here? From somewhere in the mob, a brick was hurled. The breath of its passage fanned Wentworth's cheek and behind him glass crashed again! Wentworth's smile did not waver; nor did he dodge from the missile.

"Tell me about it," he repeated to the bereaved man. "I'll see that justice is done."

"Don't listen to him!" a voice bawled out. "He's in with the crooks! Knock him down!"

This time, Wentworth spotted the man who spoke and a cold fire began to burn in his eyes. Years of underworld warfare had taught him that there was no such thing as a criminal type. Yet they had one thing in common, these men who extorted an underhanded living from the innocent—a brazen egotism and a callousness toward human suffering that must always leave its mark. That brand was upon the sly, furtive face of the man who shouted and then promptly hid behind someone else when Wentworth's eyes sought him out.

"You, there!" Wentworth singled him out. "What have you got to do with this? Trying to make trouble for other people?"

"You're all alike." The man shouted, still hiding behind one of the mob. "You rich guys gang together! Trying to stomp us under your iron heel! Bloody capitalists!"

"Come and tell me about it," Wentworth urged, his voice soft. "You other men. You don't want to get in trouble with the law! If this druggist has caused deaths, he'll pay the penalty. You know you can count on that!"

As he spoke, he deserted his post in front of the door and was shouldering his way straight in among the angry men. Clubs were lifted threateningly. Wentworth did not even look at those who menaced him. His eyes were boring into the furtive eyes of this criminal who, he knew now, was the leader. Why didn't the police come? Surely, there had been time for at least one radio car to reach the spot... unless the phone wires had been cut!

That was pure conjecture, of course, but there was something damnably suspicious about this combination of circumstances. Four deaths from this one drugstore; a mob deliberately organized by this criminal—and the police late in coming! Abruptly, Wentworth knew that his premonitions were correct. The underworld had been quiet too long and now it was stirring at last! What horror those roiling depths soon would bring to the surface he could not guess. But he did feel convinced that he was dealing with one of its first manifestations.

"Listen, men," Wentworth moved forward, thoughts racing through his keen brain. "If you harm this druggist—no matter with what justification—the law will get you. You'll pay the penalty. This man who is urging you on will run away and get off free. Why don't you ask him what he has to do with all this? Ask him *why* he cares!"

If only he could turn the attention of the mob to this one man, away from the drugstore... he could count on Nita getting to a phone soon even if those in the pharmacy wires had been cut. But she would need time.

"You're the real criminal." Wentworth was within a dozen feet of the man he had singled out. *"Tell them who paid you to do this!"*

WENTWORTH saw amazement and fear change the man's small-mouthed furtive face and it was all the confirmation he needed. He had guessed right!

"He's trying to trick you!" the man shouted. "Look, he's the owner of that store! I know him! He's just trying to trick you! Knock him down!" The man's hand flitted across his chest and stabbed under his coat lapel in a gesture Wentworth knew all too well. He would shoot without hesitation—and Wentworth was unarmed!

It was because Wentworth had approached so quietly, so fearlessly, that he had been able to enter the thick press of the mob without injury. Now, he was more afraid for these men about him than for himself. An almost superstitious fear was shaking the gunman, and when his weapon was free, he would shoot without discrimination, blindly. The instant the man's hand moved in that betraying gesture, Wentworth was in action. A quick reach of his hand caught a club from the fist of the nearest mobster and a continuation of the same movement hurled it straight at the face of the gunman!

The man, pulling his gun, almost succeeded in dodging the hurriedly thrown club. As he ducked aside, it grazed past his cheek, tore his ear. With a yelp, he flung up his left arm defensively and tried to jerk his gun into line.

Wentworth's leaping dive, started just as he flung the club, carried him headlong into the man's body. His smashing shoulder drove out the man's wind and, in the next instant, Wentworth was on his feet, the captured gun in hand. He hit once, knocking out the criminal, but he did not level the gun at the mob.

"All right, then," Wentworth said quietly. "I've got the troublemaker. The rest of you can go home and the police will see that the men responsible for these deaths are punished. I promise you that!"

The clubs were sagging in the men's hands now. That swift, efficient action, the gun in Wentworth's hand, had a calming effect. Near the doors of the store, Wentworth could see the bereaved father whose poisoned family had been the excuse for this outbreak. His heavy shoulders were bowed, his head sagging.

Wentworth felt anger surging through his own veins. Damn the criminals who could cause such tragedies out of greed! What their exact purpose was, Wentworth could not guess, but he would find out! The *Spider* must take again the trail of justice!

"Yeah, you're promising us," a man's hoarse voice broke in on Wentworth's thoughts. *"You're promising us! Who are you?"*

Wentworth smiled slightly. "You may know my name," he said. "Richard Wentworth."

His challenger's eyes widened. "Geez, yes, I know you. Sure, and—"

A shot slashed across the muted mutter of the crowd. It came from some distance away and at its sharp report—Richard Wentworth pitched forward to the pavement.

CHAPTER TWO

Skeleton Without Arms

SHOUTS of fright burst from the crowd at Wentworth's fall. For a moment, the men stood motionless, peering toward the car from which the shot had come. Then a hail of bullets whined toward them. One man screamed and, bent double, pitched writhing to the pavement. Another dropped without a sound. It was enough. With screams, the others broke into furious flight, scattering toward the dark safety of doorways and side streets.

On the ground lay four men, the two members of the mob felled by bullets; the unconscious leader and Richard Wentworth. The death car rolled toward them slowly and the metal of guns glinted at the windows; the white blurs of alert faces peered out. Wentworth had not seemed to move since his fall, but his hand remained tightly on the butt of his captured automatic. His head was turned so that he faced the approaching car. From its windows, the guns began to spit again. Two weapons were firing deliberately. The body of the man beside Wentworth jerked to the prodding leaden bullets.

Abruptly, another gun sent its crashing echoes along the street. From a dark doorway, splinters of powder flame stabbed out into the night, reaching toward the sedan. A policeman, perhaps? But there had been no skirling of an alarm whistle. Wentworth smiled thinly as he deliberately lifted his automatic into line on the sedan. Whoever the unknown gunfighter was, Wentworth now owed him a great debt.

Wentworth was as deliberate as if he stood on a target range. He dropped his muzzle into line on the windshield where he could see the white blur of the driver's face. Then a startled cry leaped to his lips! A man in the rear was crouching near the window, his right arm drawn back to throw... something. Wentworth could barely glimpse the enlarged silhouette of his fist, but he did not need to see the object the man held. It was a bomb!

If the man succeeded in throwing that bomb, it meant death to himself and the criminal he had taken prisoner. It meant worst than that—death to Nita where she guarded the druggist in his store! Wentworth's heart was pounding in his throat but his gunhand did not tremble. A twist of the wrist and the gun was bearing on that rear window. No time for nice aiming now, nor for picking a careful target. The man was in the window, and the bomb in his fist was in range. With a trigger finger timed to the exact top speed of fire for the automatic, Wentworth raked that window from side to side with lead. The gun jumped in his hand like a miniature machine gun, and—

Red and white flame streaked outward through the car windows! It thrust jagged fingers up through holes torn instantly in the roof! Behind Wentworth, the windows of the drugstore collapsed in final ruin as concussion swept over him in a great wind. It sucked the breath from his lungs and left him half-stunned. Only the urgency of his will drove him, reeling, to his feet, sent him staggering toward the drugstore even while his blurred eyes held the car. The gun in his hand was empty.

At the blast, the sedan leaped like a heart-shot deer, slammed down to veer drunkenly across the street. It leaped the curb, smashed down an iron guardfence and dropped its front wheels into a basement entrance well. Wentworth heard the crash dully in blast-muted ears, and thereafter not any sound at all. Not even a scream.

The flaming sedan leaped the curb and smashed down an iron fence!

WENTWORTH was already pushing toward the drugstore, his pace a shambling run as he forced his stunned senses to coordination. His one thought was to locate Nita. He couldn't be sure whether the shrilling in his ears was from the explosion or whether police at last were closing in. Ardently as he had longed for the police earlier in the affair, he did not want them now.

If he could get the druggist and the unconscious gunman he had left in the street back to his own house, he thought he could swiftly get to the bottom of the night's horror. Criminals knew that the police were hampered in their attempts to force out the truth; about a man like Wentworth they could not know.

There had been, time and again, rumors and stories in the newspapers which linked Wentworth's name with that of the dread lone wolf of justice whom all the underworld feared with an awful fear, the *Spider.* No one, save his few closest intimates, knew Wentworth's perilous secret—that he was indeed that swift nemesis of criminals whose guns had brought low so many enemies of society. But his captive would wonder, and Wentworth's Sikh body servant, Ram Singh, had a terrifyingly persuasive way of handling his long-bladed knives.

These thoughts were muddling through Wentworth's mind even as he plunged through the drugstore entrance, a mess of splintered glass now. Nita should be all right unless one of those bullets had gone astray, and—

"Nita!" Wentworth called sharply. "Nita, are you all right?"

He stopped at the counter, listening. There were bulletholes in the glass that shielded the telephone booth and, on a shelf, a broken bottle dribbled the last of its contents on the floor. There was a pungent odor of spilled chemicals.

"Nita!" Wentworth cried. He flung himself around the counter and into the prescription room. The phone booth… he dared a glance.… empty, thank God! The prescription room was empty, also. Then Wentworth saw a high square window that swung open, and under it a chair had been placed on the counter. Thankfulness flooded through Wentworth's heart. It had been as he had hoped. Nita must have failed to reach the police and had left that way to get help. She would have the druggist with her.

There was no mistake now about the sirens. They were still *faint* with distance, but they could close the interval quickly, as Wentworth well knew. He looped about, moving more surely now and plunged toward the front of the drugstore. He caught up a bottle from the soda fountain and a glass. He wanted to check on what had poisoned that customer and—Good Lord! Out there in the street, a man was stooping over the unconscious criminal.

"Stay just like that!" Wentworth ordered sharply and leveled his empty automatic. "Let that gun fall!"

The man twisted a white, youthful face about, managed a smile. "It's all right," he said. "I'm not one of the gunmen."

Wentworth closed up the distance with long strides and his grey-blue eyes took the summary of the man in a single keen glance. Brown eyes looked back at him steadily, and the lips, smiling above a clean-cut chin, were wide and generous.

Wentworth remembered that someone else had been returning the fire of the killers. It might very well have been this man, but he could take no chances with an empty gun in his hand.

"Drop the gun," he repeated quietly. "We can discuss the rest afterward."

The man's smile tightened, but he obeyed. "Aren't you Richard Wentworth?" he asked hurriedly. "I've seen pictures of you. Look, I'm Donald Beck, a private detective. I was coming to see you tomorrow with a proposition and I came up here tonight to... to make sure of where you lived."

The man stammered a little over his explanation and Wentworth continued to regard him with searching steadiness. Donald Beck, private detective... perhaps. It was also possible that he had been planted here to make sure of Wentworth if the others failed. Slowly a smile curved Wentworth's grim-set lips. He would soon find out, and if this man were involved with the criminals... why, there was one more source of information!

"Very well," Wentworth said quietly, "you can make me the proposition at my home. Meantime, just get that man's body on your shoulders and walk ahead of me, Mr. Donald Beck. If I find you're telling the truth, I won't be ungrateful. If you aren't—"

For seconds, Beck continued to meet Wentworth's probing eyes. There was a slight flush in his cheeks, but his voice was steady enough. "Very well, sir," he said. With smooth power, he seized the gunman's inert body, pulled it to a sitting position and, stooping, heaved it across his shoulders. "Which way?"

Wentworth felt a broadening smile tug at his lips. Beck had courage, at any rate. He directed him into the side street, on which the steel-guarded gates of his fortress home opened, and followed at a jog trot after scooping up Beck's gun. The sirens were very near; there was no time to be lost... and in the back of Wentworth's mind was a hot point of worry. If only he could be sure Nita was safe. Lord, what an end to an evening that had started out as a pleasant little social gathering to honor Nita's visiting cousin from the South—Melissa Moulin was her name.

This furious violence had started as a quiet stroll along Sutton Place after all of the guests had left save young Forbes who was calling on Melissa. Astroll, just Dick and Nita together in the Spring night. It had been a blissful relief from weeks and months of constant warfare. A relief? Wentworth laughed sharply.

He whipped a small silver whistle from his pocket and, eyes on his wristwatch as he loped along, he blew a peculiar intermittent and perfectly timed cadence of notes. Just ahead of Beck, the close-fitting steel gates of Wentworth's fortress home, which he had built partly on filled land between two piers over the East River, slid silently apart—operated by sonic-actuated electric motors. Wentworth saw Beck hesitate and shouldered him through. Instantly, the gates were closing again and, as their muted thud ran through the dark courtyard before Wentworth's home, the sirens shrieked to a crescendo and died a half-block away. The police had arrived.

"You'll pardon my precipitancy," Wentworth told Beck dryly, "but I have some questions to ask before we give the police the details of the evening."

A brawny, turbaned Sikh was hurrying toward them from the shielded lights of the building's entrance.

Wentworth motioned to him. "Conduct this gentleman, Mr. Beck, and his charge to the laboratory, Ram Singh," Wentworth directed. "Has Miss Nita come back or phoned?"

"No, *sahib,"* the Sikh replied gutturally. "Jackson went to seek thee when we heard the noises. He left just before the explosion. Hadst thou not ordered thy servant to remain on guard, I, too—"

"Jackson left?" Wentworth said slowly. "Curious that I didn't meet or see him, still..." his frown lifted. He was intensely worried over the failure to hear from Nita, but perhaps Jackson, his other close comrade in the *Spider*'s work—his chauffeur to the world—had found Nita and was helping her.

"Full protection, Ram Singh," he ordered.

"*Han, sahib."* The Sikh salaamed in acknowledgment of the order that would set the hundred electric robots at work guarding the place against surprise or invasion. From now on, no one could approach within twenty-five feet of the walls without sounding an alarm, without automatically turning on blazing floodlights and setting up defensive electric circuits in steel gates and steel-crested walls. The voltage would not kill, but it would knock a man out.

For an instant, Wentworth stood there in the darkness of the wall-enclosed courtyard with its soft tinkling fountain and its carefully tended flowers and shrubs. The softness of Spring still came to him and mellow whooping of tugs on the East River, just behind his home.

But there was no pleasure for Wentworth in the budding of the year; there could be only cold caution and ceaseless warfare, for he knew with an assurance built upon years of such battling that the night's outbreak was no isolated case. Another power was burgeoning in the underworld; another evil brain was plotting against the peace and safety and happiness of the people. For Wentworth, the tocsin had sounded and once more the *Spider* must tread in perilous ways where every man's hand was turned against him; where his only friend was the swift death that waited in his guns. God, if only he knew Nita was safe!

Wentworth swung toward the formal double doors which gave entrance to the ground floor of his home and, just inside the elegant simplicity of the foyer, he stopped. A man was coming toward him from the elevators, and the man was frowning.

"Oh, Mr. Wentworth," he said. "I'm glad to see you again before I left. I was quite worried about you—all that shooting in the streets—but I hesitated to call the police."

"Quite all right, Mr. Forbes," Wentworth told him. "Good of you to stay and keep Miss Moulin company." He had forgotten the man was in the house, had stayed to keep Nita's cousin company while he and Nita went for their stroll.

His eyes swept the man's long, somewhat dour face, probed the gaze behind the rimless nose-glasses. How long had Forbes been in the foyer here and had he seen Wentworth's prisoner? If he had, it was best that he shouldn't be questioned by the police quite yet.

Wentworth said slowly, "You're quite a student of toxicological analysis, aren't you, Mr. Forbes?"

Forbes' full lips moved in a smile. "Oh, I dabble a little in poisons. There isn't much time for it at the Eastern Drug Company's laboratories. Did I tell you I'd shifted there recently?"

Wentworth controlled a start and slowly lifted the bottle he had in his hand. It contained Aspo-Seltzer, the drink which the drugstore customer had taken just before he died—and it was made in the Eastern Drug laboratories!

He said quietly, "I wonder if I could trouble you to run an analysis on this stuff here in my lab now? It just happens to be made by the company you work for. And a man who drank it died!"

Forbes uttered a startled exclamation. "Not the man you were just carrying in here?"

Wentworth shook his head quietly. "No, I think he may be involved in the death, that's all." He masked the quick suspicion in his eyes behind a smile. Forbes apparently had not intended to mention seeing his prisoner until it was startled out of him.

"I gave Ram Singh a bit of a new restorative we're working on in the lab," Forbes was saying rapidly. "I wanted to stay and see how it worked, but Ram Singh is not... exactly affable. I didn't kno—How sure are you it was this Aspo-Seltzer that poisoned the man? Lord, old man Wister will be frantic if this ever gets out!"

Wentworth noted mentally that Samuel Wister was head of the Eastern Drug Company and led Forbes to the laboratory to run the tests on the drug. Ram Singh was working over the prisoner on a cot where Wentworth sometimes napped during experiments of his own. It was a small room off the laboratory. Beck was standing by, frowning. He looked up as Wentworth came in.

"I've seen this man somewhere before," he said, "but I can't place him. Probably on a 'wanted' list."

"Probably," Wentworth agreed. "Beck, it will be a little while before I have an opportunity to talk with you. Would you mind waiting in the next room?"

Beck moved toward the laboratory and, with a jerk of his head, Wentworth indicated to Ram Singh that he was to keep watch. Then he stood staring down at the criminal who had been inciting the mob.

IN RELAXATION, all the sly, evil lines of the man's face seemed to be emphasized. His mouth was loose, ugly. It twitched with the first hint of returning consciousness. Swiftly, Wentworth searched the man's pockets, found nothing of importance until he patted the coat and located a narrow, hidden recess close to the hem. From it, he drew an object that brought a keen look to his eyes.

A surprising thing for a criminal to carry in a secret pocket. It looked like a child's Hallowe'en favor, a tiny skeleton carved out of wood with legs and arms made out of spring wire so that they bobbed and quivered in a pseudo lifelike manner. The right arm was missing.

Wentworth weighed it on his palm. No question that this was some sort of criminal talisman, or identification emblem.

It was significant that a skeleton was used—and that the victims of these criminals had died of drugs from bottles which should have borne the skull-and-crossbones symbol of poison and, tragically, did *not!* Wentworth's hand closed into a knotted fist about the tiny skeleton. His prisoner was opening his eyes.

In a stride, Wentworth caught up a bottle on which glared the red skull-and-crossbones label of poison. He held it idly in his hand where the man's eyes would find it when they came to focus. Abruptly, the man swore and his hand ducked toward the empty holster beneath his arm. He cringed, then, like the trapped animal that he was and, slowly, his eyes came to rest on the poison bottle in Wentworth's hand.

"This bottle," Wentworth said quietly, "contains white arsenic. It isn't a very pleasant poison to take, and it doesn't kill at once. There is a lot of pain. Agony in the stomach, convulsions, then blood in your mouth."

The man licked his loose lips, "Now, listen," he said, "you ain't going to make me take nothing like that! Damn you, I ain't afraid of you! You do anything to me and the chief will take care of you. He'll finish you off, just like that!"

"Your chief is a yellow dog, like all crooks," Wentworth went on. "Even the police can't get to you here... and the river is just outside the back door. I could have my men hold you and pour this down your throat. I could sit here and watch you die... and then slide your body into the river. Your chief?" Wentworth laughed shortly. "Your chief is a punk."

"My chief is—" The man's face turned crafty. "You wouldn't dare do all that to me," he whined. "And you're just trying to pump me. Well, I ain't talking, see? You can't make me!"

Wentworth lifted his voice. "Ram Singh."

The crook cringed toward the wall as the Sikh's soft step heralded his approach. *"Han, sahib!"*

Wentworth said steadily, "I'm going to poison a rat. Hold him." His grey-blue eyes were merciless, cold, but they were carefully estimating the man before him. He would break all right. As for the contents of the bottle, it was a bitter drug that was poisonous in huge doses, but in smaller quantities would merely cause pains and nausea. Ram Singh was bending over the cot and the broad, keen blade of his knife was laid against the man's throat!

"Open your mouth, rat!" said Ram Singh, fiercely, "or I will cut a hole through which to pour this ant poison!"

"No!" the man gasped. "God, no! You can't! The Skull will wipe you out!"

"The Skull is a yellow rat," Wentworth said softly. "Who is the Skull?"

"The Skull is—" The man gagged. "The Skull is—" A powerful convulsion shook him and a tinge of blue crept into his pallid cheeks.

An oath jerked from Wentworth's lips. He sprang to a rack of bottles against the wall. He needed no more indication than this. The man was poisoned! Even while his eye raced over the bottles, picking an emetic, his mind flashed to the memory of Donald Beck bending over the unconscious man in the street; of Robert Forbes saying, "I gave him a new restorative to use..."

He whirled back to the cot... and saw that he was already too late. The man was stiffening in death, his face purple with congested blood... his tongue forever stilled! A cold anger flared in Wentworth's eyes, and he spun toward the door of the laboratory where Forbes and Beck were. He could not be sure that either had a hand in this, but both had had the opportunity. He took a long stride toward the door... and a signal bell whirred beside an annunciator there! Wentworth flipped a tumbler.

"Yes?"

"Master Richard." It was the quavering voice of old Jenkyns, his butler, who had served Wentworth's father before him. "Master Richard, there are some policemen at the south gate with a search warrant! They insist on coming in! They say there's a dead man here, a *murdered* man!"

CHAPTER THREE
Murder Charge

FOR a moment, Wentworth stared in unseeing incredulity at the blank face of the annunciator, then he laughed shortly and a gleam came into his grey-blue eyes—a gleam that might be admiration! The Skull, as the criminal now dead had termed the murder-master, worked with a swift efficiency, and an absolute reliance on his underlings. This meant without doubt that the Skull had ordered this man's death and had been sure enough of the results to tip off the police in advance! Just for that instant while he stared, wordless, Wentworth knew a quickening of his old joy in battle. If there were not such dire results from the operations of this man called "Skull," it would be a pleasure to join issues with such a clever and efficient adversary!

Now—

Wentworth's voice, when he spoke, showed nothing of the inner turmoil the announcement created. "Very well, Jenkyns," he said. "You may admit the police, but go personally to the gate and usher them in. I will receive them in the drawing room." He turned from the annunciator and threw a single Punjab phrase at Ram Singh. "Hide the body!" His gesture indicated a secret doorway in the wall of the room and then he stepped out into the main laboratory.

He was ready.

Beck was staring intently at Forbes who, a laboratory apron hurriedly donned, was bending over a test tube which simmered over a Bunsen Burner. As Wentworth watched, the tube changed from red to blue and a fine snow of white crystals began to precipitate out in the liquid. Forbes uttered an exclamation of satisfaction.

"You were right, Mr. Wentworth," he cried out. "It's poison all right! Aconitum!"

Wentworth nodded. "I wonder if you gentlemen would accompany me to the drawing room," he said pleasantly. "The police have a search warrant to serve on me and they will doubtless want to ask some questions."

"A search warrant!" Forbes' eyes widened behind his glasses, then a hint of angry red began to creep into his florid cheeks. "They have a nerve! What do they expect to find here?"

Beck's fists were knotted. "What do you want me to do, sir?" he asked indignantly.

Wentworth shrugged, but his answer was to Forbes as he drew out a cigarette case and proffered it. "From what Jenkyns told me," he said placidly, "they expect to find a murdered man. After you, gentlemen."

Forbes continued to berate the police indignantly as the elevator bore them upward to the third floor drawing room. Wentworth's eyes were apparently on the slow coiling of smoke that eddied up from his cigarette, but he was watching both men. Forbes' indignation seemed a little overdone. Beck's face was pale and intent. Wentworth touched his hand and put into it the automatic he had taken from the detective, and Beck's face flushed.

"Thank you, sir," he said. It was plain that he accepted the return of his weapon as indicative of Wentworth's trust. "Will they make trouble about the man we took prisoner?"

Wentworth shrugged. "They may. I'm sorry now that I let him go, but he succeeded in convincing me that he had no connection with the trouble at the drugstore, except to make one of the mob. I couldn't really blame him for that, though the police might."

Forbes said, a little sharply. "Funny we didn't see him go out. Do you want us to forget we saw him?"

Wentworth murmured, "Not in the least. Beck, you said you had a proposition to make to me. I think this will probably be our best opportunity. I shall be pretty busy from now on."

Beck's head jerked toward Wentworth and then a slow smile grew in Beck's eyes. He laughed, "You're the coolest man I've ever seen, sir," he said. "It would be a pleasure to serve you. The proposition—"

THE elevator door opened and Wentworth ushered the two men into the drawing room. Curled up on an end of a davenport, a book in her hands, a girl lifted an alert, small-featured face. She brushed a strand of golden hair back from her forehead.

"I declare, Richard," she called. "You startled me. Why, Mr. Forbes, you didn't go, after all. I'm so glad."

Forbes stammered something not quite intelligible, and despite his inner tension, Wentworth hid a smile. Apparently Melissa Moulin had completed the subjugation of Robert Forbes after Nita and he had left. Wentworth presented Beck briefly.

"A real live detective!" exclaimed Melissa. "Oh, I've always wanted to meet a real detective! Promise me you won't tell Mr. Forbes any of the perfectly horrid things I'm afraid you'll find out about me!"

Beck's smile was quick, "I won't if you'll promise to let me report in private." He promised. "Mr. Wentworth, sir, if you really want me to talk to you now—"

Wentworth nodded, "Go right ahead." Ram Singh had had ample time to dispose of the body, Wentworth thought, listening for the hum of the elevator which would announce the arrival of the police. He was beginning to wish, though, that he had told Ram Singh to slip the body into the river.

There was just a chance they would find that hidden doorway.

Melissa was prattling, "Jenkyns told me some policemen were coming here. Isn't it exciting?" Her brown eyes stretched very wide as she looked up trustingly into Forbes' face. "Richard, you won't mind if I stay, will you? I'm sure Cousin Nita won't object at all." Wentworth bowed to her and continued to focus his apparent attention on Beck. If only he could be sure Nita was safe! It was strange that she did not at least phone him.

"What I wanted to suggest, sir," Beck was saying in a restrained, eager voice, "was that you hire me to catch the *Spider,* or just let me work with you to that end."

Wentworth lifted a quizzical eyebrow and his grey-blue eyes swung completely to Beck. His previous suspicions of Beck returned. He had not

forgotten that either this man or Forbes had had a chance to poison the prisoner. It was possible, of course, that someone in the mob had done it also. Beck was talking rapidly.

"It's this way, sir," he was saying. "My reasons don't matter particularly, except that you can understand what it would do for my reputation as a private detective. But there is every reason why you should, sir. You've been accused a number of times of being the *Spider.* You've always disproved the charges and no sensible person ever suspected you. But as long as the *Spider* is at liberty, you're going to be bothered by these charges. Every time the *Spider* kills, somebody is going to say, 'It's that criminologist, Wentworth. He's got an in with the police or he'd have been captured long ago.'"

Wentworth smiled. "And you think, Beck, that you can succeed where the police and everyone else have failed?"

"With you to help me! Yes, sir!" Beck was standing up as rigidly as a soldier on parade. Damn it, hard to suspect him of any duplicity, but Wentworth had been deceived before this by his own quick sympathies.

"That's very flattering," Wentworth said, "but I hardly think—"

"You're going to say that you approve of the *Spider,*" Beck cried. "That he accomplishes more in the enforcement of law than all the police. But don't you see that he brings the law into disrepute? He makes the police seem stupid. He damages their morale. He hurts them with the people. And what is the *Spider* at bottom? A cold-blooded killer! What is that red seal of his but a boast that he has killed? He might as well take their scalps like a savage Indian and cut off their heads for trophies!"

"You don't believe in... killing criminals, Beck?"

"The state provides for their execution, sir, at need. And the *Spider*—how can he be so sure that he kills only guilty men, as is his boast? Is he God that he alone can tell the guilty from the innocent?"

The challenge and the fire in Donald Beck's eyes shook Wentworth, and the young detective had unwittingly touched on a sore spot. Wentworth was too intelligent not to have realized long ago these very dangers that Beck had cited. He had always been very sure before he called on his swift guns to execute the justice that so often was evaded in the courts...but was he infallible? To his own ears, Wentworth's laughter sounded a little strained.

"Fortunately," he said, "I'm not called upon to pass judgment on the *Spider.* I think he serves the people and the state better than they deserve, but—"

"Think it over, sir," Beck urged. "Has the *Spider* ever come forward when you were accused, to free you? You owe yourself and your friends the safety of definite proof that you are not the *Spider.* As long as any doubt exists you are not safe. No one that you even love is safe!"

Melissa made her narrow, sloping shoulders shudder delicately. "Oh, you frighten me, Mr. Beck!" she exclaimed. "You must be very brave to be willing to do a thing like that."

THE door of the elevator opened and Wentworth heard Jenkyns' calm voice ushering in the police. His eyes went searchingly to Melissa, still prattling. Nita had warned him that Melissa was much more than the fluffy, helpless thing she seemed. It looked very much as if she had broken into the conversation to warn him that the elevator was on the way up. Melissa was gracefully on her feet now. She clapped her hands together childishly.

"Oh!" she said. "Real policemen!"

Wentworth pivoted calmly to face the police and a swift frown dented his forehead. There were police all right, but the man who strode at their head, quick and sharp in his movements, stabbing inquisitive glances about him, was not one of the cops. It was the district attorney, Wilton Toley! In contrast to the alertness of his movements, his voice was ponderous, slightly pompous. He prodded each person in the room with his eyes as if he quizzed a stubborn jury.

"Your promptness is very courteous, Mr. Wentworth," he said, and there was a flourish like a gesture in his speech. "I have imposed on your good will to start my men searching the lower floors before talking to you."

How soon had that search started? Wentworth wondered sharply. Had Ram Singh had ample time? "Not at all, Mr. Toley," he said steadily. "I have quite a good deal to tell you, but I wonder if you will allow me to call Commissioner Kirkpatrick first? It would save a great deal of time to tell the story only once, and I fancy I shall be rather busy for a while."

"You may be," Toley murmured. "Yes, indeed. You won't think I'm discourteous, I hope, if I ask you to begin at once? I'm afraid there isn't time to wait for Kirkpatrick."

Wentworth said bluntly, "You refuse to allow me to call Kirkpatrick?"

Toley blinked, imperturbable as a judge, "If you wish to phrase it so."

Melissa tugged at Wentworth's elbow and he felt the mounting tension within him relax a trifle. No mistaking the hostility in Foley's manner, of course. Like all district attorneys, he was out to make a name for himself and, as Beck had pointed out, if the *Spider* was involved, Wentworth was suspect.

"Melissa," Wentworth said gravely, "I want to present the district attorney of New York County,

Wilton Toley. Mr. Toley, this is Miss van Sloan's cousin from New Orleans, Melissa Moulin."

Immediately, Melissa was cooing up at Toley, flattering him. Toley had difficulty in interrupting long enough to order his men to search the living quarters.

"Oh, good heavens!" Melissa squealed. "You're not going into *my* room! Why, all my... my clothes..." She blushed. "You must allow me to... tidy up a bit!" She ran lightly to the door, her small, white hands fluttering.

Toley cleared his throat, frowned, then waved a hand to the police to let it go. He swung back to Wentworth, "Who is this dead man?" he snapped.

Wentworth smiled slowly. "I was waiting for you to tell me."

Toley took two quick charging steps forward, pointed an admonitory finger at Wentworth. "Don't try to evade my question, Wentworth!"

Wentworth said, "Don't be an ass, Toley! There's no jury here for you to impress."

Toley's face whitened: his voice hoarsened. "We'll find that poor murdered man if we have to tear this building apart! You've been masquerading as a respectable citizen too long!"

Wentworth shrugged. "Provided you personally underwrite the damages, go ahead, Toley." He offered his cigarette case to Beck. "I've been thinking over your proposition, Mr. Beck. Suppose we say—it's a deal?"

"Good!" Beck cried. "The first thing is to inform the newspapers. I'll get on the phone right away."

Toley blocked Beck's path to the door. "There'll be no telephoning until I give the word," he said shortly. "Naturally anyone in this house is suspect. You'll make it easier for yourself if you tell the truth."

Beck grinned at him. "That's what my mother always taught me."

Toley's face grew livid; but his voice came out clear, edged. "You say you were going to telephone the newspapers. Why?"

"I was going to announce," Beck said easily, "that Mr. Wentworth is declaring war on the *Spider;* that he will not rest until the *Spider* is brought to justice!"

Toley laughed harshly, "That's a laugh," he said. "Why, of all the effrontery. Wentworth is—"

"Be careful of what you say, Toley," Wentworth interrupted easily. "I have witnesses. There is such a thing as criminal libel." Toley swung toward him, but what he was about to say was never uttered. A policeman slammed out of the elevator and came forward at a run. His face was red with excitement.

"Mr. Toley," he panted. "They—they found the body! *And he's got the Spider's seal on him!"*

CHAPTER FOUR
The SPIDER Walks Again

TRIUMPH was almost a smirk on the face of Wilton Toley as he whirled once more to confront Wentworth. He drew himself up to his full brief height and Wentworth could see, almost visibly, the formal words of arrest taking shape in the man's brain. Something like desperation was goading Wentworth. He had been mad to conceal the body in the first place, but he had wanted only to avoid the delay which police investigation would entail—to prevent the embarrassment of such a discovery to his friend, Kirkpatrick, the commissioner of police.

What Donald Beck had said was all too true, that each time he managed to turn aside the charges which were leveled at him, Kirkpatrick's enemies made capital of it. But this seal of the *Spider*? How in the name of Heaven had that come to be placed on the body? More of the Skull's work, without a doubt. The man was damnably clever.

"Richard Wentworth," Toley was drawing the full drama from the situation. "I place you under arrest on a charge of—"

The new opening of the elevator door cut him short and a tall man, as precise in his dress as a marine officer, stepped crisply forward—Stanley Kirkpatrick, the commissioner.

"I got your message, Dick," he said easily. "It just happened I was around the corner at the scene of that gangster raid and so I came right away. I understood it was important."

Toley glared at Wentworth. "My orders were disobeyed!" he said harshly. "That girl—"

From the doorway, Melissa Moulin ran forward. "Oh, did I do wrong, Mr. Toley?" she asked anxiously. "I didn't know. You said there wasn't time, or that was what I thought. So after I finished straightening up my room, I just called up the police. I was sure Mr. Kirkpatrick would come quickly, and—"

Toley swore harshly and Melissa put a shocked expression on her tiny face, threw back her head. "Mr. Toley!" she exclaimed. "Down home a man would be horsewhipped for using language like that in the presence of ladies!"

There was a grim smile on Wentworth's lips that had its echo on the saturnine face of Commissioner Kirkpatrick. Wentworth took advantage of the diversion to speak in a low voice to Donald Beck. "If you escape arrest," he said quietly, "stay here on guard. If Miss van Sloan comes back here, tell her exactly what happened, please, and take orders from her."

Toley threw his hands into the air in token of surrender as Melissa turned an indignant back on his protestations. Wentworth was grateful for Kirkpatrick's presence but it did complicate matters. If Toley persisted in his present course, Wentworth would have no alternative except flight. He would use that only as a last resort. It crippled him damnably to have to dodge policemen while he was working on a case and he knew, without question, that the coming struggle with the Skull would tax his resources to the utmost!

"Kirkpatrick," Toley said abruptly, "I was attempting to handle this case without interference—"

"And usurping my privileges!" Kirkpatrick took instant fire from the other's manner. "May I remind you once more, Mr. District Attorney, that it is my duty to gather evidence, yours to present it to juries for prosecution?"

"Exactly," Toley purred. "But when you neglect that duty, Mr. Commissioner, I may find it necessary to present other charges before the jury... concerning you!"

The pointed ends of Kirkpatrick's black mustache bristled. "Be careful, Toley!"

"Take that advice for yourself," Toley snapped. "I demand that you arrest Wentworth for murder!"

"Are you swearing out the warrant, Toley?"

Wentworth lounged against the wall, but he had estimated every man in the room. Forbes stood with Melissa near the French doors to the terrace. At the hall exit was a single policeman who Wentworth could reach in two bounds. Beyond that... but he did not know how other officers were distributed about the place. It made escape damnably difficult.

Toley said violently, "Yes, I'll swear out the warrant!"

Kirkpatrick shrugged, "In that case, the responsibility is on your shoulders, and I won't have to face a suit for false arrest. Dick—"

Wentworth drew in a slow breath. This was painful. It would besmirch Kirkpatrick's record if he made his escape, but there seemed no other course.

Toley was watching them keenly. "Better draw your gun, Commissioner," he said, happily. "He's a dangerous man! We just found the man he murdered here in his own house... with the *Spider* seal on him!"

WENTWORTH saw Kirkpatrick's face tighten with pain and it wrung his heart. They were fast friends, he and Kirkpatrick, but the commissioner would never swerve from his duty by so much as the breadth of a knife-edge. He had long been convinced that Wentworth was the *Spider,* and had warned him that if ever the evidence fell into his hands, he would prosecute to the full extent of the law!

Wentworth respected his rigorous attention to duty—and so made sure that the evidence was never gathered! Meantime, as Richard Wentworth, he had often helped Kirkpatrick in his battles against the underworld. Kirkpatrick was bracing himself to perform his duty. Wentworth sucked in a slow breath, gathered his energies for the dash he must make.

The policeman at the door spoke. "Maybe, Mr. Toley, you better hear about this business first, sir," he said. "Maybe I didn't tell it to you quite straight."

Toley whirled toward the policeman. "What do you mean, dolt?"

The officer reddened, "I don't have to take that off you, Mr. Toley," he said. "You ain't my boss, and even off the commissioner—"

"Tell your story, Finnegan," Kirkpatrick interrupted. "Toley, keep a civil tongue between your teeth."

The policeman grinned slightly. "Yes, Commissioner. It's like this. We found this body floating in the river—"

Wentworth felt relief like a fierce laughter pumping at his chest, but he managed to appear indifferent. He tapped a cigarette.

Patrolman Finnegan was still talking. "He had this *Spider* seal between his shoulders, and—"

"That's proof enough," Toley snapped. "We've got witnesses who saw Wentworth carrying the man into this place. They'll identify him, and—"

"Identification ain't going to be so easy,"

Finnegan said and there was a gleam of hard amusement in his eye. "This body didn't have no clothes on, and likewise it didn't have no fingers or no head! It looks like maybe he had some tattooing on his chest, but if he did, he ain't now. His chest was skinned."

With an angry exclamation, Forbes batted open the terrace doors and led Melissa outside; she seemed suddenly faint. Wentworth stared with a sick amazement at Finnegan. Such ghastly mutilation... but this was impossible! It couldn't be the man who had died of poison in his laboratory. God, to treat a human being like that. He felt the weight of Kirkpatrick's shocked stare and his head swung slowly to meet his friend's gaze. There was a pinched pain in Kirkpatritck's eye and an awful doubt. Believing as he did that Wentworth was the *Spider,* he must blame him for this, even though there was no proof!

"You say," Kirkpatrick asked the police officer heavily, "that this man had a *Spider* seal between his shoulders?"

Wentworth wanted fiercely to deny that he was responsible but anything he could say would be an admission that he was the *Spider.*

Beck jerked eagerly at his elbow. "You see, sir," Beck cried, "I told you the *Spider* was nothing but a cold-blooded killer! By God, I'll work day and night to catch him! With your help, sir, we'll succeed!"

Kirkpatrick swung his head sharply toward Toley, and there was a grimness along his set jaw that Wentworth recognized. When that drawn look came to Kirkpatrick's face, it meant that he had determined upon a course that hurt him to the heart—but it also meant that he would carry through, unswervingly, to the end!

"Who are your witnesses, Toley?" he asked harshly.

"Wait, Kirk," Wentworth pushed out words with difficulty. "Wait just a moment. Beck, you may phone the papers if Mr. Toley no longer objects. I cannot believe that the *Spider* would do such a thing as this, but I have no choice. I pledge myself to track down the *Spider. If the Spider is guilty, he shall pay!"*

Kirkpatrick's eyes were burning into his, and slowly the tension went out of the commissioner's saturnine face. He dragged a heavy hand down across his cheeks. "Yes, yes," he said slowly, "it is hard to believe the *Spider* would do a thing like that."

Toley had been watching them closely, and there was a secretive light in his eyes. Wentworth wondered if he had grasped the significance of Kirkpatrick's indignation and the reason for its abrupt termination. Kirkpatrick was not good at dissembling.

Toley's voice was purring, soft. "I withdraw my charges against Wentworth, Commissioner," he said. "Even if he were the *Spider*—and I'll admit I have no proof of it now—I can't believe that any civilized human being would perform such mutilation."

"Please, sir." The officer, Finnegan, stepped into the room. "The medical examiner was there when the body was hauled out of the water. He said it looked like a case of aconitum poisoning. He said that the mutilation had been done after death."

The tautness that had left Wentworth began to creep back again He whispered a name in his mind, *Ram Singh.* In God's name, what had he pledged himself with his promise to track down the *Spider!* He began to talk rapidly, telling of the raid on the drugstore and the things that had happened there; of the test Forbes had run in his basement laboratory which had revealed aconitum in the Aspo-Seltzer.

"We should talk to that druggist," Wentworth said finally, "and certainly Wister should be interviewed as president of the concern that shipped out the poisoned drug. I don't for a moment suspect him of poisoning his own drugs, but it should certainly be investigated."

Kirkpatrick nodded stiffly, "This is the third case of drug poisoning that has developed in the city tonight," he said, "There have been seven other deaths, besides those you know of, Dick! In each case Wister's products have been responsible!"

"Good Lord!" Wentworth whispered. "Eleven human beings killed in a single night by the poison alone! What madman can be behind this? What can he hope to gain?"

The fury that had always shaken him at the wanton slaughter of the innocent took cold possession of his soul. He had hoped that he had discovered this new conspiracy of murder at its first stages; that he could check its spread at once. The *Spider* was already too late for that, but there must be no further delay. He must run down at once the few leads he possessed.

District Attorney Toley was speaking excitedly. "I'll admit we should interview Wister," he said sharply, his face pale, "but we can't get a man of his importance out of bed at this time of night—especially since he can't have anything active to do with it. My God, what a case! When this gets to court—"

Wentworth felt contempt for Toley stir within him. In the midst of such encroaching horror, Toley could think only about his own reputation as a prosecutor; about disturbing Wister! Wentworth did not protest. It accorded with his plans that Wister should not be disturbed—by the police. It would give the *Spider* time to pay a call!

"It would be too bad to disturb Wister," he said dryly, "but may I suggest that, as a preventive measure, you should prohibit any further shipment of drugs from his concern until they can be inspected for poison?"

Kirkpatrick swung toward Wentworth. "That, certainly, will be done. I'll have men there before the plant opens in the morning. About the druggist... I've already sent men to his home. Nothing more will be allowed to go out of that store or any other to which poison has been traced. Every store in the city must make a checkup at once. By the way, Dick, I should have mentioned this before. Was Jackson doing any work for you? He was knocked out by the blast at that drugstore, and has been sent to Medical Center. A slight concussion is all, I believe."

THE buzz of the telephone cut in on his words and Jenkyns appeared in the doorway, rigid with resentment of the police intrusion; his head with its silvery cap of hair carried high. "For Mr. Kirkpatrick, sir," he reported.

Wentworth signed to him to bring in a portable phone while his thoughts raced with the implication of Jackson's injury. He must phone the hospital. He had hoped that Jackson was with Nita, protecting her! He must get rid of these men, and hurry into battle. His head jerked toward Kirkpatrick, who was handing back the phone to Jenkyns.

"The druggist hasn't reached home yet," he said. "You understood that Nita had left with him?"

Wentworth felt apprehension tauten the leaders of his throat, squeeze his heart like a cold hand. God! What had happened to Nita? Those killers of the Skull had thrown a bomb which obviously was intended to kill the owner of the store. Had they... had they renewed their attack? Had they seized Nita or... or worse? Jerkily, he voiced his apprehensions and Kirkpatrick echoed them, put out an immediate general alarm for both Nita and the druggist.

"There's no more that can be done now," he said. "I'll let you know as soon as I hear anything."

Wentworth thanked him heavily. His hands were working into knotted fists at his side, remembering the sweetness of Nita's laughter in the Spring dusk. "No alarm is going to ring in *your* district tonight," she had said. No alarm!

"If you'll excuse me," he said thickly, "I think—"

Toley seemed on fire to get away and Kirkpatrick crossed to put his hand warmly on Wentworth's shoulder. "Don't worry, old man," he said. "Nita was probably afraid some attack would be made on the druggist and is taking him to a place of safety. We'll hear from her soon."

Wentworth nodded, with an attempt at casualness. "Of course," he agreed quietly, but apprehension gnawed at his heart. What more could he do than the police were already attempting? A city-wide alarm with thousands of men on the lookout. No, the *Spider* could add little to that, even if his stern sense of duty would permit him to turn aside from the trail of the Skull. He could only hope that he could find the man responsible for these massacres—in time. In time? With eleven already dead? Wentworth strangled a sharp, sardonic laughter. It was already too late, much too late.

Forbes was leaving, too, but Beck would remain in accordance with Wentworth's orders. Wentworth moved blindly toward the terrace, found Melissa there and told her swiftly of his fears for Nita.

"I must leave the house shortly in an attempt to find her," he said. "I'll leave Jenkyns here and this man, Beck, on guard. I'm not sure that Beck is reliable. Find out for me, Melissa."

The girl's dainty face turned up to his and there was no coquetry at all in her gaze. "I'll do my best, Richard," she said.

A faint smile touched Wentworth's lips. "I fancy that will be adequate," he said. "I haven't thanked you for calling Kirkpatrick, but you have my sincere admiration. It was neatly done."

Melissa lifted a shoulder, slightly, "Self-important men are always so easy," she murmured. "Goodnight, Richard." She ran toward the French doors, paused just outside. "Oh, Mr. Beck, Richard says that you're going to protect poor little me."

There was laughter in Beck's answer. "Melissa, I'm the one that needs protection, with you around."

WENTWORTH'S face was lifted tautly toward the tender sky. He whispered, *"Nita!"* A tremor ran through his body and his face was twisted, almost ugly, with a relaxation of control that this grimly powerful man rarely allowed even when alone. It lasted only a moment, then his face was wiped bare of expression.

He swung about and paced with an easy deceptive swiftness toward another door that gave into his private suite. He did not stop there but went into the music room which adjoined his sleeping chamber and strode toward a pipe organ that filled one end of the room.

Standing where he could reach the orifices of the treble pipes, he beat on them in a soft, irregular rhythm with his palms so that a ghost of melody came forth. Then he strode toward a nearby wall panel and, as he reached it, the panel slid aside and he stepped through into a compact dressing room. He jabbed a bell-button in the wall and threw himself down before a brightly illuminated makeup mirror. His hands went deftly, instantly, to work.

A pungent liquid from a bottle tautened the skin of his face until it stretched tightly over the bones and turned sallow. A few deft touches wiped out his lips and changed his mouth into a straight gash; his nose, altered with putty, became a predatory beak. He was putting the finishing touches on that part of his disguise when a door opposite the one by which he had entered slid open. Ram Singh stepped through. He salaamed even lower than usual, and there was apprehension in his devoted gaze.

"Wah, Sahib," he said, his deep voice subdued to a murmur. "It was filthy work, but it had to be done. I found upon the rat's chest a duplicate of your own seal, master! I knew then that someone plotted against thee; that it was meant for this dead thing to be found. I... did what was necessary to keep him from being identified."

Wentworth was adjusting heavy false brows over his own, patting them exactly into place with touches of his lean, competent fingers. The Sikh flung himself to his knees and ripped his knife from its sheath, set its point against his breast.

"If I have done wrong, master," he cried, "thy servant knows how to die!"

Wentworth turned slowly from the mirror and there was gentleness in his eyes that few men had ever seen there. He said, quietly, "Thou are my child and my brother, oh warrior of the Sikhs. Who shall question what one friend does for another?" He reached out his hand and touched the hilt of the great-bladed knife. "Thy arms are without stain, thou Singh."

Ram Singh bounded to his feet and pride flashed in his eyes again. "My master has made me whole again," he said simply. "I put dynamite in the head, and that and the rest I blew to bits in the river. It was a demolition charge, *sahib."* His eyes squinted in disgust. *"Wah!* What a job for a warrior!"

Wentworth smiled faintly as he turned back to the mirror, and the things he had done to his face made that smile a menacing thing. He could not censure the Sikh, but he had made a promise that if the *Spider* were responsible—the *Spider* should pay! Grimly, he drew a lank black wig over his head and, from the mirror there stared back at him... the ominous face of the *Spider!*

"We shall want the Daimler, Ram Singh," Wentworth said quietly. "We go secretly, if possible. To Bayside."

Moments later, a long black cape draped over artificially hunched shoulders, a wide-brimmed hat concealing half his face, Wentworth sped downward by a secret stairway and found Ram Singh waiting in a cross-tunnel buried deep beneath the basement. Through it, they moved without words for a considerable distance before they entered a narrow elevator that lofted them rapidly into a private garage. The doors opened at the wink of the headlights and the heavy, sleek car of the *Spider* rolled out into the street and whirled swiftly northward.

THE illuminated dial of Wentworth's watch showed three o'clock, but the slums which jostled against wealthy Sutton Place were strangely alive. Windows showed the glow of lights and once when traffic lights stopped him, Wentworth saw a group of men about a tenement doorway where an ambulance stood. They were close together, silent, and there was a tension, almost fright in the way they huddled there, waiting. Already, the poisonings were laying their weight of terror upon the people.

While Wentworth's car stood motionless, waiting through the slow seconds for the light to change, he caught the hoarse wail of another ambulance siren. Death. Dead and dying everywhere. In the name of Heaven, what could be the motive behind the wanton slaughter of these innocents?

For a moment, Wentworth hesitated, but what could he accomplish here? Once the poison had been administered, only doctors and the hospitals could help. His was a grimmer task—to find the men behind this horror and wipe them out. The gleam in the *Spider*'s eyes was cold as death itself.

Wentworth's mind flashed back to the youthful Donald Beck and his indignation against the *Spider*—"a cold-blooded killer." Perhaps... but what was the Skull? How else could such criminals be answered than with the weapons they, themselves, elected to use? No one suffered more than Wentworth himself from the course he was forced to follow. He had his own moments of bleak questioning and self-doubt.

A wail that Wentworth at first mistook for the distant shriek of a thinner siren jerked at his consciousness and Wentworth stared fixedly at the dark streets through which the car whirled so effortlessly. That wail had a curiously human tone, and— Abruptly, Wentworth rapped on the glass behind Ram Singh, and the Daimler snubbed to a halt. At the same moment, Wentworth flung himself to the street. He had found the origin of that haunting sound. A woman ran along the street, desperately crying for help, staggering with a child heavy and inert in her arms.

"This way," Wentworth called sharply. "This way, I'll get you to the hospital."

The woman swerved toward him, stretching out the child toward him. "Oh, help me," she cried. "My baby! My little baby—" Her face was twisted with the strain of inward pain, of her violent exertion, and her eyes were frantic. Pale hair streaked back from her temples. She wore only a threadbare coat over a nightgown and her feet were bare, were bleeding. "Oh, help my baby!"

Wentworth caught the child from her arms and flung himself into the tonneau after the woman. "The hospital, quickly," he snapped. He jerked up a kickseat and laid the child across it, bent swiftly to feel the pulse, flicked back an eyelid; whipped open a compartment from which he drew a first aid kit.

The Daimler was surging across town now, racing for a hospital. Ram Singh's deep voice came back to Wentworth's ears. The Sikh was speaking in Punjabi. "Master, hast thou forgotten? Thou wearest the garb of the *Spider!"*

Wentworth's lips grew thin against his teeth as he worked over the child. Adrenalin for that laboring heart; an antidote for the swift poison which he believed he had identified. No, he had not forgotten that he wore the disguise of the *Spider;* nor that he might be identified as Richard Wentworth through this car. He had not forgotten, but if he could save this one life—

Beside him, the woman's voice ran on endlessly, "Oh, I don't understand," she was whispering. "Mary wasn't very sick—not terribly ill. Just a heavy cold, and the doctor said she'd be all right in a few days. He gave me some medicine. But now—"

WENTWORTH swore under his breath. So the pollution of poison had reached even into the offices of doctors! It was damnable fiendish—this sly death that sneaked into the homes of the sick. Where could they turn, these ailing and stricken ones, if the very healing potions turned to murder in their bodies? This child's pale, blue-tinged face, the dark smudges of shadow beneath the closed eyes, burned its way into his brain. Donald Beck should have been with him now.

A quiver ran over the child's frail body, and a faint stirring. The eyes fluttered open and Wentworth caught the breath of a sound from the pale lips. "Mother..." A great relief surged over Wentworth and he realized how tautly he had bent over the child. He smiled and turned toward the mother.

"I think your baby will be all right now," he said quietly. "Only, there must be no more strain on that heart. Absolute quiet. Tell them at the hospital that I gave her—" He detailed the treatment while the woman bent over the child, and drew it into her lap. There was the wet glisten of tears on her cheeks when she looked up.

"You saved my baby," she whispered. "You—" Her eyes widened suddenly, and she shrank back in the corner of the cushions, and Wentworth realized that he had been smiling and, in the *Spider* disguise, that made his face an awful thing.

He said, gently, "You have nothing to fear from me."

An uncertain smile touched the woman's lips. "No, of course not. You... you saved my baby. You... that black cape, your face. I know you now. You are the *Spider.* You are a great man!" The car slid to a quiet halt at the emergency entrance of the hospital.

"I won't go in," Wentworth told the woman. "Just tell them what I did and they'll take care of your baby." He swung open the door, stepped to the ground to help her down.

The woman's hand clutched his. "You saved my baby, Mr. *Spider,"* she said. "I—"

Before Wentworth guessed her intention, the woman had bowed her head and pressed a kiss upon the back of his hand. He felt the wetness of her falling tears, then she was running toward the hospital door. He stood there, motionless, staring after her, and his fingers touched wonderingly the spot where she had kissed. There was a straining lightness in his own throat... and the light of the opening door reached out into the darkness and fell across him. There was a nurse there and behind her the blue of a policeman's uniform.

For the moment, Wentworth forgot his dress, forgot that the light that flung out through the doorway was brilliant and struck across him like a spotlight. He forgot it until he heard the policeman's cry, and saw him spring forward with a hand fumbling for his gun.

"The *Spider!"* the policeman shouted. "The *Spider!* Halt, or I'll fire!"

With a wrench, Wentworth flung himself into the car and at the same moment Ram Singh hurled it forward into the darkness. Behind them, the policeman's gun poked fiery holes into the night. Once, a bullet clanged off the armored body of the Daimler, then it was gone.

Wentworth settled back against the cushion—with a slow breath of released tension. There might be pursuit, but the *Spider* would not turn aside from his mission of vengeance, of death perhaps. His fingers touched once more the spot that a mother's lips had pressed in gratitude.

CHAPTER FIVE
The Fleshless Ones

IT WAS almost four o'clock when the Daimler, with throttled motor, rolled through the dark and deserted streets of Bayside and approached the waterside estate of Samuel Wister, head of the Eastern Drug Corporation—whose medicaments had spread poison death through the city this night. In spite of the lateness of the hour, lights shone in the huge brick pile of Wister's home—one on the second floor and others in a low wing that stretched out toward the water.

So much Wentworth discovered before he and Ram Singh parked the Daimler in the shrubbery-choked driveway of a nearby untenanted house. It was a wild-seeming section to be found within the limits of New York City. Wister's home itself was shielded from the road both by a high thick wall and by close-planted shrubbery which had grown to the proportion of trees. It was possible to catch only glimpses of the house itself, set well back toward the water.

Through the cover of those trees, their shadows emphasized by the cold, lone moon that floated overhead, the black-caped figure of the *Spider* flitted as silently as the creature whose name he bore. His goal was that low wing where he expected to find Wister's home laboratory, but first he made a slow circuit of the grounds.

Hard to believe that Wister could be the criminal, less because of any knowledge that Wentworth had of the man himself than because it would seem madness to distribute the poison through his own concern. Nevertheless, the man might know something. There had to be a *reason* for this slaughter... reasons which Toley or Kirkpatrick might not be able to extract. Usually, men told the truth to the *Spider.* Wentworth's disguised lips cracked in a mirthless smile. The reputation he carried had its advantages, too.

Wentworth completed his circuit of the grounds and, with quiet swiftness, headed for the lighted wing of the Wister home. He was within a hundred feet of it when a sound among the trees ahead froze him into a motionless shadow. He drew the black cape up before his face to hide the loom of its whiteness and his eyes, fully accustomed to the darkness, gradually made out the silhouette of a man who leaned against a tree bole not twenty feet ahead. Even as Wentworth spotted him, the man began to creep toward the house!

After a moment's hesitation, Wentworth followed. The man's every movement suggested the criminal, but had he come to attack—or to consult with Wister? Plainly, robbery was not his purpose, for he went straight toward the lighted portion of the building! Wentworth's hand slid beneath his cape to loosen a heavy automatic in its holster.

Minutes dragged past before Wentworth saw that the man was crouched just beneath a window from which light streamed. If he intended murder… but there was no glint of a weapon in his hand. Tensely, the *Spider* watched the man dart aside from the window toward a door that opened into the laboratory wing.

When the man touched that door, Wentworth was not ten feet away, crouched in a clump of spirea whose white flowers were just budding into fragrance. The sweetness of their scent made the whole thing painfully unreal. Furtive shadows moving in the night—perhaps the even grimmer shadow of Death nearby—and in the city he had left men and children dying; but here, the moon poured down its silver and the bridal wreath was fragrant. Wentworth saw that the door was swinging open softly.

WHEN the slow space of a minute had gone, Wentworth followed through that doorway and paused just inside. Even his keen eyes could see nothing in the black hallway, but he caught faint music from a radio and then the slightest creak of a floorboard. He held his breath and presently there was another creak—farther away. Once more, he slipped forward, then flattened against a wall as light blazed through an open door.

"Howdy, boss," a man's voice was drawling, thin with mockery. "So you thought I wouldn't find you, did you? Thought you were too smart, and—"

The closing door pinched off the words utterly and Wentworth realized that the room into which the man had passed must be soundproofed. A half dozen long strides took him to the door, but the voices beyond were only a murmur above the muted sound of the radio.

A fierce, cold gleam was in the *Spider*'s eyes. Those few words sounded suspiciously like this were some underling from whom Wister had attempted to hide. There was not necessarily a criminal implication there; not necessarily. His hand closed on the doorknob and he pressed lightly on the portal. Wister's voice came through sharply.

"If you don't get out of here in precisely ten seconds," Wister said coldly, "I'll shoot. There's a gun in my pocket and I can shoot accurately even through the cloth."

"Aw, now, boss," the man was wheedling, "you don't want to get tough with me. *Damn you, I'll—*"

There was the double, muffled beat of gunfire and Wentworth flung wide the door, went half across the room in a bound. The man he had followed was huddled inertly against the wall where bullets had flung him and above the body bent a heavy-shouldered, dynamic man with a gun knotted in his fist. With a quick twist, Wentworth took the gun and sent Wister staggering across the room. He brought up against a high workbench.

"Just take it easy," Wentworth ordered softly, "and it may be that nothing will happen to you. It may be—"

Wister's face was solid-boned above a heavy jaw and his eyes, pale in a darkly tanned face, were narrowed with anger. "You'd have done better to attack together," he said harshly. *"He's* gone to his Maker at any rate."

Wentworth needed no examination of the fallen man to confirm what Wister had said. To a man who has witnessed death many times, there is something unmistakable in the flaccid inertia of a corpse. He smiled bleakly, and his gaze was cold, inflexible. Though he made no movement toward Wister, his voice was flat with menace.

"You may justify this killing," he said, "though the reason the man came here wants some explanation. Wister, in Manhattan tonight, a score of people died from your company's poisoned medicines. *Why,* Wister?"

Wister dragged a heavy hand across his face, dropped into a swivel chair. "God knows," he said dully. "It's ghastly. I've ordered the plant closed pending a check on all supplies." He sat with slumped shoulders; his big, squarish head with its rumpled dark hair was sagging. "You're this man who calls himself the *Spider,* aren't you?"

Wentworth made no answer. Keeping his eyes on Wister warily, he crouched beside the dead man and presently his groping hands found the thing he had expected. He tossed into Wister's lap a tiny wooden skeleton with grotesquely jiggling arms and legs... the talisman of the Skull!

"A criminal is killing those people for some greedy purpose, Wister," he said sharply. "This man is his hireling, as the talisman proves. And Wister... *this man called you 'boss'.*"

Wister's head snapped up. "Why, damn you! You're implying that I... that I poisoned those poor people!" He lurched to his feet.

Wentworth stood quietly facing him. There was no weapon in his hand. "I'm still asking," he said softly. "If I were sure, Wister, you would not still be answering questions. You would be dead with a small red spider on your forehead!"

Wister's dark face paled a little, but his angry eyes did not falter. For seconds, he held that stiff pose then, as if that brief concentration had tired him unutterably, he sagged back into the chair. "I'm long past the age when bogeymen or masqueraders frighten me," he said thickly. *"You* can do what *you* damned please. I'm making no explanations to you." He covered his face with his hands.

A knife-frown dented Wentworth's forehead. There was something peculiar here, but certainly Wister's conduct was not that of a guilty man. Wister knew that, proved guilty, he faced swift retribution at the hands of the *Spider,* yet he had shown small evidences of fright.

A flash of bright light across the window jerked Wentworth's head that way and a startled oath leaped to his lips. He knew that long black limousine gliding to a halt at the main entrance of the mansion. It was Commissioner Kirkpatrick's car! Wentworth backed toward the door.

"I leave you to the police," he said curtly. "I'd advise you to be more precise in your explanations with them."

Wister's head snapped up. "The police must not come here," he cried. "They must not. I'll see them in the morning, at my office, but they can't come here—"

Wentworth had his hand on the door and once more the puzzled light crept into his clear eyes. Wister, who did not fear the deadly vengeance of the *Spider,* was terrified at the approach of the police! It didn't make sense. No time to think of that now. Wister was suddenly snatching at a drawer of his bench. It was laboriously slow, and Wentworth could have whipped out an automatic and fired with deadly accuracy long before the drawer was even opened. But the *Spider* did not harm innocent men...and until he knew definitely otherwise, Wister must fall in that category.

Wentworth laughed flatly, mockingly, and whipped open the door. As he ducked through, his hand flicked to a leather toolkit he wore in a girdle about his waist. When he slammed the door shut, it was upon a steel wedge with reticulated teeth on its sloping surfaces. Nothing less than a hydraulic jack would open the door now! The blast of Wister's gun came faintly to his ears through the heavy portal, and a splinter of light stabbed out through the bullethole in the door.

An instant later, the *Spider* slipped out into the moonlit yard. He could see Kirkpatrick's tall figure crossing toward the entrance of the house, following by the bobbing shorter silhouette of District Attorney Toley. Wentworth ducked into the protecting shrubbery and flung himself into a silent sprint toward the nearby driveway where his car was parked. But he was not fleeing; nor was he through yet with Samuel Wister!

When he dropped over the high, thick-built stone wall, the *Spider* fairly threw himself into the car.

"Get away fast, but silently, Ram Singh," he cried softly to the Sikh. "Allow me ten minutes, then drive into Wister's place—the front door this time, Ram Singh!"

WHEN precisely ten minutes later, the Daimler drew to a halt behind the police car, an entirely different figure from the hunched, becaped *Spider* ran lightly up the main steps of Wister's home. Richard Wentworth was now impeccably dressed in dark tweeds, a light topcoat and soft felt—and his face showed no trace, other than a slight redness, of the recent makeup.

It was a perilous thing he did, in thus again so soon confronting Wister. There might be some trick of voice, some unconscious resemblance that would betray him to the man as the same ominous figure that had recently confronted him in the laboratory. It was a thing Wentworth must risk. The mystery which surrounded Wister would have to be pierced at once. Kirkpatrick's driver was crouched before the dashboard of the car, tinkering with the two-way radio. Damnation! Disablement of the set could be serious at a time like this!

Wentworth punched the bell and, within a few moments, a butler with a heavy, sleep-mottled face opened the door. Wentworth heard Kirkpatrick's crisp tones and Wister's blustering answers.

"What name, sir?" the butler asked heavily. "Pardon me, sir, is there any word of Miss Nona?"

Wentworth's keen eyes searched the butler's face, "I know of none," he said softly. "Has there been any further message?"

The butler shook his head gravely, took Wentworth's card. "God help Miss Nona, then—begging your pardon, sir."

Wentworth's eyes were half-cloaked in speculation. Those few words with the butler had given him the due to Wister's hostility toward the police, and his terror at their arrival. He strolled into the drawing room, smiling at Toley's angry glare; nodding to Kirkpatrick's quizzical regard. His eyes went past them to Wister's angry, puzzled face.

"I must apologize for this intrusion, Mr. Wister," he said formally. "We belong to some of the same clubs, I believe. Unfortunately, we haven't met."

Toley took two choppy strides toward him,

"Confound your interfering impertinence," he rasped. "You will leave at once."

Wentworth's eyes were resting on a portrait of a lovely dark-haired girl which hung above the fireplace. "Is that Nona, Wister?" he asked quietly, ignoring Toley. "May I suggest, Wister, that you are being foolish to forego the help of the police at a time like this? Especially since they are already here and, hence, the damage is done."

Wister's pale eyes strained wide. Kirkpatrick's gaze was keen as it flashed from the portrait to

He sent Wister backward across the room until he crashed against a workbench.

Wister and back to Wentworth. Toley was merely bewildered. He continued to rant.

"I suppose you don't know, Wentworth, that the *Spider* has already called on Mr. Wister!" he snapped.

Wentworth started, made his face angry. "Ahead of me again, is he? Confound the fellow... but that will have to wait. Will you tell them, Wister, or shall I?"

WISTER lifted his heavy shoulders, "I suppose this was inevitable. I don't know how you found out, but it's true! My ward, Nona Malvern, was kidnapped two days ago! I was afraid to communicate with you, Commissioner, because of the threats that were made. They were asking two hundred thousand dollars ransom and they were supposed to communicate tonight. I... haven't heard yet. That man I killed... at first, I thought he came from them, but apparently not. He was a former employee I had to fire for petty thievery. He had made threats against my life, and then—"

From the door, the butler spoke excitedly, "It's come, sir," he cried. "That man is on the phone, and—" Wister bolted into a library that opened off the drawing room, snatched up a telephone. In two strides, Wentworth reached the butler. "The other phone!" he rasped. "Where is it?"

The butler pointed toward a service door in the rear of the hall and Wentworth bounded to it, caught up the instrument.

"I'll pay!" Wister was crying. "I had nothing to do with the police coming here! It's because of the poisonings, I tell you, and—"

A rasping voice cut him short, "That's too bad, Wister. Too damned bad! We warned you. I'm warning you once more. Keep your mouth shut. *You still have a wife, Wister!"*

Wister was still shouting incoherently when the wire went dead. At the click of final disconnection, Wentworth rapidly signaled the operator to have the call traced. Not that he had much hope of success. Criminals knew too much about such matters nowadays; for instance that a call from a dial instrument could not be traced once the connection was broken.

He turned away to find Kirkpatrick beside him. Rapidly, he related what he had heard.

Kirkpatrick nodded. "Do you think there's any tie-up between this and the poisonings? I'll admit I can't see it, and Wister will close up tighter than a clam, now. Wait, Dick... before we go back into the drawing room. I have some bad news for you."

Wentworth felt his heart tighten. *"Nita!"* he breathed. "For God's sake, Kirk, out with it. Is she—"

"She's alive, and unhurt, Dick, but…that druggist was found dead of poisoning in her apartment. He was phoning when he was stricken and the operator called the police. Toley insisted that we arrest Nita. The charge is... *murder!"*

For a moment, Wentworth stared incredulously at Kirkpatrick, but the relief at news of Nita's safety was so great that laughter curved his mouth corners.

"That's ridiculous," he said quietly. "Toley can't hold Nita on any such trumped-up business as that. That druggist either committed suicide, or some poison took delayed effect on him in Nita's apartment—some more machinations of the man who is behind all these poisonings."

"I'm inclined to agree with you, Dick," Kirkpatrick nodded soberly. "How did you get wind of this kidnapping?"

Wentworth, frowning, had to drive his mind back to the immediate problem. Absently, he told of the butler's question.

"It was a guess," he acknowledged, "but Wister was scarcely in a position to be so belligerent toward the police—with all those poisonings stemming from his plant—and there was the added fact that he was awake and dressed. Obviously waiting for something. Your driver told me that you had just arrived."

"I hope that will satisfy Toley," Kirkpatrick nodded crisply.

Wentworth was a passive listener while Toley hurled questions at the obviously distracted Wister, There was little else to be learned except the details of the kidnapping: Nona Malvern had been seized from her own roadster just after a brief sail on the bay. The telephoned ransom message had been received before Wister knew that Nona had been taken.

Wister did not accompany them to the door as they left and, on the veranda, Wentworth accosted Toley.

"I'm warning you, Toley," he said, with quiet force. "Either dismiss your ridiculous charges against Miss van Sloan at once, or you'll face a damage suit that will drive you out of office! You understand me, I think."

Toley's laughter was sharp as a terrier's bark. "You may get away with murder where the police are concerned," he said, raspingly, "but you can't intimidate my office! Your lawless behavior and that of your woman—"

Wentworth took a single stride forward and there was a blaze in his eyes that sent Toley stumbling backward, pawing awkwardly at his pocket for a gun.

"You will apologize, Toley," Wentworth said, his voice dead level.

Toley had the gun out and his voice lifted shrilly. "You take one more step forward and I'll by God shoot you down!"

"Then I'll see you burn for murder!" Kirkpatrick cut in, sternly. "Put that gun away! You're behaving like a cowardly fool!"

For a moment, Toley struggled with a fury that made his eyes pop with the effort at restraint. Finally, he fumbled the gun into his pocket. "All right," he muttered, "I apologize, Wentworth, for the terms I used. But the fact remains that this lawlessness must end! I'll hold Miss van Sloan until she can prove to me—"

WENTWORTH swung away toward his waiting car. Ram Singh stood, rigid as a soldier, to swing open the door and Wentworth flung himself back against the cushions. There was an icy glitter in his blue-grey eyes, and his lips were thin with pressure. He must be careful not to let anger mislead him, but it seemed clear that Toley was motivated by some personal animosity. Did that spring from mere resentment—or was there some other, guilty reason?

Ram Singh was behind the wheel, but Kirkpatrick's car still blocked the way. Impatience goaded Wentworth. He fought to clear his mind of emotional disturbance. Nita, at least, was safe; when he reached the city, he would set his lawyers to work to free her. Nothing more could be done immediately. He tried to concentrate on Wister. The man's strange conduct was explained now; the police would set to work on the kidnapping. Wentworth's own course was plain—the pursuit of the Skull. Perhaps Nita had learned something from the druggist.

Kirkpatrick's car rolled smoothly up the drive and the Daimler followed a moment later. Abruptly, Wentworth jerked forward in the seat. Something like a white mist was rolling up through the moon-shadowed woods ahead; reaching out toward the cars in an ominous cloud!

"Stop! Sound the horn!" Wentworth snapped at Ram Singh. It might be no more than a light fog swept in from the bay, but it was strange that it should spring up now, just before dawn, and curious things had happened this night! Even as Wentworth shouted, as he tugged at the automatic nested beneath his arm, he saw the car ahead swerve violently... and then from the midst of that rolling cloud, machine guns split the night apart!

Wentworth felt more than heard the shock of bullets against the armor of his car. Men's hoarse cries filled the night, but more startling, even than the attack, were the things he half-glimpsed amid that roiling mist. There were figures that gleamed with a greenish sheen like radium, but they were not the figures of living creatures. The things that Wentworth saw behind the yammering machine guns were... *the glowing, fleshless skeletons of men!*

CHAPTER SIX
The Skull Speaks

AFTER that first shock of vision, Wentworth did not, of course, believe that there were skeletons firing those deadly guns. But, God knows, there was nothing in what he saw to contradict that fact! When the fogs, which he now recognized as a chemical smoke screen, broke for an instant, he could glimpse those figures whose bones seemed to glow with radium.

"Forward!" he shouted to Ram Singh. "Kirkpatrick's car isn't heavily armored! Cut in front of it! *Hurry!"*

With a snort of power, the Daimler surged forward. Under the skilful guidance of the Sikh, it swerved into the shrubbery and crashed through to slew broadside across the driveway ahead of Kirkpatrick's machine. Revolvers were spitting their meager flame from the police car. Wentworth flung himself to the loopholes in his own bulletproof windows and Ram Singh's gun beat out a contrapuntal accompaniment to his own careful shots.

Gun flame—

Again and again, Wentworth fired at the evanescent figures. His mind was racing with conjecture. Those figures might easily be living men under a grotesque garb, or they might be decoys to turn bullets aside from the real gunners! At the thought, the *Spider* ceased to throw his lead at those grim outlines, but hunted out the flash of guns as they flickered dimly through the curtain of fog. A yell of pain answered his second shot and, above the smashing of guns, he shouted his discovery.

"The skeletons are decoys!" he cried. "Aim at the gun flashes!"

Even as he spoke, the ambuscade was ended. The enemy guns ceased to flame and there were, suddenly, no more of the mocking silhouettes of fleshless men. For an instant, the aching silence held and then Wentworth saw a fearful thing rushing toward the car from the darkness! It floated smoothly through the air at the height of a man from the ground. A man's head twice normal size—a green-glowing skull in which fiery eyes blazed, to which bone-tight skin still adhered... *and that was all!* A bodiless skull that glided toward him!

"The Skull," Wentworth whispered to himself, even while he laid his careful aim upon the apparition. *"The Skull—"*

His gun crashed and there, in the forehead of that ghastly glaring thing, a black bullethole appeared! Still the head floated on! The gruesome jaws worked and there echoed across the scene a rasping and mocking laughter!

"Shoot, fools!" the Skull cried. "Shoot and learn

how futile are bullets against the Skull! You are doomed. Your city is doomed! *Flee while there yet is time!"*

Wentworth's bullets were tearing through and through that fearsome skull, pocking it with lead-ripped holes. Once more the jarring laughter sounded and then... *the Skull vanished!* It was as abrupt as that. One instant, the ominous head was gliding toward him through the night and the next instant, it was gone! There was nothing at all there in the blackness of the overgrown woods except the last remnants of the smoke screen vanishing among the trees.

In an instant, Wentworth flung from the protection of his car and, with freshly loaded guns, charged into the darkness.

"Lights, Ram Singh!" he shouted as he ran. "Throw lights here!"

An instant later, the auxiliary spotlight of the Daimler splashed across the underbrush. It danced over the black boles of trees, gleamed on the last remnants of the chemical mist—and found nothing else. The woods were empty, deserted. They might have been firing at so many ghosts

Wentworth swore under his breath as he raced for the gates that gave onto the street; plunged out into the roadway with his guns ready in his fist. Nothing here; absolutely nothing.

Lights were springing up in the houses scattered among their wide-spread grounds. He could hear a man calling excitedly from Wister's house. Cautiously, Wentworth spilled light from a small pocket-flash on the gravel of the street, but he could find no trace of a fugitive gunman. He whirled and ran back toward his car. In the dazzle of the spotlight, he could now see the jagged, white tears that bullets had ripped in the bark of trees, but there was not even a remnant of one of those glowing skeletons, or of the talking Skull. The whole thing was mad as a nightmare; ridiculous... and strangely terrifying.

WENTWORTH darted toward Kirkpatrick's car, heard the commissioner's voice snapping orders over the two-way radio of the machine. He whipped open the door. "No trace of their car," Wentworth said, "but the surface of the street is pretty hard. That Skull trick delayed us while they were all getting away."

Kirkpatrick's face was taut with anger. There was blood on his temple and the side windows of the car were in fragments; the bulletproof windshield frosted over. The driver was a motionless huddle.

"They got Morgan, damn them," Kirkpatrick said hoarsely. "Toley took one through the left wrist. Thanks for pushing your car in ahead of us, Dick. Otherwise—" He closed his lips rigidly, as the radio signal of the police announcer hummed in the receiver.

"Calling Car O-one-thirteen," the man said rapidly. "Come in!"

That was the call for Kirkpatrick's car and Kirkpatrick answered steadily, "Car O-one-thirteen reporting. Now in Bayside. Come in."

The announcer's voice was vibrant with excitement. "Been trying to raise you since three o'clock, O-one-thirteen. Your radio must have been out of commission. The *Spider* with a gang of other men attacked the officers arresting Van Sloan at Thirty-Third and Park. Three officers were killed and two wounded. Van Sloan was carried off. Routine pursuit. Any special orders? Come in, O-one-thirteen."

Wentworth's hand trembled visibly on the door. It was not the mention of the *Spider,* though he realized with a quick clarity that at the hour mentioned, he had indeed been in the *Spider*'s garb. He had no alibi. But Nita... he knew without the slightest question that it was the Skull who had done this, not only kidnapping Nita but striking a shrewd blow at the *Spider*'s reputation. Nita... in the power of the Skull!

He said hoarsely, "Back to New York, Kirk. If that fiend has harmed Nita—" He swung away from the car.

"Just a minute, Dick," Kirkpatrick said sharply, then spoke into the radio. "General alarm for Nita van Sloan and the *Spider.* Remember, the *Spider* is armed and dangerous. Take no chances. Announce to the papers under my name that the *Spider* apparently has stepped over the line at last and thrown in with criminals... with the criminals who are spreading poison through the city! It is war to the finish! That is all!"

His eyes burned into Wentworth's. "I have been afraid for a long time that the *Spider* would step over the line someday," he said steadily. "I believe I have said as much to you, Dick. A man cannot make himself prosecutor, judge and executioner. He cannot take the law into his own hands time and again without someday beginning to feel that he is above the law. But no man is, Dick. Not even the *Spider!* And when he kills some of my own men—"

Toley's voice was strained with pain as he clutched his wounded wrist. "Why talk in riddles, Kirkpatrick?" he said thickly. "It's plain, isn't it? Why should the *Spider* kidnap Nita van Sloan, unless the *Spider* is also—*Richard Wentworth!* Where were you at three o'clock, Wentworth?"

Wentworth could see the inflexible purpose in Kirkpatrick's set and blood-stained face. He himself was shaken with fear for Nita with the nightmare horror of the recent ambuscade. He ignored Toley.

"Wait now, Kirk," he said. "Wait a minute." He

drew in a deep breath, fought for clarity of thought. "I didn't even know Nita had been arrested until you told me there in Wister's place. You must know that. In God's name, why should I—assuming that I was the *Spider*—have to murder policemen to get Nita free from a ridiculous charge which even you did not believe? Is this the first time that a criminal has masqueraded in the *Spider*'s costume? Is the *Spider* the only one who would have reason to kidnap Nita? What about these devils that jumped us here tonight—the Skull!"

Kirkpatrick's face did not change, 'Where were you at three o'clock, Dick?" he demanded.

Wentworth shrugged, "I left home a few minutes before three o'clock to come out here. On the way, I ran into some poisoning cases; a woman with a child. I took her to the hospital." Wentworth cut off his words abruptly. In his excitement, he had committed a fatal blunder. It was true that he had rescued the woman's child—but he had worn the garb of the *Spider!*

Kirkpatrick relaxed a bit. "That should be easy to verify," he said. "What hospital? Did you get the woman's name?"

Wentworth feigned an outburst of temper. "No, and I didn't take her fingerprints! Maybe she was the *Spider!* Listen, I'm going back to New York. While we stand here talking, Nita... God knows what is happening to her! If you want me, send your men to arrest me!"

He stormed back to his car, ignored the sharp accents of Kirkpatrick's voice calling to him. He was frantic with the need for haste, and he would not be arrested now... not if it meant fighting his way clear! He flung himself into the car and his signal to Ram Singh sent the Daimler surging forward. It tore a wide half-circle through the shrubs, rocked back into the driveway and boomed through the gateway, into the street. The motor's note became deep and powerful.

AGAINST the cushions, Wentworth forced relaxation upon his taut-nerved body. It was possible that, over the repaired radio, Kirkpatrick had put out a call for his arrest, but Wentworth doubted it. That was an arrest Kirkpatrick would compel himself to make in person, if necessity ever arose. Toley would goad him with doubts.

Wentworth lifted slow hands and covered his face. There was no question as to the reason for Nita's kidnapping. The Skull wanted the leverage of a hostage against him... and that was a thing Wentworth could not permit. If he could not find and free Nita at once, the *Spider* could make only one answer to the Skull's ultimatum. The *Spider* would not, could not turn aside from the path of service—not even for Nita's sweet sake!

Wentworth pulled his hands down rigidly, took out his guns and methodically cleaned and checked them. There was utterly no expression in his face unless the rigid set of his jaw could be called that. He forced himself to consider his course of action.

If he could only arrive at the reason behind these senseless murders, he would know then where to hunt for the Skull. Aside from that, his only chance was to form direct contact with the killer himself. Nothing more could be learned from Wister, over whose home police guard was established now. Over seeming aeons of time, he recalled his temporary suspicions of Beck. That source of inquiry was still open, of course. But at best, his role must be a minor one, and remote from the Skull himself. Wentworth remembered that he had pledged himself to hunt down the *Spider*. He fell limply back against the seat and laughter that was close to hysteria pushed at his constrained throat.

Afterward, he was calmer. There was another trail, of course—the trail that the false *Spider* had left from the scene of his attack upon the police captors of Nita. He caught up the speaking-tube.

"Thirty-third and Park, Ram Singh," he ordered crisply.

From the Triborough Bridge, he turned his heavy eyes toward the skyline of Manhattan, its spires rising in graceful silhouette against the reddening dawn sky. There was majesty there that caught at the throat like grief... and deathly horror stalked its streets. How much horror Wentworth was to learn too soon.

It came while the Daimler was boring its way swiftly down Park Avenue toward Grand Central and the ramps that wove around it to bridge Forty-Second Street. Unconsciously, his eyes sought the clock between the twin arched entranceways of the ramps, and a choked curse burned on his lips. Something was dangling from that clock—something that glowed with a faint greenish light there in the dusk against the building!

Wentworth found himself straining forward tautly in his seat, his guns locked in white-knuckled fists. Swiftly, his eyes probed the entrances of the ramps, searched the street. It was deserted, and nowhere was there any hint of attack. Wentworth shot a single swift glance behind him and caught a glimpse of a car. That would be Kirkpatrick. His gaze swung back to that dangling something, and a tortured breath caught in his lungs. It was a human skeleton that swung from the clock—a human skeleton with a woman's dark, long hair blowing gently in the dawn breeze!

Wentworth beat his knotted fists upon his knees. When his voice came out, it was harsh, unrecognizable. "Stop by the clock, Ram Singh!"

He could see more now. He could see that,

though every shred of flesh had been stripped front the body of that skeleton, the head itself was intact... the face beneath that frame of dark, lovely hair was unharmed. God in Heaven, what cruelty! What fiendish madman had devised this thing! He still could not identify the face. It was too far away, too dark. *God, this thing could not be.*

From the driver's seat, the harsh outlandish curses of Ram Singh thudded against Wentworth's ears. He heard the melodious blast of Kirkpatrick's horn, then the brief muted wail of his siren. His senses recorded those things; his mind did not. All his being was centered on the desperate, shrinking endeavor to read that hidden face. Abruptly, a blade of light flicked out and touched the grisly thing. Ram Singh had brought the spotlight deliberately into play. For an instant, it glanced across the stark white bones and tossed a grotesque shadow, huge as death and as menacing, across the front of the building. Then it centered on the face.

A great cry tore from Wentworth's throat. There was a shaking that wrenched at his whole body, but he had been spared the ultimate horror. It was not Nita's body that dangled from the clock. It was that of a sweet-faced girl whose portrait Wentworth had seen no more than an hour before. The kidnappers had fulfilled their pledge and Nona Malvern, the ward of Samuel Wister, had died... *terribly!*

Wentworth flung from his car as it jerked to a halt and his wincing eyes turned upward to the poor thing on the clock. It would be horrible enough merely to find Nona Malvern dead there, but to see that stripped skeleton with the head grotesquely intact—Wentworth shuddered and turned away, staggering. It was when he turned that he saw the message that was scrawled in letters of scarlet across the face of the building:

Fools' skeletons and their faces
Will be found in public places
Unless they obey...

And appended to that crude jingle, doubly ghastly in its joking treatment of this horror, was the signature. The grinning, mocking portrait of a skull!

And Nita was in that fiend's power!

CHAPTER SEVEN
Death Marches On

IT WAS broad daylight when Richard Wentworth, drunk with fatigue and horror, made his way home at last. All trails had pinched out. There was nothing to indicate when, within hours, Nona Malvern's skeleton had been hung on the clock, nor any trace of the men who had done it. They had chosen their time well: before dawn, on a Spring Sunday and there had been almost no traffic; hence no witnesses. At the scene of Nita's kidnapping, there had been no evidence except that Wentworth had found Nita's handkerchief, and on it there were a number of red dots made with a lipstick in an eccentric pattern.

Wentworth studied the thing as Ram Singh rolled the car finally toward the house through the Sabbath-quiet of the streets, but his eyes were blurred and his mind seemed filled with lead. He tried to use the dots as the points of letters, and couldn't. They were just dots straggling irregularly across the linen:

```
•  •  •  •  •
•  •  •  •  •
•  •     •  •
   •        •
            •
```

By his private elevator, Wentworth ascended directly to his suite and there flung himself down for the two hours' sleep he had allowed himself. He could not afford the time—but he must rest. His acute mind, his lightning-swift reflexes, were slowed. In this condition, it would do him no good to track down the Skull; he would fall easy prey to

Jackson, Wentworth's ace chauffeur and aide-de-camp, served under Wentworth when the latter was the youngest major in the army . . . Just as willingly and frequently as Jackson had risked his life for the *Spider*, so has Ram Singh, full-blooded descendant of India's most famous fighting warriors!

the simplest trap. With the concentration that marked everything he attempted, Wentworth plunged himself into a blankness of spirit and mind that brought sleep almost instantly.

Promptly at the end of the time he had allowed himself, Wentworth woke of his own accord and snapped himself back to normal with a swift violent round of calisthenics and a plunge into the icy waters of his pool. When he emerged, his lithe, tanned body—marked by the scars that were the *Spider's* only medals for valor—was taut and alert again. His mind was racing. Before he could signal for Jenkyns, the old butler entered his room with a perfectly appointed breakfast table. Jenkyns' wrinkled, ruddy face was creased in a smile.

"Jackson is home from the hospital, sir," he reported, "and there is a gentleman waiting to see you. His card is beside your plate, Master Richard."

Wentworth nodded while he caught up the newspaper. "Miss Moulin?" he said. "Mr. Beck?"

"Waiting for word from you, sir," Jenkyns reported. "Mr. Beck refused to let Miss Moulin leave except on specific orders from you."

Wentworth's eyes were combing the front page, of the Sunday paper. Even the pontifical *Times* was hysterical with eight-column headlines. A hundred and three persons had been stricken with poisoned medicines overnight. Of those, eighty-five had died! Every drugstore in town had been ordered closed pending a close check on their stock. Three other wholesale distributors besides Wister's Eastern Drug Company were involved. Against that mounting toll of horror, the kidnapping of Nita and the murder of the three policemen seemed unimportant. The Wister kidnapping with its macabre, pitiful ending had come too late to receive adequate display.

Wentworth flung the paper from him and his eyes held a fierce fire as he forced himself to eat the breakfast Jenkyns had prepared. He must get back into the battle. There was a possible lead in the druggists whose stores had been the distribution points of poison. The murder of the man who had escaped with Nita the night before indicated that he might have told something… had he lived, and…Wentworth's eyes fell on the card beside his plate—the card of the man who was waiting to see him—and a startled oath rose to his lips. Then he smiled grimly.

"You may tell Mr. Samuel Wister." he said quietly, "that I'll be with him in five minutes, Jenkyns!"

IT WAS actually four minutes later that, fully dressed, his eyes as keen as though rested by a full night's sleep, Wentworth strode into the drawing room and bowed to the broad, dynamic figure which stood beside the open terrace doors.

"Sorry to have kept you waiting, Mr. Wister," he said pleasantly. "Believe me, you have my deepest sympathy."

Wister turned and there was a heaviness in all his movements. The shadows under his pale eyes were liverish, made his whole face haggard. "I come to you," he said, "because you have Kirkpatrick's ear; because I do not dare—after what has happened—to go to the police directly. There are things the police should know."

Wentworth nodded, his eyes keen on the man's face. At his invitation Wister sank into a chair, closed his eyes. "I blame myself for a great deal of what has happened," he said, without expression. "This man who calls himself the Skull phoned me a week ago and demanded that the Eastern Drug Company join a protective association with dues of ten thousand dollars a week! I thought he was a crank, and... ignored it."

Wentworth's face was impassive, but his mind leaped on ahead of Wister's speech. So that was the motive behind these poisonings, the old protection racket in a new and ghastly form! The Skull's methods were utterly inhuman—but Wentworth well knew they would prove effective! After even this one night's horrors there was not a druggist or wholesaler in town who would dare to refuse payments!

"I shall pay, of course, now," Wister's words echoed Wentworth's thoughts. "Out of humanity, I can do nothing else. My men have been working all night to discover how the poison was planted in our medicines. We have no slightest clue. The goods in our storerooms seem to be all right."

Wentworth shook his head. There was something wrong with this setup. No racketeer could hope to escape prosecution, no matter what repressive horrors he practiced. Wentworth remembered the pitiful skeleton of Nona Malvern and suddenly he was not sure. What man would testify in the face of that threat? Slowly, a cold smile crept across his lips. Well, there was a solution that would require no man's testimony in court... *the way of the Spider!* Yes, the racketeer had feared that. He had his hostage against such extra-legal action, he had… *Nita.*

The pallor of Wentworth's face matched that of Samuel Wister, but he spoke steadily. "Tell me the name of this protective association and the rest of it."

Wister rolled his head heavily against the back of the chair. "I don't know," he said thickly. "I can only hope that the Skull will give me another chance. I'm waiting for him to call, and when he does, I'll pay! As you have guessed, there was no demand of ransom for... for Nona. She was simply hostage that I would not notify the police. My wife… I put her on a ship for France this morning. Anything I can do I will willingly undertake. Just tell me."

Wentworth promised grimly and it was with impatience that he saw his guest to the door.

As soon as Wister was gone, Wentworth dashed to his rooms, caught up the handkerchief that he had found on the scene of Nita's kidnapping. The druggist, he was remembering now, had been making a phone call when he fell dead of poison. It was logical, wasn't it, that after his fright he would be attempting to communicate his surrender to the Skull? And Nita knew the trick that Wentworth had on occasion used… of picking up the static electrical impulse of each click of a dial phone in a radio receiver! Those clicks would come too rapidly to be counted mentally, but it was possible to record them, a tap of the finger for each click, *a lipstick dot on a handkerchief for each click!*

Wentworth stared at the dots again, counted them swiftly. They gave the number 34236, or conversely 63243. Wentworth shook his head. The number was two digits less than was used on New York dial telephones—but he was sure he was right. Probably, the radio had not warmed up in time for Nita to catch the first two.

Wentworth jabbed a signal button while he checked his theory. The only question was: what number had the druggist been calling? It might be as innocent as his own home. There was a light tap at his door and Jackson stepped into the room, a neat gauze bandage about his head. His strong, muscular face was pale.

he cried. "But, sir… you're not going out alone?"

Wentworth was punching into his coat again. He briefly touched the automatics beneath his arms. "Not entirely alone, Jackson!" he said softly.

THE elevator dropped him swiftly to the underground corridor that connected with the garage. Not for him this time the conspicuous black length of the Daimler. He chose a somewhat battered coupé whose worn paint job was belied by the sweet, powerful precision of the motor. Wentworth sent the car swiftly through the streets. He had communicated to Kirkpatrick the information given him by Wister and the police would make arrangements to trap the Skull should he call again. Wentworth hoped that he himself had a more direct and swift contact!

The Skull might well play a cautious game with a man like Wister, but with the lesser prey, the owners of pharmacies, he must have arranged a simpler method of payoff. Wentworth did not expect, in questioning the druggists whose supplies had been poisoned, to learn anything that would take him straight to the Skull. But he hoped to connect with an underling, and after that… after that, nothing, not even the imminent danger to Nita, could swerve the *Spider* from the stern trail of justice!

But he must move swiftly. Men were working night and day in an effort to speed the check of medical supplies, but the very fact that wholesale stocks were uncontaminated showed how cleverly the Skull was working. Even if entire stores full of

Wentworth smiled, "Not too badly hurt for work, Jackson?" he asked,

"Try me, sir," Jackson said curtly. "I'm just aching to get my hands on those mugs!"

Wentworth held out the handkerchief and explained his theory. "You can eliminate at once all exchanges whose final digit is neither three nor six," he said. "The telephone company will help. I won't have time to see either Beck or Miss Moulin this morning. Miss Moulin is to remain here for safety. Beck will await my orders by telephone. I'll call back for the information on that phone number."

While Wentworth was speaking, he had discarded his coat and was strapping on the twin holsters that carried his automatics beneath his arms. The grimness of his jaw increased. "It's possible that a gentleman who calls himself the Skull will telephone to make threats. You will know what to do. He has Miss Nita a prisoner!"

Jackson swore harshly. "I'll know what to do!"

supplies were declared harmless, the reopening of the pharmacies might well signal a new series of poisonings! Meantime, the thousands of sick persons in the city were without medicines which they must have to survive. To the scores of poison dead, there might well be added hundreds, thousands more of these victims!

The first two druggists whom Wentworth sought were, he was told at their homes, undergoing questioning at the hands of the police. At the third place, Wentworth found a man who had just limply returned from the precinct station. Terror turned the man's face grey at Wentworth's first question.

"I have a wife and child!" he cried hoarsely. "Do you think we don't know what happened to Nona Malvern and why? My wife, my child... and you want me to talk?"

Wentworth's smile was grave as he looked from the man to his wife, who stood at his elbow, twisting thin hands together helplessly. "Oh, why can't they leave us alone?" she cried. "We have done nothing. We only want to live in peace."

"Yes," Wentworth's voice was curiously gentle. "Yes, you want to live… in peace." It was for the sake of people like these that he had always been willing to plunge himself into conflict with the underworld; for their welfare, he and Nita had foregone the happiness they could have found together—because of them, Nita was now a prisoner of the Skull!

"I can't blame you for your fright," he went on. "I'm Richard Wentworth. If you read the papers this morning you know that the woman I love is in the hands of the same man who—" Stiffness crept across Wentworth's face, made his smile twisted. "The same man who did—what was done to Nona Malvern! I won't do anything so futile as promise to protect you. But I would give a great deal for one little piece of information. With that money, you could leave the city. You could, perhaps, go abroad and start over again."

The woman's hand worked on her husband's shoulder. Hoarsely, the man said, "You know what you're asking?"

"Perfectly," Wentworth nodded. "If you refuse me, I cannot blame you... but until the murderer is caught, this slaughter will go on! If you begin paying racket money, that will not be the end! I want only one little bit of information: how were you supposed to pay this money?"

The druggist was young. His high forehead was pale under the black sweep of his hair. His dark eyes showed suffering. "God help me," he whispered. "God help me... I'll tell you, but I want no pay! These murderers... listen, I don't know how I was supposed to pay. There was a protective association, and I have its phone number—"

He began to fumble in his pockets—and, from the hall behind him, Wentworth caught the rasp of a footstep! It had a furtive sound, as if the person there sought to conceal his presence! Wentworth did not wait to throw a glance in that direction. He went toward the druggist in a hard, low dive, hurled him and his wife backward across the room. In the same instant, a gun blasted out behind him. Wentworth heard the woman utter a strangled, high cry, saw her scrambling across the floor toward the room beyond.

The druggist lay where he had fallen, but whether he had been killed by the bullet or stunned by the fall, there was no chance to learn. Wentworth turned as he fell and his shoulders struck the floor in the same moment that his twin, heavy automatics thudded against his palms.

THE gunman was crouched on the stairs, hidden behind palings and newel post so that only the glint of his gun muzzle and a fraction of his head showed. Impossible for Wentworth to hit that target. But both automatics thundered in his hands. Splinters flew from the palings. The din of the guns was terrific in the narrow hall. Wentworth hit the floor and steadied himself, punched a bullet through the newel post behind which the man crouched. There was a sharp, muffled cry, then footsteps clattered down the steps.

In a long leap, Wentworth reached the railing, leaned over. He saw the man's white face twisted about to stare up at him fearfully as he ran, saw the spurt of flame from a hurriedly fired gun. Wentworth was not hurried. His left-hand automatic dropped into line on the man's left shoulder and he squeezed the trigger. Then a shout of chagrin leaped to his lips and he tried to stay the shot, to turn it aside too late.

Even as he touched the trigger, the fugitive gunman ducked his head… to the left! The bullet, striking the back of his skull, picked his feet up off the steps and hurled him in a macabre somersault. He struck the wall and lay unmoving, a broken travesty of what had been a man. Afterward, there was silence for seconds, and then, somewhere, a woman started screaming.

Wentworth went toward the druggist's apartment with long, quick strides. In the doorway, he stopped and his face twisted bitterly. He knew now that his leap had been too late; that the first bullet had sped true. Its bloody trace was there in the middle of that boy's splendid forehead. His wife—Wentworth was abruptly aware of the aching silence of the apartment! With a curse, he bounded across the room, into the one beyond. A window was open there and the black, iron straps of a fire escape were just beyond. A child's bed was empty.

Wentworth flung himself at the window. Had the

woman fled in terror with her child...or had worse happened? Had the men of the Skull attacked from both sides at once? He peered out into the back court of the apartment building, down between the wash-hung clothes lines. He saw nothing, no sign of the woman or her child; no disturbance. There was more noise now in the building, doors slamming and shouted inquiries.

Damn it, he was responsible for this thing! If he had not come asking questions—This could mean only that the men of the Skull had been following him! He shook his head. That was wrong. He could not have been trailed without his knowledge, even if the Skull followed so mild a course! Bullets from ambush would have been his portion. It meant, instead, that they were watching these druggists like hawks.

Wentworth spun away from the window. The druggist apparently had the phone number written down. If the *Spider* had been the cause of his death, the least the *Spider* could do would be to avenge him! Only it must be quick, before the police came. In the doorway, Wentworth stopped dead in his tracks. His eyes swept the room and then, with an oath, he was bounding toward the hallway again! Where the druggist had lain, there was a little red smear... nothing else. The man himself had vanished!

Gun knotted in his fist, Wentworth raced down the stairs. He paused for an instant beside the man he had slain and searched him for some clue that might point the way to the Skull's hideout. Save for the usual skeleton talisman, his body gave no helpful evidence.

For a long moment, Wentworth stared down at the man. He made it a rule never to use the seal of the *Spider* while in his own identity, but here it was more than justified. He must answer these repeated attempts to link him with the work of the poisoners, put the terror of retribution upon the Skull's men! He laid the grotesque small skeleton on the man's chest and, on his forehead, he ground in the violent red seal of the *Spider!*

From the head of the stairs, a man's voice spoke harshly, "Drop that gun, *Spider,* or I'll pump you full of lead!"

CHAPTER EIGHT

A Clue at Last

WENTWORTH did not wait for the man above to voice his threat. The instant he spoke, Wentworth hurled himself aside in the dimness of the hallway. The walls rocked with the blast of a shotgun and some of the pellets plucked at Wentworth's coat! His gun swiveled upward, and just in time he checked himself. It was a man in police uniform up there with a riot-gun! The man was plunging down the steps, the gun clutched ready in his hands. There wasn't a chance in the world of Wentworth's making the next flight of steps downward before that murderous weapon blasted at him again!

Still reeling from his first dodging leap, Wentworth threw himself at a nearby door. The flimsy portal crashed open and Wentworth pitched through, head down, doubling frantically into an acrobat's fall that would bring him up on his feet running. Once more, that terrific concussion hammered through the hall. The air ripped apart within inches of Wentworth's face; his hat was blasted from his head.

Swift as light, Wentworth's eyes flicked over the room into which he had plunged. It was empty, and its only opening was an overhead skylight! He was trapped—and out there in the hallway he had used the *Spider*'s seal! Trapped, and he dared not even allow the policeman to see his face!

It would be impossible to get out through the skylight, even if he could reach it before the policeman drew an inescapable bead on him with the riot-gun. True, a heavy pole used to open the skylight dangled from the catch. Wentworth's eyes narrowed in swift planning. His one hope—he seized the pole and started to climb up it with the frantic, exaggerated movements of fright. The pole swung erratically... and the man burst in through the doorway.

"Don't shoot!" Wentworth screamed. "Don't shoot! I'll surrender! For God's sake, don't shoot again! You got me—"

The man crouched a half dozen feet away by the door, the shotgun ready across his chest. As the pole swung wildly back and forth, Wentworth could glimpse him out of the corner of his eye, but he carefully kept his face turned away.

"Come down out of that," the man ordered. "There are three more shells in this gun and I'd like the chance to blow you to bits! You damned cop-killing crook!"

"Sure," Wentworth babbled. "Sure. I'll come down! Just don't shoot!"

He let go and dropped, sprawling toward the floor, landed on all fours within a yard of the cop and, in the same instant, he struck, he used his hands as a pivot and lashed outward with both feet at once! One foot slammed aside the barrel of that murderous gun: the other drove with neat precision against the man's jaw.

Once more, that gun spewed out its butcher's load of death! The concussion seemed to crush in Wentworth's eardrums, but he reeled dizzily to his feet. The man was out cold on the floor... and the charge had missed.

Wentworth stooped over the man. His kick had been well guided. He was unconscious, would be out for possibly ten or fifteen minutes, but no serious harm had been inflicted. Without hesitation, Wentworth caught up his hat and then heaved the body to his shoulders; ran along the hall toward the stairs. If this man had come by way of the roof—and there was no other way in which he could have taken Wentworth from behind—it meant that there was a heavy force of men below! The building must be surrounded!

Wentworth raced down two floors, then he yanked out his gun and fired two shots in the ceiling. He backed down the last flight of stars with the uniformed body across his shoulders and while he went down, the gun racketed in his fist.

"They're trapped," he yelled. "They're trapped up there!"

He heard excited shouts behind him, but did not turn his head. He fired a last burst of shots up the steps, turned and with his head low, leaped reeling down the last of the stairway. He glimpsed three men in the lower hall, another just barging in through the front door. How many more were out there he could not guess, but he knew that he had walked into a carefully prepared trap. How the criminals had managed to snatch away the druggist's body without running into the police themselves he could not understand, but—A shock ran along Wentworth's nerves. Not five feet away from him was a man in the blue police uniform. There was nothing wrong with the uniform... *but the man wore tan shoes!*

That single glimpse was enough. Wentworth knew in that flashing instant that these were not genuine police officers, but criminals in disguise! Police regulations required black shoes and no man would be allowed to go out on duty in shoes of any other color. In the same instant, Wentworth was in action. A quick heave of his shoulders hurled the unconscious man he carried against the three who were grouped together at the foot of the steps!

As they went down, Wentworth sprang straight at the fourth man in the doorway. His gun was swinging up. Wentworth's automatic was ready in his fist... but he did not fire. There was just the faint chance that this might be a genuine police officer, a late arrival. Wentworth threw his automatic and his aim was true. It caught the man's gun-wrist just as he was squeezing the trigger. Lead tore past Wentworth's side as he leaped and his fist finished the swift job.

THE high shriek of police sirens filled the air. There was no chance to get to his car, parked a half block away, and take flight. Wentworth dodged into the basement entrance of the building next door, bounded through the musty cellar. Seconds later, he drew himself out of a narrow window into the back court and vaulted a fence.

Presently, in an adjoining street, he was circling back toward the scene of the attack!

His grey-blue eyes, secretive under lowered lids, were dark with fury. Every move he had made in this battle with the Skull had been hounded by disaster, and always it was the innocent that suffered. He knew without question that it would be futile for him to try farther to get information from the druggists. Terrorism would shut their mouths. Another thought forced its way into his brain. If he had been recognized by the criminals—if the truth got back to the Skull—Nita would pay the penalty! He must work fast.

Wentworth checked at the corner of the street into which police cars were jammed now. It was dangerous to go back there. If anyone had seen his flight, they would be able to identify him at least by his clothing. And there were rents in it where the shotgun slugs had just missed his body! No matter. He had to get close. If those criminals escaped—

There were men in police blue about the entrance of the building and scores of people from adjoining houses were crowding out into the street. Some, at least, of those men at the door were the real police. Surely, the criminals could not be mingling with them! Their deception could not be carried so far. Wentworth pushed on into the street, mixed with the Sunday crowd. His eyes keenly studied the faces of the officers. The criminals were not among them.

Sharp doubt stabbed Wentworth. Had they made their escape while he circled to evade pursuit? Even while the question sprang up in his mind, one of the police came out of the building with a discarded uniform coat in his hands... and Wentworth knew! Even this chance had failed him!

Now what?

There remained then only the slender clue of the telephone number Nita had recorded on her handkerchief... and that might have been an entirely innocent call! Wentworth swung on his heel and entered a corner lunch room and made the call to his home. Jackson answered promptly.

No, there had been no phoned threats from the Skull. There had been nothing at all. But Jackson had a long list of numbers, any one of which might be the one Nita had partly recorded—twenty-five, in fact.

Wentworth swore under his breath. There was so little time, and all those numbers would have to be checked carefully lest the criminals take alarm at any one of his inquiries.

"Isn't there anything suspicious about any one of them?" he asked quietly. "Is any of them the number of a drug concern, or—"

"There is one curious thing, sir," Jackson's voice lowered. "One of the numbers on this list is the phone of this young detective here in the house, Donald Beck! His office is in the Remarque Building."

For an instant, Wentworth stared incredulously at the phone over which this message had come. Beck… the Skull's hireling? He shook his head. It was possible, of course. It was also possible that the dead druggist had simply been calling on him for help.

"Nothing else?" he asked slowly.

"Not another thing, sir," Jackson said. "Most of them are private phones."

Wentworth said steadily, "See that Beck stays there for a half hour, then have Ram Singh take him to his office. I'll be there! Find out all you can about those other phones and their subscribers without alarming anyone. And, Jackson, keep a careful watch over the place! The Skull's men are masquerading as police now!"

WINGING from the booth, Wentworth caught a taxi and sped toward the Remarque Building while his mind speculated on the possible guilt of Donald Beck. There had been suspicious circumstances about Beck before this, but the man himself seemed so frank and open.

It took twenty minutes to reach the Remarque Building and in that time the taxi radio brayed out endless alarms. The newscasters were pumping out excited words about the poisonings, swelling the terrorism by which the Skull hoped to rule. Already, they had got hold of the fact that the druggist whom Wentworth questioned had been attacked. They said the man, his wife and child had all vanished.

Horror gripped Wentworth at the thought. Good Lord, had that poor woman also been seized by the Skull? He had been sure she had merely fled to safety with her child. The memory of the pitiful remains of Nona Malvern burned like fire in his brain. He beat his fists softly on his knees with the driving need for speed. If he could track down the Skull quickly enough—

The Remarque Building was a down-at-the-heel office structure on a side street off Times Square. The elevator, when Wentworth had rung up the watchman, creaked and swayed as it labored upward. As soon as the gate had closed, Wentworth stalked on silent feet toward the door on which was painted:

DONALD BECK
INVESTIGATIONS

Wentworth's eyes swept the hallway, but found no indications of a watch kept here. The door resisted his hand and he slid out a slim hooked tool of surgical steel, a lock pick. Moments later, the bolt yielded to shrewd manipulation and Wentworth pushed the door carefully open. Something scraped softly along the floor and, inside, Wentworth stared down in amazement at the wastebasket which caught mail dropped through the slot in the door. The basket was full and overflowing. Half the floor of the room was covered with letters!

Swiftly, Wentworth caught up a handful of the letters. Each one was thick and stiff with the crackle of the paper inside… and five of those in his hand were addressed from various drugstores! Wentworth ripped open the envelopes and he stared down at sheaf after sheaf of currency! There were no letters, no messages, save in each envelope was a little slip with the name of a drugstore and the amount of money noted below it! Wentworth's hand knotted into a white fist about the money. Well, there was no longer any doubt, was there? This was the protection money the Skull had demanded of the drug stores, and this was the payoff station—*the office of Donald Beck!*

With long, silent strides, Wentworth crossed to the inner office of the detective and there was a knife-gash of a frown between his brows. He was remembering his earlier deductions. He had hoped through Nita's clue to find some minor member of the gang, for surely the Skull would not allow in general circulation a number which would lead directly to him! That would explain matters, of course. Donald Beck was merely a small link in the chain that would lead to the Skull, perhaps the weakest link. Wentworth's lips moved in a grim smile at the thought. It was a link that was soon broken!

With swift efficiency, Wentworth began to ransack the office. It was habit, engendered of long nights of secret work that made him work silently. It was experience that presently revealed, fastened beneath the desk, the ear of a dictograph! An oath sprang to Wentworth's lips and died there, unuttered, as the significance of that listening device struck him. Either the police were suspicious of Beck and had set up a plant here… or the criminals were keeping him under surveillance! That might mean the criminals doubted his loyalty to the Skull, or it might mean that Beck was innocent!

Even while those thoughts were racing through Wentworth's mind, he was in action. He did not disturb the dictograph, but his sensitive fingers traced its tiny wires under the rug to a far corner of the room where they passed through the floor! In a single long stride, Wentworth reached the window of Beck's office and eased it open soundlessly. There was a window directly below. It was partly open and the shade was drawn down tightly! It was a matter of moments to reach the hall and descend the fire-stair of this deserted building to the floor below. The door of the office beneath Beck's bore no sign. Were the men inside police—or criminals? Wentworth's lips moved in a slight, cold smile. He'd soon find out!

He had brought with him the emptied wastebasket from Beck's office, together with scraps of paper and a tattered shirt found in the desk drawer. On the metal bottom of the basket, he soon had a small fire going. He thrust it close against the door and watched the draft of that open window begin to suck the odorous smoke of the burning rag in through the crack around the door. Then he flattened against the wall to wait. Luckily, since it was Sunday, there was small chance that anyone else would be disturbed.

Now—

Tensely, Wentworth listened for the first indication that the smoke of the fire had been noticed. He held no gun in his hand, but there was an alert and eager light in his eyes. Police or criminal, his course must be the same. If it were the law, he must make amends as best he could. His acutely attuned ears caught an exclamation from inside the office and, with gloved hand, he caught up the fire basket in which only the smoldering rag remained. Footsteps beat hurriedly across the room, the door was suddenly whipped open—

INSTANTLY, Wentworth was in action. He flipped the smoldering contents of the basket in through the doorway straight at the still invisible man and charged after it. A man was reeling backward across the room, arm thrown protectively across his face. He clenched a gun in his fist! He glimpsed Wentworth and jerked up the gun.

Wentworth's fists swung in perfect rhythm. The left batted down the muzzle of the revolver. His right lanced under that uplifted arm and clicked home to the jaw! In a single long bound, Wentworth went past him toward the door of the inner office. It was empty!

Wentworth pivoted and, with quick efficiency, yanked the semi-conscious man up from the floor and bound him with his own torn clothing to a chair. Since the man worked here alone, there could no longer be any doubt. Police always worked a plant in pairs; a swift search confirmed his guess. Within moments and Wentworth held on his palm the tiny wooden figure of a skeleton! That symbol of the Skull had seemed grotesque and childish when first Wentworth's eyes had fallen on it, but now it had taken on a devilish meaning. In that bit of wood and twisted wire was an echo of the horror he had seen the night before: of Nona Malvern's poor body, and the promise of horror to come which it signified!

Wentworth turned to the reviving man and there was a cold fire in his eyes which wiped the sneer off the criminal's face. Wentworth did not speak to him. Instead, he recovered his wastebasket and into it piled scraps of paper that were scattered over the floor of the room. He snaked out a drawer of the desk and with powerful hands snapped the partitions into firewood. When he had the basket fixed to his satisfaction, he crossed to his prisoner and began to bind it in the man's lap.

"Hey!" the man said hoarsely. "Hey, wait a minute! God, you ain't going to do a thing like that! For God's sake, mister—

Wentworth's smile was wintry and thin. He struck a match.

"For God's sake, mister, give me a chance!"

With a steady hand, Wentworth touched fire to a scrap of paper on the opposite side of the basket from the man's body, near the top. It would burn very slowly from there. The man broke into incoherent pleading, his eyes strained wide as they stared down at the slowly spreading fire.

"I know you boys who work for the Skull," Wentworth said, his voice incongruously gentle. "I know you're tough, so it's a good idea to soften you up right away, before I ask any questions."

"God!" the man sobbed. "God, I ain't tough! I'm just a punk, honest. Mister, what do you want to know? Put this fire out, and—"

Wentworth shook his head gently, "I have to conserve fuel. There's just about enough to toast you nicely." He was watching the man closely. He had no intention of letting the flames actually reach him, even though he was an ally of the Skull who had done such fearful things to Nona Malvern. He didn't think he would let the flames reach him. Smoke and burning bits of paper wafted up past the man's face.

"Geez, mister, I don't know much! I'm just here to listen in on that guy's office and his phone calls. Then sometimes the boss calls me up here, see?

"That's all I know, so help me, God! Listen, I used to be a private dick and this guy that used to train with Whitey Hart came to me and offered me this job. Oh!"

He was straining his face away from the top of the basket, but a tongue of flame had come close enough to singe his hair. Wentworth flicked the flaming bit of paper away.

"I wouldn't want you to pass out too quickly," he said softly. "Is Whitey Hart the Skull?"

"He might be! God's truth, I don't know! I ain't never seen nobody except this guy that I'm talking about."

"His name?"

"Monk Deacon. *Oh, God—*"

Wentworth nodded. That much made sense at any rate. This was a racketeering trick with a new angle, and Hart and Deacon had been racketeers in old Prohibition days. He leaned forward and cut loose the bonds that held the basket in the man's lap, set it close to the window. This ex-detective wasn't hurt, and Wentworth thought he had told all he knew. He was methodically putting out the fire in the basket when the phone bell sounded briefly!

Wentworth whirled on his prisoner. "Any password for answering this phone?" he demanded harshly—waiting. The man seemed to be almost in a faint. He rolled his head, "Yeah. You say 'tibula and fibula!'"

The phone whined again. "Remember," Wentworth said softly. "If you're lying—"

"God, I ain't lying."

Wentworth caught up the instrument and imitated the husky tones of his prisoner.

"Okay, Barney," a man said over the wire. "Look, the boss wants to know: has the Cherry Hill Hospital paid up?"

Wentworth said, in a half-frightened tone, "Gee; I don't know. Look, you want to hold the wire while I see, or you want me to call you up—" He halted.

"Don't be a fool, Barney," the man said. "Look, I'll give you three minutes. When I call up, you know… see?"

Wentworth protested, but the wire went dead.

THERE was an intent light in his eyes. His prisoner, Barney, hadn't lied about a few things at any rate. Wentworth thought he could identify the voice over the wire as that of the ex-racketeer, Monk Deacon, and Barney wasn't supposed to know the phone number. The instant the other man disconnected, Wentworth was busy on the wire, getting in touch with an official of the phone company.

"Police business," he snapped, "and in a hurry. In three minutes, there's going to be a call come in on this wire—from criminals. I want it traced without fail, I'll call for the information."

As he hung up, he caught the rasp of a footstep behind him. He threw himself flat on the floor, rolled and snatched out his gun in a single swift movement. The man, Barney, was crouched by the door and he had his recovered gun in his fist! Even as Wentworth's eyes took in the picture, Barney fired!

Wentworth felt the shock of a bullet beneath his chest and his own automatic leaped in his fist. His lead sped true. Barney straightened under the punch of the bullet, his shoulders nailed to the wall. He drew in a slow whistling breath, then the stiffness went out of his joints. Neck, waist, knees sagged in one instant and he clattered limply to the floor.

Wentworth pushed to his feet and reached the outer door with long strides. He was ten stories up in the deserted building and unless the watchman happened to be near, it was unlikely the shots had been heard. He listened and caught the faint whine of the elevator. He shook his head. The creaking of the old cage would have blotted out the sounds. He turned back toward the office. He saw now that the basket had caused some of the torn clothing, with which he had bound Barney, to catch fire and smolder. That was how Barney had got free.

Wentworth crossed back to the desk and stood there tensely, the gun under his fist. In a few minutes Monk Deacon would call again and at last Wentworth would have a lead to the Skull! Heaven grant that it would be in time! There still was the problem of Beck's guilt or innocence. It would have to wait. Ram Singh could hold him prisoner. He caught the sound of an opening elevator door, but it was remote. That might well be Ram Singh and Beck arriving now. Wentworth whipped up the earphones which connected with the dictograph upstairs.

At first, there was only silence and then the rasp of a key unlocking the door, then Beck's voice: "Lord Almighty, look at all the mail! I must be getting popular as hell all of a sudden."

Ram Singh's voice lifted inquiringly, *"Sahib?"*

"Hey, Ram Singh," Beck cried. "Look, this damned mail comes from a flock of drugstores, and—Good Lord! Money! Wads of it! What in the hell—"

Wentworth was frowning with concentration. People were rarely able to dissemble with their voices. They depended more on facial expression, and he couldn't see Beck's face. Surprise and bewilderment were in his voice, no question of that. Was Beck a clever enough actor to accomplish that? Certainly, if guilty, he had known what awaited him here; would have had plenty of time to prepare his role.

The sharp ring of the phone broke in on his thoughts and he caught it up, spoke the formula into the mouthpiece.

"What's the dope on the hospital?" Monk Deacon's voice demanded.

"They paid," Wentworth answered, still in Barney's hoarse voice. "Geez, this is a sweet racket. I never saw so much dough! There must be a thousand letters up in that guy's office!"

"Don't try nothing, punk!" Monk rasped. "You finger any of that dough and the boss will hang you up like he done that girl."

Wentworth broke into protestations, but the click of disconnection cut him short. He'd been trying to stall, to gain the phone company as much time as possible. His thoughts flew to the mention of the hospital. Good Lord, were they on the racket list, too? The horror that could be wrought in a hospital by poisoned medicines was almost too awful to contemplate! The Cherry Hill was one of the largest private institutions in the city. Rapidly, he called the phone official.

"The call was traced, all right," the official told Wentworth. "It was a new installation. A private phone in the office of the president of the Guaranteed Drug Company on Third Avenue. Yes, sir, I can give you the name of the president. Here it is… Robert Forbes."

WENTWORTH thanked the man and deliberately replaced the phone in its cradle. Forbes, who had been a guest in his home no later than last night, who had given his prisoner a "new restorative" just before the man died. Yet it seemed madness that the man should use a private phone, listed in his own name, to make an incriminating call. But there was no time to waste in speculation. He thought that a personal call on Forbes was indicated. Wentworth's lips stretched thin. It was a devious trail he had to follow.

Wentworth snapped up the phone again and called police headquarters, got put through to Kirkpatrick, to whom he rapidly detailed his discoveries in Beck's office and in the room below.

"The *Spider* was here ahead of me, Kirk," Wentworth said rapidly. "There is a dead man with the seal on his forehead. A plant here might learn something. Beck? I don't know, Kirk. He seemed genuinely surprised at the sight of all this mail. No, it wasn't addressed to him personally, but to the Pharmaceutical Protective Association, with his office number." Wentworth hesitated over mention of the drug company which Forbes headed. There might be things to accomplish there with which police might interfere. But if the *Spider* went there alone… and failed?

"Kirk," Wentworth interjected slowly, "I think it might be a good idea to check on the Guaranteed Drug Company, Robert Forbes, president. No, I won't be here when you arrive. I'll leave Beck under guard of Ram Singh. No, not a word about Nita or from her. I... don't know, Kirk."

He hung up the phone and for a moment longer he sat there with his lean, sensitive hands resting limply on the desk. It had been a sorry day for Nita when they had met. Since then, her life had been harassed by violence, endangered again and again. She had been tortured… Wentworth's hands flattened tautly on the desk and he pushed himself to his feet. He paused a moment over the man he had killed, to imprint the seal of the *Spider.* At every opportunity he must so mark the men of the Skull. The danger to himself did not matter. The Skull must learn to fear that seal.

Action now!

Seconds later, he was thrusting open the door of Beck's office. Ram Singh pivoted lithely, hand flitting toward a knife-hilt. Beck stood rigidly at the entrance of the inner office. He stepped forward immediately.

"Mr. Wentworth," he said hoarsely, "I swear to you that I know nothing of these letters or why they were sent here. I know that's hard to believe."

Wentworth nodded curtly. "Fortunately for you," he said, "I found a dictograph planted in your office and discovered that your phone has been tapped. The plant is downstairs. Unfortunately for you, the *Spider* has found this out, also. He may hunt you up to ask some questions."

Beck's jaw jutted out and his fists knotted at his side. "I hope he does," he said fiercely. "But how do you know the *Spider* has been here?"

Wentworth's smile turned grim. "The *Spider* usually leaves a calling card," he said quietly. "There's a dead man down there with his seal. Never mind that now. Listen. I want you, Beck, to take up that plant downstairs and receive incoming phone calls, if there are any. Try to get a line on whoever calls. Ram Singh will stay here with you in case there's an attack, or the *Spider* returns!" Wentworth put his eyes on the dark gaze of the Sikh, and switched abruptly to Punjabi. "This man," he said steadily, "may be one of the vermin we hunt. I expect him to desert his post and perhaps go to his masters. Allow him to do this, but follow."

Ram Singh's teeth flashed amid his thick beard and he salaamed, cupped hands to his forehead. *"Han, sahib,"* he rumbled.

THE taxi that sped Wentworth across the quiet city seemed barely to crawl. He had determined an open invasion of the Guaranteed Drug Company. There was a good chance that Forbes would be on hand, in spite of the fact that it was Sunday, since the police had ordered tests of all drug supplies in the city.

He found a watchman on duty at the entrance of the drug company's building, whose dust-filmed doors opened under the shadow of the Third Avenue elevated structure. There was a little delay and then Forbes himself came striding to fling the doors open for Wentworth. A frown marked his forehead and his eyes, blue behind rimless glasses, were puzzled. His white laboratory jacket was stained.

"Come in—come in, Wentworth," he said. "I didn't see how it could be you, but the watchman swore he had the name right. Is anything wrong?

Can I do anything for you?"

"I hope so," Wentworth told him, his eyes secretly studying the angular lines of the man's florid face. "I want to open a dispensary for pure drugs, a place where the people can come and be sure their medicines won't be poisoned while this mad slaughter keeps up. I heard by accident that you had left Wister—"

"That would be splendid." Forbes' face glowed. "I think I can guarantee the drugs. So far, we've found nothing wrong at all. This job developed most unexpectedly. I had been approached about it soon after I went with Wister, but I didn't think much about it. When all this trouble broke, the owners thought this would be a good chance to get started. They were pretty sure of their supplies and thought that if we would guarantee them, we could get established almost overnight."

They were lurching upward in the creaking elevator. "Shall we go to my lab?" Forbes asked.

Wentworth's lids drooped over his eyes. Was this a deliberate attempt to lead him away from the office where the phone was? He said, "If you don't mind, let's go where we can sit down. If your lab is like most of them, I won't find those confounded stools very comfortable. And I'm a little tired. Had you heard? The criminals kidnapped Nita last night."

"My God, no," Forbes cried, and his concern seemed genuine. "How did it happen? Was—was Miss Moulia—"

Wentworth told him steadily while he fought with a feeling of fresh bewilderment. He could find no flaw in Forbes' behavior, and the office when they entered it was empty and unsuspicious, a barren cubbyhole boxed off at one side of a loft floor.

"Who are the owners of this concern?" Wentworth asked casually.

Forbes shook his head. "That's one thing that made me hesitate over the job," he said. "I don't know. A lawyer, Oscar Downey, made the contact; said he had full powers. Downey is reputable enough, God knows."

Wentworth nodded in slow agreement, abruptly made up his mind. His eyes keenly on Forbes' face, he said steadily, "I lied about my reason for coming here, Forbes. The truth is that phone calls from the Skull have been traced to your private telephone here."

Forbes said, stuttering; "What—the Skull? My God, Wentworth, you must be wrong." He swiveled in his chair and stared at the telephone. "Damn it, man, it just isn't possible."

"There's no mistake, Forbes."

"But, for God's sake, you can't suspect me! Why, damn it, Wentworth—"

"How well do you know the building?" Wentworth interrupted. "The phone doesn't have to be used from your office. The wires could be tapped."

Forbes' face grew grim, and there was an angry squint to his eyes. He reached for the phone. "I don't know a damned thing about the building, but we'll get the police here and find out."

"If the phone is tapped—" Wentworth said softly.

Forbes swore and his hand flinched away from the instrument. "You mean they'd overhear what I say? I don't know much about this wiretapping business. But we've got to do something, Wentworth. We can't just sit here, and—"

WENTWORTH'S mind was filled with racing thoughts. If Forbes were giving a truthful account of the way in which things had happened, it would help to clear Beck, also. But there was a more important inference. This gaunt, half-empty building might well conceal one of their hideouts. It might even be the spot in which… in which Nita was held captive. This building was not far from the scene of her kidnaping. He rose steadily to his feet.

"Can you use a gun?" he asked. "Have you got one?"

Forbes shook his head, his eyes widening. "Hell, no. I haven't had a revolver in my hands a half-dozen times in my life. You mean you... you want to check up on this alone, now?"

Wentworth briefly touched the automatics under his arms. "I think that would be an excellent idea," he said steadily. "We have only to trace the wires of your phone. Usually, they would run down the elevator shaft to the basement and connect there with the underground trunks. I think… the basement is indicated!"

Forbes jerked to his feet, "I have a half dozen men working here, and—"

Wentworth shook his head, "Just you and I, Forbes."

Forbes said violently, "You still suspect me, damn it, and—Oh, very well. I can't blame you, I suppose. But you're used to this sort of thing and I'm not." He mopped his forehead. "Frankly, I'm afraid as hell of guns. I've seen what they can do to people."

Wentworth said nothing, but gestured toward the door and Forbes stalked out ahead of him. The man was not feigning about his fear, but whether he dreaded what would be found, or whether he had told the truth about guns, Wentworth could not discern. He took the control of the elevator and kept his eyes on the phone wire cable as the cage slid downward—but he did not neglect to watch Forbes. The chemist stood firmly, but his lips were pale and now and again he mopped his forehead. He grinned, sickly.

"This is nonsense," he said, "but I am afraid."

Wentworth shook his head. "That's nothing to apologize for. You show intelligence."

The cage reached the bottom of the shaft and there still had been no break in the phone wires. At Wentworth's gesture, Forbes threw the doors wide and stepped out hesitantly. They found a light switch but it illuminated only two widely-spaced dim bulbs.

Wentworth took out his powerful miniature flashlight and laid its beam upon the phone wires. There was an automatic in his other hand as he moved rapidly along the course the line followed. His footfalls were soft and his eyes swept ceaselessly over the shadowed basement. The steam pipes made grotesque shadows against the walls. The place was thick with dust that rose in slow eddying

Wentworth fought with a sense of utter unreality and unreasoning dread!

swirls where they walked, hazed and dimmed the lights.

Forbes said suddenly, "The wires go into the wall there, and we still haven't found any tap."

Wentworth's lips were grim. Instead of being relieved, Forbes should be frightened. If there was no tap, it meant that the phone was used in Forbes' office. He stood motionless and sent the lens-focused beam of his light questing over the wall. It was an ancient foundation, made of grey stone and whitewashed at some remote time.

Wentworth muted his voice, "This steam installation is comparatively recent. I'm sure this building used a furnace at one time, so there will be a sub-basement. A trapdoor—

The voice that now spoke seemed to come from a half-dozen directions at once. It echoed in the close, thick walls of the basement and it was mocking, cold, rasping.

"Precisely gentlemen," it said. *"There is a trap-door, but I'm afraid you gentlemen won't find it!"*

WENTWORTH whirled about, the muzzle of his gun questing like a dog's nose after a scent. At first, he could see nothing. The beam of his light was turned back by the haze of dust...or was it dust? Abruptly, Wentworth realized that there was vapor crawling toward them over the floor, a brownish ugly vapor the color of the dust, but strangely menacing in its silent approach. *It was gas!* Even as he grasped the import of that vapor, the lights flicked out!

In the same moment, ghastly figures began to lift out of that rolling cloud of gas: skeleton men with that horrid greenish glow to delineate their bones; skulls that gaped in fleshless mocking grins.

"Quickly," Wentworth snapped at Forbes, locking his left hand about the man's arm. "Back to the elevator. Don't mind those confounded figures. They're just decoys! Fakes!"

He was thrusting Forbes toward the elevator. The ghostly figures were between them and escape, but Wentworth ignored that… rushed straight toward them. He held his gunfire. What use to fire at these fake figures? He brushed past one and the glowing bony arm swept toward him. Wentworth felt the swish of a club past his head! At point-blank range… Wentworth fired... and nothing happened. Nothing save that the figure whirled and came after him.

Wentworth fought with a sense of utter unreality, and an unreasoning dread that shook his heart. Forbes, he realized, was screaming. The sound seemed strangely thin and inadequate... like the muted squeal of a trapped rabbit. Another figure loomed ahead and Wentworth tried to jerk up his gun. His arm seemed leaden. He suddenly couldn't feel the gun in his hand at all. Then he knew the truth. The gas was beginning to take effect! He tried to shout a warning to Forbes but somewhere in the past few seconds he had lost his grip on the chemist's arm. He could not see.

Stubbornly, Wentworth plunged on. The feeling had gone from his feet now. Something struck him heavily on the chest, Why… Good God, he was on the floor! He had fallen! He pushed at it with hands and knees that registered nothing at all of sensation. He could no longer even see the macabre skeleton figures. The blackness crept inside his brain. He thought wildly that he had been right. He had found the lair of the Skull and his very boldness had trapped him. Forbes, the cowardly one, had been right.

Wentworth heard laughter, wild and mocking laughter, and realized it came from his own lips. It was the last thing he heard before the darkness exploded.

CHAPTER NINE
The Embrace of Death

IN THE lightless room with stone walls where Nita van Sloan was held prisoner, she heard dimly the rumble of passing trains and that was the only sound to break the locked underground silence of her dungeon. She had seen no one since, hours ago, a man masquerading in the gallant robes of the *Spider* had thrust her into this cell.

Nita blamed herself bitterly for her capture. She knew that the fact was being used as a club over Dick Wentworth's head; and that he would defy the Skull. She had warned the Skull of this... and been laughed at. Heavens, how many hours had it been since she had left her home with the escort of police who accused her of murder?

The attack had been sharp and over almost as it began. Two cars had crowded up beside the police car and Nita, glimpsing the caped and masked figure in one of them, had thought that it was Wentworth himself who came to the rescue. When she knew the truth—when bullets had burned down the police—it was too late to do anything except submit. She paced her small prison and wrung her hands. Anything would be better than this waiting in ignorance of what had happened to Dick.

Nita stopped abruptly as one of those awful skeleton figures began to glow against her door. The portal had not opened, but there the thing stood. The gaping empty jaws moved and a croaking voice rasped at her.

"Leave this cell," it ordered. "The Master will speak to you!"

That was all.

Nita shuddered at the grisly thing but, as the figure faded from sight, she moved hesitantly toward the door. It swung wide and, outside in the corridor, were more of those horrid skeleton figures. The glow from their bones was the only light, but it glinted on revolvers in the fleshless hands! Nita had to remind herself that this was all trickery, intended basically to hide the identity of the men who confronted her. It was hard to keep herself convinced. While she stumbled along the pitch black corridor, as directed, the creatures moved after her. There was a musty odor of decay in the air and—God in Heaven! There was the dry clatter of bones as the *things* paced after her!

Nita stilled her rising hysteria and lifted her head proudly. She was the mate of the *Spider.* Such obvious trickery could not frighten her. Her heart thudded violently in her breast and her throat was dry. She would not be afraid. Whatever the Skull wanted with her, she would not yield!

Nita was aware presently that the close walls had opened from about her for the dry rasping of bones was no longer close and confined. Hard fingers gripped her shoulders and a gasping cry rose to Nita's lips. She fought it back as she was thrust down into a chair and ropes bit into her tender woman's flesh. Afterward, the fantastic figures went away and Nita sat in darkness, waiting... for what she could not guess. She closed her eyes and fought for the courage she knew she would need.

Moments dragged past in utter black silence and

once more Nita felt hysteria rising within her. She sank her teeth into her lips, and then a *presence* forced itself into her consciousness. Her eyes flew wide and she choked down a cry. The Skull was before her!

Nita knew that instantly even though it was the first time the apparition had appeared before her eyes. It was a face much more ghastly than any skull, for the flesh adhered to the very bone and the lips shrank back from long, bestial teeth. When it spoke, the jaws moved and the greenish light made writhing shadows across the face of the Skull.

"Woman, if you answer certain questions," the voice came, rusty and harsh. "I shall permit that you be killed before the flesh is stripped from your delicate bones. Otherwise, it shall be done *while you still live!"*

NITA shuddered, as much at the fearful tones of the voice as at the torture which it threatened—but her head was still high and somehow she achieved a smile. She made no other answer. Death and the threat of death was no new thing to Nita van Sloan. She had one hope that buoyed her through every trial... and if that hope was destroyed, somewhere she would find courage. The utmost that death could inflict upon her was the fact that she would never see again the man she loved. *Never!* Nita drew in a quivering breath. The disembodied face before her was staring with burning eyes, the lips parted and a rasping sound of laughter came forth.

"Yes, yes, I know you have courage, my dear," it said. "But why waste courage on me? I feel nothing. I am only a brain. It will cost me nothing whether you suffer or die painlessly. The information is not even particularly important, but it will make a few things easier for us. Already, we can enter Wentworth's fortress at any time we wish. If he is not already in our power, he will be within a short while. So... I shall ask you a few questions."

Nita lifted her eyes above the mountebank skull, but she could not close her ears to that croaking voice. The Skull was so sure. His words dripped like corroding acid on her courage, insidious, It was not a chance to live he offered her; that she would have instantly rejected as a lie. But a chance to die painlessly. Nita's breast lifted with a quick breath. It was madness to hope that Dick would come. She could not even guess whether he had found the handkerchief clue or, *if* he had, whether the number that the druggist had called would be of any importance. This time, Dick must fail her; he who had never failed. God, how could he find her here?

"No doubt you still hope for rescue." The Skull's voice dropped to a harsh whisper. "It would be pleasant, wouldn't it, for your lover to leap from some dark corner now to challenge me? But it would be only a challenge, woman. He cannot harm me. And my men—" He laughed harshly, and in the darkness about him, there was other rasping laughter. Figures glowed against the black wall that pressed close to Nita, the glowing bones of men. Nita shuddered and there was a sagging weight in her breast.

"I have arranged for you, woman," the voice went on, "a little demonstration of what you presently will face. This woman you shall see has not harmed me, nor has the child. But her husband was a fool and would have talked to this same lover of yours. Others must learn what it is to defy the Skull. Hard, you think? Ah, but effective. Yes, yes, effective—"

The voice died out on Nita's ears and suddenly there was light in the room. Not where Nita sat but there across the room brightness shone like spotlights upon a stage. It was empty now, that stage, save for a coffin-like box of iron that stood in its midst.

Nita shuddered and closed her eyes. She knew the torture devices of medieval barbarity all too well and what she saw was a modern "iron maiden." Once, hapless persons had been shut in those coffins of steel, lined with fearful spikes that pierced. In spite of herself, Nita stared again at the gruesome thing. There were no spikes inside this cage, but that very fact made it more ominous. For there were pipes leading into it, and valves. What was it the Skull had threatened to do? *"Strip the flesh from your delicate bones."*

Nita tried to steel herself for the ordeal that lay before her. She tried to hope.

Instead, she prayed that Wentworth would not plunge into this fearful place. Men whom bullets could not harm—but that was madness! These were mortal beings and those skeleton silhouettes were trickery! No, while she could not see them, Nita could believe that. When they shone, horrible in the darkness, her certainty wavered.

Abruptly, Nita jerked taut against her ropes. A man—it must be a man—had bounded into sight there beneath the spotlights. He was a grotesque thing, a dwarfed and twisted monstrosity of humanity with a great idiot's head and bandy limbs. He turned his head and blinked out into the darkness toward her and Nita could see saliva wet his lips. The dwarf capered lovingly about the iron maiden there on the stage, stroking it with misshapen hands, caressing the valves and pipes. He skipped out of sight and, moments later, he returned. This time, he was not alone. Behind him, her wrists chained together, he dragged a woman!

APATHY had held Nita prisoner there in her chair, but now she began to struggle. She groped for the strands of rope that bound her. Hopeless. It was certainly hopeless, but she would try.

The woman there on the stage seemed without animation, without strength. The dwarf handled her like a toy. With a quick swing upon the wrist chains, he whirled her into the gaping upright iron maiden! The woman's weight must have tripped some spring devices, for as her body struck the back of the box, metal straps snapped shut about her, holding her a prisoner, irrevocably. The dwarf capered.

"You see, woman." It was the Skull's voice, behind Nita now. "You see, there is no hope."

"Please," Nita whispered. "Oh, please. This is not necessary. Free her! I–I will answer your questions!"

The dwarf stopped before the woman. With a single claw-like movement of his hands, he ripped off her clothing. For the first time, the woman's lethargy faded. She stared about as if she awoke from some awful dream.

"But you see," said the Skull, "that is not in the bargain. This woman must die. This is merely by way of demonstration. You may earn yourself an easy death, no more than that. But it will have to be soon. I have an *errand* at certain hospitals—"

Nita was struggling fiercely, and she knew futilely, against her ropes. "In Heaven's name!" she cried. "Don't do this awful thing! If you free her, I'll talk! If you kill her, nothing—you understand me, *nothing*—will make me talk!"

There was no answer from the Skull. The dwarf swung shut the iron maiden. There was a collar that fitted tightly about the woman's throat. Her head was visible, nothing more.

"You see?" The Skull's voice was a murmur. "We must make it possible for her to be identified... *afterward.*"

Nita tore at the ropes until the blood oozed from beneath her fingernails. But her bonds did not yield at all. The dwarf stood motionless beside the torture cage, hand upon a valve while his great luminous eyes prodded out into the darkness, blinking.

"No, no," Nita cried. "In Heaven's name, is there nothing that will save her?"

"Nothing," sighed the Skull. "Very well, Mignonette."

The dwarf yelped in high laughter and twisted the valve.

Sometime during the tearing horror of the minutes that followed, Nita swooned. Even in the black shadows into which her soul plunged, it seemed to Nita afterward that she could still hear those... those *screams.* And when she shuddered back to consciousness, the rasping voice of the Skull, as unemotional as Death, was sounding in her ears again.

"Woman, which shall it be?" it said. "Will you enter the embrace of Mignonette's love, with these questions answered, mercifully dead... or will you delight Mignonette's ears with your screams?"

Nita forced up her head and stared unseeingly before her. She was aware of the dread machine there with its pitiful prey, but her eyes went beyond. "Dick," she whispered. *"Dick."* And there was no answer. There could be no answer. Her head sagged again.

"Answer, woman!" commanded the Skull. "The choice is yours!"

Nita somehow voiced words, "These questions—"

"The secrets of your lover's fortress, woman," the Skull rasped. "Already, we can open the gates, but there are still a few things we need to know. It will make a good stronghold *for* us when, presently, Wentworth is removed."

Nita's head came up proudly, "Are you so sure, fool?" she said clearly. "Do you think a mountebank and his fool can master him?" Somehow, she managed a ghost of laughter. "You choose your questions badly. *I will not answer them!"*

The Skull breathed a name, "Mignonette! Mignonette, she mocks us, I think!"

The dwarf capered toward Nita and, somewhere near, a bell whirred softly. She heard the Skull's muted voice.

"Woman, I shall need you no longer. The *Spider* has walked into our trap! He is my prisoner!" He laughed again, until the harsh sound of it beat back from the walls, until it seemed to rasp within Nita's own skull. It cut off sharply, and she knew that the Skull had gone. Before her grimaced and capered the dwarf, Mignonette, and there was greediness in his luminous eyes!

NITA shrank as his hands touched her in the darkness, as ropes began to fall away from her. She gathered her body together. Now was her chance. She was alone with this misshapen monster. When the last ropes fell free—Hope began to thrill through her. If she could only get hold of a weapon! But she needed no weapons against this small, misshapen creature. She was thankful that, long ago when first she had joined her life with Dick's, he had compelled her to learn jiu-jitsu.

The ropes fell and, with a bound, Nita was out of

the chair. Before she had fairly gained her feet, a hand closed about her ankle and Nita pitched headlong. A weight fell upon her shoulders and gouging knees drove out her breath. Half-stunned by the fall, she felt her hands knotted together behind her back and she was lifted bodily into the air!

"Ah, no, pretty one," whispered the dwarf and his breath was nauseous against her face. "Ah, no! You think because Mignonette is a cripple he's weak. You are wrong, pretty one—"

Without apparent effort, the dwarf swung Nita clear of the ground and, holding her above his head, ran toward the torture machine on the brilliantly lighted stage. Nita kicked out fiercely, trying to beat at that misshapen body, to batter that swollen head with her knees—but it availed her nothing. She was thrown viciously to the ground and the strength went out of her. When, finally, she could struggle to her knees again, the iron maiden was empty and its shining metal arms were opened to embrace her!

The dwarf bent over her, smirking. "Ah, pretty one, it is not too late. But be kind to Mignonette—"

He laughed.

Nita gathered her forces and staggered to her feet. As the dwarf leaped toward her, she fell backward and lashed out with both heels together. It was all she could do. It was her final effort... and it failed.

The dwarf skipped aside as nimbly as a goat and, an instant later, Nita felt herself on her feet, reeling backward. Her eyes widened with horror as she realized the meaning of that. She tried to catch herself... and steel bands snapped shut about her, bands whose touch burned through her clothing. She was in the iron maiden! She shrank back from them and they only closed more tightly about her. In front of her helpless body, the dwarf danced and sang a song in a cracked, thin voice hatefully like a child's.

"You can mock me, pretty one," he sang, "but no one mocks my lovely maiden. No one can resist her embrace. No one!"

He stood before her, head cocked on one side. His clawed hands reached out to her, and Nita closed her eyes. She could do no more. She knew briefly the violence of those clutching hands and then—the door of the iron maiden clanged shut! The collar closed tightly about her throat! Nita's teeth clamped on her lip. Somewhere she must find the courage to endure this. It could not last for long. Not long. Hysteria corded her lovely throat. Her bound fists clenched behind her, pressed nails into flesh. She could hear the thud of the dwarf's quick, dancing feet, his cracked, crooning voice.

Almost against her will, Nita's eyes flared open. The valve—the dwarf toyed with it. He polished it with his strange, child-sized hands that were so incredibly powerful. He glanced up at her slyly and chuckled, set his shoulders to untwist the stubborn wheel of the valve. Nita drew on the last reserves of her strength, lifted up her eyes... and nothing happened. The dwarf laughed and he was dancing around her again, tormenting her spirit. Nita felt her courage sag. She couldn't stand much more. God, anything would be kinder! Even death by that awful pain that would come at her through the hissing pipes!

A frantic hope began to swell in her breast. The Skull had said that Dick was captured...but the Skull had not returned! Was it possible that somewhere behind these thick underground walls, Dick was fighting successfully? If only she could gain a little time! This fiend delighted in tormenting her. If he thought that she was suffering, he would delay the actual release of that valve for a little while for a few heartbeats of time until he tired of the fun. Nita began to rail at him, to plead with him. When next he gripped the valve, she begged him to turn it open.

"Let me die now!" she panted at him. "Anything is better than this uncertainty!"

Her voice rose thinly, as if broken by terror. The delighted dwarf pretended once more to open the valve, watched her head strain back as she set her body for the torture... and he didn't open the valve. How long could she hold him like this? How long had this mad play been going on? Minutes dragged past without end, and the dwarf was tiring of his fun. He stood and watched her with those bright, blinking eyes, head cocked on one side.

She whispered "Dick..."

Glass crashed somewhere. It sounded almost as if it were in this very room! Nita stared out into the darkness, No, she was mad. It could mean nothing to her, nothing at all. It was a trick of her disordered nerves. Dick couldn't—a glad cry burst from Nita's lips. The dwarf at her side snarled, seized the valve and out of the roof of that pit of darkness before the stage a spear of gun flame thrust!

As if in a dream, Nita saw the misshapen body of the dwarf plucked up by a bullet and hurled kicking to the platform. She saw a man leap down where the back-glow of the lights reached, springing from an overhead trapdoor. Nita cried out. She thought she cried out a name. It was a whisper, *"Dick!"*

Darkness swooped down upon her.

CHAPTER TEN
Victory—and Defeat

SAGGING into a merciful unconsciousness, Nita did not see the second man drop through the ceiling trapdoor, nor watch the two struggle toward her as if they fought their way through swift, deep water. They moved side by side with a heavy slowness, holding their guns far out and carefully so that they could see them—side by side, Richard Wentworth and Donald Beck!

"You keep watch," Wentworth said thickly. "You got less gas. Gun faster." He reached the iron maiden and began to fumble with the clasps. "It's all right, Nita. All right now!"

She heard that.

He was frantic with the need for haste, but all his movements were made with wooden limbs. At last the clips of the iron maiden swung open and he could lift Nita tenderly from the torture trap. He gathered her torn garments about her, wrapped his coat about her shoulders and swung her up in his arms.

Safe.

Nita was stirring faintly now. "Oh, Dick," she whispered. "The Skull said you were trapped."

"I was," Wentworth told her thickly. "They were keeping their distance and letting the gas do their work. Then Beck came in and dragged me out. He got a dose of gas doing it. I don't know why the Skull's men haven't followed to finish us off. Two of us, and both groggy with gas—"

A slashing beam of light knifed down from the trapdoor and Wentworth painfully lifted his gun. A man's voice called down to him cheerfully, "It's the police, Mr. Wentworth. Where are the rats? We can't find them!"

It was a matter of minutes then before they could be drawn up through the trapdoor and taken to the open air. An intern made a rapid examination and his report.

"The gas has strained your heart, sir," he told Wentworth. "The best thing you can do is to go to the hospital for a long rest."

Wentworth smiled at him wryly, "That's the best, is it, Doctor? How bad is that strain?"

The intern shook a worried head. "I'd have to run a cardiograph to tell that, sir, but there's a definite disturbance. Frankly, it may be very serious."

Wentworth shrugged. He still couldn't make his words come quickly, but his brain seemed supernaturally keen. "I think," he said carefully, "that is an effect of the gas that will wear off when it's completely out of my system."

"A stimulant, then," the man suggested.

He started to prepare a hypo-dermic needle and Wentworth's eyes fell on the ambulance nameplate, *Cherry Hill Hospital.* A startled oath leaped to his lips. In the rush of violent action he had forgotten the phoned inquiry of the Skull about that very hospital! He had assured the Skull that the hospital had paid, but by now the Skull must know that was trickery. He gripped the intern's arm.

"Never mind that injection," he said, with something like his own crispness. "When you return to the hospital, insist on poison tests being run on every drug in the place. It's been threatened by the Skull."

He whirled toward the police officers, glimpsed Ram Singh in the background. He was understanding things more clearly now. Plainly, Beck had been suspicious of him and had followed for that reason. Ram Singh had pursued Beck and had summoned the police for safety. Certainly, he could no longer suspect Beck since the man had saved his life at the risk of his own!

Nita touched Wentworth's arm. "I remember now," she said, her voice low with anxiety. "The Skull said he had 'an errand to do' at some hospitals!"

Wentworth nodded. "I'll get hold of Kirkpatrick right away."

He moved on heavy feet toward a cigar store where he could reach a telephone.

God, what horror the poisons of the Skull would wreak in the hospitals of the city! What in Heaven's name could the man expect to gain from such practices? Surely, he did not hope to collect racket money from hospitals? Almost, it seemed the man must be killing for sheer love of slaughter!

WENTWORTH tried to hurry and an overwhelming weakness made him stagger as he moved. There was squeezing pain around his heart, physical this time and he clutched his breast. His head sagged as he pushed into the store. His lips twisted bitterly with the realization that he dared not allow a stimulant to be used. That was the horror that was at work throughout the city. At one stroke, the Skull had nullified all the years of medical research and science. Worse than that, he had turned those discoveries into torture potions for humanity!

He phoned his warning to Kirkpatrick, told him with difficulty of the battle in the drug company plant. "Forbes was with me when the Skull attacked," he said heavily, "but disappeared during the gas. Your men are hunting the Skull's gang, but so far without success. They apparently had some secret exit from the plant. God alone knows what is coming next. Yes, I'll be at my home if you want me."

Wentworth made his slow way then to the Daimler, which Ram Singh had driven, and he and Nita started home with Beck. Wentworth felt incredibly feeble and a fear was gnawing at his heart... a new and strange thing for the *Spider!*

Suppose the young intern was right and his heart was permanently strained! There was an end of all his crusades, the end of everything. With heavy hands, Wentworth opened a compartment in the car and drew out the first aid kit. It had been all right when he had used it on the poisoned child, he recalled. Nita took it from his fumbling hands and rapidly fixed it, gave Wentworth the shot. It helped.

Wentworth leaned back against the cushions and began to talk. "Beck, I am sure now that you know nothing of those racket payments you received. The police will be harder to convince, but perhaps it can be arranged. Nita, you received no intimation of the real source of income of the Skull, did you?"

Nita replied softly in the negative. Her eyes were anxious on Wentworth's leaden face. Her fingers clung to his arm.

Beck said urgently, "But there has to be some monetary reason behind all this? The Skull isn't just murdering for the fun of it."

Nita shuddered a little, remembering the emotionless mockery of that voice. It was conceivable, since she had seen and heard him.

Wentworth shook his head. "It may be," he said, "that Forbes' drugs are unadulterated and that, whether he is himself innocent or guilty, the Skull owns that company—hopes to cash in heavily when his company is proved sound. That would augur tremendous profits. Once the firm was established, it would take the other companies years to restore their credit with the public. It could be a move to drive down the value of drug stocks. God knows, they'll be down practically to zero when the market opens in the morning.

Wentworth's eyes opened keenly, "How do you feel, Beck?"

"I'm all right," Beck said sturdily, "I didn't get much of a dose of that gas."

Wentworth nodded. "I haven't any doubt at all that selling orders on drug stocks are deluging the Wall Street offices right now. Now, if we could find a few who were ordering *purchases* of drug stocks!"

Beck said softly, "By God, Mr. Wentworth, I believe you've got something there. Say the word and I'll get down to the financial district. If there's heavy trading threatening tomorrow, the telegraph people will have notified the brokers at their homes. I'll wager there will be staffs at work, getting ready for tomorrow."

"The police are going to be on your trail, Beck," Wentworth reminded him. "The only reason you weren't arrested at the Forbes plant was because no general alarm has been put out yet and those men didn't know you were sought. I'll do what I can to stave it off, but I don't know—you can't give much explanation of that racket money pouring into your office."

"None at all!" Beck said stubbornly. "They'll have to believe me, sir. Let me out at that subway station, and I'll shoot downtown. You'll be at home?"

Wentworth nodded and signaled Ram Singh to stop the car. "Good luck, Beck."

He offered his hand. "I won't forget what I owe you."

Beck's square-cut face flushed a little. "Forget it, sir," he said, and swung out of the car.

Nita waved to him as the Daimler surged forward again, then she settled down comfortably beside Wentworth and took his lean, powerful hand in both of hers. There was a cold fear within her, too, for this brave man beside her. The doctor's words had frightened her terribly. He might be mistaken, of course; once they were safe home—Rigidity crept along her nerves and Wentworth's head swung toward her.

"What is it, Nita?"

"I just remembered," she said. "Oh, the Skull may have been lying, but he said that he could enter your home at any time he wanted. He said, they knew how to get in."

"Tell Ram Singh to hurry," Wentworth said quietly.

He lifted his heavy hands and took hold of his automatics, looked down at their precise, perfectly functioning mechanism. As long as there were bullets in their clips and fingers to pull them, they would work perfectly. No heart in *them* to give out. Wentworth's lips pulled into a straight, thin line. Rest, the doctor had said. Rest. Wentworth laughed harshly.

How could any man rest when such hell had been loosed on Earth? He flicked on a shortwave radio set and heard the police announcer speeding cars to the hospitals. A sharp anxiety seized him. He switched to another channel, hunting a news broadcast.

WITH shocking suddenness, a voice blasted loudly into the tonneau. "Poison has been found in the hospital supplies of the city," the announcer said excitedly, "but not before seventeen patients had died at Cherry Hill Hospital. Four of these were undergoing emergency operations. Too late, the authorities found out that the ether had been poisoned. Three persons undergoing observation in the psychiatric ward were given quieting drugs and, instead of quieting, they turned into homicidal maniacs. One of them broke loose and reached the children's ward before he could be caught, and three of the patients there were murdered."

Nita gasped at the news. "Oh, that's horrible. Horrible! How could any human being do a thing like that?"

The announcer's magnified voice silenced her

whispered words. "Two more of those poor victims of the criminals who murdered Nona Malvern have been found," he rushed on. "This time, it was the wife of a druggist and her infant son, They had been reduced to skeletons except for the heads and faces, which were left untouched apparently so that they could be identified. There was a message attached to the skeletons:

"They say that women always talk
and cannot keep a secret—
But it's hard to talk, or even breathe
with no flesh on your brisket."

Wentworth fumblingly cut off the switch. Where would all this horror end? He was forced to admit that he had accomplished painfully little against the Skull. The discovery of the racket money at Beck's office appeared to mean little; probably was intended to be revealed as a blind for the real operations of the Skull. Oh, he had succeeded in exposing one of the Skull's hideouts, but it meant so damnably little.

The car was whirling into Sutton Place now and Wentworth handed to Nita the sonic whistle which operated the gates of his home. She put it to her soft lips and her eyes were straining ahead for the first glimpse. It was reassuring to see the severely plain wall and the mansion itself rising beyond. But what would they find inside? Nita blew the curiously varying note of the sonic whistle, timing the tones carefully, and the gates slid soundlessly open. The Daimler sped through and drew to an easy halt before the doors.

Wentworth forgot his weakness and started to leap to the ground. He stumbled, caught himself only by a violent effort, and thereafter he moved more carefully. Ram Singh and Nita were at his side in an instant; then the tall Sikh strode on ahead. There was tension in the softness of his stride, in the taut roll of his heavy shoulders. He stopped and his hand pointed to a red smear on the floor!

Wentworth rasped out an oath. They pushed into the elevator together.

"They couldn't have any reason to harm Melissa," Nita whispered. "She has done nothing, nothing at all."

Her voice died as her memory swung back, flinchingly, to the Skull. The woman he had killed in that torture machine had done nothing to him, either. She had only happened to be the wife of a druggist.

The elevator door slid open and Nita darted out, ran through the hallway calling to Melissa. There was no answer, but on the floor of the drawing room was the torn fragment of a dress, and there were more of those ominous red stains. Wentworth walked heavily across the room.

"Jackson and Jenkyns," he said to Ram Singh. "They must be somewhere here."

The tall Sikh strode off silently through the house. Nita's cries echoed emptily as she still, futilely, called Melissa. Wentworth's face was bitter and grim. Perhaps they had taken Jenkyns and Jackson with them, too, to be found presently with a taunting verse pinned to their fleshless bones. And the *Spider* was hobbled. His hands, gripping the automatics that seemed too heavy for them, were trembling with weakness. Almost, the gallant heart of the *Spider* despaired. He dropped heavily into a chair. Presently, Nita came darting back into the room.

"She's gone, Dick!" Nita cried. "The Skull—" She swayed and covered her eyes with her hands. "Oh, Dick, that torture machine—the Skull forced me to watch a woman die in it." She took slow stumbling steps and slumped down on the floor, put her head against Wentworth's knees. "Oh, Dick—"

MOMENTS afterward, Ram Singh strode into the room with the limp body of the aged Jenkyns in his arms. The Sikh's fine eyes were hot with anger. "They war on women and old men, these vermin," he said violently. *"Wah,* they are less than vermin! Lead thy servant to them, master!"

Nita drove her flagging body to her feet and bent over Jenkyns. Her voice was crisp as she issued orders to Ram Singh. "It doesn't seem too serious, Dick. He was hit over the head."

Wentworth closed his eyes and deliberately drove the horror and despair from his mind; squeezed out the last ounce of emotion. They might have crippled the *Spider's* body, but his brain was still painfully alive. He must revise his whole campaign against the Skull—do it swiftly and well. He lay like a dead man, his guns resting on his thighs, face drained of blood. He was like that, still unmoved, when Jenkyns aroused.

He could tell little. He had heard the sonics whistle blow in the street to open the gates and set about preparing a quick meal. Someone had slipped up behind him presently and then hit him over the head.

Wentworth's eyes flicked open. The Skull had not lied, then. He had penetrated the intricate secret of the sonics whistle, timing and tones. It had to be precise or the gate would not operate. That was an amazing thing. The whir of the phone cut in on his thoughts and Jenkyns tried feebly to rise and answer it.

Nita forced him to lie still and herself brought the portable instrument to Wentworth's side.

"This is Beck," The young detective sounded wildly excited. "I've only checked one office, sir, but you're right. There's a landslide of selling orders. And there are a few buying orders. One of the biggest was put in by Wilton Toley, the district attorney."

"Good work, Beck," Wentworth told him quietly. "See how many other buying orders you can find. This is important!" Wentworth was smiling as he replaced the phone in its cradle. Now he knew what to do! He began to make a series of phone calls, first to his bankers.

"Richard Wentworth speaking," he said quietly. "Orders, Henderson. Get busy at once. I'll send you an unlimited order against my cash. As soon as the markets open in the morning, start buying drug stocks. I want to corner the market. Any drug stock offered, it doesn't matter. If the cash runs out, liquidate my bonds and stocks... *but corner the market!"*

Wentworth smiled at the surprised protests over the wire. "Don't let the future of the stocks worry you, Henderson," he said. "They'll be sound enough when this terror is over. Wait... one more instruction. I want all of the purchases made in my name. Make no attempt to cover up my identity and don't withhold information if the newspapers get in touch with you. That's all. Yes, of course, I'll confirm it in writing within the hour."

Nita was staring at him without understanding as he went rapidly on with his calls, getting in touch with brokers and financial men. To each one, he gave the same order, with the same instructions, that all was to be done in his name.

"But what in the world, Dick?" Nita cried. "Everyone will suspect you now! Already, a lot of blame has been put on the *Spider!* If you buy in these stocks—"

Wentworth smiled grimly, "Yes, of course, dear. Now if you'll play at being my secretary for a while, and call a telegraph boy, we'll get out these written confirmations. They won't go the whole distance without them because they'll want proof of the orders. And I want them to go the *whole* distance!"

For a long moment, Nita stared at him. There was a question in her eyes.

Wentworth laughed, sharply. "My mind is all right, Nita," he said. "Don't worry. They've crippled the *Spider*'s body, but they haven't stopped me yet!"

Presently the work was done and the orders dispatched by a messenger boy. It was within five minutes of that time that the signal bell of the gate sent its summons through the house. Ram Singh strode quickly to an electrical device which permitted him to see what lay outside the gate. He turned stiffly.

"The police, *sahib,"* he said softly. "Kirkpatrick *sahib* and the man, Toley. Many uniformed men."

Wentworth smiled faintly. "Very well, Ram Singh. Admit Kirkpatrick *sahib* and the man, Toley. No one else."

Nita crossed quickly to his side, "This is trouble, Dick," she said. "Stanley Kirkpatrick wouldn't come like that if it weren't, without calling you."

Wentworth pushed to his feet, put his arms about Nita. "Yes, dear," he said, "it is undoubtedly trouble. The Skull is trying his best to frame me, with Toley's help. I may have to run for it—I may."

"Not alone!" Nita cried. "Dick, you can't leave me again."

For a moment, Wentworth held her close, gazing down into her worried eyes. Then he bent and kissed her softly. He made no other answer to her cry. "Dear, will you go and play on the organ pipes with your hands? Have the door of the secret room so that it will open at a touch."

NITA went swiftly and the elevator doors opened. Toley bounced out and there was triumph on his sharp, narrow face. Kirkpatrick followed him more steadily, a worried frown on his forehead. He paused just inside the door and knuckled the pointed ends of his mustache, a habit of his.

"Dick," he said quietly, "you will order Ram Singh to admit my men. I did not care to force the issue."

Wentworth shook his head. "There was no search warrant, I believe? I think we'd better let matters rest like this for the moment."

Ram Singh stood, with folded arms, just inside the room. His dark eyes glittered as they roved from his master to the two men he had admitted.

Kirkpatrick said sharply, "Dick, this is not your usual greeting."

"This is not your usual method of visiting me," Wentworth told him quietly. "My friends are always welcome. Are you my friend today, Kirk?"

Toley said shortly, "Enough of this foolishness. Arrest him, Commissioner."

Wentworth stood warily poised. The pain was in his breast again from the quickened beating of his heart. He had guessed right then. His voice was even, sardonic. His eyebrows lifted with a quirk of mockery.

"I believe it is customary," he said gently, "for a prospective prisoner to be informed of the charges lodged against him?"

Toley braced his short, vibrant body. "Sure, I'll tell you, Mr. *Spider* Wentworth. There are more than a hundred counts of murder against you, signed with your own little seal. And don't think *you* can beat it. I've been busy today."

"Busy buying up drug stocks, Toley?" Wentworth asked gently.

Toley's face grew fiery red. "That's my business, damn it. Don't try to evade the issue. I had bullets dug out of the trees out at Wister's place and identified mine and Kirkpatrick's. The others are yours. They were fired from the same gun that killed the man at Beck's office building and the man in the apartment where the druggist was killed. You killed them both, Wentworth, and you put your seal on them both."

Kirkpatrick came slowly forward, and he placed himself so that Ram Singh could not come at his back.

"Richard Wentworth, I arrest you on two charges of murder," he said, his voice stiff, emotionless. "Hand over your guns!"

In the doorway, Nita cried out sharply, "I'll shoot the first man who moves!"

CHAPTER ELEVEN
Fugitives

TOLEY whipped around toward the door and stared, bug-eyed, at Nita with a small automatic held competently in her right hand. Ram Singh, at a word from her, laid his hand upon the handle of his great-bladed knife. Wentworth kept his sardonic smile, but there was warmth now in his heart. Nita has not seized control through any doubts of him, but to place herself definitely outside the law. Now, unless he took Nita with him, she would be arrested and jailed as his accessory. Perhaps, even that would be better.

Wentworth cut off his thoughts. There was no time to delay. He lifted his hands and drew out his guns. His arms had that same tired weakness in them, but he didn't think either of these men would know that.

"Thanks, Nita," Wentworth said quietly. "Now, take their guns and go... to the place you know. I will join you. Ram Singh, go and guard the *missie sahib.*"

Nita did as he bade her, then behind Kirkpatrick she stood to peer toward Wentworth with questioning eyes. There was doubt and fear in her glance, but Wentworth only smiled and motioned her on. "I'll be with you in moment," he said.

Toley was ranting, but Kirkpatrick stood, stiffly indignant and silent, until Nita and Ram Singh had left the room. He was facing Dick, not ten feet away and their eyes met... and held. Kirkpatrick's eyes revealed their pain, but the set of his mouth showed no tendency to swerve from his duty.

"I'm between you and the door, Dick," he said steadily. "It is my intention that you shall face this charge of murder. I know that, innocent, you have fled the police before this in order to continue battling against criminals. Now, you have not that excuse. We have the criminals under lock and key."

Wentworth started. "What are you saying, Kirk? What criminals?"

"We will have confessions by morning," Kirkpatrick pushed on. "Beck and Forbes were in this together. We have them in prison and it is only a question of time before they tell their whole story. The evidence against both of them is too powerful for them to hope to escape."

Wentworth shrugged. "About Forbes, I don't know," he said. "Beck is innocent. There is stronger evidence against Toley here than against anyone else."

Kirkpatrick's gaze did not waver. Wentworth said, "Ask him why he's buying drug stocks. Don't you see that all this racketeering business is a blind? It's merely to cover up the real purpose which is the wholesale purchase of drug stocks at the ridiculously low figure to which they'll drop. There can be no permanent impairment of their value, and—

"How did those criminals know you were going to Wister's, so that they could set up that elaborate trap for you? Surely, you did not tell them. If you suspect me, remember that Toley said he would not go until the next day. Toley would have discovered which men were most likely to talk among the druggists, so he would know which needed to be silenced. He knew that Nita would be arrested, and there must have been some advance warning there or else she could not have been waylaid on the way to police headquarters."

Toley laughed with sharp mockery. "You can't be very sure of my guilt, Mr. *Spider* Wentworth. I'm still alive."

Kirkpatrick said, "All right, Dick. I'm coming after those guns now."

"Stop, Kirk," he ordered softly.

Kirkpatrick's face tightened, but he did not check his slow stride forward. Desperation pumped at Wentworth's lungs. He could not risk a personal encounter with Kirkpatrick with his heart in this condition. If his heart did not fail, he would be so weakened as to be an easy conquest, unless… his trigger finger whitened with pressure.

"Go ahead and shoot." Kirkpatrick's face was suddenly twisted.

Wentworth squeezed the trigger. The heavy blast rolled across the room. With a scream, Toley whirled and went racing wildly out of the room. He collided with the door jam, fell, was up and running again in a heartbeat. He had not waited to see what happened.

WENTWORTH had indeed fired, at point-blank range, but just before he squeezed the trigger, he jerked the muzzle high. In the same instant that he fired, he leaped forward. As he had known must happen, Kirkpatrick had winced and closed his eyes at the shock of that gun blast so close to him.

Wentworth needed that instant's advantage. He swung the gun barrel lightly at Kirkpatrick, planning to knock him out. The gun landed, but Kirkpatrick was instantly grappling with him. In his anxiety not to hurt his friend, Wentworth had miscalculated. He had not struck hard enough.

Kirkpatrick's arms were like iron bands about him and there was no strength in Wentworth's body. "For God's sake, Dick," Kirkpatrick whispered. "Don't make me do this! Surrender!"

Wentworth wrenched, and there was no use at all. He pulled the only trick he could. He let his body go suddenly inert and sagged with all his weight against Kirkpatrick's grip. The hold did not loosen, but the commissioner was thrown off balance. As he stumbled forward, Wentworth wrenched an arm free and struck again. This time it was hard enough.

Wentworth stood, sobbing for breath, above the prone body of his friend. "I'm sorry, Kirk," he whispered. "Damned sorry, old man."

He turned away and his feet dragged. He staggered and thrust a gun-filled hand against the wall for support. There was a darkness before his eyes and helpless anger shook him. It was a vicious thing that the service to which he dedicated himself stood always between him and happiness; between him and his friend. He would never regret the service, nor his purpose, but sometimes it was hard.

His left hand was pressed hard against his chest. This was the bitterest blow that any criminal ever had struck against him, to leave a man whole and unwounded and helpless.

What the hell? He was lying on the floor. Damn it, he had to get on! He began to crawl. Figures were rushing toward him. He tried to lift a gun and heard Nita calling to him, felt the strong arms of Ram Singh about him.

"Seaplane," Wentworth gasped. "Go up the Sound until it's dark, then double back to—to—

The darkness crowded in irresistibly this time, washed over him in waves that, presently, took on a strange rhythm. He identified it at last: it was the motor of the plane, and they were in the air. He opened his eyes and saw Nita's face.

"All right," he whispered. "It's all right now."

He slept.

WHEN Wentworth awoke again he was in a room he had never seen before and, moments after he opened his eyes, Nita came energetically in and bent over him. "I drugged you," she said calmly. "Otherwise, you'd have kept right on going and killed yourself. I couldn't really let you do a thing like that."

Wentworth grinned up at her. "I guess I'm relieved of command," he said. "Where are we? How much time has elapsed? What's happening?"

Nita laughed at him, and relief was apparent in her tones. "I believe you're going to be all right, Dick, as soon as the full effects of that gas have left your system. I haven't dared to have a doctor in.

"All right, I'm going to answer your questions. We're in North Carolina, in a tourist camp just outside Wilmington. We've been here two days. You've been awake before long enough to eat, but the drugs kept you from remembering, I guess. As for what's happening, I don't know. I haven't seen a newspaper or listened to a radio. I sent Ram Singh back to New York with the plane."

Wentworth's smile faded. "Two days," he said slowly. "God alone knows what could happen up there in this time. The police—"

"The police," Nita told him firmly, "are better able to fight the Skull than you are—for the present. You're staying right here until you're strong—if I have to sit on you!"

Wentworth stared up at her fixedly for a moment, then smiled again as the color flooded Nita's cheeks. But his smile was a transient thing, and was replaced by that same worried frown. "You're right," he agreed, "or you would be right if it weren't for my plans. You see, I wanted the Skull to find me. He has to... and he has to take me alive, or there will be no profits for him. I have to go where he can find me."

Nita leaned over and touched a cool palm to his forehead. It was plain she did not understand.

Wentworth moved restlessly. "Don't you understand, Nita?" he asked. "If my orders have been followed out, I should have what amounts to a corner on the drug stocks, by this time. The Skull was counting on making that corner himself. The only way he can cash in on the profits of his murders now is for him to find me, alive, and force me to sign over the stocks I hold to him. When he does that—"'

Nita's face was wholely grave now. "I understand, Dick. I'll get some newspapers, if you'll promise to try to sleep while I'm gone. Please try to realize, Dick. Unless you're strong, all that work will accomplish nothing at all. When—when the Skull captures you, you have to be strong enough to fight and win."

Wentworth said quietly, "I promise." He thought his mind would be too full of whirling thoughts and plans, but sleep came quickly.

When he awoke he was much stronger and the newspapers were beside him.

As he read, his face grew grim and stern. The deaths had continued to mount in New York. Drugstores, reopened after careful check on their contents, nevertheless were still found to have poison stocks. A sneak-thief, caught exchanging a poisoned bottle for an innocuous one from the stock of a store, had said the *Spider* forced him to do it! Toley was rampant with his accusations that Wentworth was the *Spider,* and made the most of his evidence of the bullets. He glossed over the loophole in his structure—that he could not prove the bullets taken from the trees had come from Wentworth's guns! Nor had he stopped there. He was demanding the removal of Commissioner Kirkpatrick for allowing Wentworth to escape!

There were headlines on the stock market and editorial attacks on Wentworth for his attempts to corner the market to "reap the profits of wanton murder" as the editorials put it.

Nita came in then. "I have some of yesterday's papers, too," she said. "Both Forbes and Beck were released on writs of habeas corpus and Downey is their lawyer. Beck is saying now that he was duly elected head of the druggists' protective association and that the money in his office was their dues."

Wentworth stared at Nita, digesting that news. "He can get away with that if the druggists support him in the story," he said slowly. "And with the menace of the Skull, and what he has done to that poor woman and her child, I think the druggists will."

Nita nodded. "They already have, but I thought Beck was innocent."

Wentworth let the papers sag from his hands. "He saved my life when the Skull was trying to kill me," he said simply. "The Skull could bring the same type of pressure to bear upon Beck. I may be wrong, but I think Beck rather went off the deep end over Melissa...and the Skull has her a prisoner. I hope... she's still a prisoner."

Nita said slowly, "I heard a radio report while I was in the city. An epidemic of typhoid has broken out in New York and the first five persons inoculated, with what they thought was typhoid vaccine, died in convulsions... *poisoned!*"

Wentworth's fists clenched whitely. He said, with effort, "Nita..."

Nita's head bowed. "Yes, Dick," she whispered. "I know you must go... But, oh, Dick, I'm afraid... afraid..."

CHAPTER TWELVE
Captured!

THE narrow street was crowded from wall to wall with people. They stood rock-silent to listen to the hoarse-voiced man who harangued them.

"It's the fault of them bloody murderers in City Hall," he bellowed. "They can get us good medicine, if they want to. All of them are getting medicine, ain't they? And what do we get? We get poison."

Another man stood below him in the car on which the speaker was perched. "Nice going, Plug," he whispered. "You got them going."

A howl from someone in the mob, "To hell with the city bosses. Let's go tell them off. Let's go get the medicine before we're all poisoned like dogs."

Another voice took up the cry. The man called Plug looked down at his companion. "I tell you when the Skull plans a thing, it's done well—ain't it, Bumper?"

The crowd was echoing the cry now. The speaker on top the car raised both hands. "Come on, boys, I'll lead you," he shouted. "On to City Hall!"

He jumped down off the car and began to stalk through the mob. People followed him. There was a low mutter of anger. It mounted like the pound of storm-driven waves, and now there was the tramp of feet, too. The mob was on the march. Beside the car where the man called Bumper stood, a number of men drew together. They were all grinning.

"It's like taking candy from a kid," one said.

Bumper nodded. "Sure. There'll be three mobs coming at City Hall. The cops are sure to get wind of it and it will go on the radio. Then—

"Then we got the *Spider,* eh, Bumper?"

"You said it, Whitey. You can't fool the Skull. This guy, the *Spider,* will come out to try to stop the mob. It's just the sort of damn fool thing he likes to do. When he does—"

They piled into the car and it pushed into the rear of the mob until it reached a corner, then circled to get ahead of the marching, shouting people. There were indignant, bitter faces in that mob. Men who had lost loved ones and others whose families were ill with diseases they dared not treat with medicines. Clubs materialized in their hands and bricks and cobbles were clenched in ugly fists. They thought they were men with a grievance, this toy mob that the Skull had blown into life.

It was another mob on another street that Donald Beck saw. He heard the angry mutter of it before he caught sight of its leading, ragged ranks. He hesitated, then ducked into a phone booth and called the police. Afterward, he trailed along in the wake of the mob. His face was pale and set when he saw the three mobs, marching from different directions, swirl into Broadway and head downtown. The buses were stopped, and cars skittered from the path of the march. Windows were smashed by quick-flung rocks.

When the mob was within four blocks of City Hall, a battered small coupe swung out into the middle of Broadway from a side street and stopped. Instantly, a door opened and a man got out, climbed

(OVERLEAF) "Lynch the *Spider*!" They shouted.

rapidly to the roof. He stood there then, arms uplifted in a commanding gesture. There was a long black cape swinging from his shoulders, and the wide brim of a black hat was drawn down over his eyes. His voice rolled out, powerful and deep.

"Stop this madness, men! You are being led by murderers and criminals! Stop before you are slain—*The Spider commands it!"*

At the corner beyond where the *Spider* had taken his stand, an automobile started out into the street, then skittered back out of sight. The men inside it burst into excited laughter.

Bumper shook his small head. "We got to take him alive. Wait."

The *Spider* had no guns in his hands, and his eyes were keen as they swept over the mob.

"Listen, men," he urged, his resonant voice carrying easily through the mutter of the mob. "When have I ever lied to the people? When have I failed to serve them? I tell you that you are being used as tools by the very men who have poisoned your families!"

A young workingman near the front of the mob thrust forward, shaking a club angrily. "He lies!" the man shouted.

"This *Spider—he* is the one who killed our people. The papers say so. He is the poisoner. Lynch him. Lynch the *Spider!"*

For a moment, a stunned silence gripped the crowd, then the cry took hold. Everywhere, voices tossed the phrase back like echoes. "*Lynch the Spider!"*

Somewhere, a revolver cracked, and Wentworth heard the bullet hiss past him, but he did not flinch. Except by accident, he knew that he would not be killed. The men of the Skull would see to that. He lifted his hands to shout at the mob, and then his eyes narrowed. What he wanted was to turn aside the mob from City Hall, wasn't it? That and submit to capture by the men of the Skull?

Well, this was his chance. If they chased the *Spider* to lynch him, the mob would string out along the narrow side streets. Many of them would weary and turn away and there would be no one left to urge them on toward City Hall. As for the rest... the *Spider* would take his chances.

Wentworth began to run. It was a foolhardy thing he did and he knew it. Nita was two blocks away on a side street, waiting. But he dared not lead the mob toward her car.

Abruptly, a car carrying a half-dozen men swirled into Broadway and cut down the street toward which Wentworth was heading. The *Spider*'s taut drawn lips grimaced into a smile. If he had miscalulated now, he was finished. His guess was that those men would be the killers of the Skull. If they proved to be either the police or members of the mob—

His breath was already short when he rounded the corner with the mob in full cry behind him. A rock bounced off the pavement at his feet; another skimmed past his shoulder. Wentworth's eyes searched desperately, saw the car just ahead. He whipped out a gun, sprinted toward it. As he sprang to the runningboard, he jammed the gun against the head of the driver.

"Get going, and get going fast," he ordered.

The man's face went grey. "Sure, sure," he whimpered, while he fumbled with the gear shift. "Geez, you don't need to do that to me, *Spider.* Me, I drove here to save you, soon as I heard that mob yell. I think you're a swell guy. Sure, I do. Don't I, fellows?"

There were other men in the car and they all nodded hurriedly. "Sure, you do, Bumper. We all do."

One of them opened the door. "Get in, *Spider."*

Wentworth's face was grim as the car whipped forward.

He thrust his gun back into its holster and, at the same instant, one of the men struck him from behind. Wentworth fell limply to the floor. He heard the men burst into cackling laughter, and after that nothing for a long time.

WHEN Wentworth regained consciousness, it was with a rush. For moments, he could not place himself, and then the darkness of the place in which he was bound and the harsh, rasping voice he heard snapped the whole thing clearly into his mind. He swung his aching head and caught his breath.

The room in which he found himself might have been a replica of the loft building sub-basement in which he had found and rescued Nita. A pale greenish glow of light showed him that... shone, too, from the Skull that seemed to float in the darkness off to one side, whose voice had brought him back to his senses. He knew that his arms were bound painfully behind him and the pressure of his knees together revealed that they had found the hidden gun which he had hoped to use in extremity.

But it was not these things that drew the gasp of dismay from his stoical heart. Before him were two glass cases that duplicated the iron maiden he had seen before. In front of these stood a man with a flexible metal hose, a man though he seemed but a framework of glowing bones. And in those shimmering beautiful glass cases that he knew were torture coffins of death were two women—Melissa and *Nita van Sloan!*

"So you see," the Skull was saying smoothly,

"there is no hope at all, Wentworth. None at all. It was plain that you would suspect trickery, Wentworth. The guileless way in which you stepped into the car indicated that if nothing else. So we merely looked for whoever would be trailing you... and found her. A pity—yes, a pity."

Wentworth drew on all his stamina for resistance. Once he had done what the Skull would require, there could be no hope at all. There was yet a little shred of hope. He had told Nita to get in touch with Ram Singh and have him in turn trail her, but at first they had not been able to reach the Sikh. It was just possible Nita had succeeded after he left. He had wanted that double insurance passionately, but this trap had been sprung so soon after they had flown to New York that there had not been time to make sure.

"I am offering you, Wentworth," said the Skull, "the same alternative which I made to the woman. An easy death in exchange for what I wish."

Wentworth forced a smile to his lips.

"It would be most unwise for you to persist in murder now, Skull," he said, "since you wish to remain incognito. Surely, you did not think that I would depend on a single trailer? The police are undoubtedly surrounding this building now."

The Skull laughed. "If you refer to the Sikh, do not build your hopes too high, Wentworth. We contented ourselves with shooting him."

"I see," Wentworth acknowledged quietly, "and you want, of course, a transfer of my holdings in drug stocks."

Wentworth's eyes, under lowered lids, were questing over the room. His wrists were secured by ropes and other ropes bound him to a post. He was within a half dozen feet of the glass cases in which Nita and Melissa were prisoners.

Nita turned her head and smiled at him bravely. Melissa was pale, but her head was resolutely high. There was no one in sight save for this ghostly head that floated in space and the man with the flexible hose whose purpose Wentworth could guess only too well. The Skull had not had the time, or the facilities, to reconstruct his iron maiden, but he had an admirable substitute.

Wentworth said quietly, "I have more things to bargain with than that, Mr. Skull! There are certain papers on their way now to Commissioner Kirkpatrick, which could be intercepted since I asked him to hold them for me. Certain papers which contain some very fine circumstantial evidence, such as the way in which the sonics whistle that opens my gates was duplicated. Why, when so much that went on in my home was known, a certain visit made, of course, in the line of duty, was ignored by the Skull."

Behind him, he was working on the bonds frantically. If he could only wet the ropes, he thought he might succeed in stretching them enough... just enough.

The Skull laughed harshly.

WENTWORTH laughed, too. The ropes were stubborn, but how could he wet them? How... he found out that the post was rough. It wouldn't saw through the ropes in anything less than an hour. But there were splinters that would cut flesh, and produce... *wetness.* Even if he got free of the ropes, what could he hope to accomplish—unarmed, and facing the Skull? Undoubtedly, there were many more men within call.

"Reproducing the sonics was simple for you, eh, Skull?" he said. "Simple for any man who is a wizard at electrical gadgets such as these fake skeletons you hang about."

"Not all of them are fakes, my friend." The Skull spoke softly. "There is, for instance, the skeleton of Nona Malvern and of that other woman and child."

"Not all of the men are fakes," Wentworth acknowledged. "Some merely wear dark clothing with the bones painted on in phosphorescence. And you are not always merely a painted wooden box with a voice wired into it. I think that now, for instance, you are merely wearing a dark robe and that you are present in fact."

"Is this evidence?" Impatience marked the Skull's voice. "Make an end... and sign the paper. I promise you a quick death. And the women. A head shot before you are stripped of flesh. Come, surely that is magnanimous of me?"

The splinters had not produced as much blood as Wentworth had hoped. He tore the flesh of his wrists. "To get the sonics that opened the gate," he hurried on, "you merely set up a recording device when you staged that riot near my house on the first night. You have been clever, and there is damnably little evidence against you. But once the finger of suspicion is pointed, the police can find evidence."

The Skull was moving toward him now, and his hands came out from the black robe he wore, producing a piece of paper. "You will sign this, Wentworth," he said shortly.

Wentworth said quietly, *"Go to hell, Mr. Samuel Wister!"*

The Skull stopped and the hands that were holding the paper trembled the least bit.

Wentworth was frantically struggling with the ropes. His hands were slippery now and the ropes were stretching just a little.

"Do you think, Wister," he said sharply, "that you can conceal all the evidences of the ambuscade among the trees on your place? The piercings in the tree trunks which, lighted up and seen through your gas cloud, looked like skeletons? The wire cable on which you floated your Skull must have been anchored somewhere. The police will find those things, Wister, when they open the papers I have mailed them. They will find that you had been using the money of your ward, Nona Malvern, and that will tell them why you killed her."

"You can't know that," the Skull whispered. "It isn't possible!"

Wentworth laughed sharply. His left hand was almost free. "No, I'll admit that was guesswork, Wister, but it had to be something like that. A clever dodge, too, to turn suspicion away from you. And that visit to me the next morning, revealing things you intended should be found out anyway; poisoning your own drugs because no one would suspect you of doing such a foolhardy thing. And you own the company which Forbes heads—*don't you, Wister?"*

WENTWORTH strained violently, and his left hand slipped out of the ropes. The Skull caught the movement and started to leap back… too late. Wentworth's left hand flew out and fastened into the throat beneath the plaster casque of the skull. His fingers bit in deeply, and he pulled the Skull toward him while he strained to wrench his right hand free.

He saw the Skull's hand jab under the robe and knew that it would come out with a gun… and he could not dodge. He was still roped fast to the post. He had only one hand, and he must not release that hold. His shoulders hunched as he threw strength into that arm, increasing the pressure.

The gun whipped out of Wister's pocket and Wentworth yanked the man toward him just as the revolver blasted. The bullet struck in his thigh. Frantically, Wentworth wrenched at Wister's throat. That wound would drain him of strength and Wister was bringing up the gun again. Frantically, Wentworth wrenched at his right hand, still bound to the post. There was a tearing pain that shot to his shoulder… but the hand came free.

Wincingly, Wentworth swung that injured right hand at Wister's body and the gun spat flame again. The bullet caught Wentworth in the body this time. He felt numbness spreading over his chest, but the ropes were dropping down about his feet. He tried to take a step forward and stumbled, Wister wrenched free, ran toward the darkness. Wentworth struggled up and his leg gave way again. The gun spat lancing flame toward the *Spider*, but Wister's aim was not good this time. Not good enough.

Wentworth's breath was sobbing in his throat. He could not reach Wister, could not overtake him with his wounded leg. And, no matter how poor Wister's aim was, he could finish the execution easily enough from a safe distance. Desperately, Wentworth's eyes swung about the dark cellar. Probably, Wister was going for more men.

Wentworth's gaze fell on the stiff figure with the hose before the glass cages which held the girls prisoner. The figure had not moved. Eagerness sent Wentworth scrabbling toward it, as he guessed at the truth. Wister had not dared allow one of his men in the room while he forced the stock transfer from Wentworth. Probably, he had intended to lie and say he had not obtained it. At any rate, this figure poised before the cages was a skeleton—a human skeleton swung on delicate, almost invisible wires from the ceiling.

With a final scrambling leap, Wentworth reached the skeleton and seized from his hands the length of flexible metal hose. There was a valve. Even as Wentworth's hands closed upon the hose, the gun spoke again. Wentworth cried out and pitched limply down before the glass cages where Nita and Melissa were held inexorable prisoners.

Melissa had fainted. Nita was sobbing, crying out frantically as she struck her fragile hands against the glass that imprisoned her. If only she could break free! The Skull was coming forward at a run now. He held the gun in one hand, in the other the stock transfer.

"Don't worry," he rasped at Nita. "He isn't dead… yet I'll wring enough life from him to sign this paper, and afterward—"

The gun was wary in his hand. He was watching for the slightest movement on the part of Wentworth. But when Wentworth moved, it was with explosive force, like the release of a tightly coiled spring. He sprang sideways like a crab and as he moved, the hose in his hand opened with a prolonged, strangled hiss!

There was an instant when the Skull's prolonged scream was all terror, and there was another when it changed to a shriek of utter clear agony. After that, there was no sound at all for a long, long space. It was in that sobbing silence that Wentworth heard distinctly the battering axes upon metal doors. His eyes swung to Nita. That could mean but one thing… the police.

"Dick," Nita sobbed. "Oh, Dick, you won, but… but you wore the clothes of the *Spider.* Your guns—"

"The guns are gone, stolen by the Skull," Wentworth panted. "Good lord, he shot me with my own gun."

"But he captured the *Spider,* Dick," Nita cried. "The police must know that."

Wentworth was weak with the increasing pain of his wounds. "Yes," he said thickly, "the police know that. The police—"

WHEN the final door crashed down, Donald Beck was the first man through. He crossed the room in a rush and stared at the grim signs of the fight. On the floor lay a man with a shattered false Skull over his head and his chest… his chest was stripped bare of flesh. Near him, Nita and Melissa were huddled over Wentworth, who seemed unconscious with his wounds. And in one of those ominous glass cases was the skeleton of a man—a skeleton about whose feet lay the remnants of the *Spider*'s black cape and hat.

A cop said, "Geez, look, he got the *Spider.* It's *got* to be the *Spider!* The crooks we caught say the Skull was in here all alone with the prisoners."

Donald Beck was on his knees beside Wentworth. "I hope you can forgive me, sir," he was pleading. "I—I made a mistake all along. I thought that you were the *Spider.* He was in league with the Skull. He kidnapped Melissa. Now, I can tell the truth about that racket money. Melissa, dear—

Melissa smiled up faintly, "You were wonderful, darling," she said. "How did you ever find me?"

Beck flushed, "I saw the *Spider* and followed him. That's all."

Nita was bending over Wentworth and she bent low, whispering. "The wounds aren't bad, Dick. You can beat Toley's evidence easily now that we can prove Wister was the Skull, and… and his bullets are in your body. We just tell them that it must have been Wister's bullets he dug out of the trees."

Wentworth's smile was faint. He reached up his uninjured arm to pull Nita down to him. "Please, Nita," he said, and his smile grew whimsical. "It seems to me that I'm a hell of a crimebuster, having to get shot with my own gun to clear myself. Can't you—won't you—please tell me I'm wonderful, too?"

Nita laughed, softly, and her lips told Wentworth in a way that left no doubt at all what she thought.

THE END

Also coming in **THE SPIDER #7**

A mighty leader organizes the Underworld in

Green Globes of Death

An epic exploit of America's best-loved fiction character!

Strains of soft music were wafted through that ballroom where society had foregathered in a gala masquerade ball. Richard Wentworth attended as the dread *Spider*, nemesis of the Underworld, and his friends laughed at his daring impersonation. Never dreaming that he was in truth the famous lone wolf anti-crime crusader who fought always in that grim no-man's land between Law and lawless. Nor was the *Spider* laughing that night, for grim necessity brought him here, seeking his shrewdest and most valiant foeman—the Fly! Once more that furtive, gold-hilted knife was drinking innocent blood. Once more the Fly, supposedly slain, had united criminals in a determined army of pillagers and butchers. Armed with a horrible green vapor, they were ravaging the richest city in the world, spreading ruin and dishonor and death. And the *Spider*, lone-handed, hampered even by his best and dearest friends, must battle against terrific odds, and against the yearning of his own brave heart!

Can the Fly, whom all thought dead, have returned to life?

Can Richard Wentworth, hindered on every hand, win this grimmest of all battles?

Can the *Spider*, a huge price on his head, hunted by every man, succeed in saving the people he loves?

NO OTHER FIEND PREYING ON MANKIND IS SO HEARTLESS AND SAVAGE AS THE MAN WHO CALLS HIMSELF THE FLY. NEVER BEFORE HAS ANY CRIMINAL SO NEARLY SUCCEEDED IN MASTERING THE *SPIDER!* AN EXCITING, FEATURE-LENGTH NOVEL, COMPLETE IN THE MARCH ISSUE OF

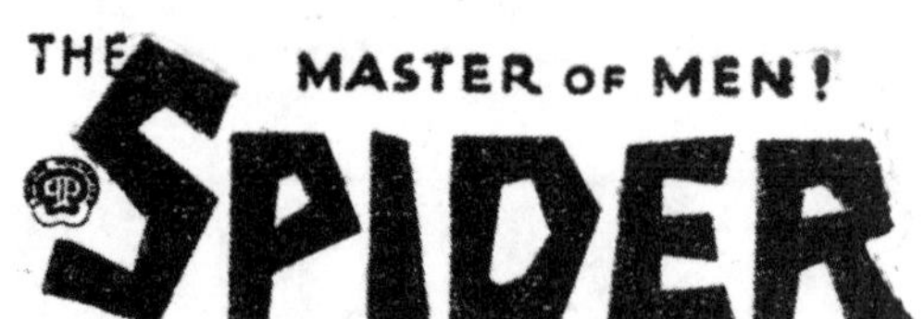

THE SPIDER AROUND THE WORLD

Though Richard Wentworth's pulp adventures seldom took him outside North America, The *Spider*'s exploits were still enjoyed by readers in the Netherlands, Mexico, Great Britain and Argentina.

In 1942, A. G. Schoonderbeek released Dutch editions of *Prince of the Red Looters* and *Empire of Doom* in its Raven-Reeks hardcover mystery series, followed in 1946 with paperback translations of *Satan's Death Blast* and *City of Flaming Shadows*.

In the early 1960s, Amsterdam's Internationale Romanultgaven released paperback editions of two 1938 novels retitled *De Gemaskerde Krankzinnige* (*The Masked Lunatic*) and *Doretta Overtroeft De Gangsters* (*Doretta Outdoes the Gangsters*).

From the collection of Hillebrand Komrij

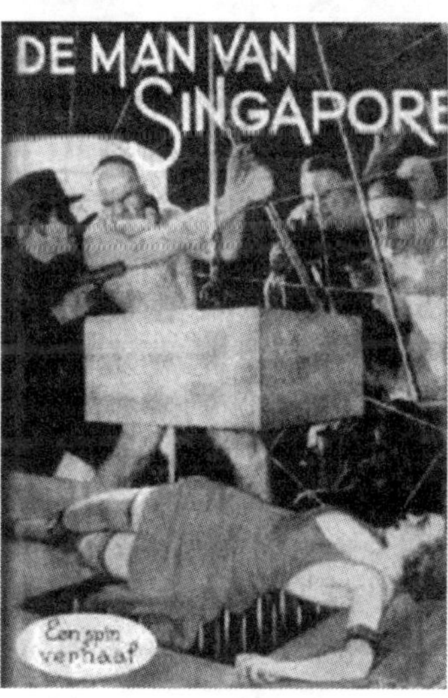

Clockwise from left: 1946 Dutch paperback translations of *City of Flaming Shadows*, *Satan's Death Blast* and *The Man from Singapore* plus later editions of *When Thousands Slept in Hell* and *The City of Lost Men.*